DIVISION

Jim Mosquera

The Sentinel

Division

The third book in the Chandler Scott series.

Mosquera, Jaime (Jim) Jr.

Division / Jim Mosquera

ISBN: 0-9832966-5-0
ISBN-13: 978-0-9832966-5-2

The text type was set in Adobe Garamond Pro

DEDICATION

To the United States of America

The third book in the

Chandler Scott series

Part I

Convention

CHAPTER ONE
UNREST

Chandler's documentary exposed the seedy underbelly of the country's efforts to suppress domestic unrest. After the release of the reorientation camp video and the revelation of the Elysium Protocol, the Jefferson administration faced great pressure to have his proposed panel give the American public something in which to believe. Civil liberty critics suggested the government targeted the underclass and the lower middle class for these camps. The president convened a panel with a heavy military footprint. The American public held the military in high esteem after 9/11. The military rose to be the most respected part of the federal government.

Some feared the public's adoration of the uniform could make them overlook their accountability. The increased use of unmanned aerial vehicles (UAV) and artificial intelligence limited the body bags seen on the nightly news. Eisenhower's warnings about the undue influence of the military-industrial complex were a distant memory. There was now the added concern of former military staffing positions in the president's cabinet and security apparatus, positions often held by civilians.

President Jefferson's security and intelligence leaders possessed vast military experience. These military men knew all along what occurred in the reorientation camps and the meaning of the Elysium Protocol. These men saw the country slipping away and felt they needed to bring order, albeit with more benign means — mental reprogramming using virtual reality. Army doctors involved with Cerebrum Technologies perfected the technology that sought to make domestic detainees more patriotic, more submissive, and more compliant.

Littered among the president's top advisers were former military brass — Director of National Intelligence (DNI) Gerald Burkemper retired as an Air Force general. Department of Homeland Security (DHS) Secretary Victor Haydon served in the Air Force as a general. The National Security Advisor (NSA), Trent Carter, had a brilliant career in the Marine Corps and retired as a general.

The Secretary of Defense had fallen ill in late November, which led to his replacement by Trent Carter. A former naval intelligence officer, Eric Greich, filled Carter's NSA role. The military-industrial connection extended to the Secretary of State, who'd served as CEO of the nation's largest defense contractor.

While the president's top advisers didn't comprise the investigatory panel, they had a heavy influence in deciding its composition. They advised against revealing too much for fear of giving domestic or foreign terror suspects information about U.S. counter-terror methods and procedures. They suggested delaying the panel's report. They reasoned that over time the American public would move on to other matters if they fed the media information about economic progress and economic slogans — the Plan for Prosperity and the We Are the Future campaign.

We Are the Future posters depicted a man, woman, and child standing in front of the Stars & Stripes looking upward and right. The Jefferson administration hoped to rally the public around family and flag. They bombarded the media with public service messages about the patriotic campaign. A visitor to the nation's capital couldn't escape the messaging in government buildings and public transportation. Sports leagues carried the messaging within their own apparel. Public universities offered economics courses with case studies featuring the Plan for Prosperity.

The president's men thought it important to cheerlead these patriotic campaigns to maintain the nation's morale during the continued economic crisis. If that approach didn't work, they would distract the public with more attention on the War on Terror versus Islam and cyber hackers, with foreign hackers receiving an extra dose of venom.

For some in the foreign hacking community, it became a matter of sport to break into U.S. companies or the government. The FBI had uncovered a sophisticated malware scheme that robbed U.S. banks of some $300 million. The same Russian hacker was allegedly responsible for a ransomware attack that disabled thousands of computers in the United States. The government offered a $10 million bounty, though there was never any expectation of his extradition, not with the protection offered by the Russian government who hired the same hacker for espionage against Georgia and Ukraine. He was part of a larger band of hackers who saw it as their patriotic duty to hack the United States whether or not the Russian government paid them. As long as they didn't disturb domestic networks in Russia, the local authorities left them alone.

On the political front, the Supreme Court had given the president until the end of 2021 to resume the undecided election of 2020 in the House and Senate. In early December 2021, the president had made plans for Congress to proceed. Then the bond market crashed, sending interest rates soaring to levels not seen since 1980. Since the U.S. Treasury had shifted the maturity of most debt to shorter terms, higher interest rates impacted new debt obligations, skyrocketing financing costs. Businesses also felt the pinch with soaring rates on short-term paper. The stock market took a dive and other world markets moved in sympathy. The Global Settlement Bank, an organization responsible for U.S.

economic policy, called an emergency meeting in Geneva with the financial leaders of the developed countries. Financial Stability Board (FSB) Secretary Malcolm Holloway and the Treasury Secretary would represent the United States. World leaders agreed to put even tighter controls over their economies to stabilize the crisis.

Nameless, faceless hackers took advantage by wreaking havoc in the nation's capital. The government thought the hackers were state-sponsored. The hackers may have just been individuals seeking to harm the USA. Some may have been hired by nation-states on a contract basis to carry out the attacks. Unlike previous hack activity, neither Omni nor the Five Tribes claimed them. Attributing attacks in the cyber world had always been challenging. It came down to one of three scenarios for the authorities: identifying who did it, identifying who did it and convincing the hacker, or identifying who did it and convincing the world of the hacker's identity. The Jefferson administration struggled to do any of them.

Fearful Congressmen and women retreated to their districts despite President Jefferson's call for their appearance in the nation's capital to resolve the 2020 election. The president's staff encouraged him to let the Congress retreat. Congressmen didn't feel safe, and neither D.C. nor Capitol police could guarantee their safety with increased lawlessness in the city. Protests became more violent and patriot groups had descended on the city to maintain their own version of law and order. It was unknown when Congress might reconvene.

The Secret Service felt wary about keeping the president safe in the White House or Camp David during the disruptions. The disruptions included the city's power grid and its automated vehicle fleet. The airports of Reagan National and Dulles had also seen a curtailment of traffic.

Amid all the chaos, Senator Matt Geringer and Senator Alfonso Chancellor, both of the Independent American Party (IAP) had mustered enough support in the state legislatures to convene an Article Five convention. Though an Article Five movement had been in play for several years, the 2020 presidential election and Jefferson's executive action had been the catalyst to see it through to fruition, albeit with a great amount of coaxing by Senator Geringer. This convention would move forward in Colorado in early February 2022.

As the president and his staff met in January 2022, they would face a new crucible in their efforts to hold the nation together.

***

The Situation Room or Sit Room comprised a 5,500 square foot complex of rooms in the West Wing of the White House. It had a relatively small conference area and an intelligence management center. The Sit Room housed National Security Council Watch Officers sitting on curved, dual-tiered rows of computer terminals where they received many data worldwide. There were also five secure video rooms, a secure feed to Air Force One, and in a style befitting Get Smart, private phone booths resembling cones of silence.

The president normally sat at the end of a long, wooden conference table, forming a horseshoe, with six chairs on each side. On the wall opposite the president hung a large, ultra-high definition video monitor, with similar monitors flanking the walls on both sides of the room. The newly adorned Sit Room included still images on the side monitors of the We Are the Future campaign — the characteristic man, woman, and child standing in front of the flag, looking up to the right.

The meeting began with a review of the Morning Book,

which contained a copy of the National Intelligence Daily, the State Department's Morning Summary, diplomatic cables and intelligence reports. The president held court today with DHS Secretary Victor Haydon, FBI Director Ralph Elliott, and Secretary of Defense Trent Carter, recently named to this post. The sullen-faced team semi-balanced the horseshoe with three members on one side and two on the other.

In January 2022, the focus turned towards domestic matters. A hack on the system authorizing EBT benefits unleashed civil devastation in cities like St. Louis, Detroit, Chicago, and Baltimore. The breakdown led to the flash-mob looting of supermarkets and other businesses. The social contract of bread and circuses in the urban zones had broken down and the public responded. With big screens, Internet, and smart phones, the circus show could always go on as long electricity flowed. The EBT hack broke the bread portion of the social contract. Food distribution happened as it did a hundred years earlier, via physical transport, creating a vulnerability in the system. Supermarket trucks stopped going into the urban core. Hunger and desperation gave rise to food riots. With social media and cell phone ubiquity, urban youths were the vanguard of these riots.

"I suppose I should have the Secretary of Agriculture here today but, it's beyond her," the president commented as the main video monitor showed a webcam stream of the riot in Chicago. The violent orgy made him look away.

Secretary Haydon chimed in with a cold, leveled delivery. "Sir, the press is calling this a 'food riot' but I wouldn't suggest using this term."

The president scoffed at Haydon's attempt to sanitize the disturbance. He raised his voice, yielding to his irritation. "You know, since I've been president, this administration has been dogged by one f'ing hack after another. We can't win, can we?"

"Mr. President, with all due respect, this is a new frontier for us. Sure, we're the big gorilla in the room, but these gnats are many and just multiply after we swat them. We can't just nuke the room or we'd kill the gorilla," Burkemper replied.

The president didn't want metaphors; he wanted solutions. The solutions seemed distant at the moment, given the disturbing images on the video monitor.

News cameras captured rioters throwing shopping carts and trash cans into an intersection. Timid drivers stopped in front of the obstructions. The mob swarmed the stationary vehicles and yanked the terrified drivers out while they desperately clung to their steering wheels. Outside the protection of vehicles, they were beaten and robbed. One looter stripped off a woman's pants and raped her. As she rolled over, viewers saw her bare bottom, raw from the sexual violation that occurred on the rough concrete.

The rioters caused harm other than punching and kicking. Many had knives and other homemade weapons. Others armed themselves with 9mm pistols and AK-47s.

Emergency medical personnel, in a scene reminiscent of the violence in Ferguson, Missouri, found themselves unable to assist those needing treatments since they also came under attack.

The main video monitor changed to an overhead display, shot by a drone, hovering over Chicago's South Side. Homeland Security was assisting local law enforcement with aerial surveillance.

"I guess I don't get where all the Chicago PD is while this is going on?" The president threw his hands in the air in disgust.

This would be a question for FBI Director Elliott, who steadied himself, shaken from the images he'd just seen. "Sir, the ranks of Chicago PD thinned after the civil rights violation trials and scrutiny from the Justice Department. Candidly, many of them just stopped patrolling these areas and are reluctant to go in."

"There's another problem too, sir. Mobs are forming more dynamically than in the past. These urban youths are using social media to just pop up in places where the police aren't. They're more like a flash mob, albeit one revolting against the EBT network crash. But they have no idea about network hacks, and they don't care," Secretary Haydon added.

Just as Chicago PD cleared one intersection, the mobs appeared at another. The flash mobs were occurring within law enforcement's OODA loop, also known as Observe, Orient, Decide, Act, which gave them much quicker reaction time than the police. Mobs had learned lessons during confrontations in other cities and now received aid from professionals who descended into the chaos.

"Why don't we just jam electronic transmissions in these neighborhoods?" the president asked, thrusting his pen against a stack of papers. He looked at no one in particular with his query.

"We could, sir, but then the people who aren't rioting and calling for help will be cut off. Besides, not many homes have landlines and even those are not reliable with outside plant being vandalized by rioters. No good options there, sir," FBI Director Elliott replied.

Rioters were moving to new areas like the suburban borderlands. Formerly safe supermarkets and stores were coming under attack by mobs armed with knives, pistols, and AK-47s. Police living in these suburban areas were unreliable since they were protecting their own families.

The former NSA Director, Trent Carter, who now served as

Secretary of Defense, had heard enough. He placed his clasped hands on the table and began his delivery with gritted teeth. "Sir, I hope you see the reason for the reorientation camps. We could have the military mow down all these animals but that would be real bad press for us. I honestly think we need to scale these camps to handle many, many more people. Once we haul them to the camps, when they come out, they'll never act like a bunch of untamed animals again!"

The secretary's callous disregard dismayed the president. He prioritized public relations over humanity.

He threw a despising glance at Carter. "These are people, Trent, human beings, not animals for God's sake!"

Carter recoiled, showing some contrition for his remarks.

The news of the reorientation camps stunned the president last year. He felt betrayed by his staff for keeping them hidden. Carter championed them and touted the favorable outcomes. Watching these webcam feeds steeled the president's resolve that he needed to take action, yet he remained conflicted about sending these rioters to the camps.

Despite the panel convened to study the reorientation camps, the president's advisers didn't feel inclined to dismantle them. They considered the matter a public relations problem needing resolution. Besides, part of the American public supported them as a humane way to have people fall in line with the nation's patriotic-inspired plans. As far as Carter was concerned, if someone wanted to be part of the future, they needed to follow the plan or face reeducation.

The president expected the special panel to come up with an alternative to the Elysium Protocol. The managed death of a bad reeducation effort was not just a public relations problem.

The Elysium Protocol was a method of euthanizing mentally

damaged camp participants. Those suffering adverse effects from the protocol were told they were going to a place that would put their souls at rest. That place included a virtual reality simulation and the administration of powerful drugs.

The men in the Sit Room understood that what they were witnessing on screen could play out in many cities, and not just because of an EBT hack. Divisiveness had split the nation far beyond just economic inequality. Ideologically, there was a great chasm.

Carter wanted as many people as possible on the same page. He understood the camps and other VR mind control efforts were the key to having a compliant society.

Cerebrum Technologies was at the center of these efforts. The government had already placed its tentacles in the company through funding from IQT, or In-Q-Tel, a non-profit venture capital firm investing in high-tech companies that supported the intelligence gathering of agencies like the CIA. Using the letter "Q" in the name paid homage to the fictional character in the James Bond series, who supplied Agent 007 with an assortment of gadgets.

The Department of Homeland Security had awarded a contract to Cerebrum to develop mind control modules for insertion into popular virtual reality games used by youths and adults. The unsuspecting players received a dose of reorientation programming designed with patriotic themes in mind; all designed to support the nation's Plan for Prosperity.

"Before I forget, I wanted to update everyone on the condition of the vice president. His doctors are not hopeful, so please keep him in your thoughts and prayers," the president's face saddened. Tears welled up in his eyes, though they didn't escape. The adviser team averted their eyes towards their notes.

18

A longtime friend of President Jefferson, the vice president had fallen ill in late December with a bacteria strain known as CRE. This class of drug-resistant bugs was impervious to any FDA-approved antibiotic. Doctors treated him with high doses of known antibiotics and could not nurse him back to health. His life remained in the balance. At least one member of the presidential succession wouldn't be able to serve if called upon.

The state of unrest in the country had made the president's military-laden security team lean towards more authoritative measures to restore order. This posture would challenge the president in the days ahead.

CHAPTER TWO
GETAWAY

Chandler had over two months to reflect on Habakk's Halloween morning comments at the Battery, about the United States of America remaining united. Habakk suggested that freedom came from the ability to choose. The separatist and secession groups were attempting to exercise their freedom and choices, to the dismay of the Elite. Those in power responded, with public support, by imposing more authority. The battle waged between the opposing forces of nationalist fervor and those stifled by the weight of government's heavy hand.

Chandler had made his own choice. After discovering the true nature of the reorientation camps, he released a documentary about secessionist and patriot groups made with his deceased partner, Arturo Dutari.

Some Americans felt the camps were a humane way to reeducate people to fall in line with President Jefferson's plan to rescue the economy and, by extension, the nation. They considered the Elysium Protocol an unfortunate, though acceptable consequence of a treatment, which could harm the patient, no different from an outcome of chemotherapy and radiation killing a cancer patient. It horrified others that government had stooped to such barbarism, barely above the cleansing efforts of the Third Reich.

With the nation divided on the camp revelation, the Justice Department treated Chandler's trespassing at the camp with kid gloves. They charged him with a Class C misdemeanor and fined him $5,000 — he served 30 days of probation. The Jefferson administration wanted to make a point about Chandler's trespassing, though not in a punitive way.

He could still live his dream. The dream now included a love like he'd never experienced before, a love that withstood the stress of his investigatory work. This love understood that his work had a higher purpose. During his undercover stint in the reorientation camp, he discovered a dark side of love, dreading that something would go wrong, and the suffering he caused her. He missed her familiar scent, the feel of her bosom, the tingle of her hair on his cheek, the rich color of her blue eyes — oh those eyes. He wanted to take his last breath looking at her.

Chandler Michael Scott was born on October 19, 1987, infamously known as Black Monday in financial circles. Destined to live his life around turbulence, a single mother raised him in Texas. He later received a journalism degree from the University of Missouri followed by a Master's at the School of Advanced International Studies (SAIS) at Johns Hopkins.

He'd spent most of his professional life working at El Mundo, an international TV network based out of Argentina, where he eventually hosted his own show that focused on financial and political events. El Mundo became a victim to international organizations that wanted it to parrot themes supporting the Global Financial Union, a coordinated plan to rescue the United States and other economies. The Global Financial Union had been kept secret from the public until Chandler revealed it in a rogue video released on the Internet with assistance from the enigmatic hacker group, Omni.

After getting fired from El Mundo, he worked as an indie journalist. He and his partner developed a documentary about secession and patriot movements within the United States. Unlikely to sell the documentary to a domestic network, he offered it to the Singaporean Financial News Network in the fall of 2021. Details of the reorientation camp caused reverberations domestically and worldwide.

He needed time away now, a time he could spend with her. They got reacquainted socially and physically. Their flight took them from Chicago's O'Hare to Denver, whose airport terminal's design foreshadowed the Front Range of the American Rockies that sat immediately to the west. Their journey took them south to Colorado Springs. Electrical towers stood guard over the prairie on their drive down Highway 25. The wispy, golden grass bent away from the strong northern wind that also coaxed their vehicle down the highway. Small hills erupted from the stretches of golden grass like irregular mole tunnels in a suburban yard. The tunnels came to an abrupt end as the Front Range served as a reminder of the mountain's authority over the prairie. Standing watch over Colorado Springs stood Pike's Peak, a mountain Arianne had summited as a youth. She wanted to climb it again, though this time with less effort.

They drove to the summit after plows cut through the snow drifts. The clear day allowed for a 360-degree panoramic view. They could see jets below them flying over the Air Force Academy. He stood behind her, his arms wrapped around her waist. Even through her coat, he felt her taut frame. Somehow the thin air bothered neither. They stood on top of the world, at 14,000 feet. The possibilities with her had no limit now.

Their trip took them back to Denver where they traveled by train to the towns of Fraser and Winter Park, two enclaves in a valley in Grand County resting at an elevation of 9,000 feet. These towns, supporting the skiing industry, enjoyed growth in the early 2010s before the economic shocks arrested their development. Incomes varied with a service economy littered with lower-wage workers living communally and higher wage earners owning the area's top real estate — a chasm reflected elsewhere in the country. Low wages were not always a problem for young adults, discovering who they were, planning their next move. Some had no interest in discovery and just wanted to live among people like themselves.

Winter Park's permanent residents wanted to escape the madness of cities and suburbs and had a difficult time identifying with patriotic campaigns like We Are the Future. The rest of the country had been separating for years. It was more than just red, blue or purple states. The country had been segregating by smaller geographic areas that, in many respects, reflected a tribal arrangement.

Arianne was an accomplished skier. Her family spent many a winter break in Colorado, Utah or California, wherever the powder was fresh. Chandler, raised in Texas, would feel as comfortable skiing a green trail as he would roping a calf, though he'd never roped a calf.

The couple embarked on skiing the Seven Territories of Winter Park, Arianne more than Chandler. Chandler found it intriguing that a ski resort would separate itself into "territories." Separation had been the theme of Chandler's documentary — secessionists and separatists, who wanted their own space. Some Americans feared the Geringer-sponsored Article Five convention would hasten secession. Others worried the Cascadia Movement and California Sí, two secession efforts, would further split the country.

While Arianne skied the moguls on the Mary Jane Trail, named after a local lady of pleasure, Chandler made camp at a watering hole perched at 10,000 feet. He enjoyed the solitude, admiring a peak that sported the contours of a bear claw on its side. He interrupted his seclusion when he removed his sunglasses and ski mask, revealing his identity. He spent the next hour chatting with skiers and taking selfies with admirers of his documentary.

After a day of falls, slides, and tumbles, Arianne took pity on her man and drove him to Hot Sulfur Springs. The heat of volcanic rock pushed out through fissures in the earth's crust and heated the mineral-laden water, so welcome after a day of getting bucked off a steer or tumbling down a mountain, in Chandler's case. The relief of the hot pools was fifty paces outside the warm confines of the dressing area. In their swimming suits, with only a soon to be frozen towel covering their shoulders, the two scurried towards the first tub in the sub-zero weather.

"Holy shit! This is colder than a cast iron commode!" Chandler yelled, as he took rapid, baby steps towards the first pool.

"Chan, don't touch the railing, it's covered with-" Her warning came too late.

Chandler's hasty entry into the pool led him to grab the ice-coated railing. He fell face first, taking a gulp of sulfur-laden water. The embarrassment proved momentary. He was happy to be warm.

"Are you OK?" She nuzzled him and parted the hair from the front of his forehead.

He coughed and grimaced, expelling the foul chemical elixir. "It's funny how just a second ago I thought my blood was about to freeze and now I'm getting as hot as Hades. Yeah, I'm good."

The bench in the pool allowed submersion to his shoulders. She straddled him. He melted into the embrace. The dancing moonlight played with her blue eyes. It was a gloriously cold and clear night. The stars dotting the sky were as bright as their future. Their love had never been in doubt. It just had obstacles

24

from Chandler's work as a journalist.

They each had a different upbringing. Hers was one of privilege. He featured a single parent, a mother, occupying both roles and the occasional economic hardship. She traveled extensively in her youth. He was making up for the provincialism of his childhood with his professional need for adventure. Their lives had achieved a balance.

"Let's go to the next one." She stepped out of the pool and grabbed her stiff towel, motioning him to follow.

Normally, her figure served as easy bait to follow just about anywhere. In the subzero temperature, outside of the water, he had to strategically plan which pool to visit next. The next pool might be full of patrons who, like him, were not eager to leave the warm confines.

"Where's the next pool?" he asked, still immersed to his shoulders.

She bounced on her toes. "I have no idea, but I'm not gonna sttaandd outtt heerree talkiiing."

She took small, rapid steps towards the nearest pool. He followed moments later — as fortune would have it, there was space for them.

After being in the hottest of the pools, she made an impulsive move. She stepped out to make a snow angel, front side and back, on the fluffy, white powder surrounding the pool.

He emerged, exposing his torso to watch her theatrics. "Arianne, what are you doing?"

Snow became encrusted on her damp auburn locks. "It's really not that bad. Come, try it."

He sunk back into the pool.

After a few more seconds of flapping her arms, she joined him in the pool. The other soaking patrons coaxed him to follow her lead. Surely someone who'd been in danger before wouldn't be afraid of a little chill. On most occasions, she followed him. This time, she turned the tables on him.

He relented and to his surprise, the experience didn't put him in cryogenic suspension. When he came back to the hot pool, he felt his skin tingle. It was the same feeling he had when he first realized the deep love he felt for this woman. They walked hand in hand to the next pool, feeling no chill. They smiled. Their teeth didn't chatter. They weren't in any hurry.

After the experience in the hot springs, they retreated to the adjoining resort with a bottle of Riesling. It was a great finish to a busy day.

***

The next day's adventure included a snowshoe walk along an alpine forest trail. He followed her again. Flickering rays of sunshine breaking through the thick canopy settled in Arianne's auburn locks.

She guided him on this walk. He'd never worn snowshoes. Though he had big feet, the snowshoes felt like walking with water skis. He was comfortable with *these* types of skis.

"Chan, just walk normally," she urged him to give up the goose step.

He obliged, transitioning to more of a slide step. "Yeah, this is easier now."

Her mood turned serious during a pause over a creek bridge. "I always thought I wanted to have a big family, you know. Now I don't know. I mean, how can we bring children into this world after what you discovered in that camp?"

They'd had discussions about their future on this trip, although children had not been part of them. Chandler had no siblings, so he envisioned his own family with two or three children.

Chandler flicked powdery snow off the bridge rail, watching it float into the rushing creek. "Yeah, I know. With the Article Five and these other movements, the country's gonna change for sure. I agree with you on one hand, but on the other, Habakk has forced me to think about the future and how I might shape it. Part of that has to include a family, don't you think?"

She shrugged, deciding to save this conversation for another time. She tugged on his gloved hand. "Come on, let's keep walking."

The heavy snow on their branches made the pines trees languid. The aftermath of economic and political crisis made the American psyche equally languid.

Recent magazine caricatures of Uncle Sam, depicted with a tear squeezing out of the corner of his eye, reflected the melancholy felt by many. Ironically, the dead trees, unburdened with snow, stood prominently on their hike, commanding attention.

When they stopped to listen to the forest, they heard nothing, only the ringing of their own ears. The wind remained absent on this walk. The occasional snowfall off pine branches spread a fine mist, obscuring the trail ahead.

A political mist obscured the path for the nation, threatening the foundation of the United States of America.

CHAPTER THREE
COS

It had taken months of planning and traveling to state capitals. Colorado Senator Matt Geringer, the father of the Independent American Party (IAP), saw his dream of an Article Five convention come to fruition.

The tall, lanky Matt Geringer sported cowboy-rugged, chiseled looks, and a considerable mustache. He could have been the Marlboro man, except he didn't smoke. He could have done the voice-overs for beef commercials. If he were a singer, he'd be a bass. An avid outdoorsman, he felt as comfortable on a horse herding cattle as he did negotiating a double black diamond in Steamboat Springs.

Born in the early 1960s, the Renaissance Man label could apply. In high school, he played a leading figure in stage productions and strummed the rhythm guitar in a teenage band. After high school, he tried his luck on a ranch as a cowhand. Three years later, he returned to academic pursuits. He completed a degree in Criminal Justice at the University of Colorado in Colorado Springs. The state university in Boulder later called, where he earned a law degree.

He served as a criminal defense lawyer in Denver for many years, a member of the city council and eventually state Attorney General. His arrival in Washington as senator coincided with the great financial crisis of 2008. During his second term, he mounted a run on the Republican ticket for president in 2016. By the time of the Republican convention in Cleveland, no candidate had enough delegates to secure the nomination. After a contentious battle, Geringer wouldn't be his party's representative. Influential party leaders suggested a run as an independent. Geringer thought it a good idea, but wanted something deeper and long-lasting. He wasn't looking for a one and done. That year marked the birth of the Independent American Party or IAP, a party focused on becoming a legitimate challenger to the Republican and Democrat parties in future races. Though Geringer lost in the general election, his strong performance solidified the party's standing and helped them win seats in the 2018 House and Senate races when more voters from the Republican and Democratic parties defected.

The nation would convene an Article Five convention with the sponsorship of the Convention of States (COS) project. After the president's historic decision to freeze the results of the 2020 election through executive order, Senator Geringer and Senator Alfonso Chancellor, the IAP nominee for president in 2020, laid the legal groundwork to challenge the president.

First, they tried impeachment. While the House drafted articles of impeachment against President Jefferson, the mostly Democratic Senate didn't find him guilty. A Supreme Court challenge also proved unsuccessful. Getting two-thirds of the states to agree to an Article Five convention was no small feat, and it proved to be the most difficult challenge of Geringer's career. The growth of the IAP and the other prominent third party, the Theocracy Party, made the task a little easier.

The Article Five convention focused on returning power to the states. Article Five represented a constitutional path for altering the law of the land. Other groups in the country wanted to take the law into their own hands and separate themselves from an increasingly authoritarian state. Some states felt as if they no longer shared the same beliefs or culture as their brethren. Senator Geringer stood in staunch opposition to secession, or separatist groups and wanted to follow the Constitution.

Congress, given the opportunity to decide the location of the convention, opted to leave that to the COS project. The legislative bodies took no serious interest in the movement, considering it a civics exercise with no teeth.

Both the COS and Geringer agreed to hold the Article Five in a remote location during February 2022 — a frigid proposition. They expected a disruption from Jefferson supporters and others who feared the result of an Article Five. They reasoned it would be more difficult for disruptive influences to materialize during the depths of winter.

Throughout the course of 2021, the COS project and its commissioners were reluctant to speak to media for fear of having their efforts sabotaged with a propaganda campaign unfavorable to the Article Five. The term "runaway convention" would cause the most alarm with state legislatures who feared the convention was nothing more than a ploy to take over the republic via nefarious, allegedly constitutional means.

Once the required number of state legislatures had voted to participate, the COS welcomed as much press coverage as they could get. They hoped the coverage would flourish into a constitutional renaissance. Much of the mainstream press opted to stay away from the convention for fear of running afoul of the Jefferson administration. Many in the mainstream media felt the convention was an affront against the We Are the Future campaign and the Plan for Prosperity.

Though the COS needed thirty-four states to approve the convention, all states sent representation via "commissioners" to have their voices heard. States like California, Oregon, Washington, New York, Maryland, Massachusetts, Minnesota, and Illinois were reluctant to send anyone, yet thought it wise to have a commissioner present. Each state could send as many people as they wanted, but could only cast one vote.

The COS would debate three main topics: a balanced budget amendment, term limits, and the all-important limits of federal government power. The latter topic spurred great interest after President Jefferson's executive order.

The protesters gathered in the town Winter Park, Colorado around the Grand Mountain Conference Center (GMCC), the site of the convention. Joining Jefferson administration supporters were the John Birch Society, the National Association of Gun Rights, and the Eagle Forum — strange bedfellows. Protesters established camps on the outskirts of nearby Fraser due to the limited lodging available in this town and the adjacent Winter Park. They clogged the main thoroughfare, Highway 40, already narrowed from impressive snow banks made by plows.

Security created other strange bedfellows. Colorado State troopers and a contingent of Winter Park and Fraser police offered a limited presence outside of the GMCC. The Honor Brigade provided the rest.

The Honor Brigade, a patriot group, emerged after the 2008 financial crisis. Their membership comprised former military, law enforcement, and firefighters, among others. The U.S. military prohibited active servicemen and women from joining such groups. The Brigade's mission was to protect the Constitution and help their members during natural disasters and civil disturbances. They didn't try to hide themselves or their stated intentions.

The Honor Brigade's commander in Colorado, with a call sign of "Big Dog", offered to provide security for a reduced charge. It was an offer which the GMCC, Senator Geringer, and the COS gladly accepted. Honor Brigade plainclothes security would outfit themselves with concealed body armor, black 511 tactical pants, black boots, and white, long sleeve shirts. Each would carry a concealed pistol in the rear waistband. This Honor Brigade security detail, numbering some 100 men and women, would hide in plain sight, inside the GMCC.

In an interview with an alternative media rag, the Article Five convention's president, George Lincoln, offered his thoughts on the historic event from the Great Hall of the GMCC.

"We're happy for Americans to see the Constitution at work. We want them to get used to seeing more of these conventions. For a nation that's approaching the grand old age of 250 years, we'll need more of these. George Mason said that these gatherings should be easy and regular, like a company board of director's meeting. We know the nation is on an unsustainable course. The cards keep getting stacked higher and higher. Which card will knock down the stack? That's what we don't know."

When asked about the mounting secession and separatist movements, Mr. Lincoln didn't see any significance to them. History would decide if Lincoln was right or whether the current movements were apocalyptic first notes in a symphony of implosion.

***

With the Article Five convention beginning the next day, Chandler said goodbye to Arianne at the train station in Fraser. The spartan train depot provided little comfort to waiting passengers. The mountain winds punished those who made the walk from the tiny waiting area to the platform. The winds blew much snow in the air, creating a mini-blizzard. The interruption wouldn't last long, perhaps a week, until the convention ended. They would see each other in Chicago soon.

After watching her board the train, and receiving her air kiss, he headed to the GMCC to have dinner with Senator Geringer and Axel Schultz, Chandler's long-time mentor and confidant. It had been months since they'd been able to enjoy each other's company. Tonight, they'd enjoy a relaxed meal at one of the GMCC's restaurants, The Alpine Spoon. Axel and the senator arrived before Chandler and were chatting over drinks.

Geringer stood first to greet him, putting his hand in a vise and slapping his shoulder. "Chan, great to see you! Where's your better half?"

Chandler wiggled his fingers to restore feeling. "Oh, she's headed back to Chicago. She didn't seem interested in all the festivities. In law school, she had a whole unit on Article Five, so I guess she's had her fill for at least half a lifetime."

Axel stood and shook Chandler's hand. His normally stout grip seemed a little soft. "Hey, Chan. I'll have to agree with the senator. I think I'd rather sit across from your better half."

"Yeah, you and half the other men in America. We spent a bunch of time together already the last few days." Chandler winked at his mentor, hoping to signal the romantic adventure he'd just finished.

The three men sat down, Chandler next to his mentor, and on cue, the waitress, a statuesque woman of Eastern European descent, came to get Chandler's drink order.

"Ah, just surprise me with a local brew. Nothing real stout, though. I'll take anything up to an amber color."

She acknowledged him with a warm smile. Axel stole a long look as she walked away.

Chandler chided him. "Axel Schultz! Eyes over here, please."

"I told you a long time ago, a man's never too old to look, right, senator?"

"Axel, you had to put me on the spot so early, huh?" Geringer replied. "I only have eyes for my wife…most of the time."

The three enjoyed a laugh.

"I do want to thank you, Matt, for inviting us to the convention, though I'm not here in any official capacity," Chandler said. He would have had difficulty playing journalist after his distraction with Arianne.

"I wouldn't have it any other way. You've put yourself on the line for the American public many times now. Whether people agree with what you did, they respect you. I know journalists get a bad rap sometimes, well maybe more than sometimes." He creased one corner of his mouth, only clear by the movement of his mustache. "Democracy needs your profession, perhaps now more than ever." Geringer's voice trailed off towards the lower end of the hearing range.

"Thanks, Matt. And thanks for your help with the Justice Department. Axel was afraid I'd get charged with more than just a simple trespassing charge for the reorientation camp thing."

Senator Geringer persuaded the Attorney General, a Jefferson appointee, that Chandler's incursion served the public good. While he trespassed on federal government property, he exposed something that America deserved to see.

"It's true that my association with you has caused me grief with members of Congress, heck even members of my own party. I don't have any more political aspirations beyond serving my state in the Senate and my party."

Axel, who could always steer a conversation in the direction he wanted, broke the thread. "Matt, what's the mood in D.C. right now? Congress on a self-imposed sabbatical due to security concerns? Even I didn't see that coming. I thought the nation's capital would be a safe place."

Geringer savored the ale he had just swallowed before

answering. "Me too. If it weren't for this convention, I'd be there. My wife wanted to come home. She didn't feel safe where we lived. The riots in Baltimore were a little too close to her. That EBT hack sent the city over the edge. Which, reminds me. I wanted to ask you. Your friends at Omni. I presume they had nothing to do with this, right? They usually leave their calling card." He frowned at the prospect.

Omni, the enigmatic hacker organization, could be a friend to some and foe to others. Axel had contacts in the hacker organization who often provided him information of which intelligence agencies would be jealous. Omni had helped Chandler uncover the Global Financial Union, a worldwide plan of economic and financial cooperation foisted on the United States by executive decree.

"No, sir! That's not their style or their M.O. If anything, they would have done the opposite, that is, put more credit in user accounts," Axel responded with a vigorous defense of the organization. The group had been a constant source of contention between the two men.

"Honestly guys, you know I've always had my reservations about Omni. They're not exactly squeaky clean. If I was running for president, I'd be lambasted for having even a peripheral association with them," Geringer replied.

The waitress, Svetlana, returned with Chandler's beer. This time Axel tried hard to keep his focus on his dinner companions. He stole a look as she left.

Chandler steered the conversation after Axel's prurient glance at her. "Short of starting the IAP, this has to be your biggest accomplishment, pulling this convention together. I mean, how long have they been trying to do this?"

"Years," Geringer answered. "Realize though that just getting this thing to happen is but a small step." He fondled the end of his considerable mustache, pondering the convention's challenges.

The Article Five convention would need to produce actionable amendments emerging from the three topics discussed in subcommittees. Each state would review and debate each amendment and there would be broad discussion before the entire convention. If approved by vote, the amendment would ultimately need ratification by three-fourths of the states. All these steps were necessary before an amendment became part of the Constitution.

"And now you have the Cascadia Movement and California Sí that have gained more support after my documentary release," Chandler lamented.

"Yes, that was an unfortunate consequence of your documentary. It has emboldened groups that were more on the fringe. Cascadia and Cal Sí have been around a few years, but the camp revelation and Elysium swelled their ranks overnight," Geringer offered as he stared into the beer glass he swirled.

Axel rose abruptly, rubbing the bridge of his nose. "Keep talking guys. I'll be right back."

"You OK, Ax?" Chandler asked, concerned by the stressed look on his mentor's face.

"Yeah, yeah. I'm fine. Continue." Axel walked towards the restroom.

Chandler waited for Axel to be out of earshot range. "I wonder if he's under the weather. He's got to be the healthiest person I know. His diet and exercise are impeccable."

"Yeah, I know I can't afford to be sick this week," Geringer offered, rubbing his neck. "Anyway, how much do you know about the Cascadia Movement?"

"I've read a little, but am far from an authority on it."

Cascadia referred to a region of the Pacific Northwest of the United States and Canada. The Cascadia Movement encompassed the states of Washington, Oregon, northern California, and the Canadian province of British Columbia. The group saw itself as distinct culturally, economically and environmentally from the rest of the United States and Canada. The group felt that having regions that wanted to secede from two countries offered them a unique appeal. The states of California, Oregon, and Washington had already held secession referendums that received the support of 65% of residents. In Canada, the Cascadia Party had been piling up seats in the Legislative Assembly of British Columbia. The province's Premier and Lieutenant Governor were both from that party.

Cascadia already had their own environmentally themed flag with three equal horizontal stripes and a Douglas fir in the middle. The upper stripe represented a blue sky. The middle white represented snow and clouds, while the lower green depicted the forest and fields. The lone Douglas fir symbolized endurance, defiance, and resilience, all qualities necessary to mount a secession from the United States and Canada.

Canada also faced secession pressure from the Parti Québécois in the Province of Quebec, which had a longer history. Secession fears troubled America's northern neighbor.

Chandler had no idea the movement had this strength and depth. "Holy cow, Matt. I wonder if Cascadia sympathizers will be here."

Axel returned to the table. He rubbed his forehead, attempting to conceal his knitted brow.

"All's well, Mr. Schultz?" Geringer asked.

"Yeah, guys. Continue." Axel took a large swig of cold water, gritting his teeth with the resulting head freeze.

"I was just telling Chandler about Cascadia," Geringer offered.

It was Axel's turn to contribute. "I've been watching that group. For the longest time, they were dismissed, though the last few years have brought them out. More people are aware of what's going on with them. That's tricky with California given that there are two active secession groups."

California Sí, or Cal Sí for short, the other secession movement, came to prominence in March 2019 with a referendum vote directing the state to leave the Union. Beginning in 2017, organizers of Cal Sí opted to work with the Cascadia Movement to enhance their chances of a successful referendum. Many Californians already viewed their state with northern and southern territorial boundaries. If there were just one referendum for either Cascadia or Cal Sí, it would have less chance of success. Californians went to the voting booths, knowing they would have two choices. Cal Sí gave voters an opportunity to join the southern half of California and the states of Arizona and New Mexico in a new republic.

California Sí based its support on appealing to those residents who felt that California served as a milk cow for the rest of the country. They felt their existence as a U.S. state no longer served their best interests. On issues ranging from peace and security to natural resources and the environment, they felt their state would be better off as an independent country. The alignment with Arizona and New Mexico highlighted the large Hispanic population centers common to all three states.

"I have to be careful how I say this since I don't want to see any state break away, but it makes sense, at least for them, that California did it this way." Chandler paused for a reaction from

Geringer that didn't come. "The break between northern and southern and their association with either Cascadia or Cal Sí seem to fit them politically and culturally. Do you think these secession movements will come up at all during the convention?"

"No, not at all. The convention is focused on the three topics and whatever amendments emerge. Anything else would be a rules violation and in some states, is punishable by jail time," Geringer replied with his voice trailing off again. There were few restaurant guests around them, so the senator's low-frequency delivery was not a problem.

Svetlana returned to take their order. Senator Geringer and Chandler ordered as if they'd not eaten the entire day. Axel opted for a small salad.

There would be no staring when she left the table this time.

"Geez Ax. Matt and I are as hungry as moths on nylon sweaters and you're ordering like you're cutting weight for a wrestling match. What's up?"

"Ah, you know, I'm just not that hungry right now. Don't worry about me. I could still do more pull-ups than either of you sad sacks," Axel replied, with unmasked pride covering his face.

Chandler had little doubt about his mentor's strength and would no doubt lose a pull-up competition to him.

"Guys, I hope the next few days are uneventful, honestly. I just want to get a few amendments out of this convention so the states can vote on them. Then I want to head back to Washington so we can finally settle the 2020 election. I want Jefferson to keep his word about that. Problem is, we need to get Congress back there and few want to go cuz they don't feel secure. If it's just the same to you, let's talk about something else now."

"I agree," Chandler replied while holding his glass in the air. "Let's toast to friendship and what will hopefully be a better year in 2022. We need a good year, guys."

Three glasses came to a high point in the center of their table. The clinging melody of the glasses made the three smile.

***

The morning of February 7th of the year 2022 would be a historic day for the United States. On this day at the Grand Mountain Conference Center (GMCC), located between the towns of Winter Park and Fraser, Colorado, the nation would hold the long-awaited Article Five convention. While they had held a simulated convention in colonial Williamsburg, Virginia, in 2016, an inadequate number of states had signed on for the real thing. Through the fierce lobbying of IAP Senator Matt Geringer, prompted by the executive action freezing the results of the 2020 election, the state legislatures took notice and reached the needed threshold.

The Great Hall of the GMCC would be the epicenter of this convention. Behind the modest main stage hung a room-sized Stars and Stripes. Next to Old Glory were two monitors that showed the convention's agenda. On the stage sat the president of the convention, Mr. George Lincoln, from the state of Utah, and below him, a secretary and two clerks who kept track of details and recordkeeping. The pole-mounted flags of the United States and the state of Colorado flanked Mr. Lincoln. The Sergeant at Arms sat obscured behind a small table holding the flags of all represented states.

The delegates, also known as commissioners, representing the states, sat alphabetically at white, cloth-covered tables. They arranged themselves in a fan-like pattern facing the stage. There were three seats available for every state. Other support staff, invited guests, and media sat or stood in a cordoned area behind the commissioners. In this area sat Senator Geringer, Axel, and

Chandler in plastic folding chairs. The Convention of States (COS) project filmed the proceedings from three different elevated camera positions and provided the feed to other networks. Honor Brigade security team members stood near exits, forming an inner ring of protection. Other Brigade members roamed the corridors outside the Great Hall and near the GMCC entrance.

Mr. Lincoln thanked everyone for their attendance and reminded them of the historic significance of their gathering. A roll call directed by the secretary followed. Once the roll call established a quorum, the day began with a prayer. Everyone stood and most bowed their heads.

Everyone remained standing for the playing of the national anthem from overhead speakers, after which time Mr. Lincoln led everyone in the Pledge of Allegiance.

"Please have a seat." Lincoln waited for the rustling of several hundred people to die down. He remained standing. "Commissioners. You are here today representing your state in a very important but often forgotten constitutional process. We look to our past to secure our future. The question we face is whether we can govern ourselves. Let's show the nation and the world that American democracy works well. We are a solution as big as a problem!" Lincoln bellowed. His face beamed with pride and satisfaction. He'd always had his doubts about the COS making the event happen.

The convention gave him a rousing applause.

The first order of business involved the committee reports. These committees were central to the convention's purpose. There were three committees, each discussing the topics of fiscal restraint, term limits, and executive jurisdiction. Each committee would deliver a proposed amendment or amendments that would be subject to review and debate by the convention. Only if approved during the convention would the amendment proceed for ratification. If ratified by three-fourths of states, the amendment would become the law of the land.

During the motion to adopt the committee report for term limits, a Utah commissioner raised an opposition. Lincoln gave the floor to the commissioner.

"I oppose! We strongly urge the committee to repeal the 17th Amendment. Our state delegation was under the understanding that this would be a resolution." The delegate stood during the outburst and pointed at the audience while doing so.

The Liberty Convention sponsored the 17th Amendment repeal. They were a group from Utah seeking the repeal to have U.S. senators elected by state legislatures. In their estimation, this would give more voice to the state. If the elected senator abrogated the wishes of the state legislature, they would call him or her back from Congress. They felt the way to solve the term limits issue was through the repeal of the 17th amendment. Few states shared that opinion.

"I would ask the commissioner from Utah to confer with the committee leader for further discussion," Lincoln shot back.

"Mr. President, I-" the Utah delegate persisted.

"Please, sir. You need to follow our rules of order. Have a seat!" Lincoln continued, this time standing to remind the commissioners and the rest of the convention about the agreed upon Mason's Rules of Order.

The side conversations of other commissioners became too loud for Lincoln, who banged his gavel. He needed to do this several times before the noise subsided.

In the audience sat the amused Chandler Scott. "That Utah delegate, I mean commissioner, looks like he could start an argument in an empty house."

Geringer, sitting next to Chandler, offered his thoughts. "I'm sure you'll see emotion here. I spoke with that Utah commissioner yesterday. That gentleman teaches a ten-week class on the Constitution. That's a big issue in his state, the 17th amendment repeal. He knows his stuff."

"Is he a professor or a lawyer?" Chandler asked.

"That's the interesting thing. He's actually a ditch digger, or as he put it, he gets to play with adult toys. Sharp guy. He likened many of these constitutional efforts to herding cats. You know, everyone wants to be a leader and not a follower."

"They have you to lead them, senator. Right Ax?" Chandler turned towards his mentor seated his opposite side. "Ax?"

A distracted Axel took a moment to answer. "Oh, yeah. Of course, we know what a great leader the senator has been." He fumbled with some papers on his lap.

"You doin' OK, Ax?" Chandler inquired. "Is that a scorecard you got there?" He snickered.

Axel reassembled the papers, stacking them vertically on his lap. "Yeah. I'm fine. Just a little short on sleep from last night. These are just some things I printed out from the COS website."

"Can't blame being tired on a long night of drinking at the strip club, huh?" Chandler teased, poking him with his elbow in the ribs.

"Chandler, I don't think people drive up here for that kind of thing. Skiing and cannabis shops, maybe. Not strip clubs," Geringer added, with a hint of waggish humor.

The commissioners spent the rest of the day listening to the various amendments drafted by the three committees.

Day one went as planned, uneventful and mundane, just as the COS wanted. Many of the assembled press availed themselves of long lunches, as did Chandler and Axel. Day two would be different.

***

The second day began much like the first. After the roll call, convention president, George Lincoln, led everyone in prayer and the Pledge of Allegiance.

Much discussion centered on the fiscal restraint topic on day one. During the continuing discussion, things got interesting.

Commissioners directed their attention towards the audience, where support staff waved their hands in unison. It resembled the communication on the floor of a commodity exchange.

Mr. Lincoln frowned, banging his gavel. "I would like to ask the commissioners to be respectful of those with control of the floor. There is plenty of space outside the Great Hall to have private conversations."

A clerk scurried to whisper something in Lincoln's ear, using his hand to muffle any sound picked up by the microphone. Lincoln covered the microphone with his hand as well. After a few seconds, Lincoln's face stiffened. The clerk froze, awaiting instructions that were not forthcoming.

In the audience, Chandler, who sat between Geringer and Axel, poked his finger at the former asking for clarification. "What's going on Matt?"

Geringer sat up, peering over the audience in front of and behind him. "I don't know honestly. Whatever it is, it's causing grief."

Axel, who had been playing with his phone, offered clarity. "I think it's the convention network. It's down. But I think it's more than just the computer network." He pulled his other device out of his bag. "I've had problems with my tablet too."

Chandler tapped on his own phone. "What do you mean?

Please, do tell."

"I think there's something going on with the cell network too," Axel replied, rubbing the bridge of his nose. "I noticed yesterday there was some other traffic floating around the wireless LAN network that seemed out of place."

Chandler turned towards his mentor, his mouth agape. "How the heck would you know that?"

Axel looked across Chandler towards Geringer. "Senator, with all due respect to you, I had my suspicions about government spying going on here. Spying, that is, on private communication between the commissioners and their support staff, and maybe more than that."

Geringer leaned over Chandler, who played communication bridge between the two men.

"What are you getting at?" Geringer raised his voice both in defense and over the disquieted audience.

"Despite your best intentions to bring this convention to life, I thought our intel agencies would be very interested in things here," Axel replied, gathering his thoughts for a moment before continuing. "Here's what I suspect."

The were some within the Jefferson administration that considered groups like the COS Project part of a broader effort, not unlike the secessionists and separatists, to undermine the stability of the nation, albeit through constitutional means. The hawkish elements of the administration viewed this convention as an affront to the Plan for Prosperity (PFP). Jefferson and his supporters felt strongly that the 2020 election results needed deferment to see the PFP through to its successful implementation. The domestic security team around the president felt that gathering intelligence from this convention could help mount a successful propaganda campaign, refuting

45

their action to the American public.

Geringer, his elbow still resting on his thigh, looking through Chandler, offered his own assessment. "I suppose, in the back of my mind, I thought they might do something like this. I hoped the truth would prevail. We're not hiding anything. We invited the press and it's being filmed."

Chandler's neck had been rotating as if watching a tennis match. He fixed it on one player to relieve his ache. "OK. Let's say what you're saying is true, Ax. How the heck do you think the government is pulling this off?"

Axel pulled a notepad out of his bag, placing it on his lap. His stern demeanor alerted Chandler that a detailed explanation was forthcoming. "There's a group called Tailored Access Operations or TAO, part of the NSA. They have this sub-group called root9b. They're not far from here in Colorado Springs. They collect intel for military ops, but with all this internal dissent going on, they've been asked to collect very specific intel from groups like the people in this convention. They don't just cast a wide net like the NSA did with Prism." Axel illustrated his point by sketching a diagram on the notepad. "There is a treasure trove of intel in this hall."

Axel wrote terms like "Ragemaster", "SurlySpawn", "Sparrow", and "Software Defined Radio."

Privacy advocates who knew about TAO thought it a better alternative than the mass data collection of Prism. Rather than collecting everything from everyone, TAO sought to focus on specific, legitimate targets — except no one knew what made a target legitimate. Under the principle of mass surveillance, everyone was a target, which meant there were no specific targets. TAO, in theory, was supposed to be better.

Even with targeted surveillance, the public didn't feel like they had any more privacy. In the novel, "1984", Winston could hide from the cameras by going to the corner of a room. His action let authorities know where he was. The surveillance apparatus of the United States didn't like it when people covered their digital tracks either — it made them look like they were hiding something.

"I suppose I shouldn't ask how you know so much about TAO since I probably already know the answer," Geringer nodded and rubbed his considerable mustache.

"Your instinct is probably spot on, senator. Organizations like Omni can only survive if they play the spy versus spy game like any other intelligence agency," Axel replied.

Omni had been a great source of intel for Axel and the newsletter he published for investors. He never credited his intel to this enigmatic hacker organization, however. Omni had tipped him off to expect significant intelligence gathering during the convention.

"OK, so are you going to explain this sketch and the terms you wrote down?" Chandler tapped his mentor's notepad.

Chandler would have to wait. A shouting match erupted among the commissioners.

A representative from Colorado accused a California commissioner of being a government spy or a plant for one of the California secession movements. The two delegations sat next to each other.

"Mr. President, I would like the floor to address an issue that's been brought to my attention. Please!" the Colorado commissioner bellowed, standing and flailing his arms.

"I'm sorry, sir. This is not the time for this discussion. Please have a seat," Lincoln yelled, his hand squeezing the microphone.

Anyone wanting attention needed to stretch their vocal

chords above the amplified murmur in the Great Hall.

The Colorado commissioner remained standing, jabbing his finger in Lincoln's direction. "No, sir. I won't!" He spun to face the audience. "These proceedings are being compromised and everyone here should know."

The secretary ran to whisper something in Lincoln's ear. Whatever he said made him accede to the Colorado commissioner. He banged his gavel. When the noise didn't abate, he blew an air horn whose piercing sound quieted the hall. "The gentleman from Colorado has the floor."

"Thank you, Mr. President. It has been brought to my attention that one of our colleagues from California is not who he appears to be. Someone in our delegation noticed that our legal counsel's screen was being copied to the delegate's screen from California."

Axel had an explanation and pointed to a box he'd sketched, identified as "Ragemaster."

"Ragemaster? Sounds like the name of a band," Chandler suggested, strumming his fingers on an air guitar.

Ragemaster was a spying tool embedded within a computer screen's video cable that reflected the screen's image to a nearby radar unit. The attorney supporting Colorado used a large external video monitor from their laptop so other members of the delegation could see her screen better.

"The device is tiny. Maybe a quarter inch long. When the attorney hooked their laptop to this external screen, she unwittingly sent everything displayed to the collector device," Axel explained. "At least that's what I think."

The commissioner from California stood and shot back at his counterpart from Colorado. "Mr. President. I must protest this false accusation!"

48

"You sons of bitches from California never wanted to be here, anyway. Why don't you just go home! We don't need you anyway!" the Colorado commissioner yelled.

Axel wondered if the commissioner from California worked for the NSA in an undercover capacity.

The rest of the convention hall exploded with side chatter. Lincoln lost control. He banged his gavel on the table, hoping to avoid the air horn. "Ladies and gentlemen. Please, let's restore order!"

A delegate from Missouri stood up and claimed that private communication between her team and herself appeared on a network news website an hour earlier.

Axel poked Chandler in the ribs and pointed to another term on his notepad, "Sparrow."

"A bird?" Chandler feigned a bird call with his hands.

Axel showed no amusement. "Sparrow is a wireless LAN collection device running with software known as BLINDDATE that collects Wi-Fi transmissions."

"A bird on a blind date? Where do they come up with these names?" Chandler snickered.

"You're focusing on the names? Come on, Chan." Axel shook his head and twisted his lip.

"Ax, chill out, man. I'm just trying to add some humor into what is quickly becoming an erupting volcano." Chandler smiled as he patted his mentor on the shoulder.

Senator Geringer, distracted with convention floor turmoil, had not paid attention the conversation beside him. "Guys, please excuse me. I'm going to see if I can find out what's going on."

Axel reached across Chandler to grab the senator's arm. "Matt, I suspect I'll be able to find out more than you can. This has the fingerprints of TAO, the NSA, or some random hacker, and who knows, maybe someone from the Cal Sí or Cascadia Movement. Some of those guys are from Silicon Valley, so I suspect they may have helped the NSA develop some of these tools and may be using them now for their own purposes. This place is dirty."

An aggravated Geringer mumbled something in a low tone before snaking his long frame through the crowd towards the exit.

Axel had other suspicions. "There's another NSA division called ANT. They-"

"ANT? Like the insect?" Chandler made a crawling motion with his fingers.

Axel delivered a playful slap to Chandler's head. "I think it stands for Advanced Network Technology. If TAO's usual techniques don't work, they use ANT to get into networking equipment, mobile phones, and computers. I think they're deep into the security architecture of a bunch of devices. They put their malicious code into the BIOS, like straight onto the motherboard."

"What's so special about BIOS?"

"With a computer, someone can run a virus scan and declare it clean. Hell, even if they put in a new hard drive or new operating system, the ANT malware's still there. It's like Rasputin — it never dies!"

Chandler shimmied his shoulders. "Creepy."

Axel wanted to investigate everything further. "Come on. Let's go back to my room and we'll look into this."

He tried rising from his seat before Chandler pressed down on his thigh.

"Shouldn't we just wait for whoever provided the network connections here? They should fix it."

"Are you kidding me? This will be beyond them!" Axel's face

stiffened and he moved Chandler's hand from his leg.

"You've got that look about you. I guess it's time to put the chairs on the table, huh?"

"Yeah, I have an idea." Axel, lightheaded from standing up too quickly, steadied himself by grabbing Chandler's shoulder.

Chandler rose to brace him. "Ax?"

"I'm fine. I just need to eat something."

The two made their way to the exit. A few in the audience approached Chandler to shake his hand. He was a more recognizable figure now, receiving praise from some and scorn from others. Some who wanted to praise him found him unapproachable, fearing a reaction from the federal government.

Mr. Lincoln, realizing that chaos had made the convention proceedings moot, blew the air horn and suggested a two-hour recess.

Though his directive suspended the meeting, the shouting continued.

***

Chandler and Axel retreated to the latter's hotel room in the GMCC. Axel grabbed a protein bar from his bathroom counter and chewed it with vigor. He finished the entire bar in just over a minute.

He declared himself fit for duty. "That's better."

"That's so unlike you to have these low blood sugar events. Did you not eat breakfast?"

"No, I just wasn't hungry. Come over here so we can investigate this thing." Axel motioned Chandler towards the work area in his suite.

Axel opened his laptop and brought up a secure chat application, one that had served him well in many instances. He looked to open a secure channel with his contact at Omni, the genderless Phish. He'd never met Phish and didn't know their country of residence. Based on the broken language via text chat sessions, he presumed English was not their native tongue.

"I always thought you needed to set things up ahead of time with Omni. Are they just going to be here waiting for you?" Chandler asked.

Axel cursed under his breath when he had to enter the connection information several times. A dark screen followed with a single flashing cursor. "I arranged with Phish to be available for a couple of days. It cost me a little DigiNote and some information." Axel referred to the digital currency loathed by governments worldwide and the preferred currency of the Darknet and the underground economy. DigiNote was one of several blockchain digital currencies circulating through cyberspace.

Chandler turned his head and arched one of his eyebrows. "Define 'a little'."

Axel waved him off. "Never mind."

Chandler texted Arianne during the ten minutes he waited for the reply from the remote side. A single, high-pitched beep came from the small laptop speaker.

REMOTE > HELLO AXEL. WHAT YOU NEED?
LOCAL > YOU WERE RIGHT ABOUT HACKING AND SPYING HERE AT COS. THOUGHTS?
REMOTE > NOT OMNI. NOT FIVE TRIBES. MANY PLAYERS. YOUR GOVERNMENT AND OTHERS WE THINK.
LOCAL > TELL ME

The information dump that followed overwhelmed the men.

Omni confirmed Axel's suspicion of the TAO's tentacles wreaking havoc on the convention floor. Phish told them that government agents might be present in the convention hall using tools like Ragemaster and Sparrow. They were also using a wireless keystroke logger known by the name SurlySpawn, which tapped the line going from the keyboard to the processor. This tool gave the user access to logins and passwords to the otherwise secure COS server.

Another spying tool called Genesis was a GSM handset with a Software Defined Radio that allowed the user to record RF spectrum in a tight vicinity. Genesis was compromising cell phone conversations in the Great Hall. These cell conversations could then be downloaded to an integrated laptop. An organization like TAO would have reams of data to analyze with this tool.

Phish also indicated there were other brute force hacks being waged by nation-states and idle hackers wanting to cause problems just because they could. Idle hackers could be a nuisance. Nation-state attacks were disruptive.

Disruption by individual hackers would take the form of spear phishing. Phishing attacks could consist of legitimate-appearing emails with an attachment containing malware. Once the user opened the attachment, it would compromise the system by destroying or stealing data.

REMOTE > ALSO REMEMBER "UMBRAGE".
LOCAL> UMBRAGE?

"UMBRAGE" was the name of a CIA false flag program designed to make the agency appear as if they were hackers operating from another country.

Phish also reminded them that it was difficult to prove who did the hacking, since individual hackers or nation states jumped around from hijacked devices that they used as a spear in attacks.

LOCAL > THANK YOU FOR THE INFO. BYE.
REMOTE > YOU ARE WELCOME. BYE.

Axel closed his laptop and turned to Chandler. "So probably the disruptive acts where delegates had problems getting into their devices or lost data were due to individual hackers just causing trouble.   The network problems because of foreign, state-sponsored hacking. The pure intel gathering would be the work of TAO. Delegates wouldn't have a clue about what TAO was doing.   It also wouldn't surprise me if someone from the California secession movements was involved."

"We got a big ole hole in the fence here," Chandler offered, placing his hands on his head.

"Your metaphor is most appropriate. There are all kinds of security holes here. It's real dirty in that Great Hall. I don't agree with what TAO is doing, but I understand their motivation."

After 9/11, the NSA sought to prevent what in their minds would be the next Pearl Harbor. That presumed attack would be more than just a nation-state bombing a naval fleet or terrorists flying planes into skyscrapers. Modern warfare extended the battlefield to cyberspace. The NSA collected it all so they would know it all. They considered the COS Project something that could morph to threaten their own existence.

"So, what's the answer here?" Chandler asked, throwing is hands in the air.

His nervous toe-tapping annoyed Axel, who put his hand over Chandler's knee. "Relax. I need to talk to Geringer and make

54

some recommendations. I'm sure the COS folks had no idea how much attention they'd attract from all sorts of actors."

"What are you going to tell him?" Chandler's foot moved again, this time his heel.

Axel looked at Chandler's bouncing leg and shook his head. "I'll tell him exactly what we learned from Omni and the steps they need to take to stop all this nonsense. They won't like it but if they want this convention to have a modicum of success, they're going to have to listen. And it's going to have to be more than just things like laptops and cell phones. There are so many Internet-connected devices now that even more mischief is possible."

Axel explained the vulnerability of Industrial Control Systems (ICS) connected to the Net. He gave an example of a hack to a refinery in Texas that caused part of the facility to catch fire.

"I think it was in 2016 that I was researching a particular company, an oil company for my readers. They'd been having problems in some of their refineries and I wanted to figure out what was going on. That's when I found this guy who ran a search engine called KIDO."

Chandler stood in a martial arts pose. He held one leg bent in front of him and raised his hands near ear-level, his wrists bent forward. "The ancient oriental fighting art of KIDO!"

"You definitely have the comedic routines going. Will you please sit?"

"Sorry, Ax. That's what love will do for a man."

Axel grabbed Chandler's arm, coaxing him to sit down. "Anyway, KIDO drew this global map of all sorts of connected devices like buildings, webcams, factories, dams, and, of course, refineries. The guy running KIDO told me that many of these ICS were built for engineers to access them. The thing is, they were never built for security. He used KIDO to show me how easy it was to walk right into an electrical substation in France."

Axel feared the GMCC's Internet-connected devices would be vulnerable to hacks on power, illumination, and HVAC systems.

"Have they fixed all these holes?"

"Who knows? And that's the problem. Hackers know this and governments know this. Ironically, there's this organization called the National Cybersecurity and Communications Integration Center (NCCIC) that protects US cyber assets. If they notice a hack on a system, they send a team out to work with the victim."

"Strange isn't it. The government hacks and then protects us from being hacked. What a strange world we live in."

"Indeed, it is, Chandler. Indeed, it is. Let's go find Geringer."

***

They found Geringer in a meeting room in a corridor outside the Great Hall. He had just wrapped up a conversation with the COS contingent from Colorado. No one looked happy.

Chandler exchanged greetings with Colorado delegates on their way out of the room while Axel made his way towards Geringer.

"Matt, glad we caught up with you. We must chat," Axel said, breathlessly.

The lanky Geringer plopped his cowboy boots on the table and folded his hands behind his neck. "Axel, I'm already worn out and this thing has just started. Hopefully, our chat can infuse me with a little spark."

Geringer motioned for him to sit.

Axel retrieved a notepad from his bag, the same notepad used to detail tools he suspected were being used for spying in the Great Hall.

"I can't promise you a spark, but I hope to give you some clarity on what happened earlier."

"I'm all ears."

Axel sketched out what he thought was occurring, breaking his mechanical pencil's thin lead several times. He also discussed his cyber chat with Phish.

Geringer straightened from his former reclined position. He placed his clenched fists on his hips. "You know how I feel about Omni. Yeah, they've helped before, but in the back of my mind I always wonder if they're feeding you a line of bullshit, covering their own tracks."

Chandler cracked the door to the meeting room and peered in. "Have you guys seen any hackers around here?"

Axel waved him in. "Close the damn door! I just briefed Matt."

Chandler took a seat opposite Geringer, next to Axel.

"Tell me again why you think Omni is clean here," Geringer urged.

"I've worked with these guys for years. Sure, I don't always agree with them, though to date, they've given me every reason to trust them. No doubt they're an enigma. At their core, they're all about fairness, or at least their conception of fairness and liberty. It doesn't fit their profile to mess with this convention."

"You know, everyone's got their own damn version of fairness and liberty now," Geringer said, shaking his head. He wagged his finger at Axel. "What do you think would happen if I called the NSA and told them to stop hacking the convention?"

"I know. I know. Let me add one more detail to get you more stirred up. It wouldn't surprise me if the North Koreans had a hand in this too. Ever heard of Bureau 121?" Axel inquired.

"No."

Axel went back to his notepad.

The North Korean government sponsored Bureau 121, a group of young hackers with special talents in math and science. These young cyber soldiers received their education overseas or in Pyongyang. For a poor country, it was far less expensive to develop a room of hackers than a weapons program. This approach allowed them to choke enemies in full secrecy without the saber rattling of threatened missile launches.

Axel punctuated the explanation with a confident tap of his pencil on the notepad. "Call the NSA and let them know the North Koreans were meddling anywhere in our country and you'll get their attention."

Geringer's eyes radiated defiance. "You're dreaming. Besides, that wouldn't solve all our problems and they won't accept you or Omni as a credible source."

"Fine. That may not solve your problem, but if you want any chance of continuing this event, you need to look at this disturbance as having three components. Our own government is spying and collecting intelligence that I know will be used against you in a propaganda campaign. They'll spin the COS as some sort of runaway convention, that you're threatening the Constitution. The second component has incursions from nation-states like North Korea. The third is just hackers with nothing better to do, causing disruptions. Oh, and maybe a fourth with California delegates."

"I'm not doubting that all these could be players, presuming Omni is not covering their own ass. What would you have me do? And don't say something stupid about the NSA."

Axel folded back the pages on his notepad and stowed it in

his bag. "I would tell Lincoln to suspend the convention for a couple of days to sweep everyone's electronic devices, especially for implants. Have the Honor Brigade review their access control procedures. The one you're not gonna like is to isolate the convention from the Internet. They can set up a network with only internal access. They can use their cell phones, though I'd recommend encryption for messaging among themselves." Axel glanced at Chandler with his next suggestion. "I suppose they can download the Maxwell Tech encryption package."

Maxwell Technologies, the firm owned by Arianne's father, developed an encryption technology for use on cell phones. The government tried blocking its release on national security concerns. The federal government asked for a backdoor into the software, which Maxwell refused to grant. Lawyers for both sides continued to litigate.

Geringer had a look of stark resignation. "I suppose I shouldn't be surprised this is going on. It's our world, sadly. Let me talk to Lincoln. I'm sure he has his own thoughts, though I have to say, your solution is the quickest way to get this done. I'm just not sure how Lincoln's gonna make it happen."

Chandler beamed with pride, placing his arm around Axel. "Yep. If Ax comes up with a plan, you can take it to the bank!"

Geringer stood and the other two did the same. "Guys. Thanks. I've got some work to do. Try to stay out of trouble for a couple of days." He winked at them, shook their hands and left the room.

"Chandler, I'm tired. I'm just going to order room service. Hope you don't mind."

"I'm good. I'll figure something out."

He didn't look forward to a couple of idle days.

***

The next morning, Chandler's room phone startled him, making him roll over in his king bed, reaching instead for his cell phone thinking he'd set an alarm. Back in his Manhattan apartment, the wake-up call would come from Venus, his digital assistant. When the fog lifted from his brain, he picked up the handset on the nightstand, clearing his throat.

"Ah, hell, hello?" He ran his fingers through his thick mane.

"Chan, you might want to check out what's happening outside the conference center. It's going to be an interesting day!"

Chandler ran his hands through his hair again. "Ax? What, what time is it?"

"Time for you to get up. Meet me in the lobby in 15 minutes. Can you do that?"

"Yeah sure."

Twenty minutes later Chandler ambled down to the lobby. "Sorry, I'm a little late. I had to grab some coffee." The java gave him needed focus and sense. He cradled the beverage with both hands, trying to extract warmth. The bitter air from the outside seeped in every time someone came through the lobby's sliding door.

Axel gestured towards the entrance. "Look at that!"

Colorado state troopers were struggling with a new batch of protesters who formed outside the Grand Mountain Conference Center. The only people being allowed in were those staying in the hotel portion and delegates to the COS. A Colorado militia group known as the Centennials added to the tumult by clashing with some protesters.

Militia groups were a source of consternation for the federal government and Americans who felt they were bent on revolution. Contemporary militia groups were born after the incidents in Ruby Ridge and Waco. Painting all militia groups with the same brush wouldn't tell the whole story.

On one end, militias prepared for Armageddon or an ultimate battle with the feds. On the other, were groups focused on civil preparedness in the event of natural disasters with their ranks eager to lend a hand to state National Guard forces. The Centennials were but one group within a larger constellation of militias in the state of Colorado. Even within a state, harmony among militias was not a given. Often there were competing interests with many chiefs and few Indians.

Colonel Randy Walker led the Colorado Centennials. Colonel Walker had a stint in the U.S. Army. After leaving the armed forces, he replied to an ad in Soldier of Fortune magazine requesting mercenaries in the former Rhodesia. Colonel Walker risked his life for $2,000 per month. He returned to join civilian life, operating a construction company. In 1999, he started the Centennials in his home city of Denver. The Colorado Centennials included nine brigades and a total membership of 500.

"So, this group, the Centennials, what's their angle?" Chandler asked, leaning towards Axel.

"Supposedly, they're here to help the state troopers who probably don't want their help. From what I can tell, none of them are armed, though this is a conceal carry state. Truth be told, the Honor Brigade is inside handling security and with the extra crowds now, it might not be a bad idea to have the Centennials helping. That is, if the state troopers let them," Axel explained.

Before Chandler could ask the next question, Senator Geringer appeared with the leader of the Honor Brigade, Big Dog.

"Hey guys, can you join us over here?" Geringer motioned them towards a walled-in business center connected to the lobby.

Geringer waited until everyone was in the room before taking a final peek outside and closing the door.

Everyone stood.

"Senator, you look like you have a burr under your saddle," Chandler offered.

Geringer ignored the idiom. "Chandler, Axel, I want to introduce you to Big Dog. He's leading the security detail here. He also leads the Honor Brigade in the state. I think you'll have an interest in what he has to say."

Members of the Honor Brigade often identified themselves only through their call signs. Chandler's first exposure to the Honor Brigade came in the documentary he made the prior year. He met a mountain of a man named Mack Crockett in Idaho, though he never identified his call sign. Big Dog was not tall, though powerfully built. Though the temperature outside hovered near zero, Big Dog wore a black polo shirt exposing three prominent tattoos.

On top of his left forearm, just below his watch, he sported a black panther, its jaws in the attack position facing a snake wrapped around the feline. On the outside of his right forearm, he had the inscription "We the People", the preamble to the Constitution. The inside of the right forearm displayed the second amendment, the right to bear arms. Big Dog didn't wear his emotions on his sleeve — he wore his beliefs on his skin.

Big Dog served in the artillery in the U.S. Army before retiring and starting a security company, hence the COS's request for his services.

Big Dog greeted Axel and Chandler with firm handshakes. "Nice to meet you all. Mr. Scott, nice job on the documentary.

You did the nation a great service by exposing that camp. Sorry that your partner, Mr. Dutari, passed away before you released it."

Chandler pointed towards the drop ceiling. "If I know Arturo, he's probably up there laughing at me for being charged with trespassing. And please, call me Chandler. You call me 'Mr. Scott' and it brings back memories of being in front of that federal judge."

The men shared a brief laugh.

Geringer broke the levity. "Let's sit. Big Dog has some intel for us."

Everyone sat in a normal position except for Big Dog, who had his chair's backrest in front of him.

"The Honor Brigade has this thing we call a 'Phantom Program' where people can join our group somewhat anonymously, and I'll leave it at that. Within this program, we have people from law enforcement, active duty military, FBI, and even some in government. We call these people Sentinels."

Active duty military couldn't join groups like the Honor Brigade. Those taking the risk did so surreptitiously within the Ghost Program.

"Interesting. Back when I worked for El Mundo, the name of my show was 'Centinela'," Chandler offered.

Big Dog smiled. "Yeah, I do recall that. Anyway, these Sentinels allow us to collect good intel. Someone told me last night that a California delegate is a secessionist from the California Sí movement."

"I guess the commissioner from Colorado knew what he was talking about when he fingered the dude from California," Chandler suggested.

Big Dog had more. "I wouldn't be surprised if there wasn't

63

someone from the Cascadia Movement in that delegation, too. I've not confirmed that."

"Axel, I related your suggestions to Big Dog and he's in agreement," Geringer said.

"Oh good. What did Mr. Lincoln say?"

"He's meeting with Big Dog this morning to discuss revised security procedures and background checks. It will be up to each state to decide who remains in their delegation. If California wants Cascadia or Cal Sí people, that's their call. They'll be out in the open now and they'll be expected to abide by the rules of the convention, otherwise Lincoln will expel them."

"Senator, I wanted to know if the convention was gonna do anything about the Centennials, that militia?" Big Dog asked, bouncing his torso against the chair.

"Not sure I can do anything. They're not causing any trouble and candidly, they are helping the state troopers manage the crowds. I'll talk to their leader, Colonel Walker, and make sure they don't overlap with the Brigade," Geringer replied.

"Good. I don't know the Centennials and in all honesty, I'm always suspicious about militias," Big Dog added.

"Well, who knows Mr. Big Dog, you may find they could be helpful someday," Chandler grinned.

Big Dog threw a quizzical glance at Chandler, brusquely rising from his chair. "Gentlemen, I need to scoot." He bid his newly formed acquaintances farewell.

"Guys, I need to do the same. Stay out of trouble." Geringer followed Big Dog out the door.

"It seems everyone's leaving," Axel said, following in Geringer's steps.

That left Chandler alone. He pursued Axel a few steps before his chest met someone's open hand.

"Chandler Scott?" the stranger asked.

"Whatever it is, I didn't do it!" Chandler shook his head.

"You're right. So, you haven't done anything yet, but I hope you will."

"Just don't ask me to trespass on federal government property."

The stranger extended his hand. "Chandler, my name is Jaden Casey and I'm the president of Veritas. You might consider us an alternative news organization. So, we're online and we publish a monthly magazine. Are you free for lunch or dinner today?"

"Ah, I guess." With the cessation of the convention, he had the time. "What's this about?"

"I have a proposal I'd like to discuss with you. Not here. So, dinner tonight?"

"Yeah, sure."

"Meet me at Cozens Cafe. It's just up the road a mile or two towards Fraser. Let's say 6:00 pm?"

"Yeah, I can do that."

Jaden shook his hand before departing. "Cool. See you tonight!"

This proposal would alter the trajectory of his life and others.

CHAPTER FOUR
VERITAS

The mainstream media (MSM) and alternative media had waged a battle for many years, a battle that intensified during 2016 when Jefferson won his first term. That election campaign featured a spirited discussion about fake news. MSM fought the smaller, alternative outlets who favored a decentralized approach. MSM felt threatened by the increasing influence of the smaller media outlets.

Another problem for MSM was the increasing number of people who got their news from social media. The popular social media site, Connections, grew to become a primary source of news for many. Anyone with a camera and a keyboard could proclaim themselves a journalist. The editorial scrutiny that existed in the traditional model had no place with solo journalists. Aspiring journalists posted stories in Connections referencing other websites. This invariably led to sensational news, creating conflict between supporters and detractors of the Jefferson administration. Connections' management attempted to scrutinize the news themselves with little success — that was not their forte.

Chandler took the free shuttle to Cozens Cafe to meet Jaden, who already had a booth.

Jaden Casey appeared to be about his age, average height and build with what was no doubt a constant beard and longish hair.

"Chandler, glad you could make it," Jaden extended his hand to greet him.

A waiter descended on Chandler the moment his bottom hit the seat, requesting his drink order.

Tonight, he'd have club soda with a twist of lime.

Chandler pivoted from the waiter to Jaden in short order. "You've intrigued me with your proposal for sure."

"So, before we get there, let me tell you about Veritas, who we are, what we believe in."

Veritas sought to capture the growing audience of those shunning the MSM. Veritas' motto was "vincit omnia veritas", or truth conquers all things. They believed the further a society drifted from the truth, the more it would hate those that spoke it.

This was also Chandler's personal motto and how he built his reputation at El Mundo, not afraid to throw cold water on the banquet guests.

Chandler's former employer had been co-opted by organizations like the International Relations Council and the Global Settlement Bank. The public had become increasingly distrustful of the MSM, and Chandler's expulsion from El Mundo only strengthened that opinion.

After Chandler's documentary received critical acclaim in alternative media circles, it became clear that these outlets posed a competitive threat to the MSM. MSM survived with advertising dollars. Their goal was to get in front of the largest number of eyeballs. The advent of small, high definition cameras and news that the public sourced from the Internet allowed small shops like Veritas to find their niche.

"I feel like I've been operating in my own niche since my last story at El Mundo and my documentary last year. I mean, look at how I had to release them," Chandler related.

"So, people's distrust has precedent too. Ever heard of Operation Mockingbird?" Jaden asked. He opened a web page on his phone and handed it to Chandler, who cradled the device in his hands while he reviewed the page.

Operation Mockingbird, a CIA effort begun in the 1950s, placed news with unwitting reporters, cited over and over by other sources. The placement served the agency's propaganda efforts.

Jaden clarified Mockingbird further. "It's a great way to spread information and eventually the public can be easily brainwashed into believing it, whether or not it's true. And now, with social media, that information spreads faster than any virus known to man. We believe journalism can be an invisible government. Look at the way the media spun your story about the reorientation camp discovery. You were loved by some and hated by others who focused solely on your illegal trespassing and breaching our national security interests. Never mind what you discovered. It's like that wasn't important. It really was a great deflection, you know, get people to take their eyes off the ball."

Chandler nodded in agreement.

His partner in the documentary, Arturo Dutari, was, in fact, an intelligence operative for two countries, Panama and the United States. Chandler maintained his partner's cover. He wanted to keep that detail from Arturo's family. Some media outlets wanted to give Chandler his due for the documentary, though they were fearful of running afoul of the Jefferson administration. Jefferson supporters would brand these outlets as unpatriotic. Many felt the camps were necessary to hold the nation together and didn't weigh them in the same regard as prisons or torture chambers.

"I know what you mean. When I worked on my last story at El Mundo, I kept butting heads with my boss. I just don't feel like I should have to ask permission to cover something. I tend to agree that having a decentralized press can keep the system more honest."

In their chatter, they'd neglected to review the menu. The

waiter came by to take their order and both men scrambled to place it. Chandler echoed Jaden's order.

"So, our feeling is that in order for democracy to work well, citizens have to be skeptical. That's where we come in. We'll investigate that skepticism. We're citizens too, right?" Jaden asked, shrugging his shoulders while spreading his arms.

Chandler tapped the ends of the menus on the table before stowing them in a wooden receptacle.

He nodded. "Yes, we are."

"I think there's another important role for an outlet like Veritas or I should say media. It's all about the unknown unknowns or those things we don't know we don't know."

Chandler lifted one eyebrow and lowered the other. His lips parted in a gasp of astonishment. The look would have made a great emoji.

Jaden grinned. "Put it this way. The public doesn't need mainstream media to resolve the known unknown or things that they know they don't know. So, if I asked you how many games the Mets won last season against left-handed pitching, you probably don't know that off the top of your head. At least I hope not. But I bet you'd know where to look it up in just a few seconds."

"Yeah, if I was in my apartment, my digital assistant, I call her Venus, she'd tell me."

"Precisely!" Jaden beamed. "And if I asked you how much the country spent on the military last year, you might go to the Pentagon's website to search for that number. Or you'd ask Venus." He winked.

"Yeah, if I was bored and had nothing better to do."

"So, the unknown unknowns are what you discovered in the reorientation camps. Someone could search on that term and probably come up with something, assuming the government didn't block the terms in the Reperio search engine." Reperio was the most popular web search engine on the Internet. "But if you searched for Elysium Protocol, you'd get nothing! Think about it. Even Omni didn't know or they would have released something."

Chandler's eyes widened. "So, I understand what you're saying. The unknown unknowns. I learned a new, ambiguous term today. Something unknown," he cracked. "Alright enough about knowns and unknowns. Tell me about your proposal!" He put both elbows on the table, resting his chin on his clasped hands.

Jaden reached for his bag and pulled out a folder, placing it on the table.

"I'd like for you to come work for us. You'll have full control of stories you want to cover or those that we ask you to. Though there are people out there that don't like what you did, our staff feels you're as credible a journalist as there is right now. And even better, you work pretty well by yourself. We don't have a big staff and who knows, we may never."

Throwing a wary glance at the folder, Chandler leaned back. "Hmm, I thought that's where you might be headed."

"So, the other thing is, we want you to start right away, right here, at the convention."

Chandler's jaw dropped. "Holy cow! That's faster than double-struck lightning! You don't waste any time, huh?"

Jaden chuckled. "Your expressions kill me. Yes, right now. You have a great relationship with Senator Geringer who spearheaded this thing and you're already here. So, I don't think you'll make the money you did at El Mundo. We're not that big yet."

Veritas received its funding from web ads, subscriptions, and private donors who pledged to keep the news organization around for a little while.

Chandler didn't address compensation thinking Jaded tucked the offer in the folder. "Where would I be based out of? Where are you based out of now?"

"Funny, you ask. You could be based anywhere in the U.S., really. I'm in Orlando and the rest of us are scattered all over. True decentralization," Jaden said with unmasked pride.

Chandler delivered a polite clap. "That's pretty cool, dude. That would make my girlfriend really happy. I'm in Manhattan and she's in Chicago."

Jaden flicked the edges of the folder, further tantalizing Chandler.

"I know I've hit you with a bunch of stuff in a short time. I'd really like for you to consider my offer and hopefully accept it soon. The convention will restart in the next day or so and I'd like you to cover it."

"I get that. The thing is, I've never heard of you guys. How many people actually see your work?"

Exposure had never been a problem for him at El Mundo and with the documentary. He wasn't sure how many people would follow him in this rag.

"So, I expected that question and have brought some stats for you to browse. You can take them with you." Jaden opened the folder and pulled out reams of charts and graphs.

Chandler scanned without reaching for the papers remaining in the folder, wondering if Jaden would address them.

"Oh! And here's the actual offer." Jaden pulled out the rest of the documents, creasing his face into a large smile. "Here, go ahead and look at it."

A relieved Chandler exhaled. "You're saying all the right things. I'll need to review this tonight." He grabbed the folder and thumbed through the statistical detail, thinking it impolite to review the offer in front of his potential employer.

"Here comes our dinner," Jaden said, spying the incoming tray. "Enough of this. Let's talk about something else."

The two men enjoyed the rest of their dinner, reminiscing about stories each had covered.

Before Chandler would make this decision, he'd need to discuss it with two important people in his life, Arianne, and Axel. Chandler understood that journalistic trust had to be earned, it couldn't be imposed. He felt like he'd earned it and now was once again time to put it to work. He hoped his girlfriend and mentor could give him good counsel. Perhaps his destiny rested with Veritas.

***

"Hey!"

"Hay is for horses." Chandler's humor streak continued in his phone conversation with Arianne while lying in bed.

"I've missed you and I just left."

"I more than miss you. I want you, all of you, every day." Chandler's declaration got him excited. He rolled over on his stomach.

"We're not having phone sex tonight. Tell me about your day."

"You know, we've been talking for months about being together, living together in the same city. The documentary last year took a toll on us, I know, but you know that was just a temporary gig until I could find something more permanent."

Her cautious anticipation grew with what she hoped would follow. "Yeah, and?"

He rocked on his elbows. "And I think I found something that would be good for us. I could live in Chicago. We could live in Chicago!"

"Oh my God, Chandler! Really? What's the catch?"

He rolled over onto his back. "There's this news organization called Veritas. They offered me a position and they want me to start right away, covering the convention. All their people are scattered, so it doesn't matter where I live. It seems like a good fit."

He'd yet to read the packet Jaden gave him.

"At least they have a great name for a news org. Did you accept?"

"No, I wanted to run it by you among other things I need to do."

"I'm glad you thought of me first. You've grown so much, Chan. I bet you're gonna talk to someone else though too, about this job."

"I always said you're as bright as a shiny new penny. Yeah, I wanna run it past Ax to see if he knows anything about them. I'd never heard of them."

"Axel has been so good to you. He's done a lot for you, professionally and personally."

"He has. I can't imagine what I'd do without him. I'm trying to contain my emotions about this. I don't want to get my hopes up if this thing is a dud. I need to go see him. Think about me tonight when you go to sleep. Love you!" He puckered his lips. "Mwah."

"I will. Good luck with Axel. Love you! Mwah."

He flipped out of bed, put on his shoes and scampered out of his room and headed to Axel's.

He knocked on the door with such force that he bruised his

knuckles. "Ax. It's me. Open up!"

Axel, in his bathrobe, opened the door with a look of contempt. "Whatever happened to calling first?"

A breathless Chandler moved right past him and plopped down on the edge of his king bed. "OK, here's what's going down."

Chandler offered details about Jaden Casey and Veritas and what it could mean for his life with Arianne.

Axel appeared pensive after Chandler's monolog. "Life is so short. I remember when I was your age, living in San Jose. I was running my own company. I'd met the lady I thought would eventually become Mrs. Schultz. Everything was good. The next few years were great. I sold my first company and bought another. I'd made great investments. But Mrs. Schultz, she got away. I should say, I let her get away. I was this high-flying stud in Silicon Valley. Everything I touched, it seemed, turned to gold except our relationship that I turned into a lump of coal. I had everything, everything that is, except a family. Then one day I looked at the calendar and we're talking about the 2020 election. 2020! It seemed like just yesterday I was voting in the 1976 election in New Mexico."

Axel sat on a chair near his bed, looking down towards the floor. Chandler, sensing there was more, didn't interrupt.

"I'm not trying to get off-topic here. I listened carefully about the Veritas opportunity. I've heard of them. They're new, trying to make a name for themselves. I don't know if they'll ever become the next El Mundo, heck they may not have those aspirations. I do think they'll be around at least for a little while. I know some of their investors. I can't tell you who they are, but one of them subscribes to my letter. They're old like me and want their grandchildren to have a future in which they can believe."

"The future is getting harder to see these days, that's for sure."

Axel lifted his head and locked eyes on Chandler. "Listen, the mainstream media's flesh is becoming gangrene. I think they're rotting from within. After what El Mundo did to you." Axel knitted his brow. "I think there are still good journalists in the mainstream, but I'm afraid their advertisers and the federal government have gotten to where they're exerting too much control. Plus, these people in the media are swinging between journalists and government, so they have to comment on an administration that they were loyal to just the day before they got hired for TV. It's all about eyeballs. Attention has become the world's new currency. I don't think this is what journalism should be."

Chandler appreciated the perspective, though his anxiety had manifested by his constant repositioning on the edge of the bed.

"All right, I can see that I'm wearing you out," Axel observed in mild frustration.

Chandler forced a smile. "No, Ax. It's all good. You know how much I value your wisdom. That's what mentors do, right?"

Axel radiated warmth at the compliment. "I guess what I'm saying is, consider taking the job. You and Arianne have a love. I can see it. I can feel it. A love that can withstand what you need to do."

"Need to do?"

"You're a superior person who's been in an inferior position. These last two years have elevated you. I'm not suggesting you'll be the President of the United States. I just mean that the public needs people they can believe, right now more than ever. You're as good as or better than anyone. Arianne fully understood this after she saw the documentary. She knows what's at stake. This is an opportunity for both of you. Don't waste it."

Chandler had never seen his mentor engaged in so much self-reflection. Axel had never confessed much, if anything, about his love life. "I know, I don't want to lose her and I almost did last year. I should probably get going, you look tired."

Chandler squeezed his mentor's shoulder on the way out.

The walk back to his room went at a snail's pace as he thought about Axel's words.

Democracy needed a skeptical citizenry. Chandler hoped that working for Veritas could feed into this skepticism and allow the public to judge events for themselves.

After arriving in his room, he reviewed the packet of information. This opportunity wasn't about money, although Jaden's offer would keep him well in the black. The rest of the packet affirmed his decision.

He texted Jaden Casey, accepting the offer. His first assignment the next morning would be a meeting with the leader of the Colorado militia known as the Centennials, and their commander, Randy Walker.

***

While the militia movement in the United States accelerated after Waco and Ruby Ridge, the financial crisis of 2008 increased their participation. Militias also started catering to a broader audience. The 2016 election proved to be perhaps the most divisive ever. Many voters, fearful of the country's direction, threw their support behind Benjamin Jefferson, a businessman from California with limited political experience. Most of the nation's militias focused on helping the community in times of natural disasters but continuing economic problems made them fear a societal collapse. The talk of secession and separation from groups like the Cascadia Movement and California Sí only heightened their worries.

Chandler met Colonel Randy Walker in a private meeting room next to the Great Hall. Colonel Walker's weathered face suggested someone who'd spent time in the great outdoors, either through his profession or hobby. In Walker's case, it was both. After leaving the military, he became a soldier for hire in the former Rhodesia. When he finished his military adventures, he joined a construction crew and eventually would own his own firm. He enjoyed all manner of hunting. A man of average height and build, Colonel Walker appeared to be in his early 60s. If he sported any ink on his body, it remained concealed under his clothing.

Chandler sat across the table from Colonel Walker, who dressed in civilian attire. He took out his phone to record the interview and laid it flat on the table.

Walker shot him a baleful glance. "What are you going to do with that?" He pointed at the phone.

"I thought I'd capture our conversation on it," Chandler said, continuing to set up by flipping a paper notepad.

Walker shook his head. "I don't know. When I talked to Mr. Casey, he didn't say nothin' about recordings."

A Denver newspaper reporter who portrayed the group as hell-bent on overthrowing the government had victimized the Centennials. In another instance, the group received what they thought was less than fair coverage by a local TV station, although they were helping a charity on the day of filming.

"Well wait a second, he didn't tell me anything about that," Chandler protested, lifting his torso.

Walker crossed his arms and turned his head. "You want to talk, turn that off. The *only* reason I agreed to talk to Veritas is because you seem like you're a straight shooter. You'll do right by us and that kinda stuff. I just don't want a recording to show up somewhere on the Internet and have all kinda whoop ass coming down on us, OK?"

Chandler stowed the phone in his shirt pocket.

"Now you ain't recording from in there, are you?" Walker pointed at his pocket.

"Huh?"

Walker grinned. "Just kiddin'"

Chandler would do a great deal of writing.

"Colonel, I spent time last year speaking with groups not happy with the government and their authority. I never talked to any militias, though. What makes your group different?"

Colonel Walker took a deep breath before answering. "That's probably the hardest thing for us. There are many militia groups all over the damn place, you see. A lot of folks have ideas about what a militia means and that kinda stuff. Look in the U.S. code, it will tell you all about an unorganized militia. Read the state statutes and they talk about militias too. Us Centennials, we abide by the law, you know. We're there to help the National Guard. During Katrina, those boys down there had the Cajun Navy helping evac folks. Job one for us is to help when needed."

"Admittedly, there are militias out there that just seem to want to pick fights," Chandler retorted.

"Yeah, for sure. That's not us. We want to be able to help." Walker paused. "Now if we ever have an invader come in to try to take things over, we'll fight to protect our land, our country and we'd expect everyone to do the same," he continued, in a cold, leveled tone.

Chandler tapped his pen, thinking about a follow-up to that response. He rubbed his chin before arriving at his question. "So, would you say the waves of illegal immigrants are invaders?"

Walker knitted his eyebrows and searched the room for a

good answer. "Look, we gotta protect our borders and we gotta let the government do that and that kinda stuff. But we make it too easy on those fence jumpers when they get here, handin' out all sorts of welfare. Maybe if we stop that, they won't come here as much. Now those other people, that's a different story."

Chandler tilted his head, scratching it with his index finger, and frowned. "Those other people?"

"Yeah, those refugees. I know some of those folks are coming over here cuz they have civil war in their country and that kinda stuff. The men doing that, they're cowards. They should go back home and fight. That's what we'd do. Do you think the Centennials would just run to Canada if there was a fight in Colorado?"

Chandler presumed the question rhetorical and didn't answer. The long pause suggested the Colonel expected one.

"Ah, I suppose the right answer is, no?" Chandler arched his eyebrows.

"You damn right it's no." Walker gave the table a sharp smack. "Don't think that every Centennial is former military just wanting to go out and shoot shit up on weekends. We have engineers, doctors, lawyers, janitors, truck drivers, union, non-union. We don't give a shit how much money you make or what you look like. We'll find a place for you."

"Are there minimum requirements? I mean, what do you expect from each person?"

Walker asked for Chandler's notepad and pen.

"Let me write down something for you. Everyone one of our members is supposed to keep 2,000 rounds of rifle ammo and 1,000 rounds of pistol ammo. Food and water for 90 days."

Walker wrote some other requirements before returning the notepad and pen.

"As far as training goes, not everyone can pass rough and tumble military style training. A lot of these guys and gals ain't in real good shape and that kinda stuff. We do have training for everyone, though. We're lucky here in Colorado, there's enough wide-open space for our training exercises. Speaking of which, we have a session this afternoon, not too far from here if you want to cover it."

Chandler didn't expect this bonus opportunity. With the Article Five convention in hiatus, it would be a great opportunity for him to get deeper into the story. It would be an opportunity few would receive.

"Yeah, that would be great!"

"Good, then meet me in the lobby around eleven. Dress warm cuz we'll be outside."

"Outside?"

"Shit yeah. Where else would we be? We train according to the season."

"Ah, yeah, of course. Where else would it be?" Chandler offered with mild sarcasm. He hoped his ski wear would do the trick.

***

Chandler and Colonel Walker drove in the latter's large SUV to an area near Grand Lake, some thirty-five miles north of Winter Park. A wealthier member of the Centennials owned substantial property near the town where they conducted outdoor training. In the Colorado mountains, the weather changed from the previous day's chill. The high today would reach a balmy 20 degrees Fahrenheit.

The Centennials had established a training compound that included a woodland course and a mock suburban complex. They wouldn't allow video or audio, but Chandler could report on anything he saw, as long as he kept out of harm's way — these would be live fire exercises.

The gravel parking area near the compound's entrance had four-wheel-drive vehicles of all stripes: pickups, large SUVs, and small SUVs. Male and female Centennials were staging their gear for the day's exercises.

Colonel Walker called everyone, including Chandler, to muster near the compound's entrance. They felt it was important for them to assemble as an organized unit, especially if called to serve with the National Guard.

Chandler's posture and foot position received a gentle nudge from the Colonel. The Centennials opened with a prayer and then the Pledge of Allegiance, acknowledging a flag perched atop the suburban portion of the training complex. Someone standing behind Chandler repositioned his right hand to demonstrate a better saluting position. After breaking muster, the Centennials returned to their vehicles to grab their gear.

The Colonel paired Chandler with a Centennial with the call sign, "Red Fire", who stood every bit of six and one-half feet tall. Red Fire wore a white coat over a gray hoodie and a stocking hat. A Molle system vest over the hoodie held ammo, a radio, and a pistol. His pants were also white. Dark, tactical sunglasses, paired with the head covering, cloaked any emotion. An ample amount of facial hair covered the rest of his visible face. A dog tag identified his social security number, blood type, and religion. He covered his hands in flame resistant tactical combat gloves with touchscreen capability. Combat boots covered his big feet. Red Fire carried a G36 rifle with a white butt and muzzle, proper for the surroundings.

"Colonel says you get to follow me. Stay close. These boys are shootin' real bullets," Red Fire's lips parted into a sinister line of stained teeth. The low tone of his voice suggested someone who'd enjoyed many cigarettes. Unlike Senator Geringer, Red Fire could pass for the Marlboro man.

"Yes, sir!" Chandler's deference met with a long, cold stare. He wouldn't get any breaks from this Centennial.

The mock suburban complex featured a series of rooms, built from plywood and rudimentary doors on bare concrete slabs. Since the complex had no roof, residual snow laid a thick carpet on the slab. A group of four Centennials stormed one of the rooms, rifles drawn, to perform a clearing exercise. After entry and clearing, Colonel Walker followed them to grade and provide guidance. Red Fire wouldn't be part of this drill, so Chandler stood next to him, observing and keeping quiet.

Next to the suburban setup, the group had an outdoor range with mock targets, both human and animal, at various distances. Recent snow covered the base of most targets. Chandler watched several Centennials fire an assortment of pistols and rifles. Hot shell casings made small clouds of steam after landing on the packed snow.

A female Centennial offered Chandler the opportunity to shoot an AR-15 at a target of buffaloes. After firing a few rounds, he realized he posed no threat to any nearby wildlife. The gun's owner slapped him on the butt for his effort. Red Fire snickered, shaking his head at his partner's inadequate skill.

"It takes practice, rookie. You ain't never shot nothin' before, have you?" Red Fire slapped him between his shoulder blades, forcing an exhalation.

Chandler lowered his eyes. "Ah, maybe just a couple of times."

Those times were shooting squirrels at his grandfather's house in Missouri with a small gauge rifle.

The woodland course proved challenging. The group started near a junked mid-sized car, pocked with bullet holes, with the number "1" spray painted on the rear quarter panel. Each member of the group squatted behind the passenger side near the engine and took aim at a distant target. After firing a couple of rounds, Colonel Walker ordered them to move to the next position. The depth of the snow made the trek to the next target slow and cumbersome. Chandler, trailing Red Fire, longed for the snowshoes from his hike with Arianne.

Chandler was sucking air in the 9,000+ feet altitude, compounding the test. After arriving at the next spot, his partner ordered him to hide behind a large pine. Red Fire set up behind a V-shaped gun stand where he laid down, placing the rifle in the stand's vertex, taking aim at a target 300 feet away. A "Don't Tread on Me" flag found refuge next to the stand. He exhaled slowly and fired 2 rounds.

A nearby spotter, wrapped in a white camo blanket with field goggles, spoke into his BaoFeng dual-band, two-way radio, "Red Fire. Two Hits. Clear!"

Red Fire looked at the spotter and yelled, "That's how you do it, bitches!" He waved Chandler to follow him to the next station. "Come on rookie."

The next exercise took Chandler by surprise. The spotter gave him an AR-15 and ordered him to follow Red Fire's instructions.

A wedge-shaped plywood structure formed the next shooting station. Red Fire ordered Chandler to squat behind him, facing the opposite direction in a defensive position, while Red Fire laid down across the wedge. Red Fire's muzzle sat four feet off the ground on the wedge's high side. He fired three rounds at a distant target.

"Hey rookie, now pretend someone is coming up behind me."

Chandler didn't know what to do next and turned with his rifle pointed at his partner.

Red Fire threw a despising glance at his partner. "Don't point that gun at me, dumb ass. Fire the motherfucker the other way!"

Chandler squeezed the trigger on the semi-automatic rifle and knocked a small branch off a pine a few feet in front.

"You are one green son of a bitch, ain't you?" Red Fire asked rhetorically. "Come on, let's go to number four. Give that rifle to the spotter before you hurt someone!" Red Fire pointed at another Centennial standing nearby. He'd seen enough of Chandler's marksmanship.

They advanced through ten more stations before completing the exercises. A warm bonfire welcomed them back by the suburban complex, where Chandler enjoyed hot coffee and sandwiches with Colonel Walker and Red Fire. Indoors didn't exist in this training compound.

Chandler would now use his notepad, kept in his coat during the exercises.

He asked Red Fire a question he'd been meaning to ask all day. "What's your real name, by the way?"

Militia members who didn't want to reveal their names were called Squirrels.

Red Fire grabbed a rolled-up piece of paper and placed it near the edge of the fire. "Colonel, I guess you didn't tell the rookie, did you? I'm a Squirrel." He used the flaming end of the rolled paper to light his cigarillo.

Walker grinned. "Yeah, Chandler. He keeps his name private from everyone outside the Centennials."

Chandler pivoted to the next question, not wanting to press

84

the issue. "Understood. OK, here's a question I think some of our readers may ask. Do you think America is afraid?"

Red Fire had removed his sunglasses in the minutes beyond sunset, revealing dark brown eyes with deep crow's feet in the corners. A shadow flashed across his eyes. A frown covered his face.

He sucked on his cigarillo, releasing an ominous cloud towards the fire. "Shit yeah. I think everyone's afraid of something. Mostly now, I'm afraid of Washington. I voted for that son of a bitch, Jefferson, in 2016. He said the right things. He knew we were hurting out here. I figured with his business background he would help. All he's done is make himself king, you know?"

Walker chimed in. "I think America is afraid of groups like ours. They think we're trying to overthrow the government and that kinda stuff. Unless they come to my house to take my gun or ammo, we'll be just fine." He patted his holstered revolver.

Red Fire rearranged logs on the fire with a walking pole, his cigarillo dangling from his mouth. "We buy the same guns and ammo as the government. That way we know we can still buy it somewhere."

"So, Red Fire, what makes you afraid of Washington D.C. or is it the president?" Chandler asked.

"I guess maybe I ain't so much afraid as angry at them. They've taken stuff away from America. Our jobs, our land, our money. Now they're tryin' to sell everyone with that horseshit We Are the Future. Who they kiddin'? And that damn Financial Stability Board is in my shit with paperwork, I can't use cash like before. It's fucked up, man!" Red Fire answered, hurling his cigarillo in the fire.

"Chandler, for sure, a bunch of our members ain't as well off

85

as before. That's made them even madder when they see government getting bigger and their opportunities getting smaller and that kinda stuff," Walker added.

"What would you say to someone who thinks a bunch of militia groups that don't trust each other or the government shouldn't be armed to the teeth? Doesn't that make everyone less safe?" A curious flush came across Chandler's face, highlighted by the roaring fire.

"I saw this interview on TV years ago. This Congressman said that we should join the non-violent peaceful movement to make the country more democratic. I resented him saying that since it ain't like no Centennial's been violent and been arrested and that kinda stuff. Our representatives are supposed to speak for us, but they haven't been worth a shit either. We're just trying to look out for ourselves and that kinda stuff. We don't want no trouble with no one either. Who knows, maybe that Convention of States, maybe something good comes out of that." Walker surveyed his weary team. "Let's get these boys and girls home. It's gettin' late." He stood up and called the Centennials to stand muster.

Walker stood in front of his brigade, allowing everyone to fall in. "At ease. Nice job. You showed well in front of our visitor today. Those of you able to go back to the COS, get with me when we dismiss. Our motto."

Everyone, save for Chandler, said in unison, "Forged in a fire lit long ago, stand next to me you'll never stand alone."

Oddly for Chandler, despite being around more weaponry than he ever had before, he felt safe. His gut told him these Centennials would make their presence felt in a useful way. Now he just needed to remember everything he saw today since he could only take notes while sitting by the fire.

Part II

Escape

CHAPTER FIVE
EXODUS

The president met with his security team in the Situation Room.

The authorities had not quelled the civil disturbances in large cities. The enraged mobs realized law enforcement couldn't stop their mayhem. The police were playing an endless game of Whack-a-Mole. Riots were breaking out and vanishing at record speeds. Not only did social media accelerate a riot's life-cycle, it also spread the message of law enforcement's impotence to other cities where peace had prevailed. Compounding the security problem were scores of men and women, and former military, trained in urban warfare from their service in Iraq and other Middle East nations. These former warriors had experience in the art of irregular warfare and conflict in dense urban environments. They took part in the riots or aided the rioters.

The disturbances continued to test the president's tolerance. "Gentlemen. Solutions please!" He grabbed the edge of the conference table and squeezed, the tendons on the back of his hands erupted from his skin.

FBI Director Ralph Elliott spoke first, "Mr. President. Local police are being stretched thin, they're tired, overworked and as you know, some of them haven't been paid due to budget problems. Some are staying home with their families." Elliott and the others knew that local law enforcement, even with supplementation by the National Guard, were not getting the job done. These mobs were on a different level.

The president's relationship with his national security team had become strained throughout the latest ordeal. Unlike his

89

economic rescue plan, there were no magic formulas to solve the crisis.

The president glared at Elliott. "Mr. Director, I suspect everyone's tired these days, especially the people who still need to go shopping for food and can't get there for fear of being assaulted by an urban youth swarm."

"The National Guard is doing what they can. We've also sent in non-lethal weapons to disperse these crowds. They're using sponge rounds, foam rubber baton rounds, and these new crowd control munitions," Elliott pointed at one of the side screens in the Sit Room after fiddling with his electronic tablet. "Over on this monitor, sir."

The president cast his eyes on the screen. "What's new about them?"

"Sir, it's an explosive munition that sends 600 rubber balls out at high speeds. It will inflict blunt trauma," Elliott asserted. He changed to another slide. "On this image, you can see the Sting-Ball Grenade, which does something similar using rubber pellets."

"That can't feel good," the president commented, squinting his eyes. "Thanks, Ralph. We can't have the Justice Department investigating hundreds of police departments for excessive force. Had enough of that three years ago."

Elliott hoped the president would move to someone else — he wasn't providing lasting solutions.

Trent Carter, the newish Secretary of Defense, had grown indignant listening to the non-lethal approaches to handling the riots. Non-lethal weapons had their application within population centers. They filled the space between "shouting and shooting" and they sought to keep tensions from escalating. "Mr. President, if I may. I realize we can't just send the Army to clear

90

out a whole city and it's clear local law enforcement even with the National Guard cannot quell this thing but-."

The president extended his right hand, halting the secretary's response. "Hold on there, Trent. We can't afford another instance of martial law especially if it's with federal troops."

Carter filled his lungs with the air of tired, stale solutions being offered to the president. "Please sir, hear me out." He raised his index finger. "These riots are organized. Let's treat this problem militarily. If this was an enemy, I'd cut off their communications. They're successful since they can communicate. I say cut 'em off at the head, figuratively." He smashed his fist into his palm.

The president, amused by his theatrics, allowed himself a sly smile. "What do you have in mind?"

Carter had his own tablet that he used to bring up slides in a monitor behind him. He and his team had been working on this plan.

He stood and used a laser pointer for emphasis.

"Let's say this is one of the cities." Carter darted the laser pointer on a slide illustrating the urban destruction. "We jam cell frequencies in a defined area, like here and here." He clicked something in his other hand to change the slide. "Or another option is to order the communication carriers to cut off their towers or shut down their access back to central offices or data centers." He sat back down for the last slide. "Law enforcement can still use their licensed radios or satellite radios, as the case may be."

"But what about non-rioters? What would they do for communication?" the president asked.

"I only propose this for a short time. Maybe one week. This would give law enforcement a breather and a chance to catch up.

The police could make public service announcements and carry messages. Over-the-air television could still provide vital communication."

The president nodded in approval. In his mind, though, they also needed to consider keeping these rioters and their coordinators from coming together in another city or perhaps the same city.

Carter had anticipated this concern. He suggested using the rioting cities as a testbed for drone dusting. The government could drop drone dust over an urban area, much like a crop duster over a farm field that would stick to civilians. This dust could provide valuable information for local law enforcement, FBI, and DHS personnel for tracking mob movement and capturing organizers. The dust contained motes, or tiny sensors collecting information well beyond people movement. This included temperature, radiation, and magnetic fields.

"Sounds pretty draconian Mr. Secretary, draconian but hopefully effective. We've got to stop these riots." The president nodded and turned his attention to the FBI Director. "Ralph, work with Trent on this. Get on the horn with the chiefs of police in the affected cities and the governors of those states. Make it happen." He pointed at Elliott.

"Yes, sir," Director Elliott replied.

"Victor, you too," the president pointed at the Secretary of Homeland Security.

"Yes, sir," Secretary Haydon replied.

Carter could barely conceal his delight. He tired of tiptoeing around civilian problems when they threatened the nation's security. More and more, the Department of Defense had turned their attention inward, towards the American public.

"Who's next?" the president asked, tapping his hand on the

table.

Newly appointed NSA chief Eric Greich took his turn. "Mr. President, we're getting very good intel from our TAO and ANT groups about the Convention of States in Colorado. We've also got someone embedded there. He's posing as a delegate. They've stopped the convention for a couple of days. They realized they were getting hacked and otherwise disrupted."

"You mean, we're hacking them?" the president asked, his eyes widening.

Greich offered a sheepish grin. He was the new kid on the block who no doubt took his direction, at this stage, from his deputy. "Ah, no, sir. Not exactly. I wouldn't call it hacking. We're just collecting intel. They won't know we're doing that."

Little did Greich know that Axel Schultz had already suspected them.

The president's forehead puckered. "Sounds like hacking to me. Jesus, I can't wait for the day when all this hacking crap ends. America's gotta be sick of all these wars!"

Jefferson's Chief of Staff, Drake Hutchinson, had already crafted a plan for countering proposed amendments that came out of the convention. He wanted to lobby key states to make sure the proposed amendments never saw the light of ratification. The TAO group's efforts were key to revealing amendment nuances not made public. Even if nuances didn't exist, Hutchinson had a propaganda campaign ready.

"Mr. President. If Mr. Greich is done and speaking of hacks, I need to brief you on cyber events occurring with our infrastructure," DNI Gerald Burkemper announced.

In 2009, an explosion destroyed a turbine in a Russian dam three times the size of Hoover Dam. Though the Russians claimed the explosion was accidental, a subsequent hack of the

U.S. Department of the Interior targeted vulnerabilities of thousands of dams in the United States. That raised U.S. intelligence's attention, who feared the Russian dam had been a cyber-attack casualty.

"Sir, we've received intel that the Oroville Dam, in your home state of California, may be at risk," Burkemper stated. He slid a document towards the president, who took a moment to examine it.

"Fine, so we've got our cyber forces ready to handle any attack, right?" the president asked, throwing a wary eye towards Burkemper.

"To some extent, sir. I should also note that your home state is full of dams and candidly, sir, we can't protect all of them or even most of them. The Oroville Dam is so important not just for electricity generation but also as a water supply and for flood control. And we can't just take the dam offline either without causing other problems. Many of our dams have software vulnerabilities that our cyber experts have known about."

"So why didn't we address them?"

"Well, sir, if we did, we'd have to notify the software manufacturer who'd patch it up and then that would close our entry points to foreign and domestic operators who we're spying on," Burkemper said, timidly.

"Hmm. We keep the vulnerability a secret to give us a back door. And yet, our enemies can use that same back door. Quite an irony I'd say." The president shook his head.

"Unfortunately, sir, yes."

The president pointed at FSB Secretary Malcolm Holloway for the next update. "Malcolm, you're up."

Holloway, just back from his emergency economic summit meeting in Geneva, straightened his tie and sat erect in his chair.

"Mr. President, the meeting with the Global Settlement Bank was productive. We spoke about the urban chaos here at home. One thing that's clear is the use of cash in these riot zones is thwarting law enforcement efforts. These urban cores have their own little underground economy going on. Forcing everyone into electronic money would make it harder for these rioters to function. When we implemented the Global Financial Union, we agreed to allow the public to have a small amount of cash. That was important for those without a bank account and the older folks. Cash is proving hazardous to the security of these cities now, sir. During our meeting, we decided that we should accelerate the timetable for getting rid of cash."

"You're right, cash and DigiNote are not helping us," the president nodded.

DHS Secretary Victor Haydon interrupted with an important update on airspace violations in D.C. and around Camp David.

Washington D.C. received a Special Flight Rules Area (SFRA) designation. The FAA restricted the area around Reagan National airport (DCA) in a thirty-nautical mile radius up to 18,000 feet. Camp David enjoyed its own radius of three nautical miles, extending to 10 nautical miles when the President of the United States was in residence. Most often, violations of restricted airspaces were due to pre-flight planning errors by amateur pilots, and navigation or communication errors, with no hostile intent on their part. Lately, however, the violations were increasing in frequency, implying more nefarious intentions.

In the D.C. area, pilots could also receive a warning from a Visual Warning System (VWS), which comprised a flashing laser. The alternating red and green lights directed civilian aircraft to turn away from the laser shot from the ground. Drone traffic would render the VWS useless.

"Mr. President, there have been too many cases recently where a small craft violates airspace. The FAA tried to keep this quiet, but it leaked. That's another reason members of Congress are not eager to return. Last month, if you recall from your Morning Book, the FBI and DHS were able to stop a small Cessna from taking off. It happened to be loaded with a chemical bomb that the pilot intended to drop over the city. This Islamic terrorist was on a suicide mission. Now we have a problem with drones capable of carrying small payloads."

DHS and FSB buildings in Virginia were recent victims of grenade-carrying drones.

DHS had deployed drone guns around federal facilities. The guns were 13-pound rifles that fired no projectiles. These guns jammed drone communication systems and had the capability of redirecting the flying craft to its operator or to a safe area for destruction. Since the drone gun operated on publicly accessible radio frequencies, it could cause disruption with consumer grade electronics. DHS figured they'd cross that public relations bridge when it became a problem.

"Sir, in light of these violations and other security events, Secret Service and Homeland Security strongly suggest your immediate evacuation," Haydon asserted.

"To where?" the president asked.

"There are several locations possible. At this time, however, we suggest Cheyenne Mountain."

"For how long?"

"Not long, sir. Give DHS and the FBI a week or two to get things settled here in D.C. We've got plans and then you and the rest of Congress can return to do the people's work."

The president engaged in an argument with Haydon and Carter. President Jefferson didn't want it to appear that he too was abandoning the nation's capital. He'd already discouraged his children from visiting the capital, and his wife pressured him to leave for their safety. In the end, his wife's insistence swayed him. She'd be happy to leave Washington, though she wouldn't be happy with their destination.

***

Carolyn Jefferson, the president's wife, proved to be a cooperative traveler when told by her husband that they needed to abandon the White House. Camp David was not on their itinerary. When he told her they wouldn't be returning to their home state of California either, well, those were fighting words.

The Jefferson motorcade departed, with no announcement, to Joint Base Andrews, where they boarded Air Force One with a destination of Peterson Air Force Base in Colorado Springs, Colorado.

Air Force One, code name "Comet", referred to any Air Force aircraft carrying the president, though typically it referred to the 747 carrying tail codes 28000 and 29000. The jet afforded travelers 4,000 square feet of space spread over three levels. With midair refueling, the aircraft had unlimited range. Of most importance, the secure communications equipment on board allowed Air Force One to function as a mobile command center connecting the president to many world leaders.

Moving the president entailed two other backups to Air Force One, though on this trip they would use only one. C-17 cargo planes carried the presidential limo, also known as "The Beast" and 2 backups. They sealed the Beast to protect against chemical or biological attack. Also on board the cargo planes were armored SUVs for transport of Secret Service and White House staff, and several helicopters, including Marine One. Given recent budget cuts, the presidential traveling detail, inclusive of equipment, was slimmer.

The president and Secret Service had only senior advisers, including his Chief of Staff Drake Hutchinson, on this flight. The press didn't receive notification.

The president sat comfortably behind his desk, wearing his Air Force One jacket. Inscribed in cursive, on the left side of the jacket, was his name with the presidential seal on the opposite side. Chief of Staff Drake Hutchinson sat across from him, looking concerned.

"Mr. President, I hope the First Lady is not too upset about the quick exit." Hutchinson also had some apprehension about leaving without telling the press corps, since a contingent normally flew with the president. He and the White House communications director were active in managing the press.

"Drake, let's just drop the formalities, at least for this flight. I know you're less worried about Carolyn than you are about your press buddies."

"You know we're gonna hear something about that."

The press had been compliant with the Jefferson administration. Hutchinson wanted to keep it that way.

Jefferson didn't want to talk about journalists. Instead, his escape from D.C. made him reflect on his presidency.

"You know Drake when I ran for president in 2016, I thought I could come to Washington and make a difference. I'd been in charge of large companies. I served on the boards of others. I thought that kind of experience could really make a difference. Of course, I knew the donors expected something from me. Hell, I've given it to them and more. How many of those people have jobs in my administration now? I'm sure they're doing back flips about the Financial Stability Board."

Jefferson's creation of a brand-new, cabinet-level department in 2020 brought a litany of compliance mandates. The regulations swelled the ranks of consultants and legal experts who kept that department off their clients' backs.

"Mr. President, sorry, Ben, you're tired. I understand."

The president shot him a glance of doomed resignation. "No, you don't, Drake. Here I am, the most powerful man in the world, or so they tell me, and I'm sneaking out of our nation's capital. I know the press will make a stink about not being here. I'm just following the orders of our security team, right?"

There was a tacit agreement between presidential administrations and the press that they would always know the president's whereabouts in a national emergency. Jefferson had just broken that unspoken covenant.

"I'm a little worried about buggin' out of Washington, but you know what? At the end of the day, it's the military and cabinet that needs to know where you are. Besides, the press is afraid of saying anything derogatory about you. If someone runs a story putting you in a bad light, they'll have another news organization, members of your party, or who knows who else come out and attack them for being unpatriotic. That Plan for Prosperity and the We Are the Future slogan were genius."

Hutchinson pointed with pride at his Plan for Prosperity pin on the lapel of his sport coat.

"You can thank Secretary Holloway for that. He's so brilliant. At the same time, I've placed so much trust in him, the Global Settlement Bank, and the International Relations Council and look what I've gotten." Jefferson tilted back in his chair staring out the window at the landscape 35,000 feet below. "The economy is still sputtering, our people are rioting, and our cyber security leaves us vulnerable."

Hutchinson leaned in. "Ben, things are improving. And I

know you don't want to talk about this. The reorientation camps have worked and are working. Even after that journalist, Chandler, what's his name?" He snapped his fingers.

"Chandler Scott."

Hutchinson tilted his index finger towards the president. "Yeah, that's him. Even after he released the documentary, the opinion polls showed your numbers were as strong as ever. People need to feel secure and they need to feel Washington cares about them. You've done that, Ben."

"But at what cost?" The president lifted his palms out to the side. "When you described the evolution of the camps and the Elysium Protocol, I felt like Dr. Frankenstein. By the way, how close are we to publishing the report I promised the American people?"

The assembled panel developing the report was dragging their feet. They understood that press members hostile to Jefferson would rake them over the coals regardless of the report's findings.

"I'd say we'll have something within the next month. I want to do a thorough review after DHS and the FBI have their turn. They'll keep the classified detail out of it and I'll make sure it's worded properly to continue to ensure your plausible deniability. We need to make sure the conclusions continue to emphasize patriotic themes, support the Plan for Prosperity, that sort of thing."

"Sure. We can't tarnish our plans and slogans, can we?" The president rolled his eyes with sarcasm.

"Ben, I'm not sure I understand the contempt. We're executing your vision. Just think of where this country would be if you hadn't frozen the 2020 election? That sort of governing paralysis makes a nation vulnerable. If you think we're vulnerable now with hackers, man, I'd hate to see what would have happened with Congress fighting for who knows how long electing a president."

"Well, we better secure D.C. by the time I get back so Congress can come back and finish the election. The Supreme Court gave me a deadline and we're beyond that now. I don't want to test the sensibilities of the American public too much longer with the election freeze."

"The public and even members of Congress understand now that your executive order was in the best interests of the nation. You carried the plurality of the popular vote and electoral vote. You should win the election in the House, even with a GOP majority. I talked to GOP members who are afraid of voting against you for fear of angering their constituents, many who view you favorably as someone who stabilized the country."

"I hope you're right, Drake. I'm going to go lie down for a few minutes."

The president retreated to his quarters, where his wife was already napping.

An hour later, the president received a distressed call from his chief. "Ben, Mr. President, sorry to disturb you. We have a situation. Please come to your conference room."

The president went to the lavatory to wash his face and hustled to the conference room where he met his Secret Service detail and his chief — everyone had a look of palpable concern.

Air Force One was cruising over western Kansas when a civilian passenger jet got too close. Whenever the president flew on Air Force One, there was a large block of restricted airspace surrounding the aircraft.

A well-muscled Secret Service agent, dressed in all black, briefed the president. "Sir, we received notification from air traffic control in Olathe, Kansas that Air Force One has traffic behind us within the restricted airspace."

Another agent standing next to him nodded in agreement.

"They're also not responding to the VHF/UHF guard frequencies. They've gone dark. It appears they've stayed behind us and are following. We don't know their intentions or capabilities," Chief Hutchinson added.

"So, what are we doing?" the president asked, placing his hands on his hips.

The Colorado National Guard scrambled two aircraft, F-16C Fighting Falcons, from the 120th Fighter Squadron of the 140th Wing from Buckley Air Force Base in Aurora, Colorado. Lt. Dustin "Dirty" Meyers and Lt. James "Hammer" Williams piloted interceptor aircraft coming to Air Force One's defense. A short time later, they were near the rogue civilian jet.

Per protocol, the F-16s approached the civilian jet on its left side. The first interceptor piloted by Lt. Williams rocked his wings to signal an intercept — the international sign to get the civilian pilot's attention. In response, the civilian craft was expected to remain predictable with a constant altitude, heading, and airspeed. They should then rock their own wing in acknowledgment. This didn't occur.

The expectation was for the civilian pilot to talk to air traffic control or move to the 121.5 frequency where the interceptor craft could speak to the pilot. This didn't occur either.

Lt. Williams attempted communication with the rogue craft. "Aircraft November, 5, 9er, 4, Bravo, Foxtrot, you are in restricted airspace. You are ordered to turn south immediately. If you do not follow these instructions, you may be fired upon."

Still no response.

The interceptors relayed the situation to the Air Force One pilots who then communicated it to the president via speaker phone in the conference room.

The president paced while Secret Service agents and the chief watched. He gnawed hard on his gum. "Is there anything else the F-16s can do before they take action?"

By this time, pilots on Air Force One had patched Lt. Williams into the conference room.

His voice rose above the background white noise of his aircraft. "Mr. President, this is Lt. James Williams. There is one more thing we can do. Stand by."

Lt. Williams flew in front of the aircraft and fired flares. Lt. Meyers followed with the same action.

The civilian craft maintained altitude, heading, and airspeed — still no response.

The white noise hummed in the conference room speakerphone before the pilot spoke. "Mr. President, this is Lt. Williams. They are still not responding."

"Is it possible that the pilot is unconscious?" A concerned president asked, leaning into the phone.

Losing cabin pressure in an aircraft could lead to hypoxia. Such a low oxygen condition would incapacitate passengers and crew.

"It's possible, sir. ATC told us the civilian craft adjusted their course when Air Force One did the same a few minutes back. They're not unconscious in there unless they have someone remotely piloting the craft," Lt. Williams replied.

"Mr. President. This is Lt. Dustin Meyers, let me get a closer look. Stand by."

Lt. Meyers got as close as he could to the civilian craft and made an assessment. The speaker phone fizzled and popped before Lt. Meyers spoke. "Sir, the pilot's just looking straight ahead. There's a co-pilot next to him. Neither one's moving. I can't see their faces real well. They've got to know what we're doing."

Lt. Williams attempted communication with the craft several more times without success.

The Agent in Charge recommended action. They'd been dancing with this civilian aircraft for too long. "Mr. President, we can't wait any longer."

President Jefferson remained unsatisfied. "Lt. Williams. It's just a civilian jet, right? It's not like they have any weapons on board. Isn't that right?"

"Yes, sir. It is civilian, but we can't guarantee your safety. These pilots are a couple of stiffs, or they're choosing to ignore us. Too many unknowns, sir."

Chief of Staff Hutchinson had heard enough. He stood right next to the president and blocked his pacing, holding out his arm. "Mr. President, civilian aircraft know the drill. This is no friendly. They've been given every opportunity to break off."

The First Lady made her way into the conference room and remarked on the stiff look on everyone's faces. "Honey, what's going on here?"

"Carolyn. Go back to our quarters. I'll be there shortly. OK?" He pointed towards the rear of the aircraft.

"Ben, talk to me!"

He put his arm around her and ushered her out the door. "Carolyn, please. I need a moment. I'll be back there in a minute."

She'd seen that look before. One of the Air Force One staff walked the First Lady back to the presidential quarters.

The president wanted one last opportunity to remove doubt. He leaned in again towards the phone. "Lt. Williams, I presume we have no options left?"

"No, sir, we do not. I recommend we take immediate action."

The president stared at his chief and Secret Service agents. A doomed expression covered his face. He dropped his chin before giving authorization. "Go ahead. Do what you need to do." He turned off the phone and walked out of the conference room. He squeezed his eyes, wincing at the order he just gave.

Lt. Williams locked on to the civilian jet and fired an AIM-9 Sidewinder missile, removing the threat.

***

Air Force One landed at Peterson Air Force Base fifteen minutes later. The base shared an airfield with the adjacent Colorado Springs Municipal Airport. Peterson also housed the North American Aerospace Defense Command (NORAD) and the United States Northern Command (USNORTHCOM) headquarters. Since 1987, the base also served as the location for Air Force Space Command (AFSPC) headquarters. AFSPC's mission focused on space and cyberspace capabilities.

High winds grounded Marine One, mandating vehicular transport in the presidential limousine, the Beast.

The president's motorcade took them the fifteen miles through the southern portion of Colorado Springs to the Cheyenne Mountain Complex — a Level One security facility more strict than the Pentagon. The complex sat under 2,000 feet of granite and could sustain a direct nuclear hit, an electromagnetic pulse (EMP), chemical, or biological attacks. Cheyenne Mountain was a place of constant twilight, where there was always someone awake.

If the president was safe anywhere in the country, this was the location.

The motorcade ambled a thousand feet up a restricted road

from the city below, streaking past the official, guarded station located a mile and a half away from the main entrance. Support buildings flying the U.S. and Canadian flags sat just outside the main entrance, including Building 100, home of the 721st Security Forces Squadron — the guardians of the facility.

The last vestige of natural light would disappear as they drove into the tunnel marking the entrance to the granite mountain.

The president and his detail continued through two sets of twenty-five-ton blast doors towards the formal entryway featuring the insignias of its four tenants. It's fifth would be the President of the United States (POTUS). The 721st Security Forces Squadron manned the security window announcing a Force Protection Condition Bravo, suggesting a predictable terrorist threat.

Air Force General Wallace greeted the president with a salute at the security window. "Mr. President, welcome to Cheyenne Mountain. We've got your quarters and conference room prepared for you to stay as long as you need."

President Jefferson, still reeling from the missile strike against the civilian aircraft, returned a weak salute. "Thank you, General Wallace. I hope not to be a guest for too long."

Cheyenne Mountain could withstand most any mayhem occurring outside its walls. The facility still required precautions for unforeseen events from within. As the presidential detail walked towards the VIP suite, the general pointed to an escape hatch used during a complete emergency. The president and his staff would crawl out of the granite mountain through this hatch in the event of an emergency.

The president and the First Lady settled in their quarters. The remaining presidential detail dispersed to suites and other quarters.

An hour later, Jefferson met with his chief of staff in a conference room also known as the alternate command-and-control center.

The room had polished oak tables arranged in a U-shape. At the top of the "U" were two large screens flanked by U.S. and Canadian flags. The left screen displayed the Battle Cab Traffic Situation Display, a visual representation of air traffic over the United States. The right screen showed concentric circles overlapping a map of Washington D.C. outlining restricted airspace, the same airspace violated in recent days by unauthorized craft.

Jefferson and his chief sat at the bottom of the "U" shape.

The president stared at the large video displays, rubbing his temples while contemplating his inbound flight from Andrews. "Drake, how are we going to handle, you know, that civilian aircraft incident?"

"Sir, we had no press on board and frankly, I don't think you should mention it to the First Lady. Did you?"

"No. I didn't want her to feel threatened, especially since we fled the White House." He rotated his chair towards his chief. "She's already on edge about being here and not back home in California."

"Look, I'll make sure we contact the FAA and put a lid on the event. They can craft a good cover story. The last thing we want to do is give anyone the idea that the president got threatened." He wrote a note on a small pad.

"Drake, the thing is, that plane, they never took any aggressive action. Maybe it was just a pilot out for a joyride, a thrill seeker. Maybe it was just someone's odd form of protest. I do have people in this country who loathe me, you know. It's possible they weren't trying to hurt me, just scare me. You heard the F-16 pilot. He called them a couple of stiffs."

"Would it make you feel better if you knew they were droids?"

"Droids?" Jefferson inquired with studied care.

The military used droids equipped with artificial intelligence for hazardous missions.

"Sir, I have no idea. If it makes you feel better. I'm just sayin'."

"Drake, please!"

"Look, you have many fans that admire what you've done. Mr. President, you really need to move on from this, please," Hutchinson suggested, in a distant, balanced voice.

The president offered a few weak nods. Despite his chief's plea, he'd have a hard time letting go of it.

He knew that being president was more than a popularity contest. He needed to lead, even if it meant being at odds with the public. The civilian aircraft encounter and other disturbances made him question his effectiveness.

CHAPTER SIX
ABDUCTION

The president enjoyed an unexpectedly good night of sleep in his ultra-dark Cheyenne Mountain suite. So much so, that he came up with an idea that he hoped would assuage the public's ill feelings about his administration.

After receiving his morning briefing by video in the command–and-control center, he floated the idea to his Chief. "Drake, the Convention of States is not far from here, right?"

"It's not. Maybe a three, four-hour drive. On Marine One, much shorter." He winked. "Why do you ask?"

"I was thinking. Wouldn't it be a good gesture if they saw the President of the United States being supportive of something like the COS? The whole process is in our Constitution, Article Five. It could just reinforce that I don't think I'm above the law. Would make for a great photo op." An enthusiastic smile reached the corners of his mouth.

The appearance of the President of the United States (POTUS), Benjamin Jefferson, at the convention could draw paparazzi eager to scoop the mainstream press.

The tension started in the chief's jaw and made its way down his neck. "Sir, I have to object. We have an intel operative there right now. You'd disrupt their operation. Also, remember the press doesn't know where you are, which is what we want. If you go there, everyone will know. We're trying to keep you safe, remember?"

"I can't argue with anything you said. It's just an olive branch. I think it will be good, just for an hour or so." The president's lips parted, revealing his pearly whites.

The tension continued towards the chief's shoulders with his boss's insistence. "Mr. President, I know you feel guilty about what we had to do with that civilian plane. Look, they're trained on that sort of thing. It's not your fault, sir."

Jefferson had not intended on reliving that memory. He lowered his eyes towards the table. "It's more than that Drake."

"Let me say one more thing. The Secret Service will totally flip out when they hear your plan."

Jefferson lifted his eyes. "Don't forget. They work for me. They have to keep me safe no matter where I go."

The chief called in the Secret Service agents assigned to Jefferson and informed them of the travel. Naturally, they were in opposition. The Special Agent in Charge called Washington. A conference call between the agents and Jefferson turned heated. He reminded everyone that he was the president. The presidential detail would head to Winter Park.

An hour later, Jefferson, his chief and Secret Service agents boarded Marine One from the complex's heliport with a destination of Winter Park. A separate chopper left Peterson with an armed military detail.

Colorado state troopers were none too thrilled to learn of Jefferson's unannounced visit. They had enough trouble handling the crowds in town and around the Grand Mountain Conference Center (GMCC)

With no airport in Winter Park or Fraser, Marine One landed at the Grand County - Grandby Airport located 20 miles north of the convention. Jefferson rode to the convention in the back of a Colorado Highway Patrol vehicle to the dismay of the Secret Service.

The crowd outside the GMCC realized there was something different going on with the approaching procession of state trooper vehicles, the cherries on the roof twirling in their customary white and red pattern.

Large men wearing earpieces emptied from the first vehicle. They dressed in dark suits without the accompanying overcoats mere mortals would need in the bone-chilling weather. These were no state troopers. The dark suits worked with local police and troopers to clear a path for Jefferson. The next set of cars included military personnel, armed to the hilt. They formed a buffer around the quieted crowd. Inquisitive spectators probed the troopers, the suits, and the military personnel for more detail. The security detail ignored their queries.

When Jefferson and his chief emerged, you could have heard a pin drop. The silence lasted but a second.

The crowd erupted into a mixture of applause, cheers, jeers, and catcalls, including words not fit for young audiences. One young lady broke containment and rushed towards Jefferson to snap a selfie. A Secret Service agent grabbed her by the arm before Jefferson asked for her release. She got her selfie.

Journalists in the lobby recognized the unexpected visitor, snapping pictures and yelling questions. The presidential detail made haste towards the Great Hall, the site of the convention.

Chandler, Axel, and Geringer sat awaiting the resumption of the convention delayed by cyber mischief and combative delegates. The secretary and clerks seated in front of convention president Lincoln pointed towards audience members seated behind Chandler. A clerk whispered to Lincoln, whose eyes cut towards the doors leading into the Great Hall. His lips thinned. The clerks looked as if they'd seen a ghost. The din of the audience grew, prompting Chandler, Axel, and Geringer to turn in unison towards the distraction.

"Is that?" Chandler pointed, speaking to no one in particular.

Geringer craned his neck at first, then unfurled his long, lanky frame, standing to get a better look. "Oh, my God!" His hand covered his mouth.

Axel remained quiet, taking in the disruption.

"Holy cow. I bet he's about as welcome here as a skunk at a lawn party," Chandler held his nose.

Geringer excused himself and strode towards Jefferson. He talked his way past Secret Service agents towards Jefferson, who by now was speaking to someone in press row.

After the president finished with his first press interaction, Geringer confronted him and his chief engaging in an animated discussion.

The convention resumed after Lincoln banged his gavel.

"Ax, what do you think the odds in Vegas would have been for all this?" Chandler was no gambler, but even he would have taken the bet.

"Even better," Axel raised his finger. "How many people would have taken that bet?"

Jefferson made his rounds through the press. The commissioners, most of whom were not fans, paid little attention to him. After one interview, he dispatched his chief to reach out to Chandler. The chief had no interest in doing so, still harboring ill towards Chandler for the documentary about the reorientation camps. Jefferson reminded the chief who he worked for.

While engaged in conversation with Axel, Chandler felt a tap on his shoulder. He turned and felt the piercing stare of a contemptuous Drake Hutchinson. After shaking his dead fish hand, he introduced Axel.

"Mr. Scott, let me get right to the point. My boss, the president, asked me to come over so he can speak to you privately. Believe me, this was not my idea." Dark blood flowed into his indignant face.

His derisive tone angered Axel, who thinned his lips and puckered his brow.

"He wants to talk to me?" A wide-eyed Chandler pointed at himself.

Hutchinson butted his fists against his hips. "Mr. Scott, will you, or won't you?"

Chandler looked at Axel as if seeking approval. Axel shrugged.

"*Maybe I really don't have a choice,*" Chandler thought. The beating in his chest quickened.

"Mr. Scott!" Hutchinson barked.

"Ah, yeah, I suppose. Where's this going down?"

Hutchinson pointed his rigid arm towards an exit door. "It's going *down*, over in one of those meeting rooms. Come with me."

Chandler arched his eyebrows towards Axel, who did the same.

He followed Hutchinson outside the Great Hall towards a meeting room where two Secret Service agents stood guard. Well-armed military personnel were also nearby. A Secret Service agent patted him down and the other circled a wand around him. They opened the door, revealing Jefferson relaxing in a leather chair on the opposite end of a table.

Jefferson walked towards him and extended a firm handshake. "Mr. Scott, very glad to make your acquaintance."

Chandler took a cautious step. His voice trembled. "Mr. President, ah, nice to, nice to meet you." His eyes darted around the room, wondering if another surprise awaited him. He'd done nothing to merit this meeting with the president, instead, he'd earned a lifetime of demerits. He wished for a stick of gum to quell the nervous tapping of his thumb against his leg.

Jefferson didn't appear as formidable in person as he did on television. Chandler stood taller by at least a couple of inches. He looked older in person. No doubt the last couple of years had taken their toll. Chandler waited for him to take his seat before doing the same. He placed his hands on the table in plain view, as if waiting for inspection.

Jefferson slurped coffee from his Styrofoam cup, pursing his lips in reaction to its heat.

"Mr. Scott, you and everyone else are probably wondering what the hell I'm doing here. I thought long and hard about what this country's been going through the last couple of years. It hit me that all these patriotic slogans, my Plan for Prosperity, We Are the Future, I need to get out and spread that message myself. Malcolm Holloway, my FSB secretary, a brilliant, brilliant guy, probably the smartest person I know. But he's a policy guy, no personality really. It's hard for people to connect with him."

Chandler would know after interviewing Holloway during his time at El Mundo. "This is a promotional tour for you, sir?" He remained disquieted being with the president.

Jefferson enjoyed a brief laugh, almost spilling his coffee. "Oh no, let's just say it's your president trying to connect with the people a little more."

"*Maybe he's testing me? Is this a trap?*" The expected ass chewing about the Global Financial Union or the reorientation camps didn't materialize.

"You definitely picked an interesting group to connect with." The president's laughter assuaged Chandler.

Jefferson appreciated the understatement. "Without a doubt, I'm probably the last person they expected to see. I didn't even know I was going to be here myself. I mean, what are the odds?"

Chandler gapped his mouth, given his own speculation earlier about that probability. "Ah, sir, I appreciate this time with you. I guess I'm wondering what we're trying to accomplish." He alternated pointing at himself and Jefferson. "Me and you."

"Of course, of course, you've been out at the forefront of reporting the last couple of years."

"Oh no, here it comes!" Chandler's face contorted.

"And I thought that you'd be an ideal person to transmit my message. I could give you an exclusive interview. The public, or I should say those that don't support me, could get a better understanding of what my administration faced and what I'm trying to do. You can write or say whatever you want. No censorship unless there's something classified or involving national security."

Chandler, nervous as a whore in church, didn't know what to do or say. The leader of the free world sat in front of him, offering him unfettered access. A story like this would put Veritas on the map. Yet, he looked fit to drop with apoplexy.

His facial paralysis unnerved Jefferson, who leaned forward, tapping on the table. "Chandler? You still with me?" He waved his hands to break his trance. "You OK?""

He snapped his brain out of seizure, squinting his eyes, tilting them up. *"Surely there's a catch here. There's gotta be! Oh, what the hell!"* His jaw tightened, making his next words jagged.

"Yesss, sssir. Ah, yes, I am." Chandler tried to maintain his composure by straightening in his chair. "What did you have in mind?" He sat on his fidgety hands.

"I'm staying at Cheyenne Mountain right now. I thought-"

Chandler popped up as if his chair had delivered an electric shock. "Cheyenne Mountain? Is there some sort of nuclear threat?"

Jefferson grinned. "There is a threat, but she's staying with me in Cheyenne. The First Lady wasn't real happy about leaving D.C. and shacking up here in Colorado."

"Whew!" Chandler scraped the tips of his fingers on his forehead.

"I thought we could start with a tour of Cheyenne Mountain. You could meet some of the brass there, you and I could spend some time on the flight down, and talk a little more over dinner. I'd have someone drive you back. Sorry, I can't let you take Marine One."

"OK, when would we do all that?"

"How 'bout now?"

Chandler wished he'd been a gambling man. "*These odds just became more absurd. Jefferson shows up at the COS, asks for my time, and grants me an exclusive one-on-one interview. How can I say no?*"

"Sounds like a plan, sir. Let me go to my room to get my tablet and coat."

Jefferson stood and walked towards Chandler's end of the table, shaking his hand once again. Chandler shook it with less apprehension this time. "Great! I'll send someone to get you. We'll leave via the service entrance. My guess is the crowd's bigger now out front. You know how it is with the Secret Service."

He didn't.

An hour later, Chandler traveled with the leader of the administration that had been the object of his enmity in the much-heralded documentary he'd released a few months earlier. He would have bankrupted Vegas with this bet.

***

The president's motorcade took him, Chandler, and Chief of

116

Staff Hutchinson in the same state trooper vehicle back to Grandby Airport. Marine One, a Sikorsky VH-3D Sea King, took off on a sunny afternoon in the Grand County valley cruising south at 150 miles per hour towards the Cheyenne Mountain heliport.

Chandler sat between Hutchinson and a Secret Service agent along the fuselage. The president sat perpendicular to them, stretching his legs on the seat in front of him.

Hutchinson ignored Chandler, spending his time checking messages on his phone. He'd only felt hostility from the chief. The Secret Service agent focused on his job. It offered a good opportunity to start the dialog above the din of the whirring rotors.

Chandler leaned towards Jefferson. "Mr. President, what do you think needs to happen for Congress to get back in session and what everyone will be talking about, the vote in the House?"

Jefferson retracted his legs and waved him towards the now vacant seat. Chandler unbuckled. Hutchinson threw a glare as he made his way towards the boss. Jefferson grumbled about his chief's attitude.

It was a bold first question for Chandler to ask after sitting now face-to-face with him on Marine One. He pinched himself, making sure he wasn't in an alternate universe.

"Chandler, the cyber disturbances have to be brought under control. They're all afraid there. I didn't want to leave D.C. It didn't set a good example. My intelligence team said it was for the best, and I couldn't argue with the Secret Service. It's comforting to know that the guy you were just sitting next to," Jefferson pointed at the agent, "would be willing to take a bullet to save your life." He paused for a moment, admiring the Rockies below. "I have no doubt that we'll still have cyber-attacks. The members of Congress just need to feel more confident and honestly, accept some risk, albeit minimal. I think in another week, we'll be back at it and as you said, we can finally settle the election."

"You feel confident about the outcome then?"

"Nothing's guaranteed. Even though the GOP has the majority in the House, I think a lot of them would be hesitant to vote for my Republican challenger, Mrs. Scarborough, in the middle of all the civil disturbances not to mention the cyber ones. Continuity is important now. The House also knows that I carried more popular and electoral votes. That counts for something," he offered with pride.

Before Chandler could get in the next question, Marine One dipped, creating that hollow feeling inside its passengers' tummies.

"What the hell?" Hutchinson broke out of his cell phone stupor.

"Just a moment, sir." The Secret Service agent opened the folding door to the cockpit to confer with the pilots.

"Drake. Settle down. You know how it is flying through these mountains," Jefferson said, confidently.

Nearby, the peak of Mount Evans punctured the sky with Summit Lake reflecting its majesty. Hutchinson had been on many copter rides with his boss, including Afghanistan. They didn't need to fear a ground-to-air missile in these mountains.

The Secret Service agent returned with an announcement. "Sir, the pilot indicated trouble with the avionics and other flight controls. He's working on the problem."

"Thank you. Drake, I guess we're going to need an appropriation for new choppers," Jefferson said, with a droll smile.

The government had contracted with Sikorsky for a new model scheduled for service in 2020. Due to cost overruns and budget cuts, the company postponed delivery until later in 2022.

The president had every confidence the craft, flown by two pilots from "The Nighthawks", would make it safely to Cheyenne Mountain. Even if attacked, Marine One could defend itself with ballistic armor, missile warning systems, and anti-missile defenses. A decoy Marine One took another route back to Colorado Springs. If all else failed, the 120th Fighter Squadron, a unit of the Colorado Air National Guard's 140th Wing out of Buckley Air Force Base in Aurora, Colorado patrolled the skies on the way to Cheyenne Mountain.

Regardless of all the chopper's capabilities and safeguards, he didn't want another experience with airspace violation.

"This is nothing Chandler. Drake's forgetting the bumpy ride we had one time coming back to the White House from Camp David. My wife just about lost her lunch that day." Jefferson concealed a smile behind his covered mouth.

Chandler didn't have many helo rides on his resume.

"Now where were we?" Jefferson asked.

Before Chandler could begin, they heard a high-pitched sound that rose above the whirring rotor. It got louder. It sounded like they were inside a beehive.

Chandler peeked out his window and pointed to a dense swarm of dark objects surrounding their craft.

"Hey Drake, what is all that?" Jefferson also pointed out his window.

Hutchinson turned to look out the window behind him and shrugged.

The swarm of dark objects moved as a single unit, though there were hundreds of them.

The Secret Service agent walked towards the cockpit to talk to the Nighthawks.

Meanwhile, the objects had piqued everyone's curiosity since they had their noses pressed against the windows.

"Sir, the pilots have informed me that we're dealing with a drone swarm," the agent offered in a cold, leveled tone.

Jefferson looked towards his chief for answers. He creased his forehead and opened his palms. "Drone swarm?"

The equally confused chief, lifted his shoulders.

Homeland Security, DEA, ICE, and the FBI used the domestic drone fleet for surveillance. Like the CIA fleet overseas, military personnel piloted the drones. Presuming one pilot per drone, the easy conclusion pointed to several hundred pilots operating the high-pitched nuisances.

"Sir, I have no idea. I can't believe the military would practice something like this around restricted airspace. And I didn't think we had these many drone operators," Hutchinson said.

While Marine One could thwart conventional attacks, a drone encounter was another matter.

This drone swarm consisted of various-sized craft. The largest had the diameter of a basketball. The smallest was the size of a cell phone.

The drone movement didn't appear controlled. A typical drone required a link to a ground controller and another to a satellite providing position and time used for navigation. These drones moved like a flock of starlings with their own collective intelligence. Despite their proximity to one another and to Marine One, they avoided collisions.

This swarm didn't have hundreds of pilots or even a single pilot. These drones operated with their own consciousness. They had a mission to complete.

120

Marine One bobbed and weaved like a prizefighter, attempting to avoid collision with the nimble swarm.

Chandler tightened his seat belt. His mouth grew dry with fear.

The Secret Service agent did the same, bracing himself on the armrests. He showed no fear.

Jefferson showed remarkable calm despite the flight disruption. "Sorry, Chandler. This is usually not part of the entertainment. Let me patch in." He tolerated this more than having to order a takedown of a civilian plane.

He grabbed a headset and plugged it into a jack on his armrest.

One of the pilots shared disturbing news. "Sir, we don't know who's operating these drones. We've never seen anything like it. If enough of these were to hit our rotors, we'd be in trouble. And our navigation is being disrupted too. I'm afraid we may have to put down soon."

Drone use had brought a new dimension to warfare. Jefferson never had to tell the press or the public about drone strikes. Drones didn't risk military lives, obviating the need for debate. Their surgical precision allowed the United States' involvement in an invisible, perpetual war. Drone warfare was something Americans just read about or watched on declassified film on the Internet. Despite their familiarity, the public never understood the horrors these nameless, faceless weapons inflicted.

"What about the F-16s on patrol?" Jefferson asked.

"Sir, there's more. We received a message on a frequency we don't usually monitor. We've been given coordinates to land Marine One."

Jefferson cupped his hands around the headset, asking for a repetition.

The pilots repeated the instruction to land the helo.

"Or else, what?"

"They've threatened to bring us down, sir."

"Can't we jam these drones?"

"That's another problem, sir, they don't seem responsive to this. It's like they're operating with their own intelligence."

Autonomous systems were part of the military's 3rd Offset Strategy. This strategy established the parameters for the next stage of warfare. The U.S. had been developing this technology for unmanned aerial vehicles. The swarm enveloping Marine One was beyond its capabilities.

"Who sent the message telling us to land?"

"We have no idea, Mr. President."

Chandler noticed Jefferson's countenance morphed into a clenched jaw and petrified, unblinking stare. This ride had unscheduled entertainment. The grip of fear clamped his throat, making him take short gasps of air. His mouth became parched. He thought of Arianne and the beautiful moments they'd enjoyed. He thought about his mom and their time in Texas. The reality of his predicament slapped him in the face.

During the F-16 Falcons' trip to intercept the swarm, they met their own problems. Another drone swarm greeted the jets as they approached Marine One. These drones were larger and armed with small air-to-air missiles. The jets from the Colorado National Guard opened fire with their 20mm Gatling guns, a 6-barrel system firing 6,000 rounds per minute. Like the swarm surrounding Marine One, these drones operated autonomously. While the F-16s shot down many of their foes, the swarm remained intact, with maneuverability exceeding the Falcons'. The drones shot all four Falcons out of the sky, their pilots ejecting safely.

The decoy Marine One encountered another swarm and couldn't render assistance.

The pilot relayed the bad news about the F-16s. "Sir, for your safety, we're going to put down at these coordinates. It's not far away and we can relay the position to our people."

Another layer protecting the president was a team of Delta commandos and FBI hostage rescue agents. Their choppers were already in route towards the coordinates given by the perpetrators.

Jefferson realized the danger in continuing to fly and figured the Delta team could easily rescue him. "Very well, make it so."

The pilots started towards the coordinates before receiving another message telling them to follow the swarm and ignore previous coordinates given.

They relayed this new order to Jefferson, who pressed the headset even harder against his ears, more out of tension than for acoustical reasons. "What? Why?"

"We don't know, sir. We should be able to just relay new coordinates just as easily. Under the circumstances, it won't really matter. I suggest we just follow the swarm."

They followed the swarm. When they tried to relay the new position to air traffic control and the commando team, their communication systems stopped functioning — their radios had power but were otherwise useless. Their flight transponder was inoperative. Still, the pilots hoped they could relay their position once they restored radio communication. This would prove false hope.

Another drone swarm repelled the Delta commando and FBI hostage rescue teams. These teams opted to take a circuitous route to Marine One's last known position and then headed for the designated landing coordinates fed to them by Marine One's Nighthawk pilots. They were unsuccessful in locating it.

Back at Schriever AFB, on the plains near Colorado Springs, the 50th Space Wing had their own problems. This base had no airplanes or runways and carried the nickname, "Master of Space." They controlled the constellation of satellites that included GPS, Milstar, or secure satellites for military communication, and the neighborhood watch birds that looked over other satellites providing early warning about threats. Of this constellation, the GPS was the most important, providing service to billions. There were twenty-four active GPS satellites with another ten in reserve. The eight people controlling these satellites were up to their ears with cyber problems. Without GPS, the U.S. military reverted to Vietnam era capabilities. The entire state of Colorado and surrounding areas experienced a GPS blackout.

When the Nighthawk pilots tried to evade the swarm, one of the drones crashed into the fuselage. Though not enough to cause damage, it proved unsettling and demonstrated the ultimate danger faced if the swarm enveloped the rotors.

Marine One descended slowly into a heavily wooded area that had a small clearing adequately sized for landing.

"I guess I'll call the First Lady and tell her I'll be late for dinner." In his attempt at macabre humor, Jefferson didn't realize his phone had no signal.

Neither did anyone else's.

For Chandler, it seemed surreal that he found himself in the middle of a hijacking. He never in a million years figured that this could happen on domestic soil. He got more than he hoped for with this exclusive interview. Little did he know how much one-on-one time he'd get.

***

They had a smooth landing, albeit in the middle of an alpine forest. The helo's rotors sprayed the powdery snow in a fine mist around the aircraft.

The drone swarm had flown away just as quickly as it appeared.

Everyone stared at one another, the next move uncertain.

The Secret Service agents drew their weapons before opening Marine One's door. A rush of winter's fury swirled inside the cabin, washing over Chandler's face. He listened to the forest's emptiness. It didn't beckon him. The truth of their predicament had not been revealed.

The agents peered into the empty forest. One of them walked down the helo's steps while the other covered him. The next one followed. Their first steps on the snow-covered terrain proved slippery. These men would take a bullet for POTUS, yet they couldn't see a threat. It was a temporary calm.

Beams of intense green light shot from eye level between the trees. They weren't expecting to protect themselves from a disabling light. Several masked men holding hand-held green lasers, an ocular impairment weapon used in military operations, charged from the forest's cover. Another group of men snuck up on the agents from the opposite direction and disarmed them. They fired no shots.

The Nighthawk pilots, unable to communicate, left the cockpit to help the agents. They had better footing, though they met little success after being struck by several Sting-Ball Grenades. The rubber pellets exploding out of the grenade inflicted blunt force, disabling the pilots long enough for the group of men to subdue them.

Jefferson, Hutchinson, and Chandler watched the capture with great apprehension.

Hutchinson opened several compartments and looked under

his seat.

"Drake, what are you doing?"

"Sir, we have to defend ourselves," replied an agitated Hutchinson.

"You wouldn't know what to do with a weapon if you had one. Besides, you, the anti-gun advocate, are looking for a weapon?"

Chandler appreciated the irony. He'd talked to people in the secession movements that feared a gun grab. The Centennials expressed the same fear, and so did the Honor Brigade.

He thought a weapon would be useful right now. The marksmanship he displayed during the Centennial training exercise would at most scare branches on nearby pine trees.

Their captors had restrained the Secret Service agents and Nighthawk pilots. The wind continued to stream into the cabin, yet no one had breached the helo's entrance.

"Chandler, what do you know about guns?" Jefferson asked.

"Not much, sir, though I shot an AR-15 the other day," he replied with a timid grin.

"Hmm. We have three men inside of Marine One who don't know much about guns and four people outside who do, that are now tied up. I hope these people, whoever the hell they are, mean us no harm. Let's go out there and see what these men want." Jefferson unbuckled, deciding to lead by example.

Hutchinson blocked his path, extending his arm. "Sir, how can you be so sure?"

"Don't you think we'd be dead by now if that's what they wanted?"

Chandler shared the president's opinion. His unquantifiable fear clenched his throat and he would not banish it waiting inside the helo. He'd been in touchy situations before, including a story

126

in Afghanistan when an IED had exploded in front of his car.

Jefferson pushed past Hutchinson and ordered Chandler to follow him out.

Chandler drew cold air into his lungs, the unmistakable pine scent gave momentary comfort, reminding him of his walk with Arianne.

There were a dozen masked men outside the helicopter. The pilots and Secret Service agents sat, their wrists and ankles bound.

Other than their masks, nothing suggested these men were but a group of guys snowshoeing in the forest. They arranged themselves in a semicircle around the bound pilots and agents.

Jefferson approached the men, coming within a few feet of their center. Chandler and Hutchinson were back a couple of steps.

"You've made your point. What do you want?" Jefferson assumed an offensive posture, hands on hips.

The masked men remained silent.

Hutchinson took an aggressive step towards them, waving a fist. "Now look you sons of bitches. This is the President of the United States. You gotta realize what sort of trouble you're in!" His spittle landed on the snow-covered forest.

The silent men stared straight at them, their eyes, noses, and lips popping out of their ski masks. Only the winter wind made a sound in this forest.

A frigid Chandler leaned towards Jefferson and whispered, "Sir, what's our move here?"

"Until these guys say something, I'm not doing anything." He folded his arms, fixing his cold stare on the captors.

The president's cool and resolve impressed Chandler, whose heart beat forcefully.

One of the masked men stepped forward, handing Jefferson

an envelope. A defiant president tore open the letter and read it aloud. "Please change into these clothes and shoes."

Another man stepped forward with three trash bags and handed them to Chandler, who confirmed the clothing and footwear.

Hutchinson wanted no part of it. "Why should we? Who the hell are these jokers? Screw you!" He flipped them the bird.

The men showed no perturbation.

The reality of their plight was becoming clear. They weren't going anywhere until they complied, and they'd surely freeze to death if they didn't.

"Drake, let's just do what they say. I'm sure they're looking for us. Stay calm." Jefferson grabbed a bag from Chandler and walked back into Marine One for the clothing change. Chandler followed.

Hutchinson engaged in a stare down with the men.

"Drake! Get in here!" Jefferson yelled from the top step of Marine One.

The chief complied.

If Jefferson had any sort of anxiety, he didn't show it.

"Sir, I take it you've been trained for this sort of thing?" Chandler asked while donning his new clothing.

"I have been advised to stay cooperative in these situations, though to be perfectly blunt, I never thought I'd be taken by my own people," he answered, pressing his lips tightly into a thin line. "I'm sure the Delta commandos will find us soon enough." He slapped Chandler between the shoulder blades. "Let's go." He glared at Hutchinson. "Come on, Drake."

The three walked out of Marine One dressed in jeans, flannel shirts, and snow boots. One of the masked men patted each one down. Hutchinson proved less cooperative and got restrained by two others.

Three of the masked men stepped forward and chucked winter jackets and hats at them. One of the masked men pointed ahead, motioning the three to follow someone in the distance.

Several masked men carried the Secret Service agents and the pilots, still tied, back into Marine One and left them with thermal blankets, wool stocking hats, and gloves. One captor opened the engine compartment and yanked out a few parts.

Jefferson pointed at the bound men. "What's going to happen to them?"

One captor nudged him towards the man in the distance.

They began a one-hour march on a trail through the deep snow and falling temperatures, arriving at several large SUVs and pickup trucks with tinted windows. The masked men blindfolded the hostages before they stashed them in the vehicles.

They would hear the first words from any of the captors' mouths. "Don't worry about your men. We'll call their position into local law enforcement. They'll be fine. And don't take off your blindfold," said a captor with a throaty voice.

No one replied. They were mentally and physically exhausted.

Jefferson and Chandler sat next to each other. The captors dispatched Hutchinson to another vehicle.

The uneven terrain jostled the unbuckled men.

Chandler wiggled his eyebrows, hoping his blindfold would move. It didn't.

He leaned to his left, sensing the president sat next to him. "Sir, how are they going to find us now?"

"I don't know. I get the feeling we'll be late for breakfast too."

None of the captors spoke during the ride, allowing the men to converse freely.

"If they ask for ransom, I guess my value will be $10 and yours will be too high to count. Or maybe I should have priced it in Mundis?" Chandler suggested, playing off Jefferson's humor. He reasoned the president was using humor to maintain their spirits.

The Mundi was the world currency introduced with the Global Financial Union, which became central to the Jefferson administration's economic recovery plan. Chandler's rogue video, while he worked for El Mundo, uncovered this unknown aspect of the plan.

Jefferson found humor in the commentary. "Well played, Chandler. I don't think we ever reviewed a scenario where I get kidnapped in Colorado."

"Will the vice president make a ransom decision?"

The public knew the VP had fallen ill, though they did not understand the severity. "We haven't made this public. I'm not sure how long he'll be around. The doctors are out of answers."

Chandler dipped his head. "Sorry to hear that, sir."

"Do you have a girl, Chandler? Someone you're close to?"

"Yes."

He'd thought about her often during the ordeal. The memories of her were helping to sustain him.

"Does she have a name?"

"Yeah, sorry. It's Arianne. Arianne Maxwell. Her family owns Maxwell Tech."

"Ah, I see. We've been fighting them in court for a while. Is it serious?"

At this point in their brief relationship, the proverbial elephant — the chilling documentary — remained in the corner.

"As strange as this is going to sound, making that documentary last year almost finished us and then brought us closer than ever." Chandler tiptoed around the documentary minefield.

"How so?"

Chandler remained amazed that Jefferson would want to speak so freely in front of these men. He didn't know if he took this approach for his own sake or Chandler's. It would be time to coax the elephant out of the corner.

"Well, sir, during my undercover work at the camp, we were incommunicado. I couldn't take the chance that someone would be listening to us over the phone. The weeks I spent in the camp obviously made me miss her. Listening to the emotional aches of those working in the camp and then some patients made me realize what she meant to me. When I finally saw her, it was like watching a beautiful sunrise on the beach. Everything seemed just right in the world. For her, she realized how important my work was to me and its impact on the country."

Jefferson didn't immediately respond. He nodded his head with slow, steady deliberation before speaking. "I watched your documentary."

Chandler felt his Adam's apple sink into his stomach. He also wondered if the captors were listening, or if they cared.

"The people around me kept me in the dark, you know, plausible deniability. I expected a strong reaction to my executive order freezing the election. What people forget is the economic mess I inherited. No one offered any good solutions. The Fed lost credibility, we were losing jobs, the stock market crashed. I wasn't going to just sit there and watch the thing implode. When I finally got a decent solution, we were close to the election. I know Congress and that would have been a mess finishing the election there. Too much partisanship, you know. I was also fearful that a new administration would dismantle our recovery." His voice rose as he explained himself.

The masked men riding in the vehicle's front murmured.

"Mr. President, I think people knew you were between a rock and a hard place. The issue was your executive power reach."

"Chandler, I would do the same thing again. I just didn't see a way out. The country had already been dividing for many years, going back to probably 2009. My regret, though, is that I've set in motion forces that government no longer seems to be able to control."

Jefferson realized that his government tried to do too much at one time. His actions had invited retaliation and pushback. Chandler didn't expect this candor from the leader of the free world.

The bumpy ride smoothed measurably. No longer were their heads bobbing up and down and sideways.

A long ride followed. The hum of road noise made Chandler doze off.

The caravan pulled into a large warehouse. Bay doors closed behind them. The three captives stepped out with help from the masked men, who then removed their blindfolds. They averted their eyes, ducking bright overhead lights. An enclosed office resided one hundred feet ahead. Stacks of empty pallets and boxes were visible at the opposite end.

Their captors lined them up side-by-side, execution style.

Chandler's beating heart quickened. *"Surely we're not gonna get shot here. They could've done that in the woods."* He looked at his masked captors with a terrified, dilated stare. His bladder reinforced his fear.

"Where are we? Is this about money? Did you at least send a ransom note?" Jefferson's questions were unanswered by the reticent men.

Some masked men walked into the office and removed their

masks. Only the backs of their heads were visible. They spoke with someone sitting at a desk and received something in an envelope. The formerly masked men inspected its contents and nodded. They donned their masks and headed back towards the captives.

Behind the masked men walked another masked group of people. These masks were plastic, not wool stocking hats pulled over the face. As they came closer, Chandler had a flashback to the documentary.

Almost all the masked men drove off. A couple stayed behind, standing guard near the warehouse's bay doors.

The new captors, the ones wearing plastic masks, approached. The painted, swirly mustaches and thin goatees bewildered Jefferson and Hutchinson, though not Chandler. These masks had a mischievous grin.

One of them spoke. "Welcome Mr. President." The speaker's tone was gentle and melodic.

They all bowed in unison, combining their dip with an artistic flare of the hand.

"You must be the chief of staff, Mr. Hutchinson. Welcome." No one bowed.

Hutchinson scowled and looked away.

"And you, of course, Mr. Chandler Scott." The group followed with polite golf applause.

Jefferson's patience had worn thin. "Now look. I don't know what this is about or what game you're playing." He wagged his finger at the men with painted masks. "This has gone far enough. Take off those stupid masks. I demand that you release us immediately and you might receive some leniency from a federal judge."

One of them replied, "I'm sure you have many questions. For

now, I invite you to your quarters for the evening." He gestured towards the office.

"For the evening?" Hutchinson asked.

"Yes, you'll be spending the evening here. We have cots and air mattresses and some food and drink for you. There's also a bathroom. I hope you will be comfortable tonight. We'll speak further in the morning."

The man speaking would have made an excellent book narrator. The three captives, however, no longer wanted to be part of this tale.

These masked men escorted the three towards the office where, as described, they had set up quarters for them.

"Who they hell do these guys think they are? Sir, we should just make a break for it and see what happens," Hutchinson demanded.

The masked man who walked beside the chief shook his head, emitting a chuckle.

"Drake, will you get rid of your commando attitude? You saw how far I got. Let's cooperate. They haven't hurt us and honestly don't seem threatening."

The chief thrust his hands in his pockets with irritation.

Chandler had remained silent about the identity of the new captors and thought it proper to go with Jefferson's approach of peaceful cooperation. "They won't hurt us, sir."

"How do you know that?"

"Sir, you said you watched my documentary?"

"Yes, I did."

"Then perhaps you forgot when I described my meeting with the person wearing the Guy Fawkes mask?"

"Oh yes, like from that movie, V for Vendetta."

"Mr. President, given everything that's happened with the

drone swarm, the incident in the woods, and now these men wearing Guy Fawkes masks, I think I know who's behind all this."

"Guy Fawkes?" Jefferson asked, sarcastically.

Hutchinson didn't appreciate the pause. "OK then, spill the beans!"

"This is the work of the Five Tribes."

***

Word arrived in Washington, D.C. of the president's abduction.

Secretary of Defense Trent Carter called a meeting with the president's top law enforcement and intelligence advisers to devise a recovery plan. They met in the Situation Room.

Carter assumed the president's normal position at the end of the conference table.

"Mr. Director, what can you tell me so far?" Carter directed his question to FBI Director Ralph Elliott.

"Mr. Secretary, all I can tell you at this point is that local law enforcement, and that includes Denver PD and the Colorado Highway Patrol, are combing large areas on the ground. We've got military choppers and the Delta commandos scanning the last known position of Marine One and the governor's dispatching the National Guard. It's dark now, so that is complicating our search."

"And the football?" Carter added.

"It's safe," Elliott replied.

The "football" referred to a forty-five-pound satchel containing verification codes used by the president to confirm his identity to the military for a nuclear missile launch. The vice president also had a football, and one remained in the White House.

DHS Secretary Victor Haydon followed. "I've got my people

involved too, Mr. Secretary."

"Thanks, Vic. I wanted to let everyone know that the Secret Service agents and the Marine One pilots are being rescued. Apparently, an anonymous source gave the precise GPS coordinates of Marine One's location. We've got a chopper headed that way now," Carter said.

"They didn't trace that call? Whoever called that in knows what's going on," FBI Director Elliott asserted.

"It must have been a burner phone," Carter replied.

The other urgent matter involved addressing the press and the public. Once President Jefferson appeared in Winter Park, speculation ran wild about the reasons for his presence. They worried there would be leaks about his abduction.

"Mr. Secretary, we need someone to talk to the press. The VP we all know is near death and the Secretary of State is on the other side of the globe. Trent, it needs to be you," Secretary Haydon suggested.

The VP's illness had muddied presidential succession. The next two in line were the Speaker of the House and the President of the Senate. The Speaker and President of Senate were part of the congressional exodus from the nation's capital. Other complications existed. The Speaker of the House, Republican Janice Rossi, assumed she'd been born in the United States. Within the last month, on her deathbed, Speaker Rossi's mother revealed that she'd been born in Italy. They had to flee Italy just after the Speaker's birth when her father became enraged that another man had sired her — she had not. When the Speaker arrived in the U.S., one of her relatives forged a birth certificate. The revelation had not hurt Rossi's standing among constituents who empathized with her mother's struggle as a single parent. The revelation disqualified Speaker Rossi from the line of succession.

After the disclosure of Speaker Rossi's birthplace, the press looked into the next person in the succession order.

The President of the Senate, Democrat Michael Dean, had always passed himself as a natural born American citizen. It turned out he was born in Canada to a drug-addicted mother who gave birth in a homeless shelter just across the border from Buffalo. His mom cleaned up her act and had always claimed giving birth in Buffalo. The presidential succession would exclude Senator Dean.

That left Secretary of Defense, Trent Carter, as the highest ranking, in-country, government official.

Carter was a military man with little patience for the formalities of engaging the press. "I'll prepare a few notes and walk over to the Briefing Room."

After an hour of receiving more updates from the rescue teams in Colorado, Carter, the FBI Director, and DHS Secretary walked to the Briefing Room. There they met a throng of anxious reporters and the White House Press Secretary who was waiting to receive direction from someone.

Secretary Carter recognized the press secretary with a curt nod and took to the podium, pausing in front of the American flag that would be behind his right shoulder as he addressed the gathering of reporters.

"Mr. Secretary! Mr. Secretary!"

He adjusted the microphone and cleared his throat. He waved his arms and pushed his palms towards the floor, attempting to settle the gathered press corps. Carter waited for the din of their pleas to subside.

"First, I know it's late for everyone and I wanted to brief you on what we know. We can confirm that President Jefferson has been abducted along with Chief of Staff Drake Hutchinson, and journalist Chandler Scott. The president was on his way back from the Convention of States meeting in Winter Park, headed to Cheyenne Mountain. Marine One set down in an unknown location in a heavily wooded area of Colorado. At this juncture, we've received no communication from the abductors. Marine One, its pilots, and the Secret Service agents appear to be unharmed. We do not know the president's condition. Rest assured that we are marshaling all available forces to find the president and bring his captors to justice. I'm in charge, here, now. I will entertain a few questions."

"Secretary Carter! Mr. Secretary!" The press corps, normally seated when asking questions, all stood, waving notepads or pens clutched in their hands.

Carter pointed to someone in the first row.

The young lady waited for the ruckus to die down. "Mr. Secretary, can you tell us why the president was headed to Cheyenne Mountain? That's a nuclear bunker. Shouldn't the American public have the right to know if we're under imminent nuclear attack?"

Carter shook his head. "Let me be perfectly clear." He pointed a defiant index finger towards the crowd. "The United States is not under any nuclear threat. Let me repeat, we are not under nuclear threat. We dispatched the president to Cheyenne to hide his whereabouts given the events in D.C. over the last few weeks. You don't see Congress here, do you? Now the cat's out of the bag since everyone knows why the president headed to Cheyenne."

Another reporter followed. "Mr. Secretary, why was the president in Winter Park? The Article Five convention is being held there. Isn't that awkward given that a reason they're having this convention is because of Executive Order 14666?"

"I'm sorry, I don't have that answer."

"Mr. Secretary! Sir! Secretary Carter!"

Carter pointed to someone towards the back. "Mr. Secretary, are you assuming control of the office of president? Is that what you meant when you said you were in charge?"

Carter cleared his throat and blinked his eyes in rapid fashion. He didn't realize his statement could be subject to misinterpretation — press briefings were not his strength. "The vice president is unable to discharge his duties. The Secretary of State is overseas and by now everyone knows the situation with the Speaker and Senator Dean. I've taken control of the functions of the Executive branch for the moment until we can ascertain the president's condition."

"Are you saying the president might be dead?"

"No! I'm not saying that. We're still quite early in this operation. We'll have more updates for you throughout the night. Please be patient. Thank you."

Carter walked in measured steps off the podium and out the rear door of the Briefing Room. Reporters continued to yell.

He walked towards the Oval Office where he would sign orders he felt were necessary for the continued safety and operation of the federal government.

He declared a state of emergency in D.C., Virginia, and Maryland. He ordered federal government facilities in D.C. to go offline immediately. He would allow no Internet access for government employees. Couriers protected by members of the military would shuttle secure messages between government facilities in the region. Plain old telephone service, what remained of it, would still be allowed under limited circumstances. Communication with federal offices nationwide would occur through an isolated military network. Messages required printing and armed escort delivery.

Another veil of executive authority fell upon the nation.

***

Carter returned to the Situation Room a couple of hours later where he met with NSA Eric Greich, DNI Gerald Burkemper, DHS Secretary Victor Haydon, and FBI Director Ralph Elliott. Joining via secure video were the Joint Chiefs of Staff. The room had a decidedly military feel with everyone in the room, save for FBI Director Elliott, having served.

This would be a late working night for the president's men.

Once again, Carter assumed the president's chair. He wanted everyone to understand that he was in charge.

He directed his first question to the FBI director. "Any updates, Ralph?" He didn't look at the director, opting instead to review a security bulletin — multitasking was the order of the moment.

"Mr. Secretary, Denver PD, and the Colorado troopers are still combing a one hundred square mile area around the landing spot for Marine One. The weather conditions are tough and it's dark. Choppers have widened the search beyond this area. Nothing yet." Elliott leaned towards the table, expecting some reaction from Carter.

Carter never lifted his eyes and moved on to Haydon. "Secretary Haydon, I meant to ask this earlier. Can't we just track the president with the subcutaneous transponder?"

DHS offered subcutaneous transponders to key members of the government and their families. The Army and Marines had already adopted these implants for some of their soldiers.

"The First Lady objected to the implants for her and for the president," Haydon replied.

"How ironic," Carter answered as he broke his gaze from the security bulletin in his hands.

"Mr. Secretary this declaration of the state of emergency, which I presume you meant martial law, I'm not sure we were quite ready for it," Haydon said.

The president or Congress had the authority to declare martial law nationally. Secretary Carter declared the state of emergency in the District of Columbia, Maryland, and Virginia without consultation with the governors of those states who normally would declare it themselves. It remained unclear if Carter would send the military to those states, take charge of the state National Guard, or order the governors to do it themselves. Government sought to avoid using the term "martial law." During Hurricane Katrina, the governor avoided using those words and it allowed the state's forceful removal of residents from their homes and suspension of certain laws. According to the Supreme Court, the words "martial law" carried no precise meaning.

Director Elliott chimed in. "Are we confiscating guns? I know they did that during Katrina. Are we suspending Habeas Corpus?"

"I'll address that here in a second. I've called the governors and I think they'll cooperate. If they don't, I'll invoke the law passed under Bush 43 that allows the president to take charge of the state National Guard."

"But that's the president's authority, Mr. Secretary," Elliott replied, his forehead puckering.

Carter waved the objection away. "Ralph, someone has to act as president. If the state National Guard doesn't want to cooperate, I'll send in the military. This is why I have the Joint

Chiefs with us." He gestured towards the large video monitor. "I need you to start planning for military enforcement of this emergency or martial law or whatever we're gonna call it."

The Joint Chiefs nodded in unison.

Carter continued. "We'll impose travel restrictions with roadside checks. We'll have curfews and compulsory identification. Search and seizure will occur without warrants. Yes, we will suspend Habeas Corpus. For now, we will only confiscate weapons as part of search and seizure. That may change. This should help things in Baltimore. Frankly, I don't know why the governors in the states with all the urban unrest haven't declared emergencies yet in their whole state."

"Mr. Secretary, did you take this action because of the abduction of the president or some other reason?" Secretary Haydon asked.

"Vic, at this point we don't know who's responsible. We don't have a ransom demand. I have every reason to believe this was a hostile act from a nation-state. Everyone in this room knows that Islamic terrorists lurk in our cities. We just haven't found them all. Look at how distracted we are right now with the urban riots. What a perfect time for someone to attack while our guard is down. We can't show the world that we're weak," Carter emphasized. His neck stiffened and his nostrils flared.

The Joint Chiefs took umbrage at the suggestion they weren't battle ready.

Carter mollified them with praise. "I'm confident in our military, all right? Look, we may have foreign agitators among the rioters. That's what agitators do. They dramatize injustices, stir up anger and otherwise cause chaos. The people in those urban areas don't realize they're being manipulated."

"That's all fine and good, Mr. Secretary, but what's your

feeling about the president? You really think a foreign government did this?" Haydon asked.

"It seems that way to me. Hell, we don't even know if he's still alive." Carter pounded the table in frustration.

"If it is a foreign government, what's your move?" NSA Eric Greich asked.

"The Under Secretary of State is hauling in about a dozen ambassadors to the White House. I expect them to arrive soon," Carter replied.

"At this hour?" Greich questioned.

"Yes. We need answers, now! When I leave this meeting, I'm going to personally call our allies to see what they know. I'll also let our foes know, in no uncertain terms, that kidnapping a president is an act of war." Carter pointed directly at DNI Burkemper for his next request. "Gerald, I want a full report in two hours with intel on all this."

DNI Burkemper acknowledged the request and asked something that had been troubling him for several hours. "Mr. Secretary, you're operating under the assumption that a foreign power is behind the president's abduction. After the executive order and the revelation of the reorientation camps, Jefferson stirred the secession hornet's nest even more. Why not consider something homegrown?"

Carter betrayed his new irritation. "Come on, Gerald! They take down Marine One, they cut off GPS, and they disturb military communication. This has to be a foreign government or an Islamic terror group working with a nation-state!"

Burkemper didn't share the Secretary of Defense's opinion.

CHAPTER SEVEN
REVENGE OF THE TRIBES

Jefferson, Hutchinson, and Chandler woke the following morning to the aroma of coffee and donuts. They rolled out of their air mattresses and formed a line by the only bathroom. The president had honors.

Several Guy Fawkes characters milled outside the office and a couple more were closer to the captives.

The Guy Fawkes man who addressed them last night would do so again this morning. "Good morning, Mr. President. I hope you slept well." He bowed, extending his hand from his forehead in a sweeping motion.

Jefferson dried his hands with a small towel. "It wasn't like my bedroom in the White House. Under the circumstances, I suppose not too bad."

Given the frozen expression of their hosts, no one could tell whether the Fawkes crew appreciated the attempt at humor. They didn't respond verbally either.

The lead Fawkes waved them towards a table nearby. "Please, gentlemen. We have coffee and donuts for you. Help yourself. There are cream and sugar for those that like these sorts of things. Oh, and we have filled and unfilled donuts for your eating pleasure." His melodic, creamy tone proved rather soothing at this time of day. Chandler imagined him hosting a morning jazz radio show.

The three sat at a table displaying the morning spread.

Jefferson experienced a rare treat with this food, stuffing his mouth with the sugary wheel. "The First Lady. Um. She made me quit eating these." He savored the cream filling. "Too much sugar according to her."

Hutchinson swiped a jelly-filled treat from the donut box. He slurped his coffee, mashed his teeth, and snarled his face, trying to annoy his hosts with his ill manners — he failed.

Chandler had no problem eating his donut with sprinkles.

"Sir, we made it through the night and I hope you can see now what I meant when I said that I didn't think they'd hurt us?" Chandler said, sipping his coffee.

The president broke from chewing his second donut to respond. "I can't believe I forgot about these guys after the incident at the Unity Rally."

The Unity Rally was an event organized by Citizens For Unity (CFU) on May Day of 2021. CFU promoted peaceful dialog about the challenges facing the nation. They welcomed all views, including those of separatists, seeking to build a coalition that could engage in frank discussion with government leaders. Part of the effort included a human ring around the Washington Mall demonstrating solidarity. For a couple of hours, it seemed the nation enjoyed a time of harmony. For Chandler and Arianne, it provided a brief respite in what had been a growing chasm in their relationship.

Everything went without a hitch until it didn't — the disruption by the Five Tribes.

Jefferson's eyes searched for an answer. "That's when that one character, the one whose name begins with 'Q', it was-"

"Quinque, sir," Chandler answered.

"Yeah, Quinque. If I recall my Latin, the number five. Interesting character. They or he even impressed the NSA. I took exception to how you portrayed him." Jefferson frowned. "Sort of how you characterized Omni."

In the middle of this abduction, Chandler found himself

talking with the president about his documentary. He speculated the kidnapping might have caused him to reflect on his administration.

"Really? In what way, sir?"

"Well for one, you portrayed Omni like Robin Hood. I think you overlook all the damage they caused. I know all about how they helped you release that video right before the 2020 election. Were you just trying to hurt my campaign?" He stared at Chandler with momentary, though unveiled, hostility.

Even though he was deferential to the president, he stiffened his resolve about his work. "Mr. President, I had a job to do, just like you did and do. We need a strong press. That's why we're called the fourth estate."

Journalism had a long history of being an important force in government, an important part of the checks and balances built into American democracy. Democracy required informed citizens. In a representative democracy, the press had the responsibility of informing its citizens and establishing a loop between government and voters.

"The term comes from the three traditional estates of the church, the nobility, and the common people. It's an old term," Chandler explained.

"Thanks for the historical reference," Jefferson offered sarcastically. "The problem I had is that we had a specific plan for releasing the information with our economic partners and the Global Settlement Bank. Politics aside, that video could have hurt the implementation of the plan."

Chandler didn't sway. "Mr. President, I don't think the press can always check with the government first."

"I guess we won't see eye-to-eye on that one," Jefferson affirmed, turning away from him.

The lead Fawkes returned, hastening the men's completion of breakfast. After getting cleaned up, he walked them to another room in the office complex.

This carpeted room belied the office's spartan accommodations and served as an odd juxtaposition to the warehouse where they had arrived the previous night.

A casual observer might confuse the room for a communications control center in Cheyenne Mountain.

Several desks butted up against one another with desktops and laptops resting on top. Ten feet in front of the desks, hanging from a dark wall, were several high definition screens surrounding a larger one. The large one was the size of a high school scoreboard. For the moment, all the screens were dark.

The three captives stood next to the lead Fawkes with the rest of the crew standing behind them.

"What are we doing here?" Jefferson demanded.

Lead Fawkes pressed his hands gently towards the ground in front of his waist. "Patience, Mr. President. Our show will begin shortly. Please turn off your cell phones. Oh, wait. We took them from you," he snickered. "Let me get you some chairs."

Lead Fawkes motioned to another Fawkian who wheeled over three high-back office chairs.

"Please, sir, have a seat and make yourself comfortable," the lead Fawkes motioned with an artful wave of his hand.

The three sat down and watched the lights dim.

Lead Fawkes moved to one of the desktop stations. He typed and looked towards the screens.

The Fawkes crew standing behind them whispered like Munchkins, as if the Wizard of Oz himself would appear.

The perimeter screens lit first, revealing a cast of characters, young adults, men and women dressed casually, some with tattoos and some with facial piercings. They smiled and waved. Most sat in front of computer screens with attached webcams. These images remained for 10 seconds and then refreshed with a new set of people. The cycling continued for a minute. There were many people on this video stream. The Fawkes crew waved back. Chandler noticed that a screen on a desktop computer in front of him showed the view inside their office, projecting him, the president, and the chief with the Fawkes crew in the background. This was the local feed.

And then an image appeared, pixel by pixel, on the big screen, becoming clear after one minute. The back of the dark, bald head and the slow rotation from side-to-side made Chandler recall his first encounter in the high-tech silo the year before.

Those on screen clapped or thrust their fists in the air. The Fawkians cheered.

Quinque had entered. It was time for the main event.

***

"Benjamin Clark Jefferson. I never knew your middle name until your impeachment last year. Mr. President, good morning. Good morning also to you, Chief Hutchinson. Nice to see you again, Mr. Scott. I hope you gentlemen had a restful night of sleep. We have much to cover today."

Quinque still sounded like Professor Stephen Hawking, though his voice had less reverberation than during Chandler's documentary. He sounded more refined.

"Mr. Quinque, I've played along now for the last day and I still don't know what you want. What are your intentions?" Jefferson asked.

"Mr. President, you may call me Quinque, no need to formally address me. We're all friends here."

Hutchinson stood from his chair and took a step towards the

148

screen, craning his neck. He swung at space in front of him. "Friends? Are you fucking out of your mind? Whatever you want to call yourself."

He felt hands on his shoulders, coaxing him back to his seat. He turned to see the frozen smile of a Fawkian. The people surrounding Quinque's screen found Hutchinson's outburst humorous. They tapped their phones, no doubt messaging each other. The Fawkians in the room hissed. Hutchinson set his lips in a stubborn line.

"Mr. Hutchinson, perhaps I'll just address you as Drake. That's how not friends treat each other. I'm sure you have many questions. This is an opportunity for us to get to know each other. First, I'd like to introduce my friends on our video chat today. I won't mention them all since I don't know them all myself," Quinque chortled.

Chandler hoped he could remember everything that he was about to witness. He sensed he would get something different from Quinque than he got during the documentary. Chandler presumed the "friends" were hackers.

"First, I want to recognize my friends that were formerly with Lulzsec who are now part of Wormhole. Please say hello."

A couple of facially tattooed hackers waved. One, with a nose ring, flipped the bird.

Lulzsec represented a splinter group from the Anonymous hacker organization. Lulzsec's claim to fame was the alleged hack against the U.S. Senate and the FBI. In the FBI hack, they targeted an information sharing organization called InfraGard that served as a public-private partnership between businesses and the FBI. They saw InfraGard as nothing more than an unpaid spying organization. Lulzsec's pinnacle came when they hacked the Sun newspaper in the U.K. who ironically had hacked the phones of celebrities. With hackers, loyalty could be fluid, hence their new association with Wormhole.

"Another important friend on the call today is Thor who originally came from the group known as Anti-Sec."

Thor, sporting long hair and patches of stubble, made a silly face and unwound a tongue that would have made Gene Simmons proud.

Anti-Sec had targeted security companies who disclosed unknown exploits in computer software. They felt publishing this information made hacking more likely.

"I also want to recognize my very special friend, Jizang, who used to work for the People's Liberation Army Unit 61398. So happy that you're embracing true freedom now, my friend."

Jizang covered his face with a cloth Chinese opera mask. He offered a brief nod.

Unit 61398, operating out of Shanghai, was the main suspect in the hacking of many Fortune 500 companies as part of Operation Aurora.

"I will not take the time to introduce everyone else. Many of the people you see are members of the Five Tribes. Some are, oh what can we call them? Yes, let's call them independent contractors for hire. And the rest are just out to have a good time."

The Fawkians in the room broke out in raucous laughter.

Chandler interrupted the laughter. "Is anyone from Omni here?"

"Ever the journalist, Mr. Scott. There could be. Yes. Possibly." Quinque replied with a synthetic chortle.

A short moment of silence followed while Quinque's screen flickered.

The lead Fawkes stepped towards a keyboard and tapped

commands after the malfunction.

"Very well. Thank you for the introductions. Now, please tell me what we're doing here and what you want," Jefferson said, leaning back and lacing his fingers on his lap.

Hutchinson glowered at the big screen.

Quinque offered Jefferson a description of the Five Tribes.

The Five Tribes espoused the belief of integrating cultures into a larger culture where everyone lived in peace and tranquility. Represented in the Five Tribes were the five major religions of the world (Hinduism, Buddhism, Islam, Christianity, Judaism), though they honored and respected all religions. They would never attack another's faith. They also used the number five to identify the four major races of the world (Caucasian, Mongoloid or Asian, Negroid, Australoid) plus anyone of mixed race.

The Tribes were an inclusive society believing in a small governing unit since technology allowed governance at ever smaller levels. They believed in a panarchic government where territory could very well be noncontiguous. Jurisdictions could overlap where two adjacent households might belong to two different panarchic governments. One could belong to the Five Tribes and the other household to another similar governmental style. It would be up to the household to decide which government to join. This structure represented the ultimate individual freedom, the freedom of political selection.

"Mr. President, as a society we've lost our tribal cohesion. It's been usurped by the State and corporations. We espouse a more natural form of organization. What we have now is a pathology of entitlement and resentment. So many feel entitled and those that don't get something from the State feel resentment. It devolves into individuals looking for something from the State or leveraging the State to get something in return. Society loses its self-reliance under that model and the public becomes addicted to consumption provided by the State."

The Fawkians erupted in applause, exchanging high-fives.

Quinque acknowledged the applause with a stiff nod before he continued. "A tribal society is a more natural form of organization. Unfortunately, the only time we witness tribal tendencies is in the face of war, social breakdown, or a disaster."

Returning combat veterans often missed the intimate bonds of their military units. They didn't miss war; they missed the communal nature of their existence during it.

Tribal customs emerged during the German Blitz of London during World War II, with people retreating to the Tube during the London bombing campaign. The stress of the Nazi bombing strengthened them.

"You see, Mr. President, people can thrive on hardship. In some ways, the hardship makes them feel useful. Americans can't turn to any tribe, they turn to you and ask you do to more for them. And now look at the mess you've created."

The hackers on the video stream yelled in affirmation of Quinque. So did the Fawkians in the room.

Hutchinson offered derisive applause. "What a bunch of drivel. I suppose we should all sing kumbaya now."

His statement met catcalls.

Jefferson waited for the noise to abate. "Quinque, I understand where you're coming from. What I don't understand is how you think this panarchic government will fit in. And I still don't know why I'm here."

Quinque's head rotated deliberately from side to side. "Mr. President, after last year, I would have thought your government would have taken us more seriously. I suppose we did not get your attention. Instead, your NSA continues to disrupt the

Darknet and US Cybercomm continues to hack us. You declared war on us and not the other way around. We're just defending our right to peaceful coexistence."

Cheers and applause followed.

Jefferson rebutted. "The Darknet is a haven for organized crime and terrorists. When I say terrorists, I mean the kinetic kind. They blow things up and kill people. I'm sure you understand why we need to defend ourselves from that."

Quinque's online supporters delivered catcalls and hisses. The Fawkians murmured.

"I understand your need to control. That's what the State wants to do. One man's terrorist is another man's freedom fighter. You're trying to maintain the kingdom and the people are revolting," Quinque replied.

"You're wrong," Jefferson replied, lashing his index finger at the screen.

"Mr. President, please look at your country. People are revolting. Look at all your separatists and secession movements."

It would be Chandler's opportunity to ask a question. "What about the Convention of States? That's not a revolt. It's an organized, lawful way to effect change."

"Mr. Scott, a worthy reply to my challenge. The convention is a laudable effort. Unfortunately, it is too late. The country is too divided. I'm sure something of importance will emerge from the convention, but it will not derail the California Sí or Cascadia Movement. And what about the Free State Project in New Hampshire? They'll remain a lawfully operating state until they can find a way out. You see, the wheels are already in motion."

"These separations from the Republic will only create an organizational mess besides other challenges," Jefferson countered.

"Very true, Mr. President. Don't discount the ability of the people to solve those problems. Remember what I said about people needing to feel useful."

"What do you want from me then?" Jefferson asked.

"Glad you asked that, sir. First, stop your attacks on the Darknet. The reason so many people are there now is because of your spying, the surveillance state, and the online companies that collect our data."

A chorus of cheers erupted from the hackers on the video stream.

The government almost broke the Darknet's back when it figured out how to disrupt TOR, freely available software for anonymous communication. Necessity became the mother of invention. Indie software developers came up with TOR's successor, ROT.

"How can you defend ROT and people browsing the Darknet? Everyone knows child porn is all over the place there." Hutchinson's anger inflamed the pores of his skin.

"Everyone has something to hide, right Drake? Far better for everyone to see who the sick bastards are rather than having them hide. Besides, our friends at Omni have done a masterful job of destroying those child porn sites. You see, we don't need you to tell us what is bad. Public shaming and self-policing will take care of that." Quinque responded.

The Fawkians clapped.

Hutchinson shook his head.

"Continuing, please leave DigiNote alone. We have no interest in the Dollar, Mundi, or any other manipulated money. We've developed technologically to need very little from the State, including money. If we need little from you, why should we be subjected to your policies?"

The Five Tribes also had plans to work with private aerospace companies to establish an array of cube satellites in low earth orbit. These satellites would connect to ground-based mesh networks that would connect to devices used for communication purposes or to conduct commercial transactions. The mesh networks would create a decentralized Internet removing the barriers to banking, government, and information. Since the satellite network would be free of government control, it promoted the vision of DigiNote or any other cryptocurrency exploding in this realm.

Jefferson had no response. A petulant Hutchinson sat sideways in his chair, refusing to acknowledge Quinque and other hackers.

Chandler broke the silence. "I don't know where you or your tribe members live. Presuming you live in the U.S., you have to expect some sort of government, right?"

"Mr. Scott, you might make a fine leader someday. It appears your mentor, Mr. Schultz, has taught you well. Mr. Scott is correct. We do require something from what you call the United States. We need physical protection. As sophisticated as we are with technology, oh and I hope our drone swarm didn't cause too much grief-"

Hutchinson came to life. "Other than kidnapping the President of the United States and having pilots eject from F-16s, no you didn't cause any grief. You son of a bitch!"

The chief came under fire from the Fawkians standing behind him, who pelted him with bits of hard candy. He hurled a piece back at a Fawkian, striking him harmlessly on his plastic face.

Quinque ignored Hutchinson's rant. "We propose a protection tax to be directed to your Department of Defense. We're not foolish enough to think we can defend ourselves, and yes Chandler, many of us live within the borders of what is now the United States. That is a fair exchange. In the future, I suspect the Five Tribes will develop its own defense force, robots with artificial intelligence and other defensive systems."

"How would we compute this protection tax?" Jefferson asked, his interest piqued at the cyber man's vision.

"Sir, you're not entertaining this lunatic's ideas, are you?" Hutchinson spread his arms in a forlorn gesture.

"I'm sure we can arrive at an equitable figure, Mr. President," Quinque replied.

"Quinque, what you ask of me is frankly beyond my scope."

Quinque's synthesized laughter spread to the others online and to the Fawkians. The irony of Jefferson's remark didn't get lost on Chandler.

Quinque reminded the president of the irony. "Mr. President, you of Executive Order 14666 freezing the results of an election. You, the creator of the Financial Stability Board. Beyond your scope? Please, sir. Have some respect for your audience."

Firm clapping followed from the audience.

"Well played, sir. Well played," Jefferson offered.

Hutchinson was shocked and wide-eyed, incredulous that his boss would compliment his captor.

"If we're not allowed freedom to coexist, you'll continue to see cyber disruptions. And it won't be just from the Tribes. Other nation-states, your enemies, will pile on, attempting to get lost in the confusion. They will enjoy watching the United States suffer since they've suffered at your hands through endless wars. It will be more than them. As you can see on this call, there are other hackers. Some cause their own mischief. Your enemies will hire others. Hackers get bored. There is nothing worse than a

156

bored hacker. They tend to make themselves not bored quickly. The Internet of Things has given hackers a new sandbox. Wait until you see what they can do there."

Hutchinson stood up and walked towards the array of screens, pointing his index finger towards Quinque. "Look you piece of shit. We're the United States of America. We don't argue or negotiate with a bunch of freaks who got kicked out of high school. I demand that you release us immediately!"

This time no Fawkian cajoled the chief back to his chair.

Quinque had the chief right where he wanted him.

"It is appropriate now for me to introduce one of my guests, my friend, Gizmo."

One screen above Quinque revealed a sock puppet. The puppet had a crudely painted face with beady eyes and an oversized mouth. The puppet floated just above a table.

"Wow, so you're like the fuckin' president, huh?" Gizmo twisted back and forth. "I don't really care much for government types. I had cops harassing me and my peeps when I was younger. You know, to me, legal or illegal is inversely proportional to right or wrong. You do wrong by me and I'll get illegal real quick. The FBI, the cops, they spend too much time watching everybody and not enough time on the real bad guys, you know?"

The sock puppet's mouth moved clumsily. Gizmo's voice came from somewhere off-camera.

"How did you get started? Being a hacker? Are you with the Tribes?" Chandler asked.

"No, dude. I'm not with the Tribes. Quinque, he and his tribe, we play games on the Darknet. Some pretty cool shit. Me? I got started in a church group. They taught me Visual Basic and it sort of took off from there," Gizmo mouthed. The sock bounced while it spoke.

"Gizmo, please tell Mr. Hutchinson what freaks who've been kicked out of high school can do?" Quinque asked.

"OK, so like I graduated, but yeah. It seems like Mr. Hutchinson didn't like walk away from his VC job when he went to work for you, Mr. Prez. A friend of mine hacked into his email and found all these investment ideas he was giving his old firm when the government awarded contracts to companies supporting the Financial Stability Board. Is that like, bad?" Gizmo's puppet attempted to arch the thinly drawn unibrow.

Jefferson crossed his arms and threw a scornful look at his chief.

The screen next to Gizmo revealed compromising photos of the chief. They showed him doing a "tango" in his birthday suit with a "dancer" in a Buenos Aires hotel.

Hutchinson retreated from the array of screens, cowering as he shuffled to his seat.

"Ah chief, too bad you didn't cover your private parts. Nothing to see there, huh? Do you offer dancing lessons too?" Gizmo mouthed.

Quinque's friends laughed in an uncontrolled, wild manner. So did the Fawkians. Chandler let a giggle slip. Even Jefferson grinned.

"I think we've covered much ground so far. Well, maybe the chief didn't cover as much as he wanted." Hilarity erupted. "Why don't we take a break? Relax, gentlemen. I trust my assistants there with you can provide for your comfort." Quinque's head bobbed and his screen went dark.

The rest of the screens remained active, though most of the hackers were no longer looking at the camera.

The Fawkians motioned for the three men to follow them to another part of the office where they had set up food and refreshments.

Jefferson had received a heavy dose from these cyber separatists who felt they didn't need him or his government. Fighting the economy, the separatists, and secessionists, and the opposition political parties had made him feel lonely the last couple of years. The lack of windows in his captors' building amplified his isolation.

***

The three men sat at a conference table where they sampled ham and cheese sandwiches, sodas, and brownies. Chandler sat between the chief and president. The Fawkians occupied another table. Others stood near the exits.

"The First Lady would be mortified if she saw how much sugar I was having," the president said, sipping his cola.

"Sir, my guess is she's worried about you right now for other reasons," Chandler said.

With Hutchinson pouting over his abduction and Gizmo's revelation, Chandler and Jefferson engaged in conversation.

"These Tribes, I must say they're sophisticated. Look at what they did to Marine One and how they defeated our F-16s. I wonder where they got all that technology." Jefferson speculated, enjoying his sugary drink.

"I've always thought that once a technology gets out of the bag, there's no stopping it. Governments don't develop everything. It's so much easier now for technology to spread too. With all this 3D printing, robotics, and AI, it may not be long for groups like the Tribes to be able to defend themselves," Chandler added.

"I agree with you. That drone swarm that attacked Marine One, they were like a plague of locusts but with some collective intelligence. Our pilots were defenseless."

Chandler struggled to understand how they were so easily intercepted by the drone swarm. He figured that radar on Marine One would have warned them somehow. The uncertainty of the whole abduction gnawed at him. He thought it possible that someone within government wanted Jefferson out of the picture. He needed to play it straight.

"My guess is the 'locusts' in that swarm were probably pretty cheap to build, so if one crashed or got shot down, who cares? I mean, how much does a Predator drone cost, sir?"

"Millions, Chandler. Millions. We're supposed to be developing these drone swarms, though it seems like the Tribes are ahead of us. I don't know how they did it either."

It seemed odd to Chandler that the Tribes could be ahead of the military with drone technology, but then he was no expert on the topic.

"But like they said, they still need government to protect them. It's not like they can stop an invading army or an incoming missile or even launch an attack on another nation state."

Chandler took a swig of his soda and belched. Hutchinson gave him the evil eye.

"You know Chandler, while you're doing your job, as you say, you've empowered these groups like the Tribes who have the balls to kidnap me. I think you added fuel to the secession movements too," Jefferson added, glaring at Chandler.

After Chandler's documentary, critics accused him of falling into a government trap. They suggested Quinque was an invention of the domestic intelligence agencies. They reasoned that creating a false flag event, or in this case a group led by a mysterious, messianic character with secessionist ambitions, strengthened government's need to expand the authoritarian state. A cyber-secession group would scare the public further,

160

who would demand more protection, this time in the cyber realm. Chandler had dismissed the critics' notions when they were first leveled.

Throughout the course of Jefferson's abduction, however, he wavered. He found it hard to believe the Five Tribes could pull off such a heist. The commandos and other members of the president's hostage rescue team didn't materialize as expected. Moreover, the abduction occurred on domestic soil.

There was also the matter of Quinque's authenticity. Chandler trusted his instincts, although the events of the last couple of years made him think the impossible was very possible. Perhaps Quinque was a government creation luring these Fawkians and hackers into a trap? It would be the perfect honeypot — create a messiah for those engaged in cyber mayhem, fool them with a bunch of rhetoric, and then trap them. Adding a credible journalist, mixing in an abduction, and engineering an escape would make the president more popular than ever. He wondered why the president reached out to him in the first place. It all seemed too convenient.

Like the drones around Marine One, questions swarmed his mind. As he swatted each one away, another arrived in its wake.

For now, he had to conceal those doubts from the person who might be part of the deception, the president.

"Sir, have you ever heard of the Journalist's Creed?"

Jefferson rolled his eyes. "Is this some sort of idealistic motto you guys have?"

"When I was in J-school, we had to learn this. The creed talks about how important it is to maintain the public trust and how we shouldn't suppress news. My old network, El Mundo, I think they lost the public's trust. They tried hard to suppress what I'd found. That's why I had to release it on the Internet. Last year, my documentary, if it hadn't been for that government whistleblower, I would never have known about the camp. But that whistleblower by himself was not enough. I had to discover the truth and I did that the only way I knew how."

The president chewed his sandwich, staring at his lap before forming his thought. "Look, Chandler, I don't have the luxury of being idealistic. Politicians get elected to do a job. Part of that job is to work with Congress. I walked into a bad situation. Congress did nothing. A think tank and an international group brought me a solution. Malcolm Holloway dropped into my lap. The country expected something from me, and I delivered. There's no question that we're in everybody's business, but we had no choice."

Chandler reflected on one of his many chats with his mentor, Axel. Axel had helped him view the world through a different prism.

"Sir, don't you think it's impossible for a few people to make optimal decisions when facing a vast array of complex issues? Complexity is increasing. I'm not attacking democracy, but the hierarchy. Malcolm Holloway and his types, as brilliant as they are, think there's a formula to solve everything. I think what you're seeing now is government fraying because of the demands being placed on it. You're trying to be too many things to too many people. And that's what gives life to groups like the Five Tribes. They're saying, 'we don't need all this from you'. Believe me, sir, I feel for the decisions any president has to make. Paradoxically, as the world has become more complex, I think you need to simplify government and not try to match the world's complexity."

Chandler stopped to reflect on how he had just lectured the President of the United States. *"Wow, did all that just come out of my mouth?"*

Chief of Staff Hutchinson stopped chewing, also surprised at the rebuke.

The president slowed his chewing, cogitating on Chandler's opinion. He'd never associated governance and complexity — the journalist had struck a nerve.

"Those camps, sir. The reorientation camps. I met a lady there. She and her husband had their lives crushed after the 2019 crash. They fell on hard times. One night, she was expecting him to get home from the casino. He never made it. No one could tell her what happened to him. With all the traffic cameras, it's like he just disappeared. It turns out he was active on the Internet, in the chat rooms. Maybe he angered Homeland Security. I don't know. He was just angry, sir. He was no threat to the country. None. He was just down on his luck." Chandler paused, blinking a tear out of his eye. "The wife, she thought he was in the camp where she worked. She looked for him. I tried to help her. He may well have been there and might have died at the hands of the Elysium Protocol."

Chandler returned a brownie to his plate. He couldn't eat after recounting the story. The lady's pain corroded his appetite.

Even if Quinque was a fraud, his time at the reorientation camp delivered a stiff dose of reality. He witnessed civilian manipulation whose stated goal was to purify their minds and make them docile. When the patient didn't take to the treatment, they unwittingly submitted to a death sentence.

"I don't know what to say. I didn't think people were just disappearing like that. That doesn't sound like the United States I know," the president lamented. He also returned his dessert to his plate. "We're better than that."

"Exactly. That's what I was getting at with complexity of

thought. Sir, there are people carrying out what they think you want them to do. Maybe at one time a single person, a president, could be the master of governing. It's easy for you to lose track of the consequences of your decisions."

"It's true. A president has to delegate so much and place their trust in so many people."

"I think it's fair to say that with the camps, it was an evil committed in the name of authority. Your authority, Mr. President."

Hutchinson stopped chewing on his food. He stood, hovering over Chandler. "I don't know who you think you are, maybe you're no better than the rest of these freaks. You're talking to the president. Didn't anyone ever teach you to respect the office?"

"Chief, I meant no harm by my comments. I-"

Hutchinson shoved Chandler between his shoulder blades. Chandler's torso bumped into the table.

Chandler popped up from his chair to look his aggressor in the eye. "You look like the kind of person who would steal a nickel from a dead man's eyes. It's people like you, greedy bastards, who are as much a problem as anyone."

Hutchinson got nose-to-nose with Chandler, evoking memories of the argument between a baseball manager and umpire. The Fawkians stopped eating to enjoy the spectacle.

Jefferson wedged his body between the two, pushing them apart. "That's enough. Both of you! This isn't helping. What sort of example are we setting here guys?"

"Sorry, sir," Chandler said. He hung his head and took his seat.

"Mr. President, my apologies. I'm tired of playing with these Tribes, these hackers. I want to get the hell out of here!"

Hutchinson took a seat on the opposite side of the table.

If the entire abduction proved to be a hoax, a false flag event, Chief of Staff Hutchinson had played his role well.

The president had been cool under fire, engaging him in conversation to assuage his fears, injecting humor when possible, and playing referee with two of the stressed captives.

No matter the result, Chandler felt he had connected with the president. Much like anyone taking the oath of office, President Benjamin Jefferson had his own ideas about how to govern. Chandler made him understand how his policies had unforeseen, downstream consequences. Government needed to reflect the consciousness, hopes, and dreams of its people. The weight of authority, coming from the cloistered Beltway, could shatter these hopes and dreams. These were further considerations for the president.

***

Secretary of Defense Trent Carter sat in the Oval Office with members of his security and intelligence team. Carter upset President Jefferson's staff who remained in D.C. for getting too comfortable in the president's chair, literally and figuratively. Carter showed fatigue from being up all night, helping coordinate the president's rescue effort.

The Oval Office, in the White House's West Wing, was 36 feet long on its longest axis and 29 feet on its shortest one. The floor displayed an alternating light and dark wood chevron pattern whose crests intersected in the middle of the room. Each president designed an oval-shaped carpet to rest on this floor. The president's desk sat at one end of the oval with the U.S. and presidential flags flanking it and the presidential coat of arms on the carpet immediately in front. Next to the lower edge of the coat of arms were two large, leather sofas facing each other.

President Jefferson requested leather since it reminded him of home. Smaller staff members felt like children sitting in them due to their extended depth. End tables were next to the sofas with two smaller leather club chairs completing the horseshoe in front of the presidential desk. If you were to look straight up, you'd see a ceiling medallion of the Seal of the United States. Jefferson also had mementos of his state of California on display, with several pictures of Yosemite National Park and scenes from the Pacific Coast Highway. Behind the large, ornate desk sat an equally ornate table with picture frames of the president's family. Behind the table was the Rose Garden. On the opposite end of the oval from the president's desk, crackling logs accentuated a roaring fire.

Carter sat cross-legged, with a folder in his lap, on a club chair at the end of the horseshoe. Next to him in another club chair sat FBI Director Elliott. On the couch sat NSA Greich and DHS Secretary Haydon.

"Mr. Secretary, what's the latest?" Carter directed his first salvo at Secretary Haydon.

Haydon also looked weary from a long night. His raspy voice indicative of someone who'd been speaking for hours on the phone. "The Colorado National Guard's been deployed and has been conducting a ground search since this morning. Local law enforcement and the state patrol are assisting with checkpoints along major roads. Denver is a mess right now. The gridlock of the weather, normal traffic, and our checkpoints has made it next to impossible to navigate that town. The Air Force is conducting aerial reconnaissance over a large area of central Colorado using drones and fighter jets. The Delta commandos are aboard choppers searching too. We've got all hands on deck."

"I can't believe that we have no leads thus far! How can the president just disappear?" Carter asked incredulously.

"The president's abduction happened just before sunset. Then there's the weather. We lost a bunch of hours to mother nature," Director Elliott responded.

Carter turned his attention to the National Security Advisor. "What's your feeling about a foreign power being involved?" Carter had dismissed that notion earlier.

"There doesn't seem to be any evidence of this, Mr. Secretary. We haven't picked up any overseas chatter leading us to believe one of our enemies was involved. I wouldn't be surprised if an Islamic terrorist group doesn't claim it soon, though. It would be great propaganda for them. But there's no evidence of their participation either."

Carter had called European and Asian allies to confer on the abduction. Likewise, he'd hauled in several ambassadors in the middle of the night, threatening them with expulsion if they had involvement or if they were withholding information that might lead to the president's rescue. The allies provided no leads and the ambassadors proclaimed their countries' innocence.

If the National Security Advisor ruled out foreign interference and nothing credible emerged from his conversation with foreign leaders, it could only point to domestic abductors. Carter was still grappling with that possibility. Presidential abductions or even abductions of VIPs were not something with which America had any experience.

"Mr. Secretary, all the information we have right now points to an internal group," Director Elliott declared.

"Who? How? This is too sophisticated," Carter challenged. He pressed his tongue against his clenched teeth.

"Don't forget Mr. Secretary, the cyber hacks coordinated with the president's abduction involved GPS and other communication. Someone hacked into our satellite network. That's what the boys at Schriever Air Force Base told us," Haydon replied. "They also think it was something domestic. It's the only thing that seems plausible now."

"Maybe these are domestic hackers sponsored or hired by our enemies? And maybe there are foreign agents operating in Colorado that took the physical action?" Carter speculated.

Greich handled this query. "That's a better question for the CIA director, the question about foreign agents. Still, the intel doesn't point that way."

The Secretary of State was due back at Joint Base Andrews soon. Presumably, he would assume the temporary role of president, though it quickly became evident Carter ran this show.

***

Fresh from playing referee, the Fawkians escorted the president, by himself, to the room with the screens. He made Hutchinson and Chandler have a one-on-one to clear the air. They couldn't afford to have this dissension while in captivity. They followed moments afterward.

The three took their seats in front of the panoply of screens still occupied by Quinque's hacker friends. As before, Fawkians formed a line behind the three men.

Quinque's image materialized in a matter of seconds on the large middle screen.

"Welcome back, Mr. President. I trust you had a nice lunch?"

"My wife will not be happy with all the sugar you served, but yes it was satisfactory."

This time Quinque's chortle seemed a more labored version of Professor Hawking's voice.

Hutchinson leaned over to Chandler, fresh from their truce, and whispered, "There's something odd about this guy. I can't put my finger on it. Almost mechanical. This is the same guy from your documentary?"

Chandler turned his head and whispered back, "Yeah, as far as I can tell."

"Why's he asking me that? Is this part of the hoax? Quinque, mechanical?"

"I wanted to know if you've given any thought to my requests, Mr. President?" Quinque asked.

"I have. I really have. Of course, you know a president cannot decide such things by himself. I am not a king."

"How ironic that you play that card now. You've been acting regally, like your own version of nobility, for some time now."

Fawkians followed that observation with polite applause.

"You've caused me to engage in self-reflection. Even so, this is a process that requires Congressional involvement. Don't forget we still have an election to finish when Congress returns. If the Tribes are involved in the cyber disruptions in D.C., you're not helping."

"I can tell you those disruptions are not entirely our work. Remember what I said earlier about other players being involved and bored hackers."

"There's also a convention going on, an Article Five convention that could very well change the way our government functions. That will take some time to play out, and there could be things out of my control then. I hope you understand that?"

"I do, sir. I hope you understand us. Please don't use that excuse as some sort of deception, giving your government more time to hunt us. Just remember, you cannot destroy us any more than the sun can destroy the shade."

Deception had been swirling around Chandler's mind. Quinque's mention of the word only made his mind spin faster.

Quinque's head turned to his right and nodded.

One of the Fawkians moved to a desktop and began typing. Another wheeled a cart-mounted, 40-inch monitor in front of the three men, connected to a pair of long cords.

"What's this for?" Chandler asked.

The second Fawkian waved his hand artfully, bowed, and took his place in the line behind them.

A new show was about to begin.

The cart-mounted monitor displayed the screen array mosaic they watched earlier. The monitor alternated between a shot of the president, Chandler, and the chief, or the Fawkians standing behind them.

The Fawkians gave a derisive royal wave to the camera while the three captives remained stone-faced.

The screen flipped back to Quinque's bald head.

"Greetings citizens of the Internet and those streaming this channel in their homes. My name is Quinque and I represent the Five Tribes. You may remember us from our visit to the Citizens For Unity rally last May Day. You may have also seen me in Chandler Scott's documentary released last year."

The monitor in front of the men changed to display Jefferson and the other two in a tighter shot than before.

"You also see that we have a special guest today, President Benjamin Jefferson. Say hello, Mr. President."

He offered an acknowledgment with a dip of his head.

"Also, here today is his Chief of Staff, Mr. Drake Hutchinson, and the journalist, Mr. Chandler Scott." The shot widened to include the Fawkians. "The people behind them in the Fawkes masks are members of the Five Tribes making sure our guests are comfortable."

The Fawkians waved, this time flapping their hands in rapid

170

fashion.

The screen switched to Quinque and the hackers.

"Joining me are my friends. Some of you may call them hackers. I prefer the term 'freedom lover'."

The "freedom lovers" greeted the Internet audience with a combination of waves and profane gestures.

"Whoever is in charge in Washington, as you can see, the president is safe and unharmed. We wanted private time with him so that he may understand our grievances. I believe he has a better idea why we invited him to this unscheduled meeting." He uttered a synthesized chuckle. "I suppose we didn't really invite him. Rest assured, he will be returned to you soon. The Five Tribes is advocating for a cyber-secession and a panarchic state. I don't suggest this for just anyone. It is a unique governance choice. We do not wish to harm the country, and we do not wish government to harm us. Please leave us alone. As I've told President Jefferson, we're willing to pay our fair share for military protection, defensive protection that is. We will not pay for foreign incursions or empire building."

"This guy! This thing! He's fraud, a phony!" Hutchinson yelled at the screen.

Chandler placed his index finger over his lips, "Shh! I don't think they can hear you. I bet the mics are off in here."

One of the Fawkians walked next to Hutchinson and put his index finger next to his temple, simulating a gunshot with his thumb.

"The Tribes want no part of your debt and your illicit plan to pay it all back. Your Plan for Prosperity is a hoax on the American public. You are just creating more debt, bailing out banks and yourselves. The War on Cash is also fraudulent. You claim you're fighting corruption and terrorism. It's all about control. We

171

don't want to be part of *your* future. These nationalist ideals you spout are dangerous. In time, we may require nothing from this country. This *will* be our choice."

The hackers on screen cheered. Some held up "applause" signs.

Chandler turned to the president. "He's being remarkably consistent in his messaging." He wanted to see how the president would react, still marveling how cool he remained throughout this ordeal, furthering his suspicions about Quinque and the government.

Jefferson nodded.

"There are others in this country that evidently need less or none of the federal government. The California Sí organization and the Cascadia Movement reflect this sentiment. So does the Free State Project in New Hampshire. I believe that state's motto is 'Live Free or Die'. This is what we all have in common — we all want to live free. I don't know what will become of these movements, nor will we try to influence them. Those ships have already left port."

"I wonder if he'll mention the Article Five convention." Chandler whispered to no one in particular.

"In the great state of Colorado, you have a group of patriots who are also seeking more freedom participating in a convention to make that so. It should be apparent to everyone watching that freedom is a universal desire. Not just physical freedom, but monetary freedom. The Five Tribes is no longer interested in using your sources of money. They have been corrupted by the very forces that thwart the other freedoms I mentioned. Please let us live our lives in peace. Don't take us lightly. Remember, we just took your president with nothing more than our advanced technology."

The Fawkians supported Quinque with loud affirmations.

"There are others on this broadcast, those you see around me, and they are not all part of the Tribes. In fact, few of them are. They also want their freedom, though in different ways. They want to use uncompromised software. Many of my friends look for vulnerabilities and report them to the software vendors, sometimes for a bounty and other times pro bono. Not your government. They find something and don't report it. It's an opening for them. They want backdoors into everything. They are constantly watching your every move. This is not freedom."

Jefferson twisted the corner of his mouth. Quinque's diatribe had touched a nerve.

"Thank you for spending a few minutes with us today. Please speak to your elected representatives and ask them what freedom is worth to them. Good day citizens."

Quinque's hacker friends terminated their connections and his image pixelated towards a black screen.

Chandler turned to the Fawkians. "That's it? Now what?"

It was time for their next adventure.

***

The Fawkes crew moved behind each man and nudged them out of their seats and waved them artfully to the warehouse part of the building. Men in ski masks placed blindfolds on the captives and ushered the three into waiting SUVs. It had been an eventful night and day. As before, Chandler rode with the president.

They began a multi-hour trip in the worsening Colorado winter to a rural area in an alpine forest, arriving an hour before dusk. When they could go no further because of road conditions, the masked men outfitted them with snowshoes and winter gear. They walked until they arrived at a clearing near a lake. The captors established a campsite complete with a large tent filled with blankets and sleeping bags. A roaring fire burned nearby with a propane stove and several boxes of rations and canteens. The masked men took away their snowshoes and began the trek back to their vehicles. Following them without snowshoes would be perilous.

"Now what?" Hutchinson yelled at the departing men.

One of them took a few menacing steps back towards the camp and pointed straight to the ground.

"I guess we're stayin' here," Chandler concluded.

If this abduction had been an elaborate ruse to fool him and the American public to layer more surveillance and law enforcement, the president and the chief continued to play it straight. It looked like they would spend the night outside in the harsh Colorado winter. He wondered if Jefferson would willingly subject himself to that level of hardship just for the sake of public relations and the expansion of his authority.

Jefferson inspected the tent and the surrounding terrain. Though the area around the camp was clear, any attempt to stray from their campsite would be treacherous given that they no longer had snowshoes. The sun had set and they had no flashlights, making the trail almost impossible to see.

"Drake, don't do anything foolish. Stay here!" Jefferson commanded. He returned to a chair placed next to the fire and patted the one next to it, inviting Chandler to sit. "Do, you have any experience in the great outdoors?"

"No, sir. Not really. We didn't do much camping while I was growing up in Texas."

Chandler gave him a quick autobiography about his childhood, raised by a single mother in Dallas.

"I had no idea about your past. Most of the time your name

came up in a meeting, my advisers were devising spin and damage control. Strange, isn't it? Now we find ourselves stranded out here who knows where and we have to rely on each other."

"Sort of like our own little tribe, huh?"

Jefferson appreciated the irony.

The restless Hutchinson prowled the camp perimeter like a sentry.

Chandler pointed in the chief's direction. "How about him? Is he an outdoor expert?"

Jefferson gave a hearty belly laugh. "Him? He grew up in Northern California and had never even visited Yosemite. His idea of roughing it is staying in a regular hotel room. He doesn't even ski. Can you imagine that? Living so close to Tahoe."

Chandler couldn't assail anyone's skiing ability given his tumbles down the slopes of Winter Park. "I'm sure he just has your best interests at heart. He's been with you for a long time. He's loyal to you. I get it."

"You know Quinque better than I do. What's your sense of what will happen now?" Jefferson asked, rearranging embers.

Chandler still harbored suspicions about the events of the last day, yet he allowed himself to believe given their current situation, isolated in the alpine forest.

"I never felt any danger. That's not their M.O. As far as being out here, good question. They left us with fire and plenty of rations. Whoever is looking for us, maybe they see this fire and check it out. Though looking at this area, we do have quite a canopy all around us and it is dark."

Hutchinson returned to join the other two around the fire.

"Well, Drake, you have our escape plan figured out?"

Hutchinson ignored his boss's sarcasm, placing his feet near the fire.

The three broke out the boxed food rations — MREs or the standard, portable, military rations.

They located the heater packet and filled it with water from one of the insulated canteens. After waiting a minute, they placed the entrée inside of that bag until their meal warmed. The evening's selection included spaghetti with meat sauce.

"This is what our troops eat while in the field. Pretty tasty, really. Not that it's better than the White House chef, of course." The president threw a playful smile at his dinner companions.

They chased the meal with hot coffee.

"Mr. President, since it looks like we're stuck with each other for a while, what did you think about what Quinque had to say, you know, about freedom, governance, that sort of thing?" Chandler asked.

He contemplated his answer, twirling the hot coffee in his cup, spilling a few drops on the snow below. "He gave me a lot to think about honestly. When you're the leader of the free world, you have all this power at your disposal. We could bomb the earth into oblivion. I can project the military thousands of miles away. Save for a few countries, we could win any war decisively. And yet, we seem to be helpless against a group of hackers. No, I don't think they could ever take over the country or even project much power, but they are, and I suspect will be, a constant thorn in our side. They expose our weaknesses. It's not like I can send the military to hunt these guys down. They're not out in plain sight. My intelligence chiefs remind me of this all the time. It's like dropping bombs to kill flies."

The president's resignation made Chandler understand the true limits of executive power in the modern age when technology could be the great equalizer.

"I can't imagine many people wanting your job. We have a

divided country so reliant on technology that it's made us all parasites of sorts. Look what happens when there's a cyber-hack. They really do expect something from you, sir."

"The nation was already divided before I got elected. It's gotten worse, and I often worry we're past the point of no return. The more I've tried to hold everything together, that authority you talked about Chandler, the more people resist. It's like pushing against the ground. Authority is making people want to leave. I don't want to be the president that presides over the destruction of the Republic. At this point, we may need to determine who's in and who's out and work with that."

Hutchinson couldn't believe these words were coming out of his boss's mouth. "Sir, you must be real tired. Let's call it a night. You'll think about this more clearly in the morning."

"Drake, don't patronize me! I know exactly what I'm saying. This problem's not on your shoulders. History won't even know who you were!"

That rebuke silenced the chief.

For Chandler, the president's words were another case of the impossible becoming possible. The practical implications of his words were another matter.

"Sir, I'm getting a little tired myself. I don't figure anyone's going to find us here tonight. That's probably why they left so many supplies for us. You hear stories of people getting stranded in places like this for days. I guess we should plan for the worst, huh?" Chandler suggested.

"Do you think Quinque and his bunch would just leave us out here without a plan?"

"My instinct tells me no. Let me get my sleeping bag set up, then I'll go grab another log. Hopefully, one of us wakes up sometime in the night to stoke the fire."

"Drake maybe you can stay up for a little bit and throw on a log before you turn in?"

The chief, immersed in his moping, didn't reply.

"Drake?"

He lifted his chin, resigned to his task. "Yeah, sure."

Without electronic devices to rouse them, they'd need to rely on their bodies for the wake-up call.

CHAPTER EIGHT
EXTRACTION

On phones, tablets, computers, and television screens all over America, the back of Quinque's bald head and synthesized voice mesmerized viewers.

A frightened Arianne worried that she had not heard from her man. She initially suspected that Veritas had him busy covering the convention.

Her return to Chicago had her on cloud nine. Now the distance between them and the Five Tribes video sent her careening down to earth.

She sought answers, calling the one person who surely would know.

"Ax! Did you see that?"

Like most of the country, he'd seen a playback of Quinque's stream during a break in the convention. He was now in his hotel room, tapping his contacts for information. "I did. I don't know what to say."

"You don't know what to say? What do you mean? Weren't you with him? How did this happen?"

Chandler had never told his mentor that he had left the convention. It had been a whirlwind after the president's arrival.

"The last I saw of him, the Chief of Staff, Hutchinson had asked him to go meet with the president. I never saw him after that. I thought he was doing something with Jaden Casey, you know, the guy from Veritas. I'm just as shocked as you are." Axel rubbed his own bald head, searching for answers.

"I know you're not his caretaker, but, but, how could you let this happen?" Arianne sobbed. "Damn it!"

Axel allowed her to release more of her emotions, which for the moment manifested as anger towards him.

"Ari, I'm certain the government is doing everything in its power to find the president. Chan's lucky to be with him."

"Lucky? Axel Schultz! What's the matter with you? He's been kidnapped for God's sake!"

Axel regretted his word choice and offered a new approach. "Let me find Geringer. The convention I'm sure is wrapped up now. I-"

"You mean you aren't there? Where are you?"

"I'm here, yes, at the convention. I meant to say that I came back to my room."

"That's not like you. Did something happen?"

"No, no. Nothing like that. Let me find Geringer and see what he knows and then I'll call you back, OK?"

"You can call me back, but I might be on a plane."

"On a plane?"

"I'm flying to Denver as soon as I can."

"The weather's not great here. Even if you get to Denver on time, you might have a hard time getting to Winter Park."

"Who knows? I may have to wait for the train then. I'm coming. Just let me know as soon as you talk to Geringer. Bye."

Axel made haste towards the Great Hall where delegate movement resembled an old TV channel when it went off the air. Axel recalled the term "ant fight" he heard as a boy in New Mexico.

He plowed his way through the mass of humanity until he found Senator Geringer. He'd have to wait his turn. The statuesque senator held court with delegates surrounding him, all talking about the president's abduction.

When he spotted Axel, Geringer dispatched the delegates and

pulled him off to the side of the hall. It was so loud he needed to put his arm around the shorter Axel to get close enough to his ear.

"Did you know Chandler left with the president?" Geringer yelled.

"No. Honestly I thought the whole time he was with Jaden Casey." Axel paused, waving his hand towards the peripatetic movement of the commissioners. "What's going on down here? This looks like total chaos."

The president of the convention, George Lincoln, halted the proceedings when Quinque's video stream distracted the commissioners. After the video became public, the commissioners debated suspending the convention until the successful return of President Jefferson. Some state commissioners suspected the video to be nothing more than government's attempt to disrupt the convention and hog the spotlight — they didn't believe Jefferson's abduction.

When Chandler released his documentary, conspiracy-minded patriots, including these commissioners, thought that Quinque and the Five Tribes were nothing more than a false flag operation sponsored by the domestic intelligence apparatus. Presenting another threat to the American public would justify even further control by the government.

Adding fuel to the conspiracy was an Omni hacker who had formerly been a government agent embedded in LulzSec, another hacking organization. When she worked for the "white hats", also known as government intelligence, she claimed she sat in a presentation where the government would sponsor, and even create domestic terror groups. She spread the word in hacking circles that she thought Quinque was nothing more than a government creation. After Quinque's video showing the president in captivity, this hacker issued a statement about her suspicions. Omni had not sanctioned her statement.

Commissioners from the California Sí and the Cascadia Movement also thought the presidential abduction to be nothing more than an elaborate hoax. They felt it was government's attempt to stoke patriotic sentiment that would quell secession talk.

"That's what we're looking at right now, Axel. This thing is being pulled in many directions."

"You don't think it's a hoax, do you, Matt?"

Geringer hooked Axel's arm, with intention of moving to a nearby storage closet.

Axel wouldn't budge his rooted his feet. "Let me go! What are you doing?"

Geringer released him. "I know it's noisy out here, but I don't want to say what I'm about to say out here, OK?"

"Fine." Axel smoothed the front of his shirt.

The two men walked into a small closet housing shelves of audiovisual equipment.

Geringer leaned his back against the door, making sure no one could barge in.

"Axel, sorry for the cloak and dagger routine. With all the speculation going on, someone in my position can't throw more kerosene on the fire."

"Very well, then. What's your feeling on this?"

Geringer struggled to find the right words, knowing he was about to open a can of worms. His fidgeting telegraphed his discomfort. "I never thought I'd see our government manipulating people's brains with virtual reality and then euthanizing bad experimental outcomes. I never thought I'd see the presidential election process suspended either. Chandler was very proud of his documentary, and he should have been. That whole thing with the Five Tribes, though…"

Axel locked eyes with Geringer, piercing them with his ire. "You're not implying that Chandler's somehow part of the deception, are you?"

He shook his head. "No, not wittingly. He's the perfect stooge. Look at the credibility he's built in the last couple of years. People trust him. Now that he works for Veritas, they trust him even more. If he comes out and says that he and the president were abducted and detained by the Five Tribes, well, that story will have credibility. That will garner sympathy for the president. It would boost his poll numbers. He knows he's got an election in the House coming up, a legislative body full of Republicans. It might be hard for a Republican to vote against Jefferson if their constituency feels sympathy towards him."

Axel hadn't considered that Chandler could be a pawn in a larger game. He felt a knot in his stomach and a pulsing in his temples. The confident, assured Axel Schultz, the closest thing to a Renaissance Man, realized that he may have let Chandler down. What Axel knew and understood as truth may have been false. Two plus two no longer equaled four. What seemed logical was not. A million thoughts flashed through his mind. If Quinque was nothing more than a government fabrication, then who knows how many of his adherents were about to meet the heavy hand of authority.

Perhaps something had happened to Chandler when he stowed away in the reorientation camp? Chandler had gone undercover for several weeks. He wondered if Chandler received a dose virtual reality programming and forgot something about his encounter with Quinque. But Axel had been with Chandler during his first encounter with the Five Tribes. That would mean he'd been duped as well. His self-assuredness dissolved.

"Axel, you OK? You don't look well."

"What you're saying is that you don't know what to believe?" Axel tugged at the lapels of the taller man's sport coat.

Geringer recoiled. "I'm just saying that we need to consider other possibilities, that's all."

"Other possibilities, huh? I didn't expect this from you, senator." Axel looked away in disgust.

Geringer placed his hand on the other man's shoulder. "I'm sorry. I'm probably not thinking real clearly myself. I don't doubt Chandler if that's what you're thinking. I just hope he wasn't part of something more sinister."

"Me too. I'm sorry for getting on your case. Everyone's stressed since we love Chandler. And I almost forgot, Arianne, she's headed here."

"Yeah, I'm not surprised. She'll probably have a difficult time getting here with the weather they're predicting."

"I know. If you hear something about the president's rescue or otherwise, let me know. I promised Arianne I'd speak to you. I'm not going to mention this conversation. No need to fill her mind with speculation."

"Agreed. I should get going. I'm not sure if the convention will be suspended again or not. But I can tell you this, we will finish. I've put too much energy and political capital into it. I can't let these commissioners down so I'm gonna have to leave Chandler's situation in your hands."

The two men shook hands. Geringer exited first.

Axel remained in the dimly lit closet, sorting his thoughts between reality and fantasy and hoping he hadn't let Chandler down. It had been a long time since he'd lacked confidence.

***

Honor Brigade leader, Big Dog, worked with his security

crew, ushering people out the Great Hall when he received a text message resembling an abducted child alert. This abduction alert referred to the President of the United States (POTUS). His message ordered him to rescue POTUS from a set of GPS coordinates. It also warned him that he shouldn't inform the federal government or law enforcement unless he wished harm to come to POTUS and his party. He first thought the text was a hoax, another hack by someone wishing to cause further mayhem at the convention. Or perhaps it served as a ploy to have him remove his security team from the Great Hall so that there could be a physical incursion.

The Brigade understood the challenges of providing security in this venue. An evacuation of participants rested foremost in their minds. If someone made a bomb threat, it would require the Brigade, working with law enforcement, to move commissioners and their staff to a secure area. Their early reconnaissance suggested the large community and recreation center a mile away. An evacuation had its own challenges with few transport vehicles available, not to mention the second vulnerability of transporting delegates.

Big Dog hailed his Executive Officer (XO) on his radio. "Proto, meet me in conference room B, over."

"On my way, out."

Big Dog arrived first, followed by Proto and another Brigade member.

Big Dog ordered the other member to stand guard outside the door.

Proto had a background in computer and network security. A veteran of the U.S. Air Force, he served time as a drone pilot and then worked for several companies as a networking systems engineer specializing in cyber security. His portly appearance and placid demeanor cloaked a Brigade member with lethal skills. Several years earlier, Proto had found himself in the middle of an armed robbery attempt in a convenience store. As the thief left the store, he noticed Proto's Honor Brigade jacket and made a threatening move towards him, saying something derisive. During the scuffle that ensued, Proto disarmed the assailant and grabbed his own knife holstered on his lower leg. Proto stabbed the robber multiple times. The local hospital declared the criminal dead on arrival. Proto turned down media requests for an interview.

Proto took a seat across from his commander.

"Look at this," Big Dog ordered, sliding his phone towards his XO.

Proto reviewed the text alert. He furrowed his brow. "Is this real?"

Big Dog curled his fingers several times, requesting his phone. Darkness passed across his eyes. A frown enveloped his face. "I don't know. We see this video of the president and then this. With everything that's gone on, I don't believe anything."

"It could be someone just wanting us to move, to make the Great Hall weaker. But if this message is real, we'd need to act quickly."

"It could be real and it could well lead us into a trap. Could be a wacky militia group fuckin' with us too." Big Dog grinned.

Proto doubted a local militia group had the sophistication to send out this sort of message. "Let me see that message again." Big Dog slid the phone back to him. Proto examined the message again and slid the phone back to his commander. He typed on his own phone and read something from a web page.

Big Dog had seen this look before. "What are you thinking?"

Proto put down his phone and peeked towards the door.

"Whoever sent this, they, ah, they knew what they were doing. I can't figure out how they did it. It looks too official, like an AMBER alert, but it's not. I think we should take it seriously."

Big Dog wanted Proto to consider another factor. "You heard all the talk out there, in the hall, about the whole Five Tribes thing being some sort of government con job. What if we get out there and act like we're rescuing POTUS and then we get blamed for his kidnapping? What if the kidnappin' ain't real and we get sucked into the con?"

Proto leaned back in his chair, looking towards the ceiling. "Jesus! Has the world gone that mad that we can't believe in anything? Are we living in a matrix?"

A period of silence ensued.

"Here's what we'll do," Big Dog ordered.

The Honor Brigade commander decided to take the text alert seriously. Since it appeared there would be no convention the next morning, he reasoned that he could leave a smaller team at the Grand Mountain Conference Center. He would take twenty of his men from the security detail and recruit another twenty members who could arrive within a short time at a designated meeting location. The forty-member Honor Brigade team would extract POTUS and presumably the other two victims, the Chief of Staff and Chandler.

They would establish a command center five miles from the GPS coordinates. Since they had no idea what they'd be walking into, reconnaissance was of the utmost importance. They had to plan for several contingencies, including anything from a con to an armed confrontation. It would take them a few hours to arrive at the coordination spot. There would be no sleep tonight.

***

A frigid night greeted the forty-member Honor Brigade team at their designated command center. The rural road leading to this alpine forest proved difficult to negotiate due to the amassed snow and the occasional fallen limb. Any further movement towards POTUS' camp would be on foot or snowmobile.

Each Brigade member dressed in a forest colored uniform whose long sleeve shirt displayed their Colorado flag designation on one shoulder and a national designation on the other. The national designation depicted a U.S. flag with the star field facing forward, representing the flag flying in the breeze as a soldier advanced. For an extraction operation like this, the members stripped away the Velcro-attached designations.

Under the uniform shirt, each team member had many base layers.

Over the shirt rested a vest equipped with a steel, rubber coated plate capable of stopping a 5.565 round from an AR-15. The vest's front side displayed an Honor Brigade patch, a U.S. flag, and the member's call sign and blood type, all attached with Velcro. The front of the vest had pouches for extra magazines and tourniquets. In a side pouch, the member carried an Individual First Aid Kit or IFAK.

For this operation, members wore fleece lined tactical pants, a winter covering and snow boots, which had a side pouch for a knife. The members also donned snowshoes.

Members carried either an AR-15 or AK-47. The semi-automatic AR-15 came with a red dot or holographic sight and a thirty-round magazine. Another ten rounds were available within the rifle's butt. The Romanian made AK-47 also had a thirty-round magazine.

Each person also brought their 72-hour bags that included such items as Paracord, Wet Fire, a Multi-tool, and a red LED headlamp. The red LED headlamp was a favorite of the Honor Brigade since it didn't dilate the pupil, making it good for map reading at night. The headlamp's limited range proved helpful in concealing someone's position.

Big Dog would coordinate the entire operation from the command center. The teams used licensed 400 MHz radios with cypher and clear text features. They also carried satellite radios equipped with texting capability and topographic maps.

First, he established a ground reconnaissance team to identify as much as possible about the extraction zone. Proto, the XO, operated a drone equipped with night vision that provided aerial recon. This would be their first look at the camp.

Proto studied the drone's pictures on his control screen. "There's a small camp. A single tent. A small fire. Some boxes stacked. I don't see any movement. Let me circle around."

Big Dog sought more detail. "Swing out away from the camp. We need to see who else is around there if there's anyone there in the first place. I haven't ruled out that we're being set up."

Proto added his own theory. "I don't know why anyone would camp in this weather. Unless they're hiding from someone. You sure you didn't piss anyone off?"

Big Dog flipped a bird at his XO.

After steering the drone around the encampment, Proto offered another assessment. "I don't see anything else. Everything looks quiet around the camp. There could be people inside the tent. I can't be sure, though. If there are hostiles, they're hiding."

It took a little while for the first ground team to report their findings. "This is Team One leader. We don't see anything but a small camp like Proto said. No hostiles in sight. Glad we ponied up for these night vision goggles. Love the green picture. The terrain's pretty rough out here. Over."

"Understood. Team One return to base, out," Big Dog answered.

The second ground team reported minutes later. "This is Team Two leader. Confirm Team One's assessment. Awaiting instructions. Over."

"Team Two, return to base, out."

At this point, they could only determine the existence of a camp without hostile players. The camp could well be empty since they had not spotted POTUS or the rest of his party. There was also the danger of booby traps.

Big Dog waited until an hour before daylight to conduct the extraction.

The extraction effort comprised five-man teams including one echelon control supervisory unit and three fire teams. Each fire team possessed a different specialty. All teams had weapons capability; one carried explosives and another had breaching capability. The third fire team had snipers that would search for a high location, offering security to the other teams. The rest of the Honor Brigade members remained with Big Dog and Proto at the command center.

Fire Team One approached from the east. Fire Team Two approached from the south, and fire Team Three approached from the north. None of the teams detected any hostiles in route and enveloped the camp. Proto continued providing aerial recon with the drone. Big Dog gave the order to penetrate the camp.

Team One, led by "Moose" breached the camp perimeter first, careful to identify any booby traps. Team Two, led by "Mountain", followed. Team Three, led by the sharpshooting skills of "Showtime" positioned themselves further away from the camp.

The sun had crested over the tree line.

Moose, who looked like he could have played tight end for the Denver Broncos, announced his presence. "Hello, I'm from the Colorado Honor Brigade. My call sign is Moose. Please come out of the tent slowly with your hands in the air."

The Brigade members heard rustling inside the tent. Chief of Staff Drake Hutchinson, crawled out after pulling up on the tent zipper. He wore a stocking hat and a parka, looking like a man who had slept little.

Moose didn't recognize the chief in his bundled appearance. "Sir, please stand up and keep your hands in the air and identify yourself." Moose had his AR-15, with the safety on, trained on the chief.

The rest of Team One surrounded the tent while Team Two established a defensive perimeter around the camp.

"Oh great. Now you guys are terrorizing us with some damn militia?" Hutchinson said in a raspy voice. He presumed the man with the gun trained on him had some affiliation with the Five Tribes. "Stop pointing your fuckin' toy at me. I've had enough of your shit!"

"Sir, please, your name?" Moose asked, maintaining his aim.

Chandler crawled out next, fully bundled in his parka.

"Mountain" from Team Two approached and pointed his AK-47 at Chandler. "Sir, please stand up and keep your hands in the air and identify yourself."

He wouldn't get a chance to answer.

Big Dog requested an update from the Team One leader. "Moose. How many packages? Over."

Moose tightened the grip on his rifle and answered his commander. "Two so far, out."

"Can you identify package sizes, over?" Big Dog asked.

Chandler lowered his arms, cupped his gloved hands, and tried to yell, before having his mouth covered by another Brigade member.

Mountain, the Team Two leader, twitched when Chandler brought down his arms. He motioned with the barrel of his rifle to raise them.

The Brigade member uncovered his mouth. "Sorry. I'm Chandler Scott."

"Who's standing next to you?" Moose asked.

"The president's Chief of Staff, Drake Hutchinson," Chandler responded, hands still aloft.

Hutchinson still thinking this was part of the Five Tribes' game, shook his head and moved his hands to his side. Moose allowed the movement.

"Can I put my hands down too?" Chandler asked.

Mountain motioned for him to drop his hands.

Big Dog still wanted an update. "Moose, Mountain, come in, over."

"Stand by, sir," Mountain replied.

Moose then asked the question on everyone's mind. "Where's the president?"

President Jefferson emerged from the tent with his hands in the air and his parka hood removed. "That would be me. Who the hell are you guys? Where are the commandos?"

Moose pointed the barrel of his weapon towards the ground and walked towards the president to get a better look.

Big Dog grew impatient with his extraction team. "Team One or Team Two. Confirm you have large package. Over!"

Satisfied he'd identified him, Moose answered, "Confirmed for large package. We also have medium and small. Out."

192

Mountain moved the flap of the tent door with the barrel of his AK-47. "Anyone else in there?" He directed his question to POTUS.

"No, that's all of us. Now, who the hell are you guys?"

Mountain and Moose shouldered their weapons, saluted, and walked to shake POTUS' hand. "Mr. President, we're with the Colorado Honor Brigade and we're here to extract you," Moose announced.

The rest of Team One and Team Two maintained watch around the camp's perimeter.

"Honor Brigade?" POTUS remarked, ruffling his hair under his stocking hat.

"Mr. President, they were part of my documentary last year. They're also providing security at the convention in Winter Park. This has nothing to do with the Five Tribes," Chandler said.

Notions he had about the presidential kidnapping being part of a larger ruse by government faded with the Honor Brigade's appearance. He didn't think they would wittingly be part of such a complex deception — unless they were stooges as well.

"Mr. President, do you need any medical attention?" Moose asked.

"No, but it will be nice to get somewhere warm. The people who left us here, at least they provided great thermal gear. Are my Delta commandos on their way?"

Moose, confused about the question, looked at Mountain who shrugged his shoulders.

"Sir, large package asking about other help, over," Moose asked Big Dog via radio.

"Ah, Moose, don't know who they are. Begin moving packages back to the command center. We're getting reports of some weather moving in. Out."

Moose shook his head at POTUS. "Mr. President, we brought snowshoes for you and the rest of your group. We need to move. We've got a long hike ahead of us."

Chandler never expected to have to use snowshoes so soon after his hike with Arianne.

Hutchinson, absorbed in his sulking, realized the armed men escorting them out of the camp were not part of the Five Tribes. He'd have to redirect his enmity.

***

Mountain's Team Two led the way. Moose's Team One had the rear guard. Showtime's Team Three lagged behind, protecting against a hostile incursion.

The trail out of the camp was narrow and snow packed. The sun, which had peeked out earlier, lost its battle with the thick cloud cover and the snow that followed. Fluffy powder covered the pine trees. They walked over tracks previously made by the Brigade team members during their entry. Occasional animal tracks dotted their hike.

Mountain resembled the character from Grizzly Adams. He and his family inhabited a remote area of northwest Colorado and lived off the land as much as possible. This included hunting wild game. He looked like the most comfortable person on the hike, no doubt honed by his survival skills. The rest of the men were keen to return to base where a warm vehicle awaited.

Chandler, doing his best snowshoe shuffle, caught up with Mountain. "Hey, Mountain. How long have you been with the Brigade?"

Mountain didn't turn around, continuing to walk. "A few years."

"What's your real name? Or can you say?"

Mountain slowed down and turned towards Chandler. He

194

lowered his voice. "My real name is Dickson."

He didn't lower his voice enough. The other four members of Team Two erupted in laughter.

Mountain broke off a branch from a tree and hurled it towards his team. "Shut the fuck up or I'll shoot you sons of bitches myself. And stop making so much noise." He fell back closer to Chandler. "For some reason, my name makes these guys laugh." He then turned towards POTUS. "Sorry for my language, Mr. President."

"No need. You should hear this one when he gets mad," POTUS pointed back towards the still brooding Hutchinson.

Mountain, or Dickson, grew up in the Arctic National Wildlife Refuge in Alaska, a region the size of South Carolina. After 1980, the U.S. government banned human occupation of the refuge, save for a handful of families who were grandfathered — Dickson's was one of them. There he learned to fish, hunt, track and otherwise live off the land. He was the ideal guide out of this forest or as a leader on a survival-based reality show.

Moose yelled from the rear. "Hey, Mr. Scott. Don't worry if you get hungry, Mountain will drop a deer for you, skin it, and roast it on a fire. Might take him about an hour." The rest of Team One enjoyed the humor.

"Keep it down. You guys are still jealous, I know," Mountain said.

That piqued Chandler's curiosity. "Jealous of what, your survival skills?" Chandler's next step plunged him into a deep hole, down to his waist. Even snowshoes couldn't save him. "What the..."

Mountain reached towards the fallen hiker and pulled him out with relative ease. "Careful there, Mr. Scott. Try to stay in the middle of the trail. These pockets can swallow a small child."

"And my leg too," Chandler added. "So, maybe they're jealous of how strong you are. You yanked me outta there like it was nothin'."

"Naw, those sorry asses are jealous cuz I won the Jubilee Jackpot!"

During the 2020 election, Theocracy Party candidate John King advocated for a debt jubilee as called for in the Bible. King suggested the debt jubilee was due in 2020 since that was 49 years after Nixon had taken the country off the world gold standard in 1971. Several states adopted the jubilee by integrating it with the state lottery system. Each week, Colorado held a separate drawing to pick winners who would be exempt from any state taxes that year. Mountain had been a recent winner.

"How nice for you. How much longer?" Hutchinson bellowed while he sloshed through the powder.

"Maybe another thirty minutes. There's more snow on this trail now. The weather's definitely getting worse. I hope we don't have a problem further ahead," Mountain answered.

It took them close to an hour before they arrived at the two snowmobiles. A Brigade member from Team One would transport POTUS, while another from Team Two would transport Hutchinson to the command center. That would leave Chandler to hike the rest of the way out with the other fire teams.

"Big Dog. This is Moose. We're sending large and medium out the rest of the way on the snow machines. Over."

"I'll send a few guys your way to rendezvous. The rest of you, get moving. The weather's starting to get nasty. Out."

Ten members from the command center escorted POTUS and his chief the last one-quarter of a mile in.

The makeshift command center included trucks and sport utility vehicles parked near a trailhead that had not seen a plow in some time. Big, heavy flakes had formed a thick carpet on the roofs of the vehicles.

Big Dog emerged from his vehicle to greet the incoming party. "Mr. President, chief, I'm Big Dog, Commander of the Colorado Honor Brigade. It's a pleasure to meet you." Big Dog saluted and shook their hands.

"Nice to meet you too. Could we drop some of these call signs? I feel like I'm in the middle of some war game," POTUS requested.

"James West, at your service." He saluted again.

Hutchinson rolled his eyes. "Great! Now you're going to tell me the guy over there is Artemis Gordon?"

Mr. West didn't pick up on the attempted humor. POTUS grinned.

Big Dog, aka West, ordered the two snow machines to retrace their path so they could pick up Chandler and other team members.

POTUS smacked his gloved hands together, attempting to warm them. "Ah, Mr. West. Who sent you and how are we getting out of here?"

"Sir, why don't you come into my vehicle and get some hot coffee. I'm sure you're freezing." He pointed towards his large SUV. "I can fill you in. Mr. Hutchinson, you too."

The three men walked to West's vehicle. West opened the front passenger door for POTUS and moved the dash-mounted laptop out of his way. He then opened the rear passenger door for Hutchinson.

After serving them coffee, West gave them details about his notification and the extraction operation.

POTUS remained skeptical. "So, let me get this straight. You got a random text message with our GPS coordinates and you were told not to tell anyone? That didn't strike you as suspicious?"

"It did, sir. My XO and I talked about it and determined we should check it out. Believe me, we examined conspiracy angles, especially after we saw the video with the Five Tribes. And honestly, sir, I'm not sure anyone would have believed us."

"You're in no way affiliated with the Five Tribes?" POTUS questioned.

Big Dog explained the role of the Honor Brigade as a patriotic organization interested in the welfare of their members, helping in times of natural disasters and ultimately repelling foreign invaders if the case arose. They were against any talk of secession and wouldn't know how to stop the Five Tribes. He understood the bad connotation about groups like his, given association with militias. He reiterated that they were not a militia.

POTUS requested the use of a phone to call for help.

Big Dog balked. "Sir, there's no coverage and we're gonna follow the instructions we got. They didn't want any contact with law enforcement. It's just these radios for now."

He remained concerned about the circle of trust around POTUS, finding it difficult that he could have been abducted in this fashion on domestic soil.

On cue, Big Dog's radio hailed him. "This is Moose, we should be there in about 30 minutes, over,"

"OK, Moose. Make sure you take small package to a warm vehicle immediately. Out."

"Mr. President, we're only here to extract you. I don't know who sent me the coordinates, although it has to be someone from the Five Tribes or someone working with them. The coordinates were spot on," Big Dog continued.

Thirty minutes later, Moose, Mountain and the rest of the

fire teams arrived with Chandler, who they ferried to a nearby pickup truck where hot coffee awaited.

They delayed their trip out of the forest when they learned that an avalanche blocked the road on which they entered. It would be a few hours before road crews cleared the blockage.

***

After warming in another vehicle, Chandler made it to Big Dog's SUV to join him and POTUS.

He entered through the driver side rear door and sat beside a sullen Hutchinson. "Hey, guys. Sorry, I mean 'guys' and Mr. President. What's the word on the roads, Big Dog?"

Big Dog's satellite radio offered the only communication to the outside world, and it displayed a weather map that looked unfavorable. "They're still showing the road blocked. I bet it will be a few hours."

"Mr. West, ah, Big Dog, I appreciate everything you've done so far but I think it's time to get my people involved," POTUS said.

"Sir, as I told you before, I intend to complete this mission as originally directed. You're safe now. I don't want to risk changin' something up from this plan. They gave us specific instructions not to call law enforcement or anyone else. I don't know why. Besides, the most we have right now is this sat phone," Big Dog twirled the device in his hand.

"I'm sure you can send some sort of alert with it?" Hutchinson asked, defiantly.

"Yeah, I can send out an SOS but to be perfectly honest, with everything that I've seen the last couple of days, my circle of trust right now is small. I'm still trying to figure out how you were brought down and kidnapped. They had to know Marine One's route, don't you think? I mean, how does that kinda thing leak

199

out?"

POTUS wondered that himself, though it became apparent that his security detail had never considered an autonomous drone swarm.

Chandler remained torn, not sure what to believe. He reasoned the Honor Brigade couldn't be part of a hoax, though Big Dog's question about Marine One rekindled his uncertainty. Perhaps the Honor Brigade was, in fact, another unwitting stooge like himself.

"Mr. President, my other concern is that if I call this in, we'll be implicated in this somehow," Big Dog suggested.

"No, I'll vouch for you. I'll do whatever it takes!"

"I don't want any unnecessary attention brought to me or my team. I know Mr. Scott here interviewed the Brigade commander from Idaho last year, and that's his choice. Me, I like my privacy," Big Dog asserted.

Proto, Big Dog's XO, tapped on the driver's window signaling that it was time to fuel up the SUV. Big Dog turned off the ignition and waited while another Brigade member fueled the tank.

Proto joined the party. The diesel odor wafted into the passenger cabin as he settled on the opposite side of Hutchinson.

The five men would have plenty of time to talk about the country's ills.

"Mr. President, if I may. Your executive order, you know the one for the election. You had to realize the hornet's nest you would be stirring up with that. The Honor Brigade is all about the Constitution and respecting the Office of the President. But when you did that, we had an emergency national meeting. We really thought a revolt was coming. I voted for you in 2016. After your order, I had to get behind Senator Geringer and the impeachment." Big Dog shared the prevailing opinion within the Brigade.

POTUS nodded. "I understand. Looking back, and after spending time with the Tribes, it's made me wonder if I'd really do the same thing again." POTUS flipped his head to look at his chief. "My advisers, they insisted I stay the course and not rely on Congress. They figured D.C. would come to a halt if they had to decide the election. I know some in Congress didn't want that responsibility. My responsibility is to keep the country safe. If the economy had gone down the tubes, it wouldn't have been safe."

President Jefferson polled the most popular votes, though he lacked the Electoral College votes necessary for reelection. He and his advisers felt that if the House elected someone else, most of the nation would rebel. There had been a discussion for many years about abolishing the Electoral College. There was also concern that a new administration would dismantle the Plan for Prosperity, further throwing the nation into anarchy.

Big Dog squirmed, crossing his hands in his lap. He felt edgy speaking to the president in such a candid way. "I understand, sir. But look at the chaos you have now. The economy. Riots in large cities. We've been busy helping our members with all this."

The Honor Brigade performed extractions in several large cities including Baltimore, Detroit, and Chicago to evacuate members trapped in their homes by civil unrest.

"You went around law enforcement to fetch them? How did you do that?" POTUS asked.

"We gather intel from our Sentinels. Sometimes they're people in your own government. To get the word out to our membership, we'll use whatever method we can to communicate. When communication got disrupted in some of the metro areas, we resorted to ham radio. Our House Protection Team evacuated some twenty-five families from those metro areas," Big Dog recounted with unmasked pride. "We also helped local law enforcement in protecting National Guard depots. When the guard gets called out, those depots are high-value targets for troublemakers."

The Honor Brigade's exploits didn't impress Hutchinson. "So, you're just saying you're a bunch of wannabe vigilantes?" Despite the Brigade's rescue effort, the chief did little to conceal his disdain.

The truce Chandler had established with the chief broke down. "Listen to the man! He supported your boss and he's telling you how people like him felt about the election."

Big Dog paid no heed to the chief's question, continuing his dialog with POTUS. "Sure, we realized you might not win in the House. But, ultimately, we're a nation of laws. Those that don't believe that are rioting in the streets now. I'm not saying the riots are all your fault. You guys have taken control of everything so that when something does go wrong, they're going to take it out on you. Does that make sense?" Big Dog asked.

POTUS' gaze froze, caught in deep thought, staring out at the falling snow.

"Mr. President?" Big Dog tried to break the trance.

"Sorry. Yes. Yes, it does make sense. Continue."

"Sir, we may be past the point of no return in America. Talking to people at this convention, most of them feel that they're the last hope of keeping the republic together. Some of them, in private, say that what they end up keeping together may not look like the United States does today. And then you have these Five Tribes characters. They don't want to be part of the country, not the way I understand it, anyway. The way they use technology and all their hacking buddies, man!"

"Yeah, we have to deal with their technology," POTUS made quotation signs, "for all the wrong reasons. Speaking of technology, was that a drone I saw in the back of a pickup?"

"Yes, Mr. President. That would be my toy," Proto declared, raising his hand.

"Toy? That is some toy. Those things hard to fly?"

"Well, sir, I had experience flying more expensive drones before I bought this one."

While in the Air Force, Proto received the 18X specialty code, designating him a Remotely Piloted Aircraft (RPA) pilot, also known as drone operators. A hefty retention bonus that awaited him after his five-year stint in Creech Air Force Base in Nevada lured him to the position. His "office" was a large "cube", as he called it, where he worked alongside a sensor operator. Proto flew the bird while the sensor operator worked the onboard cameras. Proto's missions were thousands of miles away in Afghanistan, Iraq, and ISIS-held territory. His Air Force commander often showed videos of the events of 9/11 to enrage him prior to missions.

The separation from the battlefield created an indifference that poisoned his consciousness. He asked to see a therapist and was told he'd lose his security clearance. He visited with a chaplain instead who told him the RPA pilot's work was part of God's plan. During his five-year stint, his missions killed 1,600 people. He often wondered how many innocents met their maker at his hands.

"Mr. President, with all due respect, I know how important our fight against terrorists is. It's just that I really didn't feel like a warrior. I was killing people without being vulnerable. I'm sitting in a cube thousands of miles away. My father, he fought in Desert Storm. He used to tell me about the warrior ethos, as he called it. He said drone pilots never had it. What about the implication of doing the CIA's bidding? These were civilian missions carried out by military personnel. It hit me that they could charge me with a war crime or something."

In one of his last missions, Proto positioned his MQ-1 Predator over a target in ISIS-controlled territory east of the Syrian border. When they confirmed the target, Proto fired his missile. Immediately after impact, the mission's safety observer yelled "splash" while he stood behind Proto, making him leap out of his chair like he'd been jolted with electricity. In the strike's aftermath, the sensor operator trained the Predator's camera on a man who'd had his leg ripped off. The man rolled on the ground and bled out. Afterward, the safety observer circulated the cube, backslapping and giving high fives to others who laughed at how high Proto had come out of his chair. Proto knew this chapter of his life had to end.

"We're starting them so early now too, Mr. President. These video games the kids play with. It's just gettin' 'em ready," Proto lamented.

There were blurred lines between the military and entertainment. Defense companies owned much of the intellectual property for video games. Thus, it became easier to get that mindset into the psyche of young people.

"I'm sorry to hear of your experience, Proto. Even though my military advisers told me that civilian casualties could be greatly minimized with this warfare, they never hid from their mistakes. It's clear that we have our own casualties back home, the fine people like you who had to experience a different sort of horror," POTUS added.

The discussion with Proto proved to be another valuable

opportunity for the president to break away from the bubble of the Beltway and speak with those affected by his government's policies.

POTUS engaged Big Dog and Proto in a substantive discussion for the next couple of hours on various topics of national interest. Chandler listened, enjoying the dialog. The discussion moved outside when POTUS wanted to hear from the other men and women who were part of the extraction team. The Brigade assured him they were not training to fight the next revolution. They wanted to be watchmen, ready to metaphorically blow the trumpet if they saw the sword coming. The informal town hall in the middle of the alpine forest proved enlightening for POTUS.

Mountain broke up the informal town hall announcing the clearance of the avalanche blocking their exit. Everyone returned to their vehicles and began the trek to Winter Park.

***

After the multi-hour ride back to Winter Park, the Honor Brigade dropped off POTUS at the Grand Mountain Conference Center. The convention wouldn't be in session today. The press used the opportunity to scatter to local watering holes. The few present looked on with curiosity as several large SUVs and pickup trucks rolled to the entrance. The sight of armed men exiting the vehicles piqued their interest further.

Big Dog had called Senator Geringer in route and informed him of the package they were carrying, even using the Secret Service code word "Bear" to identify POTUS.

POTUS was effusive in his praise of the Brigade and Mr. West's, Big Dog's, leadership. He thanked them all via radio before arriving.

Geringer met the detail at the entrance to the conference

center. He remained troubled by the presidential abduction. A part of his mind considered the entire event nothing more than a theatrical production for the benefit of Jefferson's popularity. The Honor Brigade's appearance quelled that thought. Regardless, he needed to maintain respect towards the office.

"Mr. President. Glad to see you're safe and sound." Geringer shook his hand and scanned his attire. "I must say, sir, I don't think I've ever seen you in this garb before."

POTUS still had on his snow boots and heavy winter gear provided by the Five Tribes. "Thank you, senator, it's been an eventful couple of days."

The press murmured in reaction to the president's appearance. They tapped their phones. The flicker of camera shutters filled the air. They rushed him like a swarm of mosquitoes descending on a lantern on a summer night.

A few state police officers and Centennials pressed forward to offer the arriving party a buffer zone from the press.

"Secret Service should be here soon. They will have an escort from the Colorado National Guard to take you back to Cheyenne Mountain," Geringer added.

"Thank you. Yeah, no more helo rides for me. Hopefully, the agents brought fresh clothes for me," POTUS said, smiling.

Axel emerged from behind the senator and jumped towards Chandler, giving him a life-threatening bear hug. "Chan! I thought I'd lost you." Axel had never been one to display much emotion, though time had softened him.

Chandler pushed him back. "Hey, Ax. Glad to see you too, but I'm struggling a little to breathe here."

Axel released him.

The two men placed their hands on each other's shoulders.

"I texted Arianne from Big Dog's phone. I told her I was fine, but not much else. We wanted to get back here before I talked to her," Chandler said.

Axel dropped his arms to his sides. "She probably told you she's headed here. I heard Denver ATC stopped incoming flights due to storms. She may not arrive until tomorrow. I'm sure you're tired and need to get cleaned up. Why don't you go to your room and we can have dinner later?"

Chandler had gained a burst of energy from his rescue and conversation with Big Dog, Proto, and POTUS. "Hang on, Ax." He walked towards the president and Senator Geringer.

Geringer offered a handshake and a slap on the shoulder. "Chandler, good to see you in one piece."

"Thanks, Matt. My interview with the president took a slight turn." He winked at POTUS.

POTUS commented on the understatement. "Slight? Mr. Scott, you were a great companion during this ordeal. You made me examine myself and my administration. So did the encounter with the Tribes and the Honor Brigade. It was good to get away from my handlers, the policy wonks, and my spin doctors and see things from a different perspective."

POTUS reached for Geringer's shoulder. "Senator, we've been on opposite sides of just about everything the last couple of years. I hope we can try to work together more. We've both been doing what we thought was best for the country. Regrettably, my cure may be worse than the disease. I've got some thinking to do."

Hutchinson would have none of it. His eyes darted between Geringer and Chandler, wary of their continued dialog. He moved to coax POTUS by the elbow. "Mr. President. It's been a difficult couple of days. Let's get you back to Cheyenne where you can get some rest and get checked out."

POTUS placed his hands on his hips in reaction to the patronizing tone. "Drake. Please!"

Geringer walked POTUS and the chief towards a conference room and informed them along the way of the action taken by the Secretary of Defense, Trent Carter. He had a Colorado state trooper stand guard outside the room.

The three men sat at a table for more discussion. Geringer figured he had a unique opportunity to confront POTUS, in private, about his suspicions and those of others.

"Mr. President, I think it's only fair because I'm sure you're going to hear something. There are people at this convention that don't believe your abduction was legitimate. Others think the Five Tribes and that Quinque character are nothing more than a fabrication by government."

POTUS didn't answer. He looked towards his snow boots, shaking his head.

"That's preposterous! You people at this convention are out of your minds. Why would we do such a thing?" Hutchinson yelled.

Geringer didn't respond, waiting for POTUS to comment.

Hutchinson tugged on the president's arm. "Now you see what I mean about this convention? These conspiracy whack jobs are the ones that are gonna fix our Constitution? Give me a fuckin' break, sir." Hutchinson's glare bore a hole right through Geringer.

POTUS grabbed a convention promotion folder left on the table, thumbing through it. He paused on a page showing a picture of George Washington. "Drake, I hope history doesn't judge my administration as the one full of whack jobs."

He turned to Geringer. "Senator, I have no doubt that people are struggling to believe what they see. I too had a hard time believing that Marine One could be brought down like that. There are questions I need to ask. I need to speak to Secretary Carter about what he's done. I hope that-"

A Secret Service detail burst into the conference room.

"Sir, we need to move you, now! Please come with us."

"Senator, I guess I have my orders. Thank you for whatever help you gave. I'm sure we'll be chatting soon. Extend my best wishes to everyone at the convention and tell them I hope something meaningful comes from their effort. The republic needs it."

The three men shook hands and Secret Service agents whisked POTUS and the chief to the service entrance of the conference center. The president didn't get his change of clothing.

CHAPTER NINE
DETAINMENT

They traveled in the valley of the private road, snow plowed into mountains on both sides, leading from State Highway 115 to the Cheyenne Mountain Complex. The president's motorcade entered "America's Fortress" passing heavily armed guards at the tunnel's ingress. They slalomed around staggered barriers placed inside the tunnel. A mile later, the thud of the 25-ton blast doors let the president's detail know they were secure. The president raced beyond the security checkpoint towards the Granite Inn, the complex's dining facility. There he met the First Lady, who'd had a couple of stressful days. They shared a long embrace.

It had been some time since he'd had a regular meal. He satisfied his hunger alongside his wife, with a tuna sandwich and ice tea. Hutchinson sat at another table.

After a shower and a change of clothes, he retreated to the alternate command and control center, a large conference room with wooden tables arranged in a U-shape. At the top of the "U" were two large, wall-mounted screens flanked by the U.S. and Canadian flags. The left screen displayed the Battle Cab Traffic Situation Display, a visual representation of air traffic over the United States. The right screen showed the concentric circles with Washington D.C. in the center, outlining restricted airspace.

The president sat at the base of the "U" with Hutchinson to his right. The facility commander and his direct reports sat opposite the chief. Secret Service stood outside the doors.

He'd arranged a secure video call with the Secretary of Defense, Trent Carter, DNI Gerald Burkemper, NSA Eric Greich, DHS Secretary Victor Haydon, and FBI Director Ralph

Elliott, who were all in the White House Situation Room. Also, joining the call remotely was the head of the Joint Chiefs of Staff from the Pentagon.

The rightmost screen in front of the president alternated between the White House and the Pentagon.

Carter occupied the president's chair and greeted Jefferson. "Mr. President. Let me be the first to say that we're happy you're safe and sound back in friendly territory."

"Thank you, Mr. Secretary. It's good to be back. Director Elliott, what do we know about the abduction and what happened with Marine One and the other security measures?"

The director wiggled in his chair. "Well, sir, we're not exactly sure how they could pinpoint your exact route back the Cheyenne. As far as the drone swarm that took down Marine One and those F-16s, my people tell me that this is a technology that may have been developed by one of our contractors."

"Mr. Greich, if Director Elliott's intel is wrong, could this be the work of a hostile foreign power?"

"Not that we can tell, sir. The only government we know that has this technology, besides us, are the Israelis. Your administration, ah our nation, has enjoyed great relations with them, so I don't think that's likely."

Carter chimed in. "Mr. President, I called all our allies on the hotline and had several ambassadors from less friendly countries to the White House. The allies had no intel and the ambassadors denied any responsibility."

President Jefferson presumed everyone on this call supported him, though he remained troubled by the relative ease with which he became a kidnap victim. The Secret Service was responsible for the routes he took and for the decoy Marine One. He kept his concerns to himself for the moment.

Jefferson asked the facility commander and his direct reports to leave the conference room. Hutchinson walked them out and closed the door behind them.

Jefferson explained to the remaining group how he felt the need to reexamine his policies. The civil unrest and worsening social mood, as reflected by the secession movements on the West Coast and cyber separatists like the Five Tribes, gave him pause. He brought up the reorientation camps, the personal interest story related by Chandler, and his conversations with Brigade members. No one could ever accuse the Honor Brigade of being unpatriotic, so he felt their opinions carried value.

"Gentlemen, we have a group meeting, a convention going on right now to the north of me. The only reason they're meeting is because of my administration. And they're doing this in total compliance with our Constitution. They've had enough and frankly, the more I think about it, I can't blame them."

Hutchinson hurled a scowl at the president. "Sir."

Jefferson shushed him.

"Mr. President, with all due respect, those people in Winter Park, they're trying to undo the Constitution, undoing the work of all who've built this great nation to what it is today," Carter affirmed, looking comfortable in the president's chair.

"To what it is today? Trent, look at what we've become. The world of my children and grandchildren will be nothing like I had envisioned. We have so many layers of security and surveillance, but the reality is no one feels any more secure. You guys couldn't even keep me safe from a group of cyber separatists." Jefferson threw his hands in the air.

"Mr. President, I'm sure we can fix whatever the problem was with your security," Carter asserted.

Jefferson thought the country's social distress resulted from blowback. The more they tried to control, the more certain groups rebelled. He thought they'd spent too much time winning over the minds of those in government instead of winning over the hearts and minds of the people, all the people.

"We've antagonized our citizens so much that some have decided they no longer need us. I think the Five Tribes demonstrate that pretty well, don't you think?"

"Sir, we'll take care of the Five Tribes and that Quinque character. We've had enough of them. I have-" DHS Secretary Haydon couldn't finish his sentence due to Jefferson's interruption.

"What good is having all these nukes and a great military when things are crumbling at home? No one wants to fight the U.S. in a war. Even our greatest foes understand the price they'd pay for a war with us. But we can't bomb our way to domestic security and we're not winning the cyber battle."

"Mr. President, have you been checked out by medical personnel in Cheyenne Mountain?" Carter asked.

Others in the Situation Room had similar thoughts, yet they deferred to Carter, who remained in charge there.

"Trent, are you listening to me? I'm fine. I-"

"Sir, if I may. We need to quash all of these secession groups once and for all. We'll find Quinque and arrest him. With regards to the convention, you know about our people there collecting intel. When that convention gets done, we'll be waiting for them with a verbal barrage. They won't know what hit them," Carter replied.

"That's your answer? More of the same?"

Jefferson's attitude raised eyebrows in the Situation Room. Hutchinson's eyebrows had already traveled well into his forehead.

"Mr. President, your tone, frankly surprises us. You were just abducted by cyber separatists and the Article Five convention wants to repudiate you. Two secession movements want to leave the country. We need to do something!" Secretary Haydon insisted.

"We have Mr. Secretary. It's not working. At the end of the day, I want to have something that looks like the USA left. It may not look like before, but we're not going down on my watch. You guys need to pay attention to what's going on out here."

An uncomfortable silence followed. The mood in the Situation Room turned grim. No one knew what to say.

The president startled his audience with his next move. "Gentlemen, I'm headed back to D.C. I will address the nation from the Oval Office to discuss what I feel should be a new vision for the country. Thank you for your time today."

The rightmost screen went dark, reverting to the restricted airspace map of the capital. The president marched to his quarters with the Chief of Staff in tow.

Back in the Situation Room, Carter's facial remolding characterized everyone else's agitation at the video call they'd just had. He would soon bring up a subject that no one would ever want to discuss.

***

The military formed the backbone of Trent Carter's career. After earning a degree in International Relations from Georgetown University, he received his appointment as a second lieutenant in the Marine Corps, rising to the rank of general. He served many tours overseas, including the first Gulf War and the Iraq occupation. After retiring from the military, he served as a State Department liaison in the Middle East and on various corporate boards. President Jefferson appointed him National

Security Advisor in 2017. He recently moved to his role as Secretary of Defense.

Carter, a patriot, dedicated his life in service to his country. His childhood in Tulsa, Oklahoma represented everything that was red, white, and blue America. As the son of a serviceman, he would always respect the Office of the President and be loyal to his Commander-in-Chief. Nothing in his training or education, however, prepared him to fight the modern forces of separatism — cyber-separatists and hackers.

His biggest test occurred early in his tenure as National Security Advisor, in November 2017. In the middle of the night on November 22nd, he received a call from his military attaché who informed him that NORAD had a confirmed ballistic missile launch by North Korea with warheads targeting to the U.S. mainland. President Jefferson would have but minutes to respond to the doomsday signal, unleashing the Armageddon fires. Carter was in the San Francisco Bay Area visiting his son for the Thanksgiving holiday. While his wife and son's family slept, Carter dialed President Jefferson, who slept at the White House. Before he could finish dialing, another call came in from his attaché. It had been a false alarm caused by a software malfunction.

The world came within a whisker of annihilation because of what software designers called the "Titanic Effect", which described how things can quietly go awry in complex technological systems. Technology complacency had made everything less safe.

Now he feared an annihilation from within, something the country avoided during the Civil War. This internal conflict had a different complexion, and its outcome looked to be more than binary. It wouldn't be a North and a South. He worried about a fracturing into many pieces with technology supporting the process.

In his mind, the alt-media and journalists of Chandler Scott's ilk were poisoning the minds of Americans. Though he valued an independent media, the needs of the nation outweighed the needs of a few journalists. Carter was one of several in the president's inner circle who felt the Justice Department should have prosecuted Chandler with severe penalties. They needed to make an example of him. Politically, Jefferson knew that would hurt him with part of the public and members of the GOP and third parties whose support he needed to resolve the 2020 election. Carter opined that Chandler's documentary corrupted the administration's Plan for Prosperity and the patriotic We Are the Future messages.

Carter's vision of America was under assault, and now he dealt with a president that appeared complicit in its unraveling. He had little time to act.

The team remained in the Situation Room chattering about POTUS' comments.

"Gentlemen, I'm not sure what the president will say to the American public, but I'm deeply worried," Carter noted.

Nobody said anything, fearful of where Carter might take the conversation. Perhaps they were fearful about breaching their oath of serving the president and country.

"Come on, guys. You heard what he said," Carter offered, pointing at the large screen in front where POTUS had just appeared.

The rest of the room dropped their heads towards their papers on the table.

Carter stood to get their attention. "Gentlemen, I'm sure everyone realizes what's at stake here. The secession movements, the separatists, this Article Five convention, and the civil unrest are tearing us apart. It's our solemn duty to protect the nation, and increasingly these threats are becoming existential. We have to stand up for the Constitution, don't we?"

After a prolonged silence, DHS Secretary Haydon spoke with resignation. "Trent, I think we all agree, but what do you want us to do? He's the president. He's within his rights to express his opinion to the American public."

Carter paced around the conference table, making a chopping motion with his hand. "Gentlemen, we are facing a grave crisis." He stopped pacing near an American flag in the room's corner. "Men of true character and honor act decisively during perilous times such as these."

"What are you asking of us, Trent?" DNI Burkemper asked.

Because of the president's abduction, Secretary Carter wanted him to undergo a thorough medical and psychological evaluation. He suspected that POTUS was a victim of brainwashing by the Five Tribes. Given the government's use of virtual reality and drugs to reeducate unruly citizens, it was plausible for the technologically savvy Tribes to have similar capability for their own nefarious aims. The mental manipulation could go a long way towards carrying out their goals with a compliant president.

Carter hoped the attending psychologist would deem POTUS unfit for duty, in which case he expected the president to resign. If POTUS resisted, he would have him detained and charged with treason or relieve him of duty based on the 25th Amendment.

The Constitution and U.S. Code spelled out treason. Carter hoped that "adhering to their enemies" would form the basis for charging President Jefferson if it came to that. He reasoned that anyone advocating for the partial dissolution of the republic was aiding the enemy.

Carter stood over his chair and pointed around the room. "It's your duty, gentlemen. Who's with me?"

DNI Burkemper's gaze could have burned a hole through the steel doors of a bank vault. "You realize what you're asking, Mr. Secretary?"

The rest of the group repeated Burkemper's question in their minds.

Carter had the look of a man about to deliver an unwelcome mandate. "Gentlemen, he'll be given a choice. If he's a patriot, he'll do what's right for the country."

"And if he doesn't?" Burkemper asked.

"Then I'll charge him with treason, plain and simple. If the Attorney General thinks otherwise, then we'll relieve him of command under the 25th Amendment. I ask again, who's with me?"

No one spoke. Some shuffled papers, unwilling to look Carter in the eye.

Carter spun his chair and waited for the rotation to stop. "I understand the gravity of what I'm asking. If you feel you don't want to be part of this, stand up and offer your resignation immediately."

Those around the table only offered calcified stares. They all remained seated, their arms rigid, anchored to the table.

Carter listened to the emptiness of the room, interpreting silence as full consent. "Very well, then. It's done!"

Carter ordered the White House press secretary to issue a statement suggesting the president was under medical care suffering from undisclosed injuries after his abduction. He took this action before the inbound Secretary of State, who he presumed would be acting president, could render an opinion on the press release.

The press would have to sort the resulting maelstrom. Journalists in Winter Park, Colorado wouldn't understand why POTUS would be under medical care when he looked perfectly fine to them. The D.C. press corps wouldn't know what to think.

Carter had just thrown the president's men into the churning propellers of a constitutional crisis.

***

Jefferson had just finished spending time with the First Lady in the VIP suite. He answered a forceful knock.

"Mr. President, they have instructed me to bring you to the complex's hospital."

Four men stood on the other side of the door. One dressed in medical garb, another in civilian attire, and the other two were security personnel in military dress.

"Honey, who is it? Is it time to go?" the First Lady asked while packing her suitcase.

Secret Service had continued to advise Jefferson to remain in Cheyenne Mountain, given the airspace violation on the inbound flight, his abduction, and the continuing unrest in some large cities. He and the First Lady wanted to return to D.C. for those same reasons. He had a different agenda now.

"For what reason? I'm fine," Jefferson replied, his arms extended on the door frame.

The man in medical garb, presumably the complex's doctor, repeated the earlier request. "Sir, I've been instructed by Secretary of Defense Carter to examine you before you're released."

The First Lady suspended her packing and approached the gathering, placing her hand on the president's shoulder. "Ben, what's going on?"

He didn't acknowledge her, instead directing his ire at the

doctor. "Everyone seems to have forgotten who the president is. Thank you for your concern. I think I'll finish packing now."

Jefferson's attempt to close the door met the physician's foot. "Mr. President, you've just been through a significant ordeal. No one has checked you out. This is not a request, sir."

The four men on the other side of the door stood poker-faced. Though he felt fine and was in otherwise good health, he realized the man was just doing his job. This was standard procedure, though the last couple of days resembled nothing standard.

He turned to the First Lady and caressed her hand. "I'll be back soon."

She didn't look assured.

He walked with the four men to complex's small hospital — two rooms separated by a partition. A pungent, antiseptic aroma blanketed the sterile, shiny examination room. A single bed with rollers sat in the middle. An oxygen tank rested on a wall. A large, plain cabinet, also on rollers, sat next to the bed. Wedged in the corner next to a foot-operated hazardous material receptacle were a nondescript sink and towel dispenser. There were several warning signs indicating the presence of oxygen.

The doctor escorted the president into the exam room. The rest of the party stood vigilant outside.

After submitting to the standard medical exam, the doctor switched places with the civilian who entered the room wearing a white smock.

"Mr. President, we're not quite done yet." The civilian in the white smock extended his arm, blocking Jefferson's progress.

"What do you mean? We just finished. The doctor didn't say anything was wrong."

"Sir, after a kidnapping, the victims often are traumatized in ways that are not immediately identifiable. This is just standard procedure, sir."

Jefferson tightened his jaw, throwing a despising glance at the man. "Look, don't throw the Stockholm Syndrome bullshit at me. I need to get back to Washington." He pushed by the man and met resistance at the door. The doctor pointed back into the examination room and the security personnel blocked his exit.

"Mr. President, please," the doctor pleaded.

Reasoning that he only delayed his departure, he acquiesced and went back to the examination table.

"Thank you, sir. I'm a psychiatrist who will perform the MSE." He tapped on his electronic tablet.

Mental status examinations or MSE determined a patient's psychological function. The exam focused on appearance, attitude, behavior, thought process, and other dimensions. This wouldn't be the first MSE performed on President Jefferson.

The psychiatrist asked him a series of open-and-closed questions, focusing on his accomplishments and regrets while in office. He then administered a series of tests completed on his tablet.

After a couple of hours of inquiry, the psychiatrist finished the examination. "Thank you, Mr. President. Please wait here for the doctor."

The psychiatrist had an animated discussion with the doctor that Jefferson witnessed behind the frosted glass on the examination room's entry door.

The doctor reentered. He attempted to hide his worry by focusing on the electronic tablet in his hands. "Sir, we're going to escort you back to your suite after which we'll send our findings to Washington."

"Your findings?" Jefferson's heart skipped a beat.

The doctor made eye contact. "Yes, sir. The results of our

exam."

"I'm fine, right?"

"Physically, you are, sir. Fit as ever."

He exhaled, blowing out his cheeks. "Good."

"The attending psychiatrist, however, feels that you've suffered mental trauma that will require time to heal."

His relief turned to anger. "That's nonsense. I'm in perfect control of my faculties." Muscles in his neck bulged. His nostrils flared.

The doctor reached towards the president, placing his hand on his shoulder. "Sir, let's go back to your suite so you can relax."

Jefferson spun away from his caregiver. "Relax? No, now I'm *not* relaxed."

He wanted to get back to the First Lady, unsettled with his departure for the exam room. He'd already been out of her sight enough on this trip.

Hutchinson intercepted him while returning to the suite. "Sir, I just spoke to the Secretary of Defense and he's informed me that you're confined to Cheyenne until further notice. What's this about?"

"I don't know but we're gonna find out. Let me go say something to my wife. Wait outside, please."

After reassuring the First Lady, the two men walked to the alternate command-and-control center for a video conference with the secretary.

Secretary Carter joined them from the Situation Room. "Mr. President, glad to hear you had a good exam," Carter beamed.

Jefferson spoke through gritted teeth. "Trent cut the BS. They told me I'm confined to Cheyenne Mountain. Who gave that order?"

Carter's lips parted, revealing his pearly whites. He

222

understood the nature of this confrontation. Never did he expect the president do go down without a fight. "Sir, the psychiatrist who examined you suggested that you're suffering from delusional guilt. You've had to deal with so much the last few years. It's more than any president has ever contemplated. Your time in captivity has made you sympathetic to the separatists and the secession movements. It's understandable, sir. Anyone would have suffered the same fate. You just need a little time. Once we get Camp David secure, we can send you there to recuperate. In the meantime-"

Jefferson stood, leaning over the conference table, lunging at the screen. "Trent, I don't know what you think you're doing. You better fix this now or you're fired!"

Carter's toothy grin and devilish eyes revealed a sinister intent. "The psychiatrist told me you'd react this way. He said it's perfectly normal. The rest of your advisers and cabinet members have been informed of your condition, as have the Joint Chiefs. We told the press that you were undergoing a medical evaluation following your abduction. Well wishes are pouring in from our allies too, sir. Everyone's pulling for you."

Jefferson grabbed a nearby pen and hurled it at the screen, holding it too long before it bounced on the ground. "Stop patronizing me, Trent!" He pressed a button on the console and ended the video call.

His accusatory stare towards the chief unnerved him. "Sir, I hope you don't think I have anything to do with this, do you?"

He seethed. He took a few moments to calm himself while staring at the screen showing the air traffic over the continental United States. "Drake, all these planes. They have people going somewhere. Business trips, family visits, vacations. When I took this job, I knew I couldn't just get on a commercial flight and go where I wanted. Now, they tell me I'm the most powerful man on Earth and yet, here I am stuck inside a granite mountain. I can't go home." He looked at his chief, showing a vulnerability that he hadn't revealed to anyone but his wife. "Do you think there's something wrong with me?"

Hutchinson had hoped his boss didn't ask that question. "Sir, it's not my place." He averted his eyes.

The president pleaded, interlacing his fingers, shaking his hands. "Drake, please."

"Well, Mr. President, you have been through a lot." He flitted his eyes around the room. "I'm sure that journalist, Mr. Scott, put thoughts in your head too. It's easy for people like him to judge. He's not trying to fix the economy and deal with people who want to leave the Union. Anyone would feel the stress and have their thoughts upended. You're only human, sir."

"No one should blame him. I didn't get the sense that he judged anyone. He reported what he saw. He didn't need to judge when he showed the reorientation camp. Everyone could figure that one out. And these people who want to leave, I'm not sure I can stop them despite all of my administration's Orwellian efforts. I'm disappointed that people think that a journalist doing his job could somehow corrupt my mind."

"You may be right, sir. But a bunch of people in Washington don't agree."

"I'm going to get my own doctor in here. Maybe then, all those fools will see that there's nothing wrong with me and that I'm up for doing this job."

***

The Secretary of State's inbound flight to Joint Base Andrews diverted to Tel Aviv to deal with a sticky diplomatic issue. For the moment, Carter controlled the reins of the executive office.

He met with his usual contingent in the Situation Room. After briefings on the civil unrest, he pivoted towards the topic of POTUS.

Carter wasted no time. "I know I asked you to take a stand with me against President Jefferson in light of his sympathetic comments about his captors and secessionists. Gentlemen, it appears there's another option to restrain the president's actions. While I urged you before to consider treason, the medical evaluation from the attending psychiatrist paints the profile of someone suffering from delusional guilt."

The rest of the room looked at one another, seeking clarification.

"I spoke with the president a couple of hours ago and explained the diagnosis. The Five Tribes and that journalist have brainwashed him into feeling guilty about everything he's done to save the country. The psychiatrist has prescribed rest and medication."

Though he didn't voice it, the secretary wondered if POTUS could benefit from a dose of virtual reality reorientation.

DNI Burkemper sought more. "What does this mean, Trent?"

"It means we will remove the president from office under the 25th Amendment. The attending psychiatrist felt that the president's actions could do irreparable harm to the nation given that he was just not himself."

The 25th Amendment dealt with presidential succession. The country already faced a crisis of sorts with a vice president near death and a Speaker of the House and President of the Senate who were ineligible to serve. With the Secretary of State caught overseas on an important assignment, the job fell to the Secretary of Defense, Trent Carter.

The 25th Amendment, ratified in 1967 in the wake of President Kennedy's assassination, formally described the procedure for a vice president to assume the office. The amendment also opened the door to remove a president judged unfit for office. Carter preferred this option for Jefferson's removal rather than charging him with treason and the impeachment process that came with it. There was still the matter of an unresolved 2020 election that needed Congress' attention.

To remove Jefferson from office, Carter would use Section 4 of the amendment. This meant most of the president's cabinet, including the Secretary of State and Defense and the vice president, would formally declare the president unfit for office due to a mental condition. Alternately, the vice president, could make his case to Congress. Given the vice president's perilous health, Secretary Carter opted for the first option.

The president could defend himself, mandating a special congressional vote. Jefferson would need to step down if his opponents could convince two-thirds of Congress. Though a formidable task, Carter reasoned that it was a more palatable and faster alternative than another impeachment. He understood that part of the public would cheer the action while others would deride it. Carter would follow with a propaganda campaign, openly questioning Jefferson's sympathies to groups wishing to split the country.

Carter continued. "I've already explained the situation to the rest of the cabinet, including the Secretary of State. Most of them have pledged support for my action."

Malcolm Holloway, Secretary of the Financial Stability Board, a department created by the president after the economic shocks, raised his hand.

A strong partner of the president, he knew the country needed to maintain its course. His recent trip to the emergency economic summit in Geneva reinforced this. He and his allies at the Global Settlement Bank (GSB) were architects of the Plan for Prosperity. The International Relations Council (IRC), part of the nation's shadow Elite, supported the Jefferson administration domestically. The IRC advised the administration on the patriotic themes necessary to further their economic agenda.

"Mr. Secretary, we're at a critical juncture with our economic plan. Everything we discussed in Geneva suggests we need to stay the course. If the president wants to deviate from our plan, well, I don't know what would happen. I'm not even sure how we'd dismantle what we've done without throwing the country into utter chaos."

The GSB and IRC had already contacted Holloway when word leaked of the president's wavering. Carter himself had fielded calls from them.

Carter didn't need more tumult right now and counted on Holloway to keep the economic ship on course. "Thank you, Mr. Secretary. It's good to know I have your support."

Holloway had another offering. "On the other hand, he is our president. He's the face of this economic plan. He's the one who looked the American people in the eye and told them he had a solution. People still want solutions to a crisis that's far from over. Who's going to carry that torch now? You?" He pointed at Carter. "Why don't we let him return to Washington and we can address his concerns?"

"Secretary Holloway, I understand your loyalty. Remember, he appointed me to be the NSA. I owe him much. But, we have to look beyond our personal loyalties. The events right now could get out of hand quickly. I'm sure President Batista thought nothing of a ragtag group of Cuban guerrillas marching all the way to Havana. His inaction gave us Castro. I don't want a repeat of that. The country cannot afford to give any hope to those who want to break up our Republic."

Holloway's dark eyes radiated disdain. He saw no correlation between Castro's Cuba and the current situation, thinking it a feeble try to discredit his concerns. For someone who was usually the smartest person in the room, the maneuver didn't sit well. He understood that he'd have to support Carter's decision.

The rest of the assembled group murmured in agreement.

"I want to remind everyone that secessions are most successful when the central government shows weakness, especially if it comes from the economy." Carter extended his open hand towards Holloway. "Secretary Holloway is right. We can't dismantle what we've done, and yes, the president is the face of the plan. But he's not bigger than the plan!"

The rest of the group, save for Holloway, applauded. Carter beamed.

Holloway sought redemption in this meeting, something that he never had to do around the president. "You had the press secretary say he was under medical care. What about those journalists that saw him in Winter Park? They're going to say he looked fine. You also haven't considered what that journalist, Mr. Scott, is going to say. They captured him along with the president. How are you going to address that?"

Because of a bill signed by President Jefferson's predecessor, the government had established its own Ministry of Truth. Late in 2016, the government created the Global Engagement Center (GEC). The GEC analyzed information, regardless of source, and determined its impact on national security. It formed a network of partners who would feed it information used to counter anti-government propaganda. The center operated under the auspices of the State Department and could acquire funds appropriated for the Department of Defense. They developed and disseminated fact-based narratives, or alternative facts, to counter propaganda. While originally intended as a vehicle to prevent foreign propaganda, domestic actors became targets of their wrath.

Carter disarmed Holloway's concern, creasing his face into a smile. "You bring up a great point, Mr. Secretary. I've been in contact with the GEC and they've assured me that they will counter any alternative news interpretation. At this point, I also don't want to alarm the public about the president's psychiatric diagnosis. We'll keep that quiet for now and reveal it when the time is right."

Carter's mood changed when one of the Watch Officers stationed in the Situation Room ferried a bulletin to him. He read it and pressed his lips into a thin line.

He raised the bulletin for all to see. "Gentlemen, one of our dams in California, Oroville, one of the turbines is spinning out of control. They're afraid it's on its way to overheating. That's over a thousand metric tons of metal, gentlemen. They've contacted the governor and National Guard."

"They can't stop it somehow? I don't understand," DNI Burkemper said.

"They can't stop it because of a software hack. They're hoping they get a ransomware call from the perpetrators so they can shut it down. That's how bad it is," Carter replied.

Given the events of the last few years, the suspects at the top of the list were the Five Tribes and Omni.

CHAPTER TEN
REUNION

He waited for her at the Fraser railway station. A more apt description would be railway pavilion. With temperatures hovering near zero, Chandler sat in a car in front of the steps leading to the raised pavilion. The day was gray and the winds howled, throwing a fine snow mist that swept over his vehicle's hood. He didn't think he'd see her so soon. Then again, he didn't expect his role in the presidential kidnapping.

Thinking he heard a train whistle in the distance, he bolted out of his car and stumbled up the snow-covered pavilion steps. Looking south, he could see the train's headlights in the distance. The train floated over the snow, the tracks covered with white powder. He stood underneath a heat lamp, staring at the sign that told him the elevation, 8,574 feet. The cloud he was on was higher than that — he couldn't wait to see her.

The train stopped just long enough for Arianne to deboard. She carried a small duffel bag over her shoulder. She didn't prepare for the wind that blew hair over her face.

She jumped on him, straddling her legs around his midsection. "Oh, my God, Chan!" The lip lock lasted several seconds.

Her legs fell to the ground and she squeezed him for dear life, placing her head next to his.

Chandler, forced into shallow breaths, dropped a Groucho Marx line. "Ari, if you held me any tighter, I'd be behind you. Let's go to the car. It's colder than you know what kind of commode out here."

He meant cast iron.

He grabbed the duffel bag with his left hand. He occupied his right hand with both of hers.

He started the car and ran the defroster. It had not taken long for a coating of snow to cover his windows.

"I can't believe I almost lost you." She'd moved next to him, leaning over the center console.

He put his arm around her. "I know you won't believe this, but I felt safe most of the time. Once I figured out it was the Five Tribes, I knew they wouldn't harm us."

When not thinking like a journalist during the ordeal, thoughts of her sustained him.

"What about when you had to spend the night in the woods?"

"The Tribes, I gotta say, they did right by us. The camp was well-stocked, we had a great tent, unbelievable sleeping bags, a fire. We were OK, really. I don't know that I'd want to do that again, but for one night, we were good."

"And how 'bout you, sleeping right next to the president. Awkward, huh?" She jabbed him in the ribs.

"By the time we got in the tent, we were all so tired. I wasn't going to be speaking much to the chief, that's for sure."

Chandler explained his confrontation with Hutchinson while pulling the vehicle away from the station.

It didn't take long for the two of them to get "reacquainted" after arriving in Chandler's hotel room.

He activated the Do Not Disturb sign. They left a trail of clothing from the entrance to his bed.

She laid on top of him. The late afternoon sun fought through her auburn locks, the glint igniting his passion. Her skin glowed. Her warm hands moved gently over his chest.

"I want you, all of you, every day, the rest of my life," she whispered in his ear.

The warmth of her breath was as essential as his own. His skin melted into hers. Their hearts beat as one. It was his favorite way to have her.

She traced her tongue around the edge of his mouth. Their bodies became united.

Swept up into a raging torrent, their ecstasy catapulted her beside him. They both remained motionless.

An hour later, he awoke first. He laid on his side. She was behind him, her arm around his waist. They had but a sheet on top of them.

He turned to her, inhaling sharply, allowing her scent to seep into his lungs. That scent offered him as much comfort as anything. He'd returned home.

A reddish glow covered the frosted trees dotting the mountain behind his room. On the other side, the sun was setting over the horizon. Darkness came quickly, forming a wicked union with the frigid air. Day and night waged a struggle, with night declared the victor.

Chandler would soon learn of another struggle. He clicked the remote in time for a news bulletin.

The White House Press Secretary has confirmed that President Benjamin Jefferson is under medical care due to injuries suffered during his abduction by the Five Tribes. The secretary did not disclose his location. We will provide more information as it becomes available.

Chandler sat straight up in bed. "What? No way!"

He woke Arianne from her post-passion slumber. "Huh, what is it?" She reached for him, grabbing his pillow instead.

"That's a bunch of bullshit!"

Arianne still didn't have her faculties. "Chan, what time is it?"

"Who cares? Did you hear what they just said?"

She sat up, with the sheet wrapped under her arms. "Why are you yelling? What is it?"

"They said Jefferson's under medical care like he's hurt. That's BS!"

"Maybe something happened that you didn't notice. When you camped overnight, maybe?"

"No. We had to walk for a while after the Honor Brigade rescued us."

"OK, so maybe he pulled a muscle or something. That might not show up until later. I remember one time-"

"No Ari. This is weird. They're not even saying where he's being held. Why wouldn't the White House let everyone know?"

"Chan, he just got kidnapped. I'm sure they want to keep his location secret."

"When he left here, he headed back to Cheyenne Mountain. Who knows? Maybe they moved him again. I'm not buying this."

She slid behind him. The sheet she had pinned under her arms fell on the bed. She massaged her bosom against his back. He straightened at the sensation. She hoped Chandler would fall on her this time.

"Come on. Let's start round two," she breathed.

He succumbed to her charms.

***

His phone roused him from his mini-slumber. He rolled her off before grabbing it from the nightstand. He didn't bother to look at the caller id.

"Hello."

"Chandler, it's me, Matt."

"Senator, what time is it? I mean, how are you?"

"I've got something that may be of interest."

"OK, shoot."

"No, not over the phone. Can you meet me in that first conference room outside of the Great Hall?"

He looked at the sleeping beauty next to him who had not budged. "Yeah, sure, I guess. Give me a few minutes."

Though he regretted leaving her, the senator's voice had a sense of urgency. The gurgles in his stomach reminded him that they had skipped dinner.

Geringer sat impatiently, his leg bounced while crossed over the other. When he saw Chandler approaching, he unfurled his lanky frame, ushering him in and looking both ways outside the door.

"OK, now I know something's going on. You, looking out both ways. What's up Matt?"

"You spent a couple of days in captivity with the president. You and everyone here saw him walk into the convention hall without help. Then we get this statement from the White House Press Office saying he's under medical care, they won't say where or for how long. I got suspicious."

"I know, I thought the same thing. That's what I just told Ari-"

"She's here now? Good. Is she doing OK?"

Chandler smiled, recalling their affection the last couple of hours. "Yeah, she's good."

"That's great to hear." Geringer's face stiffened. "An old friend of mine, he works at Peterson Air Force Base. I won't tell you the name. They supposedly were preparing for Air Force One to head back to D.C. when they received an order to stop. My friend said the order came from the Secretary of Defense. My friend pursued this further since they figured POTUS was still in Cheyenne. They were told that he was being held in Cheyenne after undergoing a psychiatric evaluation."

"It's understandable the president would have some sort of a medical evaluation after his ordeal. Does that normally include a psych one as well?"

"I don't know the answer to that. What's important is that they detained POTUS *after* the psych eval. The question is, why?"

Both men fell silent, contemplating the answer.

"Chandler, was there something about POTUS that seemed off to you when you were being held?"

"Honestly, I saw a different side of the man. I'd spent the last couple of years investigating the power brokers and the people who opposed him. And you know how Axel feels about Jefferson's heavy hand of authority. The more I talked to him and the more he listened to the Tribes or even the Honor Brigade, you could see like these veils being removed. It's like he had more clarity and awareness. I don't think he ever really sensed how his administration's policies were affecting people. It's that old thing about the Beltway bubble, I suppose."

Geringer nodded. "I have to remind myself of that. That's why it's important for us legislators to go be with the people who elected us. The president, he doesn't really do that. When he visits with America, it's usually to promote the Plan for Prosperity or to get everyone behind We Are the Future. The communication is all one way. Most of the time, they're carefully planned propaganda events. His handlers are all about making him look like the hero."

Geringer stroked his thick mustache. "There's something else going on. Secretary of Defense Carter assumed control of the White House when they kidnapped POTUS. He should have surrendered control by now. For Carter to order Air Force One grounded, there must be something else going on with POTUS. Keep this to yourself for now. I don't want you to report it until either you or I can learn more detail. I just wanted to give you a heads-up. I've got to speak with some commissioners who are asking questions."

Geringer shook Chandler's hand and slapped him on the shoulder on his way out. He took a step out the door before retreating. "I almost forgot. I confronted Jefferson about suspicions on the abduction."

"Yeah, and?"

"Hutchinson thought everyone was nuts. Jefferson started to say something before Secret Service took him away."

"Clear as mud, then."

"Yeah, just one more thing to think about. Gotta go!" Geringer left this time.

Whenever Chandler had questions that needed answers or even more probing, he turned to his mentor. He remained in the conference room, dialing Axel.

"Hey, Chan. Did Ari make it in?"

"Yeah, yeah, she's fine. Hey, are you in your room?"

"Yes, what do you need?"

"Let me come up and I'll explain."

Chandler pulled the same routine as Geringer, looking both ways out of the conference room. He didn't want to answer any questions about his time in captivity. He scurried up to his mentor's room.

Axel looked tired, with a pained expression.

"Ax, you doin' OK?"

"Just a headache. That's all. What do you want to talk about?"

They moved to the living area of the suite — the lights were dim.

"You got a hangover or something," Chandler asked, commenting on the darkness.

Axel shook his head.

Chandler explained his observation about POTUS during the captivity and relayed Geringer's intel from Cheyenne.

The normally contemplative Axel responded in short order. "The president's been under a great deal of stress, I'm sure. His doctor probably thought he needed a more thorough check after the kidnapping. We haven't talked about how you're feeling after the ordeal."

Chandler expected the usual historical perspective and other analytics. "I'm doing fine, really. Seeing Ari helped." He winked. "So, you don't find it odd about Air Force One being grounded?"

"There must be a security worry. Maybe the Secret Service made the decision?"

Chandler hadn't considered the Secret Service angle.

"Let me reach out to a couple of people and see what I can find," Axel reassured.

"As in Omni?"

Axel smiled. "Among others. Now please leave and go spend time with Arianne. She needs you more than I do."

"Oh yeah, I left her sleeping too. She's probably hungry."

"All right, keep me posted, and get some light on in here."

He made his way to the other side of the Grand Mountain Conference Center hotel facility when he ran into one of his rescuers.

"Mr. West, ah, Big Dog!"

Big Dog appeared troubled. "Chandler, glad I ran into you. Do you have time?"

His famished, ravishing beauty remained in the hotel room. He reminisced about their earlier frolicking. For the moment, though, he had to don his journalist cap.

"Yeah, what's up?"

"Not here. Let's go up to my room. My XO, Proto, is there."

They took the elevator to the top floor of the center's north wing. After sliding the key card for room access, Big Dog led Chandler into an apartment-sized suite.

"Clearly, I need to come work for you," Chandler said, admiring the surroundings.

"We gave the hotel and Convention of States a good deal, so they comped us with this room, or should I say, suite," Big Dog answered, spreading his arms in admiration of his quarters.

They moved to a spacious living room where Chandler exchanged greetings with Proto.

"Can I get you a beer?" Proto offered.

Chandler declined, moving to a chair and ottoman while the other two sat on the adjacent leather sofa.

Even though a couple of AR-15s were on a table a few feet away, Big Dog and Proto didn't show the operational tension while providing security for the convention or rescuing POTUS.

The Honor Brigade had reasons for being defensive.

They fought the stigma of association with militia groups, some of which spewed anti-Semitic messages. They didn't tolerate these views. They had a good mechanism in place to screen for people who deviated from their beliefs, though as Chandler found out in Idaho during his documentary, covert splinter groups could form from within.

While they saw themselves as patriots, they had no interest in picking a fight with the government. They shared a vision that government couldn't always provide their security.

The first instance of this vision materialized after 9/11. Expanding criminal gangs and Islamic jihadists gave them more reason for concern.

The lawlessness in the aftermath of Hurricane Katrina made them realize they needed to protect themselves far beyond the criminal enterprise. Natural disasters demanded their attention for humanitarian reasons. During Hurricane Sandy, the Honor Brigade fortified local efforts by sending truckloads of supplies into areas of New Jersey rife with post-storm crime.

To be aware of field conditions, the Brigade created a phantom network of informants, called Sentinels, providing them intel to make proper rescue decisions for their membership.

This network included law enforcement, FBI, and others within the intelligence community, who like the Brigade, shared the belief that government, despite its authoritarian bent, couldn't always be counted upon during natural disasters or mass civil disturbances.

The Sentinels provided Big Dog intelligence that corroborated Senator Geringer's suspicions about the status of POTUS.

"First of all, you didn't hear this from us, if your intent is to publish this or issue some sort of bulletin. Ordinarily, if this involved someone from our membership, we wouldn't be having this conversation. Being as this is the President of the United States, it's bigger than us," Big Dog said.

Proto shook his head in support of his commander.

"Understood," Chandler replied. He grabbed his buzzing phone out of his pocket. Sleeping beauty had awakened. "Sorry guys, continue."

"They gave POTUS a health check, but they also gave him a psych test. According to our source, the doctor that gave him the test said there were problems. Supposedly the problem was serious enough to call Washington. Then they called the base at Peterson and told them to ground Air Force One," Big Dog continued.

"What was the problem they found?" Chandler asked.

"Our source didn't know. They said POTUS is being held under observation at Cheyenne."

While Big Dog confirmed what he'd heard from Geringer, the question lingered why they'd be holding POTUS.

"You guys were with the president when he got to Winter Park. There didn't seem to be anything wrong with him!"

Big Dog and Proto nodded in concurrence.

Proto nudged his boss. "You didn't tell him the rest."

Big Dog puckered his forehead and narrowed his eyes. "Huh?"

"Carter."

"Oh yeah, jeez. I haven't even started drinkin' yet. Yeah, Carter's installed himself as king over there. He's the one calling the shots. Somethin' happened with him and POTUS that turned the cabinet against him. We're not sure what that is."

"Sounds like a power struggle," Chandler said.

"That's all I have, Chandler. I'll keep my ear to the ground," Big Dog said, cupping his hand around his ear.

Chandler thanked the men for their information and left the suite.

He had just as many questions as answers and another text message to distract him.

While eager to return to Arianne, he remained frustrated with the lack of answers about the president's condition.

CHAPTER ELEVEN
MYSTERY MAN

A few months ago, in the sharp morning sun of Halloween Day, he sat on a bench at The Battery, pondering the nation's future. President Jefferson's Executive Order 14666 had survived an impeachment, a trial, and a Supreme Court decision. Security in the nation's capital decayed, chasing Congress back to their home districts. The nation could not settle the presidential election of 2020 per Supreme Court order and Jefferson's promise.

He'd seen a different side of Jefferson after the president came face-to-face with a group who wanted to leave the Union. Jefferson also landed in the middle of the Convention of States, which surely would pursue a vast evisceration of federal power. Those encounters changed Jefferson, though to what degree remained uncertain.

He weighed the possibility that Quinque was a government creation, established to provide a foil for the Jefferson administration and to stir feelings of patriotism. He also considered the president's abduction and the feeling in the convention of a staged kidnapping to raise his popularity right before resolving the 2020 election in the House of Representatives.

Chandler contemplated the uncertainty of the president's psychological evaluation. Perhaps Jefferson suffered psychological damage before his captivity, or maybe after he returned to Cheyenne Mountain. There were many competing thoughts swirling in his mind as he made his way to his room.

He went to press the button on the elevator when a familiar

voice froze his hand.

"Chandler, great to see you doing well after your ordeal!"

He rotated, like an old gate, to confirm the identity of the person, not that he needed to. This voice came to him during times of uncertainty and doubt. It was uncanny. There were times, in retrospect, that he questioned whether the voice and the person were merely figments of his imagination, his consciousness offering words of wisdom.

Habakk stood a body length away, dressed in his usual colors, black shirt with khaki pants. Etched on his face was the incurable dulcet smile.

"I don't know what to say any longer, about you." Chandler shook his head. "You are a real person, aren't you?"

Habakk grabbed his hand and squeezed. "Flesh and blood, Chandler, see?"

"You've arrived at the center of a vortex where the Elite, government, and those opposed are swirling around, trying to arrive at an outcome, though I don't know what that will be. I've got my own vortex spinning in my brain, trying to make sense of it all."

Habakk chuckled. "That's some metaphor."

During their encounter on Halloween morning, Habakk used the term "Praetorian" to refer to the protective structure around the nation's Elite. Habakk's reference to the Elite included those in the Global Settlement Bank, the International Relations Council, the corporatocracy, and those in government supporting their aims. Often, those in government moved in and out from those other organizations.

The secessionists and separatists wanted to get out from under government's thumb by using digital currencies like DigiNote and moving their commercial activities to the Darknet. Groups like the Five Tribes wanted the Internet to return to its original, decentralized origins. They abhorred being digital serfs. Secessionists like the Cascadia Movement and Cal Sí sought a physical separation.

Jefferson's apparent sympathies rankled the Elite and some in government. They worried about what he might say to Congress and the American public. The Plan for Prosperity and patriotic slogans like "We Are the Future" were Elite creations. They stood to enjoy their continuation. Any disruption of these plans was antithetical to their aims.

"What's today's message, Mr. Habakk?"

"Chandler, by now, you should know that I'm only here to help you. That time with the president had to be instructive. You spent time with someone from the Elite who is in government. I'm sure you must have learned something?"

Chandler looked around the corner, certain that another hotel guest would come by soon. "I did and so did the president."

"But you have other worries. I can see it."

"You know me well."

"Would you like to talk about it?"

He felt a sense of trepidation about having the conversation in the middle of a hallway, shifting his eyes around the space. "Well, there's another thing buggin' me, about Quinque." He related his newfound doubts.

Habakk crossed his arms. A slight frown disturbed his habitual serenity. "Very interesting."

Chandler fidgeted, looking at his phone while another text from Arianne arrived. "By now, I should know not to doubt your wisdom. I'd like to talk about it more, but I have to ask a favor."

"A favor?" The older man raised a quizzical eyebrow.

"Yes. My girlfriend is waiting for me, in my room."

Habakk placed his hand over his gapped mouth. "Oh, I understand. You need private time with her. OK, I-"

"No, no, no." Chandler laughed. "Nothing like that. I just need to check in with her."

"If this is a bad time, then perhaps some other time? Have a good evening." He pivoted away.

Chandler reached for his arm. "Mr. Habakk. It's fine, really. I just need to get her something to eat. And myself too."

"I see. Perhaps both of you would like to join me for a late dinner. I think they're still open."

Since he'd first met Habakk in the fall of 2019 in the aftermath of the stock market crash, his interactions with him had been one-on-one affairs. Only Tomás, his assistant, had ever been around during their conversations. Tomás had evacuated Chandler from the reorientation camp.

"Wait. You mean I can bring her?" said a wide-eyed Chandler.

Habakk parted his lips into his dulcet smile. "Of course, why not?"

"Well because normally, oh never mind," Chandler said, rolling his eyes."

"Good, then it's settled." He clapped his hands. "Meet me in the restaurant as soon as you can. I'll grab a table for us."

He walked away with his half-moon glide down the hall.

"Don't you want to ride the elevator?" Chandler yelled.

Habakk waved as he disappeared down the long corridor.

Chandler texted Arianne, relating their late dinner plans. Once he arrived at the room, he revealed their dinner guest.

***

More nervous meeting Habakk than she had been with Chandler's mother a couple of years earlier, Arianne tussled with her hair in front of the bathroom mirror, trying to get just the right look.

"Your hair's fine. Leave it alone." Chandler clutched her hand, pulling it away from her auburn locks.

She yanked it back. "I want to make sure I look the right way."

"And what way is that?"

She didn't answer. Instead, she continued to preen.

Chandler watched, rapping his fingers on the bathroom door frame until she declared herself proper. Ten minutes later, they left to meet the mystery man for dinner.

They saw Habakk thumbing through an oversize menu in a corner booth, tucked away in a part of the restaurant furthest from the entrance. He wanted privacy. The lack of patrons at this hour meant their conversation wouldn't blend in with everyone else's white noise.

He peered above the menu the instant before they arrived at the booth.

"Mr. Habakk, this is my girlfriend, Arianne Maxwell."

Habakk greeted her with both of his hands around her right hand, looking her straight in the eye. "Miss Maxwell. It's my pleasure. You could stop an advancing army with your beauty. Your charm is no doubt as impressive."

She giggled like a schoolgirl, tucking her chin. "Thank you, sir."

"Chandler's told me so much about you."

She looked at Chandler for confirmation. He shrugged. She frowned.

Habakk motioned to them. "Please, sit."

Chandler and Arianne occupied the side opposite Habakk. The waitress took their drink orders. Chandler and Arianne both ordered glasses of Pinot Noir. Habakk opted for club soda with lime.

"Miss Maxwell. I'm sure you have questions about who I am. No doubt Chandler's mentioned my appearances." Habakk turned to Chandler, who nodded.

"Please, Arianne will work just fine."

"Very well then, Arianne. Chandler, you've asked me before who I am and how I appear when you need me. The time has come for me to talk about who we are."

"We? As in, there's more than one of you?" Chandler cocked his head with curiosity. It was yet another surprise.

Habakk chuckled at Chandler's inquisitiveness, placing his hand over his belly.

The waitress returned to fetch their food order. Chandler and Arianne both ordered steak. Habakk opted for the grilled salmon.

"Chandler, we, as in more than me, we go back a long way."

Habakk was a member of the secret society known as the Council for American Liberty (CAL). CAL got its start around the time of the American Revolution. A group of twelve men met in a restaurant after hours in New York County, or present day Manhattan, to discuss the monarchy's taxation policies. They coalesced as a formal group to combat the increasing tyranny of the English crown. As the Revolutionary War broke out, some of their membership, including colonials, slaves, free blacks and Native Americans, joined the Continental Army. They kept their participation in the society a secret, preferring to work behind the scenes or fight under the command of General Washington. They initially organized around a tribal structure and expanded to the Thirteen Colonies after the war. They kept their rituals to a minimum, although they were like those of Native Americans.

"Your ethnic background is Native American? I always

thought you might have been Hispanic or Middle Eastern. Your Spanish, your pronunciation is impeccable," Chandler commented.

"Thank you. My mom was Native American and my father hailed from Lebanon."

"OK, but how is your Spanish so good?"

Aside from upholding the principles of liberty and freedom, society members needed to ask themselves who they should become and how they could best serve their fellow man — to find their true calling. These decisions had to come from the member's desire. Once identified, members gave themselves fully to their calling. In Habakk's case, he chose to be a scholar in the fields of history, politics, language and religion.

"I was born in the United States, but my university studies were overseas. My Spanish accent comes from time spent studying and teaching in Spain and Latin America. I also spent time in the Middle East. I could blend in well there."

CAL was an influential society until early in the 20th century, when membership declined due to the aging of many of its top leaders. Since the society never had mass solicitation of members, their influenced waned. That was the trade-off of being a secret society. They maintained their numbers through their offspring, yet that same offspring was under no obligation to join. Members who never had children adversely affected the society unless they recruited someone else. This was part of the tension of serving their fellow man and having a family.

"Chandler, it's a theme I've mentioned to you in our previous conversations. Besides our demographic problem, we got complacent, intellectually lazy. Our quiet influence on American politics and governance faded. By the 1960s, we experienced our own crisis. Some of us stopped being involved in local politics or government. We stopped writing and educating. We stopped being active in civics. Candidly, we started becoming too materialistic. We strayed from our core values."

"And what are those core values?" Chandler asked.

CAL believed in maintaining the democratic way of life in America, preserving the nation by upholding the principles of liberty and freedom, organizing charities, opposing empire building, and fostering bonds among their members.

"If you look at the country now, you will see how we've deviated from these values. As I've told you, the public values freedom 'from' as opposed to freedom 'of' and that's what has ushered in this period of authority under President Jefferson. The public asked and received. Politicians are eager to satisfy. Eventually, the public, at least some part of them, will push back. This is where we are now."

The waitress returned with their entrees. Chandler and Arianne dug in, creating a lengthy period of silence, to Habakk's amusement.

"Sorry, Mr. Habakk," Chandler mouthed between bites of steak.

Habakk took a sip of his club soda. The carbonation made his mouth pucker. "I should also tell you that Habakk is my first name."

Chandler stopped chewing, pushing a morsel of steak towards his cheek. "Your first name? So, what is your last name?"

"My last name's not important. My father was Christian and named me after a prophet."

"A prophet?" Arianne questioned, suspending her own chewing.

On the day of Habakk's birth, a sachem, an Algonquian chief told his mother about a vision quest he'd had as a young man where he witnessed the birth of a great leader — the son she bore that day. His father took it as a sign and named him after the prophet Habakkuk, by shortening his name to Habakk. The prophet Habakkuk was venerated in three of the world's major religions, so his father believed his son's birth was important for ultimately unifying people. Despite his veneration in three religions, the world knew little about this prophet. His father viewed this mystery as an asset for his son. Chandler could attest to Habakk's mysterious nature.

Habakk displayed the behavior of his namesake as a child, always questioning his parents and ultimately, God. Over time, he grew to place his trust in both. That trust led him to follow his desire to pursue scholarly work and ultimately serve his fellow man through secret membership in the CAL.

"Mr. Habakk, ah, Habakk. I knew you were a man of great wisdom, but sheesh. Compared to you, I feel like I just fell off the turnip truck," Chandler said, scratching through his thick hair.

"Chandler, I should ride in that turnip truck with you so I could come up with my own expressions," Habakk mused.

Habakk explained their membership's distribution through different areas of government and academia. They kept no central record of their membership, making it impossible for anyone to identify the entirety of their organization. Most times, the membership resembled a chain where one member knew at most two others. Elders like Habakk had greater knowledge of membership, though even he didn't have the entire picture. The society did this to prevent saboteurs from having a target list.

"You're fortunate, Chandler. You know two members."

"I do?"

"Yes, you know me and my son, Tomás."

Chandler's mouth gapped. "I always thought he looked like you! I bet he gets the better side of his looks from his mother." He jabbed Arianne on her elbow.

"Yes, his mother was beautiful. Maria passed when he was young." He winced at the memory.

Arianne reached out towards Habakk's hand. "I'm so sorry. It still pains you."

"We met in Seville, or *Sevilla* as my friends say in Spain. I was fortunate to at least spend a few years with her." Habakk looked away from his guests to compose himself.

Chandler and Arianne were afraid to speak, keeping their heads down, playing with the remaining food on their plates.

"I'm fine." Habakk took a tissue from his shirt pocket and wiped his nose. "Please, don't let my pain end this conversation. Let's see, where was I? Have you ever wondered why I've taken such an interest in you?"

"I sure thought you were burning daylight with me."

"I take that to mean that I was wasting my time with you?" Habakk asked, arching one of his thick eyebrows.

"Yeah, for sure."

"Chandler, we've been following you for several years. A couple of other elders suggested contact. They knew that you were a man of truth."

Chandler pointed at himself. "Me?"

"Truth is of the highest importance. Only with truth can one move forward. You can continue to help our society move forward. People believe you. You won't be able to do it by yourself. That's not what I'm suggesting. But you can be a beacon of light for us. You have a talent and now you are at the center of the tempest."

"I feel honored and humbled that a society like yours would

consider me. If the rest of your leadership is anything like you, well, that's about as strong as it gets." Chandler raised his fist. "But you make it sound like this is my fate, somehow."

"Fate is fluid, Chandler. Destiny is in the hands of man. You could walk away from this dinner and never see me again if that is your wish. I just want you to consider the possibilities."

CAL hoped Chandler would be a bright light in the collective darkness and division that enveloped America. He would open hearts and minds, encourage intellectual curiosity, and spread the message of freedom. This would create more beacons of light until liberty could triumph again. CAL understood that America had willingly yielded its freedom without realizing it.

Habakk molded his hands into a steeple, placing his wrists on the table's edge. "You are a young man. As you get deeper in life, you'll see just how finite it is. Modern culture imbues us with this notion that we can be anyone we want. I believe you will find fulfillment by being yourself, by finding out who you are, by finding the seeds of possibility already within you."

Chandler, overwhelmed by Habakk's words, laced his nervous fingers through his hair.

"Isn't that a lot to expect from him?" Arianne put down her fork, eager for the answer.

Habakk patted her hand. "Chandler cannot repair what has already been damaged by the government's Eye of Sauron. We realize that. The nation will be changed, we do not know how exactly. The council cannot stop it. We need more people like Chandler in the aftermath of the changes. I hope you understand that."

"I don't know. You might overestimate me here," Chandler interjected, shaking his head, blinking rapidly.

"You need not worry about that. Let go of the outcome. If

you worry too much, it will disturb your mind. Doubt will creep in. I always gave fully of myself, but I never tried to reach for an outcome. The outcome simply is. I am comforted by knowing that I worked to the best of my ability. We only ask that you dedicate yourself to these principles and give yourself fully to the task."

Arianne gestured her head in affirmation.

This message resonated with Chandler, who'd heard something similar from Axel. He never seemed to worry about outcomes either. Axel focused on putting in the work and preparation — beyond that, he let the chips fall where they may.

The waitress returned to clear the table and take dessert orders. No one wanted anything sweet. She thanked them and wished them a good evening.

"She forgot the check," Arianne remarked.

Chandler stood up to follow her.

"It's fine. I took care of it," Habakk said.

"That's very generous of you. Thank you," Arianne said.

"Yes, thank you," Chandler echoed.

Another period of uncomfortable silence followed. Chandler and Arianne stared at Habakk, and he did the same with a gentle smile.

"Chan, I should get going. I'm sure you two have more to discuss." She leaned towards him and gave him a peck on the cheek.

He reached for her. "Wait. What?"

"I think you have more to talk about, with Habakk."

Chandler didn't sense there was more to discuss. He waited for Habakk to excuse himself so they could call it a night. Another moment of silence emerged. Habakk remained silent.

"I'll see you upstairs later. You two have a nice chat." She squeezed his shoulder and slid out of the booth.

Chandler's eyes followed her until she was out of view.

"She's a lovely woman, Chandler. Very lovely. You will need her support. Trust me. Are you ready to finish our chat from earlier?"

"From earlier?"

"Yes, when we were by the elevator."

Chandler slapped his forehead with embarrassment. "Sorry, too much stuff spinning in my brain."

He had related his concern about Quinque being a government creation whose sole purpose was to incite feelings of nationalism. If true, it would be a stain on his cherished documentary.

Habakk encircled his chin in his hand, contemplating his response. Chandler worried about what he might say.

"This Quinque has created his own version of freedom. He's asking for the ultimate in liberty. I'm sure that message will resonate with many people. It would be a risky proposition for government to create someone like that because he and the movement could escape their control in a short amount of time."

Chandler's shoulders rose, the weight of concern temporarily removed. "You're saying he's legit?"

"That's for you to decide. It will mean more if you come to that conclusion rather than me telling you. I've just offered you my perspective."

Chandler appreciated that Habakk always made him think. He led the horse to the water, but the horse had to drink. "OK, I agree. I also have my instinct to guide me."

"You do. That was something I sensed about you. Instinct and mentoring have taken you a long way."

Chandler nodded. Axel's mentoring had honed the instinct

upon which he often relied.

He then raised doubt about the president's abduction and the doubt swirling around the convention of its authenticity.

"You spent time with the president and I'm sure you saw a side of him that would be unique. How did he seem to you?"

"First of all, I was shocked that he wanted to spend time with me at all, I mean after my documentary and everything else. Once he got exposed to the Five Tribes and the Honor Brigade and he heard my side of the story, I think he changed. It's like he had an epiphany or something. He said he needed to review how government was doing things. It seemed genuine to me."

Habakk became more animated than usual, gyrating his hands. "I've always felt that the larger the conspiracy, the more difficult it is to keep secret. Consider that even if government staged it, the outcome might work in the country's favor, wouldn't you say?"

"I suppose so, now that you put it that way. But do you think they staged the whole thing?"

Habakk tilted his head and wagged his finger. "Now Chandler."

"Yeah, yeah, I know, I know. I need to decide that myself," he answered, sheepishly.

Chandler pulled out his phone after it buzzed with an alert. He noticed the late hour and surmised that he had a few things to think about after this conversation.

"Habakk this was a lot to process. I want to talk to you more in the morning if you're going to be around. Heck, you just seem to be around, if you know what I mean. You'll need to explain that."

"I was hoping we can chat further, tonight."

"Tonight?"

"Yes, I have some important information for you. It's about the president, Mr. Jefferson."

The night was still young.

***

Chandler and Habakk left the restaurant and walked into an office behind the lobby of the GMCC.

Chandler arm-blocked Habakk from taking more than a step into the office. "Wait. Is this someone's office?"

"It would seem that way based on everything we see," Habakk replied, patting him gently on the shoulder. "Please let's sit down."

They sat on club chairs in front of the office owner's desk.

"At dinner, I mentioned that our society is embedded within the ranks of government. That includes the military, too. It's possible that there may even be an Honor Brigade member within our ranks." Habakk winked.

"Really?"

"Yes, but remember, none of us know the entirety of our membership. I mention them since I know the Brigade also has membership within government."

"Big Dog told me the same thing."

"Big Dog? A talking canine?" Habakk furled his thick brow.

Chandler laughed that he'd stumped the great Habakk. "You've got too many cobwebs in the attic!"

Habakk rubbed his chin and narrowed his eyes. "Canines and attics?"

"Big Dog is the call sign for the commander of the Honor Brigade here in Colorado. He helped rescue the president."

Habakk nodded. "I see. And the attic?"

"Never mind. OK, so what about the president?"

Habakk crossed his legs. "Yes. A member of ours, I've known

her for many years, she informed me that President Jefferson's reported condition is not accurate."

Chandler's eyes widened. "In what way? I've had my suspicions too. So did the Brigade."

Habakk placed his palms together in front of his torso. "The suspicions are well founded. President Jefferson has been deemed unfit for duty and is being held against his will. His cabinet is taking action under the 25th Amendment to relieve him. The Secretary of Defense has more or less assumed control of the Executive Branch."

"This has something to do with that psych evaluation then?"

"Oh, so you know about that? Yes, that is what my contact suggested."

"Does she know if the president really is unfit for office?"

"She does not. Unfortunately, very few people really know his mental state and that is a problem. Despite our society's differences with the president, we view this as a coup. Something happened after both of you were released from captivity. You could judge his mental state better than just about anyone after your experience. I'm sure you saw a side of him to which few are privy."

"I did. I think the experience with me and the Tribes made him think about the country's direction. He suggested as much."

"My concern, and that of other leaders within the council, is how the coup may evolve. The vice president is near death and the next two in succession are not qualified. And don't forget that Congress needs to finish the 2020 election when they return to Washington. This is on top of things you're witnessing here at this convention and the secession movements."

The sobering assessment prompted Chandler to rub his forehead. "Yeah, quite a mess. What will your council do?"

257

"I'm glad you asked since we need your help."

Chandler fell back into his chair. "A secret society that's been around for over 200 years needs help from a journalist working for small news outlet?" He poked his index finger at his temple. "I think those cobwebs are back."

Habakk had conferred with other members of the CAL who understood the importance of thwarting a government coup. They too doubted Jefferson's cabinet's conclusion that he was unfit for office. They were no fans of Jefferson, yet their principles wouldn't allow them to see the presidency treated in this fashion. It was a difficult position for them to assume, given Jefferson's executive order that froze the 2020 election results.

CAL devised a plan, with the help of insiders, to extract the president from detention. Extracting him would be but a single step. They would then have the problem of what to do with him. They couldn't possibly fend off the entire government apparatus.

This is where Chandler would help. After they extracted him, CAL felt the president needed to address the nation and expose those trying to usurp executive power. He might have more to say beyond that. They considered that a coup attempt might embolden him and the public would rally around him. It would be a chance they'd have to take.

Finding the appropriate outlet for this address would be important. Someone like Chandler, who'd established credibility with the American public, would be the perfect vessel to deliver the message, or at least facilitate it.

Chandler had his own ambivalence. Jefferson's conciliatory message might embolden the secessionists, which was antithetical to Chandler's hope of keeping the country together. If the president instead lashed out, it might hasten the unraveling in another way.

"You are the key to the ultimate success of this plan, Chandler."

"The thing is, you're asking me to be complicit in the president's abduction, who is in a secure government facility. If he addresses the nation and suddenly he sounds like he's extending an olive branch to the secessionists and groups like the Five Tribes, he may well be charged with treason. And what would that make me? On the other hand, he might, as you suggest, seek to make himself more powerful." Chandler rubbed his forehead with much vigor, drawing out a shade of pink.

Habakk grinned. "Quite a Gordian Knot, isn't it?" He patted Chandler on the knee. "There is little doubt the plan has risk. I'm asking you to draw out your potential, your gifts. I can understand if you want to run away from the chaos and darkness of this world." He stretched his hands towards the ceiling as if ushering in sunlight. "If you stay, your light, your truth, can shine upon it."

Chandler's face brightened for a moment until more doubt crept in. "Won't Jefferson's supporters, you know, all those people with We Are the Future posters in their homes, think he's really nuts if he talks softly about their enemies?"

"Chandler, we don't know. You don't know what Jefferson will say. A coup is seldom an orderly transition of power and obviously, there is much disorder in the country now. Whatever the president might say, he deserves a chance to be heard."

Habakk had placed the weight of the world on his shoulders — he'd never felt like Atlas. Chandler thought he'd already used up one of his lives by dodging more serious charges after trespassing in the reorientation camp. The relationship with Arianne had blossomed, and he'd mapped out a future with her. There was the fresh and exciting opportunity with Veritas.

Someone else could fight this battle. He didn't know what to do.

"Habakk. I need to introduce you to someone important to me."

"Someone else? I thought I just met her?"

Chandler would introduce him to his mentor, Axel Schultz.

***

A bleary-eyed Axel answered the door in his bathrobe. "Chandler, do you realize what time it is? Shouldn't you be with Ari?" He eyed the shorter man standing behind him. "Who is this?"

"Can we come in? I have someone important I want to introduce to you."

He opened the door cautiously and waved the men in.

"Please let's sit over here." Axel motioned to the suite's living area.

"Axel, this is Habakk. Habakk, this is my mentor, Axel."

The two men studied each other during their firm handshake.

"Ax, I've kept something from you. The time has come for me to reveal it."

Chandler detailed the various encounters with Habakk beginning in the fall of 2019 when the stock market crashed. They had an encounter on Christmas Day that same year where the mysterious man formally introduced himself. There was the walk on a warm summer night in 2020 on the National Mall and the chat in the Battery on New Year's Day in 2021. There were other encounters in 2021, though none more important than his rescue from the reorientation camp by his son, Tomás.

Habakk described his involvement with the Council for American Liberty and their identification of Chandler as a potential member.

"He's appeared during times of questioning for me. I think

you two could have quite a conversation," Chandler added.

The information dump overwhelmed the stoic Axel. He searched the room with his eyes, trying to make sense of it all. There was one detail, one event that he could associate with this revelation.

"Last year, that person who called me, who dropped Chandler off at my condo after the reorientation camp. That was your son?" Axel asked, turning toward Habakk.

He nodded. "Yes, Tomás. He's a good boy. We're counting on him to carry on our mission."

Axel layered his hands on his bald scalp. "Wow. I've read about secret societies. I've never met anyone, though. It's an honor, sir. If your group has done what you say, the American people owe you their gratitude."

He humbled Habakk with his words. "Thank you, Axel. As I mentioned, we don't seek attention. We stay true to our principles." He placed his hands in prayer in front of his heart space.

"I can appreciate that." Axel looked at Chandler. "There has to be more to this introduction, I presume? You wouldn't be here now to reveal this society or your experiences."

Habakk explained their plan to rescue the president and what they hoped would be Chandler's role. Chandler sought an important person who could give him counsel.

"That's why I'm here, Ax. I don't know what to do. You know my situation with Ari and how I almost lost her last year. I dodged a bullet with that documentary. My partner got killed. This rescue could get me killed or imprisoned. They could charge me with treason. I don't need that kind of drama."

Axel stared off into space, probing the recesses of his mind. This went on for at least a minute.

261

"Earth to Axel? Come in please," Chandler teased, waving his hands in front of the man.

He gestured with a dip of his chin. "I was just thinking."

"Clearly."

"After you left earlier, I contacted a few people, like I said I would. I didn't get much, or at least any more than you know already."

Axel winced in pain, pressing on his temple.

Chandler winced in sympathy. "You still have that headache?"

"I'm fine. Don't worry about me." He grabbed ibuprofen from his pocket, chasing it with the water bottle on the coffee table. "I feel like I'm letting you down here, not having better intel. My sources can only confirm what you know. Sorry."

"Ax, that's cool. No worries there. I'm really here to ask you what I should do."

Axel, normally generous dispensing advice to his pupil, offered little in return. "I can't tell you what to do. You have your whole life ahead of you. You have a future with the love of your life. You have an exciting new career opportunity. I'm an old man who's on the 'back nine', so to speak, it wouldn't feel right. Sorry."

Chandler cast his eyes on Habakk, who shrugged.

He glanced back at Axel. "I guess the mother eagle just left me alone in the nest."

"Perhaps it's the mother's way of telling you it's time to spread your wings and soar?" Habakk lifted his hand towards the ceiling.

Axel shook his head, the earlier pain in his temple still clear with his narrowed eyes. "No, that's not what I'm saying. I'm still here for you, but this decision is one you should make."

Chandler needed to include someone else in the decision. After weeks of loneliness in the reorientation camp, playing undercover journalist, he vowed to be considerate of Arianne, especially if it jeopardized their future.

"Guys, it's late. I have stuff to think about. I'll have to leave. I need to talk to Arianne about this. Maybe a few hours of sleep and a conversation with her will clarify this."

"I understand. This is an important decision, possibly life changing for both of you. We'll touch base in the morning," Habakk said.

"How will I find you?" Chandler asked.

Habakk chuckled. "Oh, you really have to ask after all this time?"

Chandler gave himself a faux jab to the cheek. "Yeah, really. Maybe one day you can tell me how you do that? OK, I'm outta here."

He shook Habakk's hand and squeezed his mentor's shoulder and let himself out.

Alone in the suite, the two men stared at each other without saying a word. Axel knew. He didn't know how he knew. He knew what Habakk was about to ask.

Habakk walked over and sat next to Axel, placing his arm around his shoulders. "How long have you been ill?"

Axel covered his face. "Is it obvious?"

"My wife. She passed when my only child, Tomás, was a young boy. She had your symptoms."

"My symptoms?" He cradled his jaw in his hands.

"It's more than what you outwardly demonstrate." He removed his arm from Axel's shoulders and placed his hand over his heart. "I can feel it."

Axel, often answering other's questions, realized he was in the presence of someone special — someone of great reverence. "You can feel it? How?"

Habakk lifted his shoulders towards his ears. "I can't explain it. I've had that gift since as long as I can remember. I can often feel what others feel. It has been both a blessing and a curse. I felt my wife's birth pains. I suffered through her illness as if I had the disease myself. When my son would get sick as a child, I cried if for no other reason than he cried. I had to be strong for him. I couldn't let him see me break down like that, especially after his mother passed. You are suffering Mr. Schultz, suffering greatly and yet you're able to conceal it from everyone. It is remarkable."

"I don't feel remarkable. Not any longer. I've tried to help Chandler understand. I taught him what I know, though not in matters of love."

The two shared a brief laugh.

"Yes, Mr. Schultz. Love. It has many dimensions and is never rational. I guess that's the beauty of it."

"Indeed Habakk, indeed."

"Chandler will be fine, no matter his choice. He has great potential. You see that. He has to come to this decision on his own. That is also a principle of our council. The desire has to come from within. We cannot coerce it."

"I agree. I'm sorry we won't develop our relationship further. I know I will miss seeing Chandler and Arianne develop as a couple."

"How much time do you have?" Habakk asked.

"Not long, I'm afraid." A single tear flowed out of the corner of his eye, coursing its way through the stubble of his cheek. "Please. I ask of you. Do not tell him. I want my last remaining moments with him to be without sorrow."

Habakk reached out and grabbed his hands, warming them in his.

"Your secret is safe. Prepare for your last time with him. I sense that you view death in a different manner than most."

***

He didn't wake her, opting for a few hours of sleep instead — a good decision.

He reached over to touch her, only to grab air and mattress. Arianne was fixing her hair and makeup in the bathroom.

She noticed his head bob in the mirror. "Hey!"

"Hey, why are you puttin' on makeup?"

"Why do you think, silly? I'm doin' it for you, baby." She blew him a kiss.

He propped his head on his hand, admiring the view. "You know how many times I've told you that I love how you look in the morning, fresh-faced, and with your hair all messed up?"

"Not today. I'm sure you'll be covering the convention. I want to watch it. Get dressed and we can go get breakfast."

He walked towards her, placing his arm around her waist, guiding her back to bed. "Come here for a sec."

She spun away. "No, we're not doing *that*. I just fixed my face."

His serious look clarified his intentions. He grabbed her hand and walked her to the bed where they sat side-by-side. "Ari, we need to talk about something."

Her look sobered.

He told her about Habakk's plan to extract the president and his role.

She placed her hands on her powdered cheeks, parting her lips. "Are you sure he's being detained, as in against his will?"

He nodded. "Geringer, Big Dog, and Habakk all seem to

265

think so."

"What if they're all wrong? It would be terrible for you. You could get in real trouble."

"I know."

"What did Ax say?"

"Surprisingly little. I think he's ready to cast me out on my own, in a manner of speaking. He's been a little off since he got here. I know it had been a couple of months since I'd seen him but, yeah, he's off."

"In what way?"

"Just not as mentally sharp. Probably that headache he's had. I think he has migraines. You know him, though, he never wants to admit when he's sick. I guess he feels that getting sick is a betrayal by his health and exercise routine."

She leaned into him, putting her arm around his waist. "Honey, what do you want to do?"

"That's why we're talking about it, right?"

"I know you well enough to know that you want to do it. Once I met the mysterious Habakk, I got a feeling he wanted to meet me because he was going to ask something of you. It would have been much harder for me to accept what he would ask you without ever having met him. Clever on his part. You see what I mean?"

He agreed.

She stood, beginning a pace in front of him.

"I learned something about us when you were in that camp last year. You've never placed any limits on my career and yet, that's what I was doing to you. When I met you and fell in love with you, I knew who you were and what you did. I know you can't sit still, that you have to be in the action. That's what drives you and makes you who you are. It would be selfish of me to stifle you or change you. Even more so, what you're doing is so important for so many people. I always knew that. Accepting it was more difficult. I love you so much, I want all of you, although I have to accept your place and your role in this important time."

She straddled him, giving him a small peck on the lips. "I love you, Chandler Scott."

"I love you, Arianne Maxwell."

They embraced for a moment before she unlocked. "Let me finish getting ready and we can go downstairs." She grazed her hand over his cheek as she got up.

He grinned, staring at her snug jeans as she made her way to the bathroom.

He rolled over to grab his phone from the nightstand and called Jaden Casey, his erstwhile boss at Veritas.

"Chandler! Good to hear from you. So, any signs of Stockholm Syndrome yet?"

Chandler enjoyed the humor. "Hey, Jaden. If I develop signs, is it covered under my health insurance plan?"

"Well played, Mr. Scott."

"I wanted to let you know that I may be out of pocket for a day or two."

"Planning on being abducted again?"

"I hope not, but you're warm. Listen, I have to get involved in something and if it works out the way I think, it will help Veritas in a big way. I think you'll like what I'm gonna put together for my time with POTUS and the Five Tribes. This could be bigger than that."

"Wow! That's saying something. So, I guess I shouldn't ask?"

"Probably not. If it goes well, and with what I can put together for my captivity, it should really help launch Veritas to a different level."

"Good. So, a couple of investors called wondering how we'll cover your kidnapping. Advertising dollars, you know."

"Understood. OK, Jaden, talk to you soon."

"Later, Chandler."

They walked to the restaurant where they'd had dinner with Habakk the night before. There were more patrons. A few wanted to speak with him regarding his kidnapping ordeal. Polite, yet distracted, he struggled to maintain focus during these conversations. He darted his eyes around the eatery, waiting for the mysterious one to appear.

Arianne rescued him from a fan who wanted to chat after snapping a couple of selfies.

She ushered him to their booth. Their breakfast proved to be a restless affair. Almost always the focus of his attention, Arianne barely merited a stare while they ate. His eyes bounced between hers and the surroundings.

Lack of attention made her reach for his chin, which she put in a vise between her thumb and forefinger. "Will you stop fidgeting? He'll show up soon enough. Haven't you always told me he shows up when you least expect it?"

He couldn't disagree with her on that point. If he had to lay odds on Habakk's appearances, well, he couldn't.

The waitress handed him the check which he'd pay at the table. Frustrated by Habakk's absence, he settled the check.

Beginning their walk out of the restaurant, a familiar voice beckoned from behind. "Chandler, wait!"

Chandler twisted the corner of his mouth. "Right on cue, just when I least expected it."

"Do you two need privacy?" Arianne asked.

"No, please stay, Arianne," Habakk responded.

The three returned to their breakfast booth. There, the

mysterious one offered a detailed plan to rescue the president, even sketching it out on a napkin.

"You really think this is gonna work?" Chandler asked.

Habakk gave a hearty belly laugh. "Oh, Chandler. After getting you out of that camp, or I should say Tomás. Please have faith."

"Yeah Chandler, have faith." Arianne slid an encouraging wink in his direction.

Chandler peeked behind Habakk and whispered, "Ah, we are talking about kidnapping the President of the United States."

"This is no doubt another Gordian knot for you. I think my plan will allow us to cut it. You're ready for this moment. Now, please speak with Axel and Big Dog to get the rest of this plan ready. I will speak with the rest of the team to start things. We have much work to do."

Chandler's lips twitched into a smile, though its underpinnings concealed doubt.

Part III

Rescue

CHAPTER TWELVE
OPERATION BEAR TRAP

The president had his personal physician, Dr. Jason Pillares, flown in from his home in Menlo Park, California. He had every expectation that Dr. Pillares would find him fit for duty and challenge the earlier psychiatric evaluation.

President Jefferson was unaware that the secretive Council for American Liberty (CAL) contacted Dr. Pillares. CAL informed the doctor about the President's detention in Cheyenne Mountain for reasons that appeared nefarious at the moment. CAL never identified themselves and only sketched an outline of the plan for releasing the president from captivity. At first hesitant to cooperate with the unidentified CAL representative, Dr. Pillares relented when the contact described Jefferson's detention as a coup attempt. Dr. Pillares wouldn't be alone on this visit. CAL instructed Pillares to fly to Denver and meet his contact at the rental car facility a couple of miles from the main terminal.

Posing as an official from the Department of Defense, Habakk's son, Tomás, introduced himself to Dr. Pillares at the airport.

Tomás had experience with these types of rescue operations. Most recently, he extracted Chandler from the reorientation camp where he'd been undercover as a food service worker pursuant to the documentary. Tomás arrived to whisk him away, moments before camp security blew Chandler's cover.

The doctor and Tomás drove south on Highway 25 to Colorado Springs. Tomás briefed the doctor on the plan's detail.

Once made aware of the plan's intricacies, the doctor balked, fearing a federal crime charge.

"The president called me for a personal examination. He didn't sound happy and said he'd explain when I saw him. He kept his cards close to the vest. I still don't know who you are or who called me about this whole thing or how you even knew that I was headed to see the president."

The placid Tomás, looking ahead at the road while driving, offered his endorsement of the plan. "Doctor, I can assure you we have the president's best interests in mind. The person who contacted you offered assurances about our intentions. I believe they mentioned something to you concerning that, something that only you and the president would know."

Dr. Pillares removed his sunglasses and turned to Tomás. "Yes, and how did they know that?"

The doctor didn't reveal the detail regarding the assurances. The information had merit.

Tomás didn't break his concentration on the road, keeping his hands on the sides of the steering wheel. "Doctor, I assure you once again that our plan is in the best interests of your friend, the president, and the country. I want to make sure you understand what you're to do after we arrive."

"Yes. I'm still concerned."

"You need not be. If the plan is unsuccessful, I will not implicate you. The blame shall fall on me."

They took State Highway 115 and climbed up the snow-covered Norad Road to the Cheyenne Mountain Complex. They came upon the first guard station, located a mile and a half from the main tunnel entrance. Tomás flashed his badge and the guard waved their vehicle through.

Heavily armed guards stood watch at the next security

checkpoint just outside the granite mountain's tunnel entrance. One of them extended his hand to halt the vehicle's progress, which was already slowing with the flashing yellow lights mounted just below the 15 miles per hour speed limit sign.

Tomás rolled down his window and provided a Defense Department badge for inspection. The doctor provided identification issued by his home state of California. Another guard swept the vehicle with an electronic device and a mirror that he passed underneath. The guards ordered the men out of their rental car. Winter's fury slapped Tomás and the doctor in the face. A guard passed an electronic wand around their bodies. Another guard took Dr. Pillares' medical bag and placed it on a conveyor belt where it received its own scan.

The guard who had taken their identification walked into the small security enclosure, Building 106, to verify their identities. After a couple of minutes, the guard returned and handed their identification back to Dr. Pillares and Tomás, who by then had returned to the warm confines of their rental vehicle. Another guard inside Building 106 waved them through the gate.

Tomás made a right turn and headed towards the tunnel entrance, completing an important phase of their plan.

"What sort of credentials do you have? What's your security clearance? Were they even expecting you?" The avalanche of questions from the doctor met dulcet smiles from Tomás.

The badge Tomás flashed identified him as having a Top Secret security clearance and Department of Defense area-specific clearance known as Yankee White, Category One. The area-specific clearance allowed him access to the president. If that clearance failed, he had another badge with "codeword" security clearance. Jefferson's predecessor established this level by executive order, creating a clearance few in government possessed.

Tomás negotiated the vehicle around the staggered concrete barriers. They drove past the blast doors and walked towards the security checkpoint, once again flashing their identification. Dr. Pillares' medical bag also received scrutiny.

A security officer walked them to the VIP suite where two stoic, armed guards stood outside the president's quarters.

"I'm Dr. Pillares, the president's doctor."

The guards parted. One of them opened the door.

The president sat in the living area, watching the news on TV. His spirits livened when he saw the doctor.

"Jason, thank God!" The president rushed the doctor and gave him a firm handshake and a man hug. "Who's this?" He pointed at Tomás.

Dr. Pillares hesitated for a moment. "Oh. Him? He's with the Department of Defense. They assigned him to me for the visit."

Tomás stood several feet away, revealing his best poker face.

The president chucked the remote control towards the couch. "That damn Carter and his bullshit psychiatrist. Once this whole thing is over, I'm gonna fire him."

"Mr. President, Ben, I need to take you to the examination room if we're going to do this right. Where's the First Lady?"

The president pointed towards the bath area. "She's in there taking a shower. Let me go tell her that you're here."

Dr. Pillares grabbed the president's arm. "Actually, let's head down to the exam room right now."

The president titled his head, frowned, and twisted his lips. "What's going on?"

Tomás moved towards the president to assist the doctor, grabbing the other arm. "Please, sir."

The president wrestled his arms away from both men,

frustrated with his treatment. "Please! I don't need any help walking. As you can see, I'm just fine. Come on, Jason, you know me better than that!"

The president walked towards the door, knocked, and waited for the security detail standing outside to open it.

The three men plus one of the armed guards made their way to the examination room.

As the armed guard entered the room, Dr. Pillares rebuffed him. "This is an exam. Please wait outside." He pointed to Tomás. "You, you can come in."

The miffed guard took his position outside the exam room that had the sterile stench of disinfectant.

President Jefferson sat on the examination table, glaring at his doctor. "This is all a setup, isn't it? I call my personal doctor and he rubber stamps what the other one found. Or I guess in your case, Jason, you'll say that I'm suffering from some chronic fatigue that made me more susceptible to whatever that bullshit psych doctor said."

"Ben, please calm down. I'm here to help," Dr. Pillares said. He needed calming himself for what he was about to do to his friend.

"Bullshit!" His face revealed an unveiled loathing towards the entire exercise.

Tomás pointed a NIR LED towards the security camera watching the examination table.

Near Infrared (NIR) LEDs overloaded the light sensors on cameras, confusing operators into believing there was a technical malfunction on their end.

The doctor motioned to the president, flicking his index finger upwards. "Ben your shirt, please."

While the president removed his shirt, Dr. Pillares turned his back to him, removing a small syringe from his bag.

He nodded at Tomás, who made haste towards the president.

"Ben, I'm sorry."

The president threw a worried glance at the doctor.

Tomás held down the president while the doctor thrust the needle into the president's shoulder.

"Ow! Jason, what the fuck are you doing?" He lunged at Tomás, who held leverage over the president's shoulders. "And who are you?"

"Cover his mouth," Tomás ordered.

Dr. Pillares did as ordered. The president's eyes bulged. He twisted his head, trying to unlock the doctor's dominion over his mouth.

"Ben, try to relax. It will be over soon," Dr. Pillares said as he locked his free hand on the back of the president's head.

The president pushed the doctor's hand away from his mouth. Tomás grabbed his palms, twisting them to inflict discomfort.

His muffled yell and scared expression unnerved Dr. Pillares who cringed at the pain he was inflicting on his patient and friend. "How much longer will it be?"

"He should be out in another minute," Tomás replied, still maintaining a lock on the president's palms.

The president flailed his legs, striking the doctor on his shin. Dr. Pillares gritted his teeth, agonizing about the contusion stinging his leg.

The injection sapped him of strength. His resistance waned. A minute later, he was unconscious.

Tomás turned the president's body and laid his head down on the examination table. The doctor arranged his flaccid arms at his sides.

"How long will he be out?" Dr. Pillares asked.

Tomás had walked towards the door, checking on the security guard. "Maybe thirty or forty minutes. Maybe longer."

"And the symptoms?"

"They'll manifest soon."

Tomás had supplied Dr. Pillares with a fast-acting virus that produced fever, body aches, and other flu symptoms. The injection had another agent rendering the president unconscious and erasing his short-term memory.

Forty-five minutes later, the president awoke complaining of flu symptoms. Dr. Pillares took his temperature. It was 103.8. The president had no memory of the earlier struggle.

The doctor opened the door to the examination room and alerted the guard of the situation. The guard summoned the facility doctor who'd previously examined the president.

The facility doctor confirmed the president's symptoms. He called Cheyenne Mountain's director to brief him on the situation. The director then called the White House and spoke to Secretary Carter.

The medical staff recommended moving the president to a regular medical facility. They feared his symptoms could worsen and didn't feel that Cheyenne Mountain could adequately treat him.

Carter had one demand. He requested a minimal Secret Service detail and no announcement of his transfer. The First Lady would know only after the president's evacuation. Carter did not want to attract any attention to the transfer.

The medical staff alerted the Secret Service agent in charge and the president's Chief of Staff.

Habakk had expected all of Carter's moves. A high-ranking member of the Department of Defense, a member of CAL, had reached out to the Deputy Director of the Secret Service. The Deputy Director, fiercely loyal to President Jefferson, listened to the CAL member's charge that the president was under medical detention for reasons that appeared dubious. He enlisted the Deputy Director's support in the plan to rescue the president. The Deputy Director contacted the Special Agent in Charge to have particular agents assigned to the detail.

Dr. Pillares dressed the president in sweats and a hoodie with dark glasses to disguise his identity for travel. He and Tomás took the president via wheelchair to an awaiting motorcade of two black SUVs. Tomás showed his codeword identification to stunned agents who'd been trained to recognize the clearance, but had seen no one display it.

Tomás rebuffed Chief of Staff Hutchinson's attempt to enter the vehicle carrying the president.

The motorcade had a lead SUV with a group of Secret Service special agents only, none of whom were privy to extraction plan details. The trailing vehicle carried Tomás and Dr. Pillares flanking President Jefferson in the rear seat, a special agent loyal to CAL driving, and another special agent in the passenger seat.

The first stage of Operation Bear Trap had been successful.

**

Local law enforcement was unaware of the presidential motorcade, again to conceal attention. Secretary of Defense Carter wanted to preserve the cover story.

When the convoy merged onto State Highway 115, the next phase of Bear Trap took hold. Tomás pulled another syringe out of Dr. Pillares' medical bag and plunged it into the shoulder of the special agent in the front passenger seat. In a matter of seconds, he was unconscious.

Tomás reclined the passenger seat and pulled the special

agent's limp body to the floor of the second row. He and Dr. Pillares undressed him and did the same with President Jefferson, whose fever kept him drowsy. Dr. Pillares administered an antidote to the president intended to counteract the effect of the virus. They switched the men's clothing and maneuvered Jefferson to the front seat. They propped the special agent between them in the rear seat.

The lead car took notice. "Unit 2, what's going on back there?"

The driver of the president's SUV responded. "Unit 1, special agent Morris is a little queasy. Did you guys go out drinkin' last night?"

"Unit 2, never mind."

Ten minutes later, they arrived at Arapahoe Medical Center, just north of the airport and Peterson Air Force Base.

The motorcade entered the lower level of a covered parking garage connected to the hospital. The first vehicle's agents parked and surveyed the lot. Cheyenne Mountain notified the medical center of an impending government VIP arrival without mentioning the president. A doctor waited with a wheelchair. An agent inspected the chair and confirmed the doctor's identity.

The driver of the second vehicle jumped out to open the door for Dr. Pillares and the president, now a disguised special agent. The agents from the lead vehicle surrounded the second, forming a protective shield.

"How's Morris?" The Special Agent in Charge shot a glare at the presumed agent in the front passenger seat, slumped with a towel over his head.

"He says he feels like he's going to throw up. He said to give him a minute," the driver replied.

"We don't have a minute. What a pussy! Forget him then,"

the Special Agent in Charge said, flicking his hand.

The medical center doctor helped the person he thought was the government VIP, disguised with a hoodie, sweatpants, and sunglasses, into the wheelchair.

Dr. Pillares gave him an update. "His last temperature was 103.8. Hasn't moved. He's in and out of consciousness."

"Understood, we'll take him to a special exam room. It won't be in the ER per the instructions I received," the medical center doctor said.

Dr. Pillares, the medical center doctor and the disguised agent followed the Special Agent in Charge towards the exam room. The other agents formed a protective ring around them.

The driver of the second SUV piloted the vehicle out of the parking lot with Tomás in the back seat and the president riding shotgun. They traveled to an adjacent covered lot where they boarded a food service delivery van driven by a member of the Honor Brigade answering to the call sign, "Glock."

When the Secret Service convoy of men arrived in the exam room, the doctor removed the patient's hood and sunglasses and began the examination. The Special Agent in Charge realized they did not have the president. Dr. Pillares feigned shock. The Special Agent in Charge retraced his path towards the parking lot, brushing a few doctors and nurses along the way. He only saw the SUV in which he had traveled.

He called Unit 2, informing them of their predicament. Unit 2 did not respond.

His next call would be to the Deputy Director of the Secret Service, declaring the president missing.

Stage two of Bear Trap was in the books.

The food service delivery van took the rogue party towards West Colorado Springs, near Garden of the Gods and the

Manitou Gun Club. The club was a large, standalone, modern building nestled against a rocky hill immediately to its west.

The van pulled to the rear of the club by the service entrance.

The president was coming out of his fogginess by the time they arrived.

He pointed feebly at Tomás. "What are you doing here? Where are we? He turned to the Secret Service agent. "Wait, where is our-"

"Mr. President, we're moving you to a secure location," the special agent replied.

"Secure? Where's the hospital? Aren't we-"

"Sir, things will clear up for you in a little while."

They whisked him into a room at the gun club, owned by a member of the Honor Brigade. The club was empty, expecting the president's arrival. Only three people from the Brigade, Big Dog, Glock, and the gun club owner were aware of the president's status.

They changed the president into jeans, a flannel shirt, and a stocking hat. They threw a heavy winter coat over him and outfitted him with a pair of dark, tactical sunglasses.

"Mr. President, can I get you anything?" Glock asked.

The president lifted his glasses to rub his eyes and placed his cool hands on his cheeks. "A bottle of water would be nice. It's warm in here." He rubbed his throat. "Can someone to tell me what the hell is going on? Where's my wife?"

Tomás stepped up to answer. "Your wife is safe in Cheyenne Mountain. As the special agent said, we're heading to a secure location. You should feel better in a couple of hours. Everything will be clearer once we get to the safe house."

Glock handed the president a bottled water. "Where's Jason, Dr. Pillares?" He sipped it and coughed several times with force.

Glock placed his hand on the president's back, steadying him.

"He's at the Arapahoe Medical Center," Tomás answered.

"I thought that's where I was going."

"Sir, Mr. President, please try to relax. We need to move to the safe house. Everything will be clear once we arrive."

Glock offered the president a protein bar. "You might get hungry, sir."

"Yes, thank you."

Tomás and the agent helped a stumbling president walk towards their next vehicle, an extended cab pickup with darkened windows.

Glock locked the door of the club.

Tomás grabbed plastic ties from the delivery van and shook the hand of the special agent loyal to CAL. The agent entered through the van's rear door. Tomás bound his hands and feet — they had to create the appearance the agent was a kidnap victim. After throwing a blanket over the agent, he shut the delivery van's rear door before realizing he'd failed to grab the agent's weapon.

"My apologies," he said, shrugging.

The agent figured out why he'd returned.

Tomás grabbed the weapon, a Sig Sauer P229, and holstered it in his waistband.

After closing the delivery van door for the second time, he handed the pistol to Glock. "I believe this is your area of expertise."

Glock had not accounted for a spare weapon and was reluctant to leave his prints. He put on his gloves before grabbing it. After thinking for a moment, he put the gun in the delivery van's storage box in the front seat.

"You disabled your security cameras, correct?" Tomás asked Glock.

"Yes. There shouldn't be any record of your arrival. What about him?" Glock said, pointing towards the van.

"We'll call in his location once we're clear of the area. Probably in another hour," Tomás replied.

Glock started the pickup and turned back towards the president. "Sir, try to get some rest. We've got a little ride ahead of us."

Jefferson gazed at the delivery van, aware the special agent was inside. "You sure he's going to be OK? It's awfully cold."

"Yes, sir, he'll be fine. Remember, these guys will take a bullet for you. What's an hour in a cold van?" Tomás teased.

The three men began their long trip to the safe house, where everything would become clear for President Benjamin Jefferson.

Stage three of Bear Trap was complete.

***

Back in Washington, the Deputy Director of the Secret Service, filling in for the Director, had the unenviable task of calling the Secretary of Defense and informing him of the president's disappearance.

The secretary took the call from the president's speakerphone on his desk in the Oval Office.

He pounded the desk, demanding answers. "How the hell could you guys lose POTUS? Wasn't it a short drive?"

"Mr. Secretary, understand that we did not have our usual security detail, per your instructions."

"Don't fucking blame this on me. You told me that you could handle it with limited detail. Just tell me what you're doing right now?"

"We're locating the other agent, sir. They left his phone in the Secret Service vehicle, in the hospital garage."

"So, you lost the president and you can't find your agent.

Unbelievable!" Carter dispatched a short stack of papers to the floor.

"We need to be discreet about this now, Mr. Secretary. I can't just broadcast that the president's been kidnapped somewhere in Colorado. That would just create a bunch of chaos. We think the perpetrators changed vehicles. There was a delivery van seen exiting the parking lot of Arapahoe Medical Center shortly after the president arrived. It showed up on the security cam. We're tracking its movement on traffic cams. It appeared to be heading west."

He clapped derisively. "Well, that's a start."

"Yes, sir. We don't know who's in the van besides the president, the agent, and the man from the Defense Department, the one with Yankee White and codeword clearances."

Carter moved his mouth towards the speaker phone. "What other man from the Defense Department? Codeword? Huh?"

"Thomas, Thomas Molina. Yes, he's got codeword level."

"Who the hell is that? And what was he doing with Jefferson? And how'd he get codeword?"

"He said he was assigned to accompany the president's doctor, Dr. Pillares."

"Who assigned him?"

"Evidently, someone from your department, sir."

Carter recoiled. "Whoever did that is fired. Mr. Molina, if that's even his real name, is the one you need to be looking for. Find him and you find POTUS."

"Well, sir, that's another problem. The Thomas Molina we found doesn't work for Defense. He's in the Department of Energy and he's got a Q clearance. We didn't think anyone at DoE had codeword clearance."

The Q clearance was specific to the Department of Energy

(DoE) and was roughly equivalent to the Defense Department's Top Secret clearance. Often, the DoE tagged Q clearance with a Level 3 or Level 4 sensitivity, the highest designations available.

"Does the real Thomas Molina have any idea that his identity's been co-opted?"

"No, sir. We looked him up. He's part of a nuclear disarmament negotiation team and he's not even in the States right now."

"This sounds like a hack into the DoE personnel database."

"Perhaps, sir. The Colorado Highway Patrol is helping us. We planted a story with them that we're looking for the Chief of Staff, Mr. Hutchinson. They have the other details."

"That's good. Where is Hutchinson now?"

The chief had followed ten minutes later in a vehicle separate from the presidential motorcade. After arriving at Arapahoe Medical Center, Secret Service took him into protective custody, thinking he might be a target.

"Our agents ferried him back to Cheyenne. He's none too happy, sir."

"I don't care if he's happy. Keep him there so we don't blow the cover story. Please keep me abreast of everything. I want hourly updates."

The secretary stabbed at the phone. His next series of calls would be to the security team and the cabinet.

CHAPTER THIRTEEN
JEFFERSON STRIKES BACK

Glock pulled his vehicle into a familiar-looking warehouse in the evening with POTUS and Tomás in tow. This was the same warehouse where POTUS, Hutchinson, and Chandler met the elusive Quinque. They were back in Five Tribes territory. Chandler's former captors were essential for the rest of Operation Bear Trap. His challenge would be the resulting mediation between the President of the United States, Fawkians, Quinque, and Honor Brigade. These personalities would never willingly find themselves under the same roof, much less working together towards a common goal — undeniably strange bedfellows.

Chandler met the incoming vehicle and opened the front door of the pickup.

"Tomás?" He puckered his brow, unsure of the man's identity. Tomás clarified his memory, removing part of his disguise.

Chandler grinned and extended his hand. "Good to see the *real* you. Rescuing people again, I see."

"Indeed, Mr. Scott." Tomás nodded a smile at Chandler, pleased with himself.

Tomás had ferried Chandler from the desert of Nevada, and the reorientation camp, to Chicago in a marathon journey that ended at Axel's condominium.

Chandler moved to open the back door. The president slid out of the cab's rear, still looking worn from the virus.

"Mr. President, welcome. As you can see, you're back where you were not long ago," Chandler said as he shook his hand.

"You, and I don't know who else has a lot of explaining to

287

do." He rubbed his head to calm its ache.

Glock had walked to where Chandler and POTUS stood.

"And you must be Glock," Chandler said, shaking his hand. "Your commander, Big Dog, is waiting in the office."

"Glock? Big Dog? What is all this?" POTUS asked.

"Mr. President, let's walk back here where you can rest and get something to eat." Chandler pointed towards the office. "Are you hungry?"

POTUS took off his ski hat and brushed his hair back. "More thirsty than hungry, to be honest. But, yes, I can eat something."

The Fawkians applauded when the president walked with Chandler to the office. The new arrivals found a spread of sandwiches prepared by the Fawkians. Glock glared at his hosts with unmasked contempt.

Big Dog met them near the office entrance and reintroduced himself to the president. The group sat at a large folding table where the Fawkians served them.

On one side of the table sat Chandler, POTUS, and Tomás. Facing them were Big Dog and Glock.

Chandler detailed Operation Bear Trap, without revealing its name, as it had transpired.

"Chandler, that's a wild tale. I need more details. I need to call my wife, though, she's got to be worried sick." He rose from his seat.

Chandler gently pushed on his shoulder, resettling him. "We've gotten her a message, sir."

"How?"

"For now, you're just gonna have to trust me. We can't reveal your location just yet, sir."

"I've had several people tell me I need to trust them including this Glock character and Tomás over here." POTUS waved his index finger at both of them. "I think it's about time someone tells me who all you guys really are."

"Mr. President," Big Dog began. "We're part of the same Colorado Honor Brigade. I say 'we'," he pointed at himself and Glock, "that fetched you from the forest."

"I remember you, Mr. West, ah, Big Dog, but Glock never identified himself."

"I'm sorry, Mr. President, given what I was doing, I wanted to keep it on the down low," Glock replied.

"And you," POTUS glared at Tomás. "Defense Department, my ass. Who are you?"

Tomás interrupted his sandwich chewing, offering a faint smile.

"Ah, sir, that one's a bit more complicated," Chandler added, fumbling his napkin.

"How complicated can it be? Just tell me!" POTUS bellowed, spilling the rest of his drink.

In short order, one Fawkian rushed to his side with a towel, cleaning up the spill. Another Fawkian brought him a refill. Other Fawkians in the room complimented the other two with subdued cheers.

POTUS acknowledged both of them. "Thank you, thank you." He turned his attention back to Chandler. "OK, spill it, Mr. Scott." He paused at the irony. "All right, 'spill it' might not be the right words."

Fawkians chuckled at his self-deprecation.

Chandler spilled some information, though not all of it. The Council for American Liberty was a secret society. Habakk trusted Chandler would keep it that way. No one in this warehouse knew about the council or Tomás' identity.

"Sir, the best way to look at Tomás is to consider him a

sympathizer who is looking out for the best interests of the country."

POTUS glowered at his audience. "That's another thing. Everyone is supposedly looking out for the best interests of the country somehow. I guess I should just ask all of you to come to Washington and be in my administration!"

Fawkians bent over laughing. Big Dog and Glock remained silent, not embracing the levity.

Chandler patted POTUS' shoulder. "Mr. President, let's focus if we can on why you're here. We know a doctor gave you a psychiatric evaluation and that it pronounced you unfit for duty. We know the Secretary of Defense, Mr. Carter, is playing president right now. We know the White House Press Secretary announced that you were under medical care for injuries suffered during your abduction. And we know that you were being detained against your will."

"Yes, but how the hell did you know all that?" He spread his arms in a pleading gesture.

"That's not important right-"

"Damn it, Chandler!" He smacked his hand against the table. "Stop treating me like this! I should have all of you arrested for kidnapping!"

Fawkians booed and hissed in unison. Tomás remained unfazed. The Honor Brigade team looked fearful, as if summoned to the principal's office, except this principal carried more authority.

POTUS scowled at the Fawkians.

"Sir, I would think you'd be mad at Carter more so than us. He's the one trying to take over. He's got your cabinet lined up against you, declaring you unfit for duty. Who knows what he'll do next?" Chandler clarified.

"Oh, and another thing. We're back here in the place, with the people, that held us captive not long ago. Does that seem normal to you, Chandler?"

The Fawkians emitted a collective murmur.

"OK, yeah, that part is strange for sure but there's a method behind the madness, sir."

"I'm listening," POTUS answered, turning sideways in his chair, facing Chandler. His dark eyes drilled into Chandler's as if trying to probe inside his head, searching for a persuasive explanation.

"You need to speak to the American people, sir. Tell them what happened to you. Show them that you're OK. That will expose Secretary Carter and those supporting him. Maybe those that support him right now would feel differently if they heard your side of the story. Ask yourself why Carter did all this?"

POTUS mulled that over. "It was after that video call I had at Cheyenne. I told him about what had happened to me with the Tribes. I talked about the Article Five convention. I thought we needed to reexamine our policies. He suggested I wasn't myself. Asked me if I'd been medically checked. Maybe he thought I'd been brainwashed. Then that psychiatric quack gave me that test and said I'd suffered mental trauma. I guess they think I'm such a marshmallow that a bunch of guys wearing masks and the back of a bald head would somehow traumatize me."

Fawkians whispered among themselves, some of them pointing towards POTUS.

"Sir, why don't you get some rest? I'm sure you're still tired from the virus. Why-"

"Yeah, that's another weird thing. I was feeling great then all of a sudden I get the flu. Go figure."

Chandler winked at Tomás, who acknowledged him with a nod of the head.

"Sir, these men will take you to your room. They've set it up for you so you can rest," Chandler said, pointing to a couple of Fawkians who waved POTUS towards them.

"Fine, we'll talk in the morning and you can tell me, the President of the United States, what I'm supposed to do next," POTUS offered, sarcastically.

He walked with two Fawkians towards a room in the office's rear section that would serve as his quarters for the evening.

Chandler turned his attention to the anxious Brigade members. "Glock, I didn't know if you were going to leave here in the morning or what? I suppose you can stay for the rest. It's up to you."

"Look, Chandler. I agreed to help with all this. I'm sure you realize what kinda trouble we could get into. Kidnapping the president and all. People will think the Brigade was part of some elaborate plot to rescue him and then kidnap him again. We'd never work with a bunch of hackers or guys dressed in masks, I can assure you," Big Dog explained, consternating the remaining Fawkians.

Some of them yelled at Big Dog. Chandler quieted them, placing his finger over his pursed lips.

Glock related his worry. "When the police find that delivery van at the gun club, they're gonna start asking a bunch of questions and oh yeah, and like why the security cameras were off." He curled his lip in disapproval.

"The special agent that Tomás tied up, he won't finger you, only Tomás. The story is that he abducted you at gunpoint," Chandler answered, casting a glance at Tomás.

Tomás shrugged.

"Fine, but no one's told me who Tomás really is and how we got help from a Secret Service agent. I mean, come on, Chandler, you've asked a hell of a lot from us and kept us in the dark the whole time," Big Dog said. A frown covered his face while he thrashed his arms.

"I know and I'm sorry. It's just the way it has to be guys. Why don't we all get some rest? It's going to be a big day for us tomorrow. Come on, let's go to our air mattresses."

Operation Bear Trap had crossed an important milestone. They'd abducted POTUS and bring him to a secure location. The next day, he'd reveal his intentions, and Chandler hoped he could put to rest the lingering doubts he harbored about the president's abduction by the Five Tribes and Quinque. He couldn't bear the thought of being a dupe in a large government operation.

***

The next morning, the Fawkes crew prepared a decent breakfast spread that included eggs and bacon instead of donuts.

They served POTUS, Chandler, and Tomás at one table and the Honor Brigade at another.

POTUS remarked on the improved breakfast fare, savoring the bacon's saltiness. "Was this your doing, Mr. Scott?"

"Nope. I guess they like you more now, sir."

"And you, you don't say too much do you?" POTUS asked Tomás.

"Mr. President, I can assure you I will speak when necessary," Tomás replied, smiling, before sipping his coffee.

"Since you're my acting chief of staff, I should ask what we're going to do now." He poked Chandler's ribs.

Chandler had set up a video call with Quinque and his friends. The call had a dual purpose. Chandler wanted to establish a dialog between POTUS and the Five Tribes leader. He also needed to broker a deal with the Tribes and the hackers. Brokering that deal would be the most difficult phase of Operation Bear Trap.

Chandler wanted a window of time to settle the disruptions in Washington, like establishing a truce or a cease-fire of sorts.

"They assured me that we'd have all the right players, Mr. President."

The Brigade members were leery of any further participation in this elaborate scheme. Big Dog walked over to the other table to express his concern.

"Excuse me, Mr. President. Chandler, you know how we feel about these guys wearing the masks and these hackers. We don't agree with anything they do, they're unlawful and frankly, need to be arrested. Glock over there," Big Dog motioned towards the Brigade member at the other table, "he's gettin' real nervous, asking me questions that I can't answer."

"I'm sorry. I can't give you any more details. The reason this plan could go forward is that I agreed to keep certain things confidential. You have your *own* secrets in the Brigade. Please respect the process."

The confidentiality of CAL was foremost. Given the Brigade's use of their Phantom Program, Chandler hoped they would understand.

"Ah, Chandler, if I may," POTUS interrupted, placing his hand on Chandler's arm. "My administration doesn't agree with these guys wearing masks either. That said, you see everything that continues to happen with the hacking and the disruptions. Technology is gonna let them, or anyone else, keep pushing government away. I don't like it, but the alternative will be a bigger police state and just more battles between us. It's a vicious cycle that everyone, including me, is tired of."

"I understand, sir, but why not tackle it like the folks in the Article Five are doing?" Big Dog countered.

"Come on. Can you see a bunch of guys wearing masks or that bald head at the convention? Is there a body attached to that head?" POTUS peered over Big Dog's shoulder at the Fawkians at an adjacent table. "I fully expect that convention to produce one or more amendments that all the states will vote on soon. If approved, that's the law of the land. I may not like it, but I have to respect it."

"With all due respect, sir, you froze the election with an executive order," Big Dog reminded him.

"I did what I thought was right for the country. We'll resume that election soon, as long as my people can secure Washington again."

Chandler held up his hand. "And that's something we're going to be talking about here shortly."

"Securing Washington?" A wide-eyed POTUS asked.

"Yes, sir. Why don't we all move to the video area so we can have our call?" Chandler suggested.

The Fawkians made a reception line, funneling their guests out of where they just had breakfast. They held their hands in the air, expecting high-fives that never came.

The group walked to the carpeted room that resembled the communications control center of Cheyenne Mountain.

The Fawkians provided their guests high-back chairs. In order from left to right sat Glock, Big Dog, Chandler, and POTUS. Tomás stood on the other side of POTUS.

Fawkians typed on desktops in front of the men. After a couple of minutes, they retreated behind them. Other than whispers by a few Fawkians, the room remained silent.

As before, the perimeter screens came on first, revealing a diverse cast of characters, or Quinque's hacker friends. Most waved at the webcams. A few looked away, typing on keyboards.

One screen displayed an image unlike the rest. It was an image of a Guy Fawkes mask. Its appearance led to a buzz among the Fawkians, unsure of what to make of it.

As before, a pixel-by-pixel image materialized in the large middle screen. The dark, bald head hovered over the back of an executive style office chair.

Quinque's appearance was a signal for rousing applause and cheers from the gathered Fawkians. The hacker community joined in the celebration.

"Good morning, my fellow Tribe members. Good morning, Mr. President and Mr. Scott. And I'm sorry, I don't know the other two gentlemen sitting next to you, Chandler," Quinque asked in his synthesized voice.

Chandler waited for the Brigade members to identify themselves. They had little interest in engagement with the bald head. They preferred maintaining operational silence.

"Big Dog next to me and Glock next to him. They're with the Honor Brigade," Chandler answered.

"Interesting names. We're familiar with the Honor Brigade. Welcome, gentlemen. I understand Mr. President that you have news to share with us?" Quinque's head rotated mechanically to one side.

Big Dog's curiosity made him break silence. "Is this guy for real? He moves like a machine or like he's had neck surgery or something."

Chandler muttered back, "Shh! Let the president talk."

POTUS stood. "I do. First, I want to reiterate that I condemn everything your group does to disrupt the public."

The Fawkians voiced their displeasure. Other hackers on the screens surrounding Quinque offered their middle finger in response.

"Please everyone, let him speak," Chandler urged, standing momentarily and taking his seat.

"At the same time, I realize that there are points you've made that have merit. Events are occurring now in this country that make me think about how I'm governing. The country has responded, lawfully, with this Article Five convention. I'm one reason for that convention. I don't know if the Five Tribes and government can ever work together, but I think we can arrive at an understanding of how to move forward."

Quinque's head rotated in the other direction and nodded stiffly. "I'm glad to hear that, Mr. President. What did you have in mind?"

POTUS looked to Chandler, who was responsible for the next phase of the interaction.

"Quinque, if I may. Who is the person displaying the Guy Fawkes mask?" Chandler asked.

Quinque's head tilted down as if looking at something below. "Yes, I believe you may know this person, Chandler. They're from Omni."

Mere mention of Omni angered POTUS. The Brigade was no fan of the enigmatic hacker organization either. Chandler wondered if the Fawkes picture was Phish, Axel's contact within the group. He dared not mention the name, fearful of angering them.

"I asked Omni to join us today. Mr. President, we don't see eye-to-eye with Omni either and yet they're here in what we all hope is the spirit of cooperation."

POTUS sat back in his chair. Chandler stood, clearing his

297

throat before addressing everyone. The success of Operation Bear Trap now relied on his ability to strike a deal between hostile parties.

"As you all know, there's been a shakeup in the White House. The Secretary of Defense has assumed control and declared that the president is not fit for office. I think everyone here can see that's not the case. The president would like to address the nation, today via an Internet stream, from here, where he can show the American public that he's fine."

The Omni representative spoke from behind the Fawkes mask image. "This good. What it have to do with us?" The speaker possessed an eastern European accent.

"The nation has to finish the presidential election of 2020, which the president—," Chandler continued, before facing an interruption.

Fawkians booed and hissed. Others on the screens shook their heads. No one could tell what the Omni rep thought, his or her face concealed behind the plastic mask.

The Brigade members rose from their chairs. Chandler patted the air in front of them, urging them to sit. His first act in this play was failing. He needed to recover, fast.

"Everyone, please! Anyway, for that to happen, Congress has to return to D.C. and they can't do that until they feel safe returning to the capital again."

"What would you like from me, Mr. Scott?" Quinque asked.

"A moratorium on hacking the capital, and Maryland, and Virginia, at least until Congress can return and vote on the election."

"And what would we get in return?" Quinque asked.

Chandler hadn't discussed the offer with the president. He bent down to confer with him. The president looked perturbed, though he relented after a short, but vigorous debate.

The delay created side conversations among the Fawkians and on screen. The Brigade team was aghast that Chandler entertained a negotiation with people that were digital hooligans.

"Everyone! Your attention, please!" Chandler clapped his hands three times. "Yes. OK. What the president agrees to, is to have the NSA, CYBERCOMM and other federal agencies back off the meddling in the Dark Web for an equal period."

As soon as Chandler finished his sentence, the hackers on screen busily typed on their keyboards and phones. He discovered that one of the computers on the desk in front of him had a stream of their conference's text chatter. He noticed dissension in the assembled group of hackers. One Fawkian gave him the evil eye when he tried to get closer to the computer.

Quinque cast his gaze down, observing the text chatter.

The Fawkians had an energized debate.

Chandler sat during the delay. He suspected they were debating the offer in the private, no doubt encrypted, chat room.

"You have them talking," POTUS whispered to him.

After several minutes, Quinque ended the discussion. "You can probably assess that not all my friends are in agreement. This is not surprising for this diverse group. I do have to ask a question, Mr. President. If we allow for this cease fire and then you resume your election, how does this change things, in the long run?"

POTUS remained seated for his response. "There are no guarantees. I can only offer that we'd have the election and that there's going to be movement with the Article Five proposals. I commit to you that I will tell the American public that my administration needs to review our policies. I will admit that I've taken things too far and that I will defer to Congress."

"Mr. President, of course, if you hold your election, you may not win. There's no guarantee that the new president will follow any of this," Quinque countered.

"Yes, that's true. As I said, no guarantees. Whoever the next president is, they're gonna see that what we've been doing is not working. We have a divided country and people are so fed up that some want to leave the republic."

The chat room resumed its bustle.

The Omni representative broke the silence this time. "We understand. Five Tribes listen to him. You and other hackers causing problems all over. Some of you taking advantage of chaos. We have to fix things you break. Give them chance."

Some of Quinque's friends took offense to Omni's comments by displaying Omni's symbol, a series of concentric circles, with blood splattered over it.

Another round of chat room yakking followed.

Big Dog and Glock's eyes oozed with disdain at the spectacle.

No one could tell what Quinque thought since his head remained tilted down, no doubt reading the chatter. It would be difficult to tell what anyone was thinking when only the back of their head was visible. They would shortly know his thoughts.

"Very well. I also cannot guarantee anything. The Tribes will circulate strong messaging in the Darknet for hackers to stay clear of the capital and surrounding states. Shaming is a good deterrent for these people. But understand that there is nothing worse than a bored hacker. I must keep them busy. I have a project that may just accomplish this."

The Five Tribes had established within the Darknet, their own cabinet of curiosities. Cabinets of curiosities, also known as Wunderkammer, were collections of objects evidently containing the entire knowledge of the world. In old Europe, rulers and aristocrats owned the cabinets that became the precursors to museums.

The Tribes' cabinet included source code to popular applications and code powering artificial intelligence or AI. Quinque agreed to offer source code for often used applications so the software companies could pay a bounty to hackers finding vulnerabilities. While most hackers could get their hands on some source code, the Five Tribes' stolen code library dwarfed everyone else's. Quinque would also offer bounties for hackers finding weaknesses in ROT, the browser used for Darknet access. He would pay hackers for finding vulnerabilities in AI work being done by the Tribes. All payments would be in DigiNote, of course.

"I don't know how long they'll remain occupied, but I have challenging problems for them. After that, I cannot control what they'll do."

The "they" he referred to were members of the Tribes and lone hackers.

The Omni representative seemed happy with the proposal, knowing that his people would take a crack at the bounty program.

POTUS agreed with the proposal, though he didn't understand some of its nuances.

To Chandler's relief, Operation Bear Trap eclipsed another important milestone. He also felt more confident in Quinque's authenticity. If he was a government creation, both he and the president deserved Academy Awards. Both Habakk and Axel had told him that vast conspiracies were difficult to pull off due to the number of participants involved. If Quinque was nothing more than a government-sponsored messiah, an organization like Omni, and now, the Council for American Liberty would know.

If Omni knew, then Axel would. If the Council for American Liberty knew, then Habakk would know.

He hoped someday he'd see the rest of Quinque.

President Jefferson prepared to deliver one of his most important addresses to the nation, albeit from an undisclosed location.

***

The president had experience doing this, addressing the nation. Most of the time it was from the Oval Office, East Room, or Brady Press Briefing Room. Today's appearance would be historical. The president sat in a simple office chair. A small camera faced him. He was in an undisclosed warehouse office location, presumably in the state of Colorado. His attire would be informal, flannel shirt and jeans. His hair missed the narrow teeth of a comb. His face missed the scrape of a razor. No one would be around to powder his forehead. The lighting was adequate.

Fawkians hung a makeshift background using a dark green tarp from the warehouse. Only the president would be in the shot. There would be no Teleprompter or printed speech. Only a rough outline of what he wanted to say rested on his lap. The Internet awaited.

"My fellow Americans. I address you today from this undisclosed location, even undisclosed to me, to clarify the events of the last few days. My national security team and Secret Service evacuated me from the capital due to the continued cyber disruptions and the corresponding mayhem. Congress took the same action before my departure for the same reasons. After my arrival in the state of Colorado, I was taken, along with the First Lady, to a secure location where we would wait until they had declared the capital safe.

"I decided, against the wishes of my security detail, to visit the Convention of States Article Five convention in Winter Park. The Article Five convention's purpose is to potentially amend the Constitution. My administration, played a role in hastening this. During my visit to the convention, I spoke with many reporters and delegates. I offered one reporter, Chandler Scott, an opportunity for a lengthier interview. Mr. Scott, as many of you know, was responsible for the video released on the Internet before the 2020 election where he outlined the Global Financial Union. Last year, he and his partner released a documentary on a foreign network where they interviewed patriot and secession groups. Within this documentary, he revealed the existence of reorientation camps and something identified as the Elysium Protocol. After this documentary, I committed to a panel investigating our reeducation methods and treatment of detainees.

"While traveling to my secure location, the separatist group known as the Five Tribes forced down Marine One. The Tribes took myself, Mr. Scott, and my chief of staff to our current location, where I met their leader, via video, Quinque, and hackers. We were then taken to a secluded alpine forest where members of the Colorado Honor Brigade rescued us. The Honor Brigade returned me to Winter Park. The Five Tribes and the Brigade treated us well. No one in our party suffered injury or mental distress. The Five Tribes made no effort to brainwash me with their ideology. On the contrary, they don't foist their ideology on anyone.

"After returning to my secure location, I underwent a medical exam by a staff doctor and a psychiatric evaluation. I was pronounced fit by the staff doctor, but not by the psychiatrist who determined I'd suffered mental trauma. I disputed then and continue to dispute this diagnosis.

"During my absence from Washington, the Secretary of Defense assumed the executive role by convincing my cabinet and security team that I'm not fit for the office. This is patently false.

"I have had time to reflect on the actions of my administration and realize that we have overreached to return prosperity to our great country. Part of that overreach was the executive order freezing the 2020 presidential election. I will ask the Congress to return to D.C. within the next 72 hours so that their first action be to finish the election. I will ask my party to nominate a vice-presidential candidate given the deteriorating health of the current VP.

"I would like to endorse the efforts of the Article Five Convention of States project. This is a lawful attempt to change the Constitution. While the states may disagree with amendments coming out of the convention, they can exercise their opposition through the ratification process. Please allow this process to play itself out. Returning power to the states may be the only way to keep us together.

"I do not endorse the Cascadia Movement or the California Si secession movements. They are not in the best interests of our country. That said, if those states wish to leave the republic, I will only ask that constitutional scholars work with Congress to investigate its feasibility. The federal government will not stop their exit if that is their desire, and we have followed the proper constitutional procedures. Since we don't have a process in place for secession, it will require a great deal of patience. I ask that all states respect the process and its outcome, whatever it may be.

"The journalist, Mr. Scott, has brokered a deal with the Five Tribes, Omni, and other hackers that establishes a moratorium on cyber disruption in the nation's capital and surrounding states. This will allow the proper function of the federal government. I will immediately order our cyber forces to halt their offensive activity on the Darknet for a period equal to the hacker moratorium. We will not break the truce first.

"I am saying these words freely and not under any coercion. Romeo, Alpha, Echo, Bravo, Foxtrot, Two, Five.

"I will return to Washington after this video to continue the work of the people. Thank you and God bless the United States of America."

POTUS awaited reaction from the Fawkians, Chandler, the Brigade members, and Tomás who stared back at him in awe.

Chandler took uncertain steps towards the president, yet he beamed with pride. "Mr. President, that was amazing. You've got more guts than you can hang on a fence. I can't believe you did that without reading a speech." He patted the president on the shoulder. "You know, if this president gig starts gettin' old, you might make it as a speechwriter."

POTUS grinned. "I've been thinking about all this. I laid it out there. We'll see what happens. You never know, I may be out of a job soon."

Glock and Big Dog also came forward to shake POTUS' hand. "You did great, sir."

"Thank you. Thank you. Well, I did my part. Now, who's taking me back home? I need to go to Cheyenne Mountain to see my wife."

"I guess that would be us, sir," Big Dog answered.

POTUS got up from his chair and looked around at the Fawkians, spreading his arms wide. "To all of you, thanks for your hospitality. I know we'll never agree, but I hope we have a newfound respect for one another."

The Fawkians nodded their heads, waving artfully at their departing guests.

"Mr. Scott, I can't thank you enough. Maybe one day, over some cold beers, you can tell me how you put this whole thing together, and who really helped you. I know you had a lot of help."

"Yes, I would like that," Chandler answered. He shook POTUS' hand.

"But let's wait until I'm out of office. I probably wouldn't like what you have to say."

Only one more phase of Bear Trap remained — returning him home.

***

Secretary Carter had assembled his national security team in the Situation Room. The Joint Chiefs, the Secretary of State, the Deputy Director of the Secret Service and other cabinet members joined via video. As stunned as they were by the president's video stream, they had to confirm its authenticity and face how they would handle him now that he was apparently out of their control.

DNI Burkemper, DHS Secretary Haydon, FBI Director Elliott, and NSA Greich joined Carter in the Sit Room. The men realized their earlier decision would require confrontation, not just in the Situation Room, but also before the American public. The first confrontation would be difficult. Confronting the American public was something for which no one had any experience.

Carter paced in front of his chair, the president's chair. No one wanted to begin this conversation.

He faced the large monitor, addressing the Deputy Director of the Secret Service.

"Mr. Director, we all saw the video, the president. I want to, want to know, if you believe, if in your estimation, that was President Jefferson?" Carter's voice quivered.

The main screen flipped to the director. "Yes, sir, it was."

"How can you be absolutely sure? These Tribes, I wouldn't, I mean, they could have just fabricated this, right? I mean it is possible, right?" Carter couldn't conceal his desperation.

"Mr. Secretary, we have an authentication plan in place for such a circumstance," the Deputy Director responded.

One of the authentication methods included something only the president and the Secret Service knew. They used the call sign "BEAR" when referring to the president. The president would echo his call sign using the Army's phonetic alphabet, followed by the first letter of the month and the day of the month. For an odd-numbered calendar day, he'd recite his call sign in reverse.

"And the authentication code was correct? You're absolutely sure?" Carter asked, his eyes darting around the screen.

"Yes, sir. The president recited 'Romeo, Alpha, Echo, Bravo, Foxtrot, Two, Five'. We also put the stream through a voice analysis to confirm the pattern and it checked out," the Deputy Director added, in a cold, leveled tone.

The Deputy Director waited for the next question, which did not come. He had nothing else to offer. "Mr. Secretary, I've got to get back to setting up our detail for returning POTUS to the capital." He dropped off the video call.

Carter paced again, this time around the perimeter of the room. Other than the din of the Security Watchmen in the background, no one spoke.

Though the Sit Room had a comfortable temperature, he wore a sheen of sweat across his forehead.

"I don't know. I don't know. I wouldn't put it past these guys to synthesize his voice. They could have sampled it so many times. They could have drugged him. They may have threatened him. Who knows?" Carter didn't want to let go of the idea that the president spoke, without coercion, in his own authentic voice.

Carter's suspicions had a foundation. The firm responsible for the reeducation efforts of the camps, Cerebrum Technologies, had developed a virtual reality (VR) application that reprogrammed a user's thoughts. In the camps, domestic agitators received a VR dose, reorienting them towards support of patriotic themes like We Are the Future and President Jefferson's policies. One of the chief scientists at Cerebrum, Yitzchak Goldman, an Israeli expert in VR development, left the company under mysterious circumstances and went off the grid.

Dr. Goldman had initially developed software targeting mental illness. He hoped his invention could relieve patients from having to deal with the pernicious side effects of conventional drug therapy. He opposed the software's alteration for mass mind control efforts. He vanished without a trace. Neither the FBI nor Interpol knew his whereabouts. High-ranking members of the intelligence community suspected the doctor sought refuge with Omni.

FBI Director Elliott was familiar with the scientist's disappearance. "Mr. Secretary, I know where you might be going with this. I think you're connecting dots that we have no evidence of being connected."

"Mr. Secretary, Trent, have you spoken to the president yet?" DNI Burkemper asked.

Carter shook his head, wiping his forehead with the backside of his hand.

The president was back in the Cheyenne Complex after being dropped off at Peterson Air Force Base visitors' center by his drivers, Big Dog and Glock. They were leery of handing over the president at an official entrance for fear of being taken into custody. Visitor's center personnel identified President Jefferson and escorted him inside the base. From there, base personnel

308

drove him to Cheyenne to reunite with the First Lady. They would land at Joint Base Andrews later in the day.

Carter understood he'd have to face the president in a few hours, a meeting rife with trepidation. Even if the president spoke freely and without coercion in his video address, it was a betrayal of the country and patriots like him. He thought the president was not defending the Constitution by adopting the conciliatory tone. Carter felt the responsibility to fight for his beliefs, despite the world around him being turned upside down.

His fear of facing the president could strangle his words, but his patriotic fury would set them free in the Sit Room.

"Ladies and gentlemen, the president acted in a treasonous manner with his statements. He's brokering deals with known domestic terrorists like the Five Tribes and all those other hackers. And wasn't Omni on that video as well?" Carter turned to NSA Greich.

"Yes," Greich acknowledged.

"I ask you, since when do we make arrangements with domestic agitators like these? Tell me!" Carter pounded the table. The reverberation caused a pen to fall on his lap.

DNI Burkemper had a long-standing relationship with the secretary and challenged his assumptions.

"Trent, we've got to face this man when he comes back to the White House. I think you may have miscalculated his mental state. He appeared fine to me."

"Fine! Then he needs to be charged with treason. He betrayed the country and the Constitution." He clenched his fists, digging his nails into his palms. He bounced them on the table several times.

His aggression silenced the room. The country plowed through the impeachment and trial of President Jefferson the year before. Public opinion polls showed the president with favorable ratings despite congressional attempts to oust him from office and the continuing economic challenges. His detainment by the Five Tribes and release had only made his popularity increase. The public interpreted his latest foray with the Tribes and the hackers as an alternative form of statesmanship. The authorities couldn't keep the hackers at bay. America, if one were to believe the polls, wanted to give the president's détente with the hacking community a chance.

The Joint Chiefs agreed with Carter, as did DHS Secretary Haydon and FBI Director Elliott. The rest of the president's cabinet was split. Greich was too new to support either side with any conviction, though he felt loyalty to Jefferson who'd recently appointed him. Burkemper stood somewhere in the middle.

DNI Burkemper had a distinguished career in the military retiring in 2000 as a general in the Air Force after 30 years in uniform serving in various intelligence roles. After his retirement, Burkemper served as a consultant to the Department of Defense and the Department of Homeland Security, focusing on matters of domestic terrorism. President Jefferson appointed him to his current post in 2018. He'd been deep in the trenches in the battle against domestic terrorism, both cyber and kinetic. His office served as the hub of intelligence collection for the nation. To date, they'd reached mostly a stalemate in their battle with those creating cyber mayhem — they'd win some and lose some. Burkemper was as old school as they came, but even he realized that they were neither winning nor losing this battle.

He surveyed the room. "Trent, we all have to decide right now. But I feel we need to unite. Either he's guilty of treason or he's not. If he is, then we know what has to happen next. If he's not, then we have to decide if we can continue to work with the man and apologize to him for what we did. He may ask for the resignation of some of us, maybe all of us. We have to put the country in front of our personal feelings."

"That's exactly what I'm doing Mr. Burkemper." Carter's agitation made him draw air in short gasps. He drew a sharp breath, sucking the apprehension that had permeated the room.

They spent the next hour in a heated discussion. Some cabinet members continued to feel that Carter made erroneous conclusions about the president's health, even influencing a psychiatric evaluation. On the other hand, most everyone agreed that President Jefferson's extension of an olive branch bordered on something treasonous.

Burkemper tried to offer another consideration after an outburst by one of the Joint Chiefs. "Everyone, please!" Burkemper tapped his soda can on the table. "I want everyone to remember that with this deal Jefferson brokered, Congress should be able to return and finish the election. Consider the ramifications."

If the president won the election in the House, his popularity might increase further still and it would be highly unlikely there would be any appetite to draft impeachment articles. If he lost, then there would be a new administration under no obligation to honor Jefferson's deal or revised policies.

That point got everyone to reconsider their positions. The president's cabinet also had to acknowledge the reaction from Elites vested in the Plan for Prosperity. There was big money in supporting the plan and the suffocating regulatory environment created by the Financial Stability Board. Despite Chandler's documentary, Homeland Security had big plans for building more detention camps. The Department of Defense's cyber security budget continued to grow. There were many people with an interest in continuing the status quo, including the government's own Deep State. The president's change of heart would undermine that.

After another round of votes, Carter made an executive decision.

"We won't agree on this. The president will return to the White House soon. If we can't be unified, then I'm afraid there's only one thing left to do." He threw wary glances towards everyone.

A pause followed.

"What is that, Trent?" Burkemper craned his neck and spread his arms in a helpless gesture.

Carter pushed away from the table. "I can't serve under Jefferson's treasonous leadership. It goes against every fiber of my being. I will offer my resignation as soon as I see the president."

On the video monitor, each member of the Joint Chiefs of Staff acknowledged Carter with their own resignations.

The DHS Secretary, Haydon, pushed himself away from the table. FBI Director Elliott followed by doing the same, rolling his chair on the carpet.

One by one, each of the cabinet members echoed the sentiment on the video display.

Burkemper fought the urge, yet he succumbed to peer pressure.

Everyone in the Situation Room, save for one, sat away from the conference table, symbolizing the gulf between themselves and their president.

"What about you, Mr. Greich?" Carter asked.

Greich's appointment had been controversial, deemed too young and inexperienced for the position. He also had no allegiance and little in common with the rest of the cabinet and security team. He was the next generation. "I'll serve my president and will welcome him when I see him. I respect your positions, but I can't agree." He folded his arms.

By the end of the day, the president's cabinet was gone. So were his Joint Chiefs and the security leaders.

It was next man or woman up.

***

One by one, the resignations arrived on Jefferson's desk. A portion of his staff resigned face-to-face and handed him a letter explaining their action. Others emailed their intentions.

National Security Advisor Eric Greich joined the president and his chief in the Oval Office, sorting through the mess.

The three sat on couches in front of the president's desk.

Jefferson, normally averse to the formalities of being president, was eager to put on a suit after his time in captivity and in Cheyenne Mountain. He and the First Lady welcomed sleeping in their own beds again, though it remained uncertain how much longer they'd occupy the White House.

He faced a maelstrom. Most of his appointees had abandoned him. Had this happened months ago, he might have withered under the stress. Now he felt at peace. A quiet assurance coursed through his body.

He'd always been confident, whether living within the Beltway's insular nature or his earlier life within the sturdy walls of an executive suite. Captivity forced him out of the protective shell of his handlers and policy wonks. For the first time in his presidency, he vicariously felt consequences of his decisions.

He wrapped his arm around his chief. "Drake, I know I've put a lot on your plate, with all these resignations. I just want to make sure we have a smooth transition."

The chief tilted back, surprised by the sudden affection. "Ah,

313

yes, sir. Deputies and undersecretaries have all agreed to serve under your leadership for the time being."

Mass promotions were only part of the story in D.C.

Members of Congress were already filtering into Washington. The full House and Senate expected to be in session in a couple of days. Former Secretary of Defense Carter's efforts to secure the capital and Chandler's brokered agreement with the hacking community returned life to normal. Congress would resolve the 2020 election as their first order of business.

The Democrats nominated a new VP candidate considering the sitting vice president's health. They didn't expect him to make it longer than another few days. They nominated two-term New Jersey governor, Robert DeMarco, as Jefferson's running mate. DeMarco achieved national prominence by turning around the state's deteriorating budget and rehabilitating the state's public pension fund.

For the lone survivor of the cabinet level bloodbath, new challenges emerged. NSA Eric Greich inherited a tenuous hacker deal, which meant his organization needed to stand down for the moment.

"Eric, I know I've placed you in probably the toughest spot of all. I can't tell you how much it means to me to have your loyalty."

"Mr. President. I wouldn't have it any other way. I hope to serve you through the rest of your term."

"My term may not last much longer. My party's not in control of the House, as you know."

"Sir, you're popular right now. The public loved how you thought outside the box," Hutchinson offered. "I had my reservations, but you gotta love those poll numbers."

The beaming chief, with broad experience in marketing,

valued his boss's popularity more than anything. He had been instrumental in Jefferson's victory in 2016.

"Drake, you know Chandler and whoever helped him had as much to do with it as anyone, including me."

Chandler's experience with the president's abductions were the main story in the upcoming edition of Veritas' monthly publication. He'd have a tale to tell his readers, though certain details would remain forever buried.

The president's continuing tale would play out in a few short days in the House of Representatives.

CHAPTER FOURTEEN
HOUSE IN ORDER

The 2020 presidential election featured four candidates. President Jefferson, first elected in 2016, carried the torch for the Democrats. Kansas governor Alicia Scarborough represented the GOP. Texas Senator Alfonso Chancellor represented the Independent American Party (IAP). John King represented the Theocracy Party (TP). When the Electoral College held their vote on December 14, 2020, Jefferson had 239 votes, Governor Scarborough had 198, Senator Chancellor had 80, and Mr. King had 21.

Only the top three vote-getters were eligible for the runoff in the House of Representatives, meaning that King was no longer in the running.

For many Americans, an election in the House was proof of a constitutional failure — their votes had somehow not counted. After the 2016 election, many Americans suggested abolishing the Electoral College by constitutional amendment. That issue was not open for debate during the Article Five convention in Winter Park.

The House of Representatives last selected a president in 1825. In 1800 it took thirty-six ballots to select the president. Those events might as well have been ancient history. Americans and President Jefferson feared the impasse such a vote would create. For Jefferson, it was important to continue his economic plan, which partisan bickering would derail. Everyone's fears were more likely to be reflexive instead of reflective. Constitutional scholars reminded everyone that it wasn't the system that caused the fractured election, but the country's social

316

mood.

Once resettled in the nation's capital, the House of Representatives wasted no time in discharging their duties of electing the next President of the United States. On Monday, March 7, 2022, they began. The Constitution allotted each state delegation one vote. This meant that a state like California, with fifty-five electoral votes, carried the same weight as Alaska with its three. Having an entire state delegation come to an agreement would always be challenging.

On March 10th, after seven ballots, the mostly GOP House of Representatives elected Kansas governor Alicia Scarborough. Governor Scarborough, now the President-elect, would become the first female president in the nation's history.

The Senate vote went much quicker. The majority Democratic Senate voted for New Jersey governor Robert DeMarco, recently nominated in place of Jefferson's ailing vice president.

Two parties would lead the Executive Branch of government. The Republicans held the office of president, and the Democrats held the office of vice president. The unprecedented arrangement would be a watershed moment for American politics and governance. Governor Scarborough would be sworn in on the west front of the Capitol, facing Pennsylvania Avenue, on St. Patrick's Day, March 17th, one week later.

The country had more to contemplate than just a new president.

The Article Five convention, sponsored by the Convention of States, had developed three proposed amendments, on which state legislatures would soon vote. These included a balanced budget amendment, a redefinition of the General Welfare Clause and a limitation of the use of Executive Orders. The Convention of States project agreed to hold another convention the following year, this time in a warmer environment.

The incoming president also faced the Cascadia Movement and the California Sí secession efforts. While President Jefferson voiced his opposition, the movements felt as if he left the door open for constitutional negotiation.

Jefferson's loss had opened another chapter in his career. He'd experienced an awakening, one that would guide the rest of his life. It was his time to begin that journey.

***

Unlike the last time he addressed the nation, from an unknown warehouse location filled with Fawkians, President Jefferson had composed his words ahead of time. This would be his farewell speech. He could have addressed a live audience. Instead, he wanted to begin the transition to the seclusion he craved. He'd been in office for five years. The nation's polarity had only increased during his watch. While he still had ardent supporters, he understood that those that hated him felt as strongly as those that loved him. A Republican and a Democrat would now lead the United States of America.

Third parties like the IAP and the TP had proved their mettle and would be more influential in future races as the electorate sought representation more tailored to their needs. Ironic that the tribalism touted by Quinque had made its way into American political structure.

In the late eighteenth century, George Mason, a delegate to the Constitutional Convention, had speculated that Congress would decide most elections. With the rise of third parties, his prophecy could well come to fruition. Some feared more gridlock, while others welcomed the opportunity for coalition building.

He sat alone in the Oval Office, at his desk, and waited for the light on the camera to come on so he could fix his eyes on the Teleprompter above the lens.

"My fellow Americans. It has been my privilege to serve you for the last five years. I leave knowing that some of you support me and others loathe me. For those that support me, thank you, I appreciate it. For those that loathe me, understand that every action I took was for the welfare of this great nation. Faced with unprecedented economic challenges, I took action when others did not. Some of this action may have caused financial injury to some. For this, I am sorry. My administration also had its hand in conducting mental warfare against our citizens, which at times led to deadly outcomes. For this, I apologize.

"The new administration will face challenges, including parts of the country that no longer want to be in the Union. Others are happy to be within our borders, but would like to opt out from most of our governing aspects. Another group wants to bring change to our Constitution.

"I wish the best for President-elect Scarborough. She has been a fine public servant and patriot. I'm sure she will do her best to keep the nation together. My administration will offer her every support during what will be a difficult transition. My chief of staff, Drake Hutchinson, will remain in Washington to assist her.

"The First Lady and I will retire to our home in California, where I will engage in reflection. I will not seek nor will I accept a nomination for public office from this point forward. My goal is to return to private life and engage in philanthropic causes. I owe this country much and it is time to give something in return.

"Thank you for the privilege of serving as your president.

God bless you, and God bless the United States of America."

The light faded on the camera and his presidency. He looked over the mementos he'd amassed throughout his term. There were pictures with foreign dignitaries and celebrities. Memories of his beloved home state of California adorned his walls. There were the family photos behind his desk.

There were banker's boxes littering the floor, serving as a reminder of his imminent departure.

The president took measured steps leaving the Oval Office, where he gave a final look to the We Are the Future posters. He contemplated his own future. The nation's future would be someone else's concern now.

***

In less than twenty-four hours, the Chief Justice would swear in Alicia Scarborough as the 46th President of the United States of America.

Jefferson had removed most of the vestiges of his time in the Oval Office. The only items that remained were his treasured books and family pictures that rested on the table behind his desk.

Chief of Staff Drake Hutchinson, walked in with President-elect Scarborough, Vice President-elect DeMarco, and Senator Matt Geringer. Everyone exchanged greetings before taking a seat. His three guests sat on the couches, the president and his chief sat on the club chairs.

"President-elect Scarborough, are you ready?" Jefferson asked. Scarborough would take the oath of office the next day at high noon.

She blushed. "How can anyone be ready for this job? Were you?"

Jefferson chuckled, turning towards his chief who offered but a smirk. "Sure, I was. I read that book." He pointed at the table behind his desk.

"That book?" She looked towards his desk, attempting to locate her instruction manual.

"Yeah, 'How to be President for Dummies'," Jefferson replied.

Everyone got a kick out of that line.

Geringer started in his unmistakable bass delivery. "Mr. President, I fought you tooth and nail for the last few years. You know how I felt about your executive order. While I don't agree with everything you said in your video, the one on the Internet, it is a great measure of a man," Geringer stole a glance towards the President-elect, "or a woman, who can engage in self-reflection and look at another point of view. You did that and I think even those opposed to you appreciate that."

Jefferson leaned towards Geringer and shook his hand. "Thank you, Matt. You've been a hell of an adversary. You did things the right way, the impeachment, trial, Supreme Court, the Article Five. You never lost faith in the system, did you?"

He shook his head. "No, sir. We're a nation of laws. If we don't follow them, what do we have? That's what I tell my party all the time. If you don't like something, get involved and change it. Work within the law. We'll get a chance to see that in action when the states get to vote on the proposed amendments. That will be under your watch, Mrs. President-elect."

"Guys, seriously, Alicia for now, please. I'm comfortable with what you did, Matt, and we'll abide by whatever the states decide. Cascadia and Cal Sí, that's another matter. They have a great deal of momentum and support. That's going to be my biggest headache, I'm afraid."

Hutchinson threw cold water on her comfortable optimism.

"Mrs. Presi-, Alicia, I hate to bring this up but that panarchic state the Five Tribes wants, I don't know how you're gonna manage that not to mention all the hackers."

"True. I just think the country is tired of the endless wars, on terror, drugs, cyber bullies, you fill in the blank. Depending on what happens with the constitutional amendments, the federal government may find that it has less to work with there."

President-elect Scarborough would also have a battle on her hands with the entrenched Elite and Deep State, who had a stake in continuing the Plan for Prosperity and other Jefferson era programs.

Jefferson's Oval Office guests left after one hour. He returned to his desk and penned a letter to the incoming president and thank-you notes to White House staff.

He packed the rest of his possessions and left them in the banker's boxes for the movers, who would come soon.

The next morning, he performed the duties and formalities associated with the transition of power.

At twelve noon on March 17, 2022, on the west front of the Capitol, Alicia Scarborough took the oath of office, becoming the nation's first female president. Given the short turnaround after her election in the House and security concerns, President Scarborough opted for a more subdued inauguration. There would be no honeymoon period for her. Most presidents touted what they would do in their first one hundred days.

President Scarborough faced an hourglass that was already spilling its sand.

CHAPTER FIFTEEN
FAREWELL TO A MENTOR

Chandler would have a difficult, if not impossible, time giving an encore that was better than his first published piece for Veritas. What had started as coverage of an Article Five convention morphed into an adventure with the president, the Five Tribes, and the Honor Brigade. Veritas delayed their March 2022 magazine edition a couple of weeks to include Chandler's piece, which occupied most of the issue. The issue sold so well that Veritas printed commemorative editions. Online subscriptions soared. Veritas had to hire someone to handle the barrage of media requests.

He'd spent the last two weeks as a guest in the home of Arianne's parents, the Maxwells. He drove south from Winnetka towards Great Lakes Tower to present Axel with one of the print editions.

Axel greeted him at the door of his 55th floor unit overlooking Navy Pier. On a clear day, Axel claimed he could see three states. Today featured overcast and dreary skies. Chicago was still in the throes of winter, though the calendar said otherwise.

"Ax, hey! You doin' OK? You look kinda pale." Chandler shook his hand with enthusiasm. He was on top of the world.

Axel's firm grip was missing.

"Chan, come in. What's this?" He spied the wrapped gift in Chandler's hand.

"Arianne, she said I should wrap it."

Axel reached for it.

The playful Chandler would have none of it, speeding towards the living room where he plopped on the sofa.

He placed the gift on the coffee table. "OK, let's do this the right way. Now you can have it." He winked.

Axel played along. "Well, it's not Christmas and it's not my birthday-"

Chandler slapped him on his arm. "Hey, you never have told me your birthday!"

Birthdays were not something Axel celebrated. It wasn't an age thing. He just thought the whole idea of celebrating the day of one's birth was frivolous, except for those not yet of adult age. Now, he hoped life would allow one more.

He flicked his hand. "Are you kidding me? Forget about my birthday. Let me open this."

He tore through the paper like he might have as a youngster in New Mexico in front of his family's natural Christmas tree. The smell of pine and hot chocolate were a reminder that the holiday season had arrived. He longed for that aroma now. In the last couple of months, his sense of smell had dulled.

"Oh, your magazine. That's wonderful, Chandler. You'll be on the interview circuit now. Who knows? Maybe a book deal is in your future?" A smile crept on his mouth.

"Easy, one thing at a time. I've already told my boss, Jaden, that he shouldn't expect this sort of story every time. How can I possibly top this?"

Axel looked away. His closed eyes were a sharp reminder of his throbbing head.

His mask of indifference to the pain could no longer fool Chandler. "You've had these headaches for a long time now. Have you been to see anyone?"

He tried to brush off the question. Axel never was much for doctors. He'd been so healthy his entire life, he hardly needed them. Other than occasional trips to the dentist, which he despised, and his optometrist, he couldn't recall the last time he saw a doctor.

"Chandler, this is a spectacular time for you and Arianne. Your professional life and personal life are soaring. This is difficult for me."

"What's difficult? What are you talking about?"

He cast his eyes on the dull sky over Lake Michigan. "My parents, they were immigrants from Austria, as you know. They each taught me something that served me well later in life. I regret that I never had children or that I never married." Axel flipped his head around and tapped his guest's knee. "My manners! Can I get you some ice tea? Something else?"

Axel scurried towards the kitchen. Chandler followed.

"No. Sit." He pointed back towards the living room, stopping Chandler in his tracks. "What can I get you?"

"A tea, I guess. Ax, what's going on?" Chandler took cautious steps towards the sofa.

Axel returned to the living room and placed a tray with two glasses of ice tea on his coffee table. He passed a glass to his guest, offering a weak smile.

He took a sip before placing it back on the tray. He crossed his legs and leaned back, this time facing his guest.

"When you reach my age, you engage in self-reflection. It's natural. You look at what you've accomplished, your regrets."

"I can't see many who've done what you have. You are a true Renaissance Man. I'm sure you know that."

"Thank you. Even someone as accomplished as me still has unanswered questions. There's not enough time in life to answer all of them. A long time ago, I realized that my knowledge would be finite, while my ignorance would always be infinite."

"OK, that's fine but you're gonna be around for a while.

There are many more questions for you to answer. Especially questions from a young journalist like me!"

Chandler's enthusiasm couldn't lift his mentor's wounded soul. He uncrossed his legs and took another sip of his tea. He looked towards his ceramic floor, between his legs. When he raised his head, Chandler could see the hurt in his eyes. Though the eyes were dry, they revealed a pain that Chandler had never seen. Axel had been a rock, fearless, cool under pressure, the fountain of answers. He didn't look that way now.

"What is it? Did I do something?" Chandler pleaded.

"No. No. It's not that."

Chandler shook his mentor's shoulders. "Please, you're scaring me!"

Axel eased Chandler's arms towards his sides.

"The headaches that you've noticed, there's a serious issue there."

"Like migraines? I know you don't get headaches. So you deal with severe migraines now? Maybe it's something in your diet?" Chandler searched for answers to calm his growing anxiety.

Axel stretched the corners of his mouth, hoping to fashion some sort of smile. "No. Not migraines." He turned away from Chandler, looking out towards low cloud cover descending on Lake Michigan. Navy Pier remained hidden. "I went to the doctor a few months ago, after the holidays. My headaches were not getting better and I was getting dizzy. She recommended an MRI when I told her that no matter what I took, they did not improve." He paused.

"OK, so what did the MRI say?"

"Chandler, the MRI showed I have a very aggressive, advanced brain tumor."

Chandler dropped his head. He reached to his mentor, still

looking out towards the lake, turning his shoulders back in his direction. He didn't know what to say after the gut punch he'd just sustained. After losing color in his face, he asked the first thing that came to mind, clinging to hope.

His voice trembled. "You're gonna do radiation or chemo, right? You probably have your own therapy. How is your treatment going?"

Axel had convinced himself that he would never engage in heroic attempts to prolong his life.

"No way was I going to subject myself to chemo and radiation. Are you kidding me? My body's been strong my whole life. I wasn't about to weaken it like that. And what would be the purpose? The technology, the treatments, would keep me alive for what? For the next treatment. I couldn't live like that. The doctor didn't give me any hope either."

"What are you saying?"

"I've lived to my ultimate potential. I've accomplished everything I ever wanted to. Throughout my life, I've thought about death not to obsess about it, but to live my days like they may be my last. You know I'm not a spiritual person in the religious sense. That's because I haven't tried to look outside of myself for that guidance. I've always treated people fairly and respect everyone regardless of their station in life, that's been my religion. Sometimes, I think people's search for that sort of guidance leads to a religious or spiritual materialism."

Chandler squeezed out tears, wiping the corners of his eyes with his knuckles. "You have to do something!" He blew his nose with the napkin that had been on the table.

"I feel very comfortable letting nature take its course. The last couple of years have been a joy for me. Watching you grow as a man and as a leader. You've taken on some big things and made the world a better place. And now you have Arianne. Honestly, you two are the closest thing to family I've ever had outside of my parents. You two have a bright future ahead of you."

"I know but you, how can you say-"

Axel reached for him, clutching his arm. "I'm not afraid, Chandler. Fear is an incompetent teacher. Part of me has always been curious about the whole death experience. It's like another frontier to cross."

Axel's views of life and death were not familiar to Chandler or many others. For him, death was the other end, the counterpart, to life. In all of one's life, the only guaranteed experience was death.

He lived his life knowing the limits of time. No matter how accomplished he was in his professional life, he could never create time. Life accelerated as he aged. His contemporaries experienced the same sensation. The Earth orbited the Sun at the same rate, though it sure seemed faster. For someone who was always in control, time was something he'd never tame.

As he matured into an adult, he wondered about his purpose. To fulfill his life, he looked for achievement, whether professional or financial. When his personal life didn't take the trajectory he wanted, he poured himself further into his work. Without a family to support, that came easy, perhaps too easy.

Parents understood that when they made their children, they would die. They just hoped they didn't witness it.

He didn't make his child. The child came to him when he met Chandler while the latter attended graduate school at Johns Hopkins University. Axel would become his mentor. It would be a friendship that had blossomed over the last dozen years. He found his purpose with the charismatic, impressionable journalist to be from Texas. Chandler gave him what would be his final purpose.

He'd read that there weren't any atheists in a foxhole. While his beliefs were not overtly spiritual, he believed in a higher power and respected everyone's religious beliefs. He knew once he arrived at his own foxhole, he'd be at peace.

He'd seen people die before. They often had a wretched apprehension, appearing unprepared. Everyone knew they would die, they just didn't want to die right here, right now. Axel had prepared himself mentally for years, even in the pinnacle of health. It was easier for him. His parents were gone. He had no siblings. His parents had no living siblings. He'd maintained no ties with his ancestry in Austria. There would be no children to watch his decay. He had Chandler, and now Arianne.

Chandler had sunken in the sofa by now, filled with despair. The rock in his life crumbled before him. "How much time?"

"Not long. I have enough time to get my affairs in order."

He hoped Chandler wouldn't alter the trajectory of his life. His capacity for doing that rested from how Axel died. Axel wanted Chandler to praise his life, which would allow him to cope with the grief, a skill Chandler would need for the rest of his own life. For Axel, grief represented an awakening of sorts — something to learn. He'd learned grief and hoped that Chandler would now. Axel had awakened to his own death.

He reached towards Chandler, placing his hand on his knee. "Life requires an ending in order for things to continue. I hope that some piece of me will continue to live within you. I ask that you make your life deep and meaningful, understanding how brief your time is on this Earth."

Chandler sat up and placed his hand on top of Axel's, studying the wisdom etched in his face. "You're as responsible as anyone for who I am today."

Axel felt heartened by the comment. "That means a lot to me."

"What will you do now?"

Axel had decided to move to a hospice in rural New Mexico, his childhood home. He didn't want Chandler or anyone else he knew to see him in the final days — better for Chandler not to remember him that way.

He wanted to show Chandler his last will and testament before retiring for the day. Chandler read it and asked if he could remain there overnight. Axel was grateful to host him one last time.

In the morning, Chandler would have a surprise.

***

As usual, Axel had risen first and had prepared a simple breakfast of toast, scrambled eggs and coffee for his guest. The smell of fine Arabica beans, ground and brewed, wafted through the condo, tantalizing Chandler who slept in the makeshift bedroom that served as Axel's office. For a moment, the inviting smell made him forget the conversation from the night before.

From the sofa bed, Chandler surveyed his mentor's office for one last time. Gone were all the financial charts that lined the walls behind his desk. The desk itself no longer had his newsletter editions scattered on top. Most of the books, his treasures, he'd already boxed. Two boxes displayed Chandler's name. He wondered how many great insights and thoughts had emerged from these quarters over the years.

He'd slept in his clothes, not expecting his overnight stay. The night of restless slumber wrinkled his long sleeve shirt. He shuffled into the kitchen and stared at his mentor.

"What? Oh, come on. Please stop looking at me like that,"

Axel said as he finished setting up breakfast at his counter.

Chandler had a doomed countenance. "I'm sorry." His chin fell to his chest.

"Sit down and eat. I have someone I want you to talk to. They'll be here any minute. I wasn't sure what time you'd wake up."

Chandler sat and sipped his coffee. "Who's coming?"

Axel wouldn't tell him and only urged him to make haste. He had little appetite, mostly rearranging his food. Chandler would still need to clean up after breakfast, per Axel's insistence.

A splash of water on his face and teeth cleaning with salt and baking soda prepared him for Axel's arriving house guest.

Chandler waited in the living room, staring at a still overcast sky above Lake Michigan. A knock on the door shifted his eyes.

The familiar guest appeared, yet again, when he least expected it, although when he most needed him.

Habakk, dressed in his usual black top and khaki pants, embraced Axel and made his half-moon strides towards Chandler.

"Chandler! It's so good to see you again." Unlike any of their previous encounters, Habakk offered a warm embrace which Chandler reciprocated.

"Please, everyone. Sit down. I'll bring more coffee," Axel commanded.

"You didn't just show up here this morning, did you?" Chandler questioned while grabbing a seat.

Habakk followed, sitting in an adjacent chair. "I am a guest today of Mr. Schultz." He swung his attention back to his host. "This is quite a view here! A pity the day is so dark and foreboding."

Axel and Habakk had established a relationship in the brief time they'd known each other. Habakk's deduction and Axel's confession about his illness brought the two closer together, given Habakk's wife's similar affliction. The bond of sharing Chandler as a pupil strengthened their brief time together.

Axel returned with a tray holding a pitcher of coffee and three cups. He poured everyone some java.

"You're probably wondering why I've asked Habakk here this morning. I shared, or I should say he somehow knew about my illness when you introduced him to me in Winter Park. His insights have helped me, particularly in having a connection with you after I'm gone."

It didn't sound right for Chandler to hear the words "after I'm gone" coming out of his mouth. Axel's eventual death would make Chandler's relationship with Habakk more important now. "You know, that's the way things have always been with Habakk. I never know when he'll show up. But I'm sure glad he's here now."

Habakk offered a toothy grin. "I've always made myself available to you. Now that you know about the Council for American Liberty, you should understand my need for being discreet. I cannot telegraph my arrival."

Members of the Council never tried to call attention to themselves, speaking softly and dressing modestly. Their conservative manner hid the complexity of their minds.

"For now, anyway, you guys rescued the nation," Chandler said, cradling his warm cup. He appreciated that they started their conversation with something other than Axel's health.

Habakk lifted his cup, pinkie in the air, and sipped, twirling the coffee in his mouth. "We didn't rescue anyone or anything. Throughout this crisis, everyone's been waiting for leadership to bail out the country. At some point, we need to rely on personal inner leadership and compassion for our fellow man. If we think we have no choice, well that is a failure of imagination. Government and its leaders can't give everyone perfection. They can't eliminate risk. Everyone will be much better off accepting risk and imperfection. It will bring the nation a sense of peace. People should have a vision beyond their fears."

Axel chimed in. "The Sword of Damocles reared itself in the latest crisis."

Habakk nodded in concurrence. "Precisely. It wasn't solely the Five Tribes or anyone else that changed the president's stance. They just pushed him in the direction he was already going. I suspect he governed with a Sword of Damocles hanging over his head. Every decision he made had this specter of anxiety. I can't imagine what it must have been like in Washington after your documentary revealed the reorientation camps. It's hard to live when you're under constant apprehension. My guess is he had to wear a mask of indifference frequently, trying to hide how he may have felt, figuring he needed to do what he did for the good of the country. The country lost its innocence a long time ago and it must now deal with something that will look different."

"You mean the secessionists?" Chandler asked.

"I don't have a crystal ball. Our council has done what it can. Ultimately, we can't stop the will of the people. The will of the people can go in many directions. I'm certain the new president understands this and will have to deal with it accordingly."

Habakk took another sip of his coffee before continuing with Chandler. "You must be a bright light of liberty in the collective darkness of our society. I believe you'll have a wonderful opportunity to do that with Veritas. Educate people so that freedom and liberty will always triumph. Axel and I are both confident you can do that since you are someone of great character. Character and freedom go hand in hand. Nations that lose their character, lose their freedom. Never forget that."

Chandler nodded, though he realized that his two mentors were trying to get him to think about something other than Axel. "I don't think you came here today to talk about all this."

Habakk and Axel looked at each other for a moment before Axel dipped his head.

"Axel asked me here to help you transition. He wants you to know that his disease, his tumor, could never kill who he was. Yes, his corporal body will fade away, but his ideas will endure within you. He has loved his life and that's what he wants you to do, love *his* life. He isn't approaching his death with fear, he's embracing it and he wants you to embrace it as well."

Chandler thrust his arms to his sides. "You want me to be happy?"

"Rejoice that you have spent twelve wonderful years knowing him. Rejoice in what he's passed on to you and what you may pass to your children. Know that I will be here for you and so will the council. Maybe someday, you join us. Axel's life is behind him now. Mine is mostly as well. You and Tomás, you are the future. I can only hope that our collective wisdom can live through both of you."

The mysterious one stood, pulling down his sweater and smoothing his khakis. Habakk understood that they'd have more conversations about Axel. Today marked the beginning.

"That's it, you're leaving?" Chandler stood up as well.

"My work is done here." Habakk walked towards Axel, who had stood up also, and offered him a firm embrace. "Please let me know if you require anything in New Mexico." He extended his hand towards Chandler. "Chandler, we'll be in touch. I don't know where or how, but we'll be in touch. I'll let myself out."

Axel and Chandler stood watching him and his half-moon

slide leave the condo.

They turned to look at each other, neither man saying anything.

Axel stepped towards him, placing his hand on his shoulder. "Chan, nothing I can say will help you avoid the pain you'll feel when I'm gone. It's natural to be averse to this pain, just don't fear it, otherwise you'll suffer." He took his other hand and clutched Chandler's cheek. "Please say goodbye to Arianne for me. I know that I leave you in good hands."

Chandler reached for Axel's shoulder. "You don't want to do it yourself?"

He shook his head. "It's better this way. You should get back to her."

"I will but-"

"We should say goodbye now."

Bitter tears streamed down Chandler's face, interrupted by stubble on the way to his jaw. His feelings bounced between anger and sadness. "Now? It's still-"

"Yes, now. I want you to remember me as I am, right now. Please don't look for me in New Mexico."

Axel reached for him, wrapping both arms around him. Chandler rested his chin on Axel's shoulder. He wouldn't let go. Neither man wanted the other to hear him cry. They pushed away deliberately, averting their eyes when they broke the embrace.

Axel paced towards his office. Chandler watched him leave, knowing this would be the last time. When he disappeared from view, Chandler's gaze drifted towards the overcast sky.

From the 55th floor, he stood high over the city, yet he bobbed the depths of sorrow.

The relationship with his mentor, something for which he'd

never prepared, had ended.

He carried an ambling gait towards the living room, thinking about memories they'd made together. He grabbed his coat from the hall closet, dreading the catastrophic news he would deliver to Arianne.

***

As difficult as it had been, he respected his mentor's wishes and did not try to contact him after that morning in his condo.

Axel had written a lengthy letter offering final words of wisdom and conveying parental affection he'd experienced only from his mother. It was easier for Axel this way, to express his thoughts with the power of the pen.

Arianne joined him for a blustery walk along Lake Shore Trail, about a mile north of Axel's former condo. Chicago had a strange transition from winter to spring. Some would say there was no transition and spring never arrived, skipping directly to summer.

It had been two weeks since President Scarborough took her oath of office and a week since he'd said goodbye to Axel. Executive power had transitioned from a polarizing, autocratic figure to another who'd yet to fully grasp the tempest she inherited.

He imagined Axel transitioning in New Mexico's arid climate, watching sunrises and sunsets, reflecting on the fullness of his life, embracing his next frontier.

He wanted to watch sunrises and sunsets with the woman clinging to his arm. She accepted who he was — someone willing to explore new paths and be unpredictable.

Chandler loved her and she loved him. They opened themselves to the suffering that inevitably came with that love. She might break his heart and he might break hers. Those were both the risks and burdens, which they freely accepted. The risks and burdens were like wings that could weigh them down, yet give them flight.

It was a divided country, perhaps more than ever. Some were ready to take flight, willing to forge a separate future. There would be more acts to follow in this ongoing historical production.

What Chandler and Arianne knew and understood today could change radically. Their union allowed them to adjust to anything they might face. If there was another crisis, they'd look for opportunity on the other side of it.

They would stand together, ready to accept the test.

Read the first two books (2020, Rebellium) in the Chandler Scott series. Release updates posted on author web site (www.JimMosquera.com).

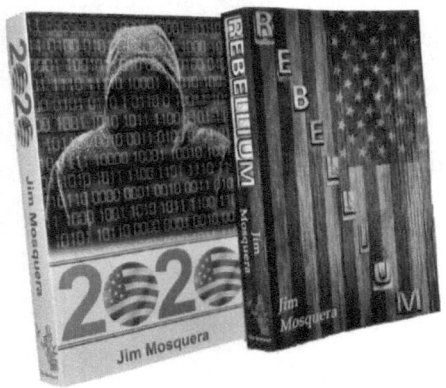

ABOUT THE AUTHOR

Jim Mosquera has an academic background in Industrial Engineering and held management positions in the telecommunications industry. Developing expertise in financial markets and economics through his own study, he produced a column in a national publication and edited a financial newsletter.

That work led to a series of books on the economy and financial crises known as the **Escaping Oz** series (Protecting your wealth during the financial crisis, Navigating the crisis, An Observer's Reflections). He is also the author of the **Chandler Scott** series (2020, Rebellium, Division, Hope).

Sentinel Consulting, a firm he founded in 2014, assists businesses with financing and debt restructuring. Mr. Mosquera is a frequent contributor to numerous financial news outlets.

SIMPLIFYING THE COMPLEX
UNITING THOUGHT
DESCRIBING THE FUTURE

His non-fiction work will make you question proposed solutions to financial and economic problems. His novels are so realistic, the stories will hit close to home.

Follow the author at https://JimMosquera.com

CREDITS

Book cover design by Jim Mosquera using edited art from the following sources:

Clouds background - Copyright: <a href='http://www.123rf.com/profile_blackboard1965'>blackboard1965 / 123RF Stock Photo</a>

Eye - Copyright: <a href='http://www.123rf.com/profile_flynt'>flynt / 123RF Stock Photo</a>

USA Flag - Copyright: <a href='http://www.123rf.com/profile_masnah'>masnah / 123RF Stock Photo</a>

Cascadia Flag - Copyright: <a href='http://www.123rf.com/profile_monkeydluffy123rf'>monkeydluffy123rf / 123RF Stock Photo</a>

USA State Map - Copyright: <a href='http://www.123rf.com/profile_silvertiger'>silvertiger / 123RF Stock Photo</a>

Thank you to Commander Griz and Lieutenant Commander Crypto of the Watchmen of America – Colorado, Freebyrd of the Watchmen of America, Keith Carmichael and Kristina Cook of the COS Project, Glenn Stonemann, Randy Sumpter, and Dr. Jason Sorens.

www.ingramcontent.com/pod-product-compliance
Lightning Source LLC
Chambersburg PA
CBHW030639260626
47157CB00007B/2408